PENGUIN

# NIGHTINGALE WOOD

STELLA DOROTHEA GIBBONS, novelist, poet, and short-story writer, was born in London in 1902. She went to North London Collegiate School and studied journalism at University College London. She then worked for ten years on various papers, including the *Evening Standard*. Her first publication was a book of poems, *The Mountain Beast* (1930), and her first novel, *Cold Comfort Farm* (1932), won the Femina Vie Heureuse Prize in 1933. Among her other novels are *Miss Linsey and Pa* (1936), *Westwood* (1946), *Conference at Cold Comfort Farm* (1949), *The Shadow of a Sorcerer* (1955), *The Snow Woman* (1969), and *The Woods in Winter* (1970). Her short story collections include *Christmas at Cold Comfort Farm* (1940) and *Beside the Pearly Water* (1954). Her *Collected Poems* appeared in 1950. Stella Gibbons died in 1989.

SOPHIE DAHL, granddaughter of Roald Dahl, author of *James and the Giant Peach* and *Charlie and the Chocolate Factory*, is a model, author, and actress. Born in London, Dahl grew up in Los Angeles and attended boarding school in England. While well-known for her modeling career and her cover appearances on UK *Vogue* and UK *Elle*, Sophie Dahl is also the author of *The Man with the Dancing Eye* (2003), a novella, and *Playing with the Grown-ups* (2007), a novel.

# NIGHTINGALE WOOD

Stella Gibbons

*Introduction by Sophie Dahl*

PENGUIN BOOKS

PENGUIN BOOKS

Published by the Penguin Group
Penguin Group (USA) Inc., 375 Hudson Street, New York, New York 10014, U.S.A.
Penguin Group (Canada), 90 Eglinton Avenue East, Suite 700, Toronto,
Ontario, Canada M4P 2Y3 (a division of Pearson Penguin Canada Inc.)
Penguin Books Ltd, 80 Strand, London WC2R 0RL, England
Penguin Ireland, 25 St Stephen's Green, Dublin 2, Ireland (a division of Penguin Books Ltd)
Penguin Group (Australia), 250 Camberwell Road, Camberwell,
Victoria 3124, Australia (a division of Pearson Australia Group Pty Ltd)
Penguin Books India Pvt Ltd, 11 Community Centre, Panchsheel Park, New Delhi – 110 017, India
Penguin Group (NZ), 67 Apollo Drive, Rosedale, North Shore 0632,
New Zealand (a division of Pearson New Zealand Ltd)
Penguin Books (South Africa) (Pty) Ltd, 24 Sturdee Avenue,
Rosebank, Johannesburg 2196, South Africa

Penguin Books Ltd, Registered Offices:
80 Strand, London WC2R 0RL, England

First published in Great Britain by Longsmans, Green and Co. 1938
Edition with an introduction by Sophie Dahl published by Virago Press,
an imprint of Little, Brown Book Group 2009
Published by arrangement with Virago Press, an imprint of Little, Brown Book Group
Published in Penguin Books 2010

3   5   7   9   10   8   6   4   2

Copyright Stella Gibbons, 1938
Introduction copyright © Sophie Dahl, 2009
All rights reserved

ISBN 978-0-14-311757-5
CIP data available

Printed in the United States of America

A Romantic Comedy for Renée and Ruth

'. . . all those endearing young charms.'

## Note

The occasional words of Essex dialect in the story are taken from Mr H. Cranmer-Byng's *Dialect and Songs of Essex* and *Essex Speech and Humour*.
All the places and people are imagined.

# INTRODUCTION

'She did not look quite a lady, which was natural; as she was
not one.' So wrote Stella Gibbons, author of *Cold Comfort Farm*,
as she introduced the heroine of her ninth book, the latterly
forgotten treasure, *Nightingale Wood*. The not quite a lady is
grey-eyed Viola Wither, née Thompson, a beguiling widow of
twenty-one. Viola is a victim of circumstance, like so many of
Gibbons' female protagonists; a shop girl orphan, married briefly
to a bumbling, bullying older man, to whom she felt unable to say
no at precisely the wrong moment. In his death she is similarly
muted, and when, with a sigh of middle-class duty, her in-
laws, the aptly named Withers, summon her from London to live
with them in their dour house in Essex, she hops on a train
in her cheap black coat and pink satin blouse, meek as a sacrificial
lamb.

Their house, 'The Eagles', runs thick with thwarted longing.
Dwelling there are two daughters, spinsters (in 1930s parlance): the
lumpen, unfortunate, thirty-nine-year-old Madge; and Tina, who at
thirty-five, with an extreme penchant for dieting, is wasting away in
every sense. Their mother, Mrs Wither, seemingly has no fight left
in her after four decades with the petty, pedantic patriarch of the
family, the hateful Mr Wither. Mr Wither delights in the casual put-
down, stamping the most fragile hope in his pitiful daughters with a
quick lash of the tongue, forbidding Marge her one desire of a puppy,
and tormenting Tina at every opportunity:

'What time did you say Viola's train gets in?' Tina asked her mother; she sometimes found the Wither silences unendurable.

'Half-past twelve, dear.'

'Just in nice time for lunch.'

'Yes.'

'You know perfectly well that Viola's train gets in at half-past twelve,' intoned Mr Wither slowly, raising his eyelids to look at Tina, 'so why ask your mother? You talk for the sake of talking; it's a silly habit.'

It is in this bleak household, in which the clocks are constantly checked to see whether the day is ending, that poor Viola is deposited. And yet . . .

On the other side of the valley is an entirely different house, a house that sings with comfort and luxury, a house that has the feeling of 'moving a little faster than other places, as though it were always on the brink of a party'. This is 'Grassmere', a polished nouveau paradise, home to the dashing Victor Spring. Victor lives with his mother, Mrs Spring, who only employs the comely because, quite simply, 'She hated plain maids; they depressed her', and bookish cousin Hetty, who despises the inertia of a moneyed life, believing 'The Eagles' across the way to contain a life full of 'muted melancholy beauty'. Oh, the grass is always greener.

Add to the cast, amongst others, a ravishing chauffeur living above the Withers' garage, his mother, a faded village beauty with slatternly ways, a Machiavellian millionaire, a fast fairy godmother named Shirley, and a voyeuristic chorus of sorts in the form of a tramp known as 'the Hermit', and you have a sense of the proceedings, because *Nightingale Wood* is, in essence, a sprawling, delightful, eccentric fairy tale.

Gibbons loved this medium, and wrote three books conjuring it in her lifetime: *My American* (1939) borrows from 'The Snow Queen'; *White Sand and Grey Sand* (1958) is influenced by 'Beauty and the Beast'; and *Nightingale Wood*, her first endeavour, makes a great curtsy to 'Cinderella'. Where she strays from the classic fairy tale in these books, and brilliantly so, is that there is no such thing as staid, straightforward good and evil. Prince Charming is charming, yes, but he's also a little dull, vulgar and complacent. Her Cinderella is beautiful and true, yet a tad apathetic. Each social stratum in *Nightingale Wood* is capable of its own brand of snobbery, which is a theme that permeates all of her books. A greying of characters that are otherwise empathetic stretches to their occasional bigotry, which is deeply jarring to the modern reader. Casual anti-semitism and racism is insidious in much of the fiction from this period, and it serves as a stark commentary on the time. Virginia Woolf, T. S. Eliot, Agatha Christie and W. B. Yeats have all been accused of perpetuating this in their work. It is difficult to fathom whether Gibbons herself held such beliefs, or if she was casting judgement (and satirical scorn) upon her culture by making reference to them in her fiction. It is worth noting that these examples are used in conversation, perhaps as a narrative example of the characters' own narrow-mindedness. To edit them out would be a denial, and so, uncomfortable as it is to stumble upon them, they remain as a harrowing reminder of what went before.

It is staggering for a writer with an archive spanning twenty-five novels, four volumes of poetry and three volumes of short stories, to be best (and sometimes solely) known for one work. *Cold Comfort Farm* was Stella Gibbons' first novel, published in 1932, when she was thirty. She had grown up in a family similar to the ones she parodied so well: she was middle class, educated, and her father was a doctor. In their local community of Kentish Town he was publicly lauded for his humanity; in private, he was a domineering and violent man. Such roots must have had a profound impact on her, regardless of her career trajectory, but to my mind they also tattoo her writing: the men in her books are regarded somewhat warily, whatever their station, and she writes of a woman's plight with sensitivity, buckets of humour, and ceaseless compassion. The women of *Nightingale Wood* each suffer suffocating consequences of their sex. Perhaps the most succinct surmisal of the 1930s female lot comes from Viola's best friend, Shirley, who says wryly, 'Vote, Marie [Stopes], perms, and all, we can't do anything.'

But with the shadows we have light, and, again, it is testament to the wily talent of Gibbons to dance between the two with her light touch. One realises that *Nightingale Wood* doesn't have just one heroine; it has many, and each is duly rewarded for her pains. There is romance galore: a transformative dress and a ball; much dizzy kissing in hedgerows and beyond; spying, retribution and runaways; fights and a fire; poetry and heartbreak; a few weddings *and* a funeral; and a fairy-tale ending with a twist.

What luxury to stumble upon this quirky book, and the fascinating modern woman who wrote it. It is a rare unadulterated pleasure, and high time for its encore.

Without further ado – I give you *Nightingale Wood*.

*Sophie Dahl, 2008*

# CHAPTER I

It is difficult to make a dull garden, but old Mr Wither had succeeded.

He himself did no work in the grounds of his house near Chesterbourne in Essex, but his lack of interest in them and his dislike of spending money influenced the gardener. The result was a poorish lawn and a plaster rockery with very little in it extending as far as the eye could reach, and a lot of boring shrubs which Mr Wither liked because they filled up space and gave little trouble. He also liked the garden to look tidy, and on a fine April morning he stood at the breakfast-room window thinking what a nuisance the daisies were. There were eleven of them, out in the middle of the lawn. Saxon must be told to get them up.

Mrs Wither came in, but he took no notice of her because he had seen her before. She sat down behind the cups as a gong sounded in the hall, and Mr Wither heavily crossed the room and took his place at the other end, opening the *Morning Post*. Mrs Wither passed him a cup of tea and a bowl of patent cereal smelling and tasting exactly like all the other patent cereals, and three minutes passed. Mrs Wither sipped her tea, gazing over Mr Wither's bald head streaked with two bands of hair at a blackbird strutting under the monkey-puzzle tree.

Mr Wither looked slowly up.

'The girls are late.'

'They're just coming, dear.'

'They're late. They know perfectly well I don't like them to be late for meals.'

'I know, dear, but Madge overslept, she was so stiff after the tennis yesterday, and Tina's just trying—'

'Fiddling about with her hair as usual, I suppose.'

Mr Wither returned to his paper and Mrs Wither went on gazing and sipping.

Madge, their elder daughter, came in rubbing her hands.

'Morning, Mum. Sorry I'm late, Father.'

Mr Wither did not reply, and she sat down. She was thirty-nine years old, a big woman in a tweed coat and skirt with strong features, a closely shingled head and fresh yet insipid colouring.

'How can you eat that sawdust, Father?' she inquired, beginning on eggs and bacon and speaking cheerfully because it was a fine morning and only ten minutes past nine; and somehow, at the beginning of every new day, there was always a chance that this one might be different from all the rest. Something might happen; and then everything would be jollier all round.

Madge did not see clearly into her feelings; she only knew that she always felt cheerier at breakfast than at tea.

Mrs Wither smiled faintly. Mr Wither said nothing.

Footsteps came draggingly yet hastily across the tiled hall, and in hurried Tina, her eyelids pink, her dull hair arranged in its usual downward wave on her forehead. She was a little person, with eyes and mouth too big for her thin face. She was thirty-five; and dressed with evident pleasure to herself in a green suit and a white ruffled blouse. The nails of her small fingers were painted pale pink.

'Morning, everybody; I'm sorry I'm late, Father.'

Mr Wither uncrossed his plump legs in unexpected trousers of a natty checked cloth, and crossed them again, but did not look up. Her mother smiled at Tina, murmuring:

'Very nice, dear.'

'What is?' Mr Wither suddenly fixed Tina with a bloodshot, drooping and pale-blue eye.

'Only my new – only my suit, Father.'

'New, is it?'

'Yes – I – yes.'

'What do you want to go buying more clothes for? You've got plenty.' And Mr Wither returned to the City page.

'Bacon, Tina?'

'Please.'

'One, or two, dear?'

'Oh, one, please. No – that little one. Thank you.'

'You don't eat enough. It doesn't suit you to be thin,' observed Madge, buttering toast. 'Can't think why you want to diet at all; you look washed-out.'

'Well, you can only go by how you feel, and I know I feel miles better—'

'*Miles* better? How can you feel miles better?' loudly demanded Mr Wither, putting down the *Morning Post* and staring severely at his younger daughter. 'A mile is a measure of length. It cannot be used to describe a condition of the human body. You can be much better, or considerably better, or noticeably better. You cannot be *miles* better, because such a thing is impossible.'

'Well then,' Tina's dry hands slowly ground over each other in her lap as she tremulously smiled, 'I feel *considerably* better since I started the Brash Diet.'

Her smile showed irregular teeth, but sweetened her face surprisingly and made her look younger.

'Well, all I can say is you don't look it, does she, Father?'

Silence. The blackbird gave a loud sweet squawk and flew away.

'Are you playing golf today, dear?' presently murmured Mrs Wither to Madge. Madge, with her mouth full, nodded.

'Shall you be in to lunch?' pursued her mother – cautiously.

'Depends.'

'You must know whether you will be in to lunch or not, Madge,' interrupted Mr Wither, who had suddenly observed in the City page a piece of news which had blackened for him a world that was never very fair. 'Can you not definitely tell your mother whether you will, or will not, be in?'

' 'Fraid not, Father' said Madge firmly, wiping her mouth. 'Give us the sporting page, will you, if you've finished with it.'

Mr Wither detached the sporting page and passed it to her in silence, letting the rest of the paper drift listlessly to the floor.

No one said anything. The blackbird came back.

A purple-black and louring mantle of gloom now lay over Mr Wither. Before reading that piece in the paper, he had been as he always was at breakfast, and at luncheon and tea and dinner as well. But now (thought Mrs Wither and Madge and Tina) Father was Worrying; and the rest of the day would be darkened.

Mr Wither's chief worry was his money, of which he had some two thousand eight hundred pounds a year. This was the interest upon a handsome capital left to him by his father from a private gas company, established towards the middle of the last century, in which the late Mr Wither had held most of the shares.

During his own working life, Mr Wither the younger, knowing little about gas but a good deal about frightening people and getting his own way, had bossed the gas company with some success: and at the age of sixty-five (five years ago) he sold his shares, invested the proceeds, and retired to relish his leisure at The Eagles, near Chesterbourne, Essex, where he had already lived for thirty years.

Mr Wither's investments were as safe as investments ever are in this world; but that was not safe enough for Mr Wither. He wanted them to be *quite* safe; immovably productive, stable as rock and certain as nightfall.

It was no use; up and down they went, influenced by wars and births, abdications and airports. He never could be sure what his money was up to. He would wake up in the night and lie in the dark wondering what was happening to it, and during the day he prowled uneasily after it in the financial columns of the Press.

He was not mean (he often told himself) but he detested to see money wasted. It gave him strong pain to spend money without a strong cause. Money was not Given to us to spend; it was Given to us to save.

Now, as he sat gazing hopelessly at his half-finished cereal, he remembered all the good money he had been persuaded into wasting. How he had disliked paying away all those fees for the girls, during the ten years when they had tried to have careers! Pounds and pounds and pounds thrown away, good money sent after bad. Art schools and domestic schools, barbola work and secretarial college elocution lessons and journalism courses, kennel-work and weaving. None of it any use, of course; all of it wickedly expensive, and what could the girls *do*, as a result of all the money that he had spent upon them?

Nothing. Mr Wither considered them to be ill-informed and inaccurate in their speech, muddled in their thinking, and useless with their hands. He had a vague feeling that Tina and Madge, having been taught so much at so high a price, ought to have been, like Sir Francis Bacon, possessed of universal knowledge; but somehow it had not worked out that way.

'What time did you say Viola's train gets in?' Tina asked her mother; she sometimes found the Wither silences unendurable.

'Half-past twelve, dear.'

'Just in nice time for lunch.'

'Yes.'

'You know perfectly well that Viola's train gets in at half-past twelve,' intoned Mr Wither slowly, raising his eyelids to look at Tina, 'so why ask your mother? You talk for the sake of talking, it's a silly habit.' He slowly looked down again at his little bowl of mushy cereal.

'I'd forgotten,' said Tina. She continued vivaciously, at the silence. 'Don't you *loathe* getting to a place before twelve o'clock, Madge – too late for breakfast and too early for lunch?'

No one spoke: and she remembered that she had said the same thing last night at dinner, when the time of Viola's arrival had been threshed out with a rousing argument about the times of trains between Mr Wither and Madge. She flushed slowly, and ground her hands together again. Breakfast was being awful, as usual. Never mind, her new suit was really becoming, and Viola was coming today; that would make a little change, and Viola's presence might prevent Father from Worrying so much and so often, and Madge from arguing with him so rudely. Viola was not an exciting person, but anyone's company, even that of a sister-in-law, was better than that of unadulterated Relations.

After reading a book on feminine psychology called *Selene's Daughters* borrowed from a school friend, Tina had decided to face the facts about her own nature, however disgusting, nay, appalling, those facts might be (the book warned its readers that the truth about themselves might disgust, nay, appal them); and one of the facts she had faced was that she did not love her family.

She had not even loved her only brother, Teddy; and that *was* rather appalling, because, for three months, Teddy had been dead.

Viola was his widow, a bride of a year, who was coming to make her home with her husband's family at The Eagles. Whenever Tina realized that she had not loved Teddy, it made her feel worse to remember that Viola, a very young girl with plenty of young men to choose from, had chosen Teddy and loved him enough to marry him. I suppose I'm unnatural, thought Tina. Of course, we never saw much of Teddy after he was grown up. He never shared his life with us, as some men do with their sisters and parents. All the same, I must be abnormal, not to have loved my only brother.

'Want me to drive you up to the station, Mum?' offered Madge, standing at the door.

'You won't be back in time, will you, dear?'

'That doesn't matter; I'll come back, if you'd like me to run you up.'

Madge loved to drive the car, but as Mr Wither said that she did not know how to, she seldom got the chance.

'Well, thank you, dear, but I've told Saxon now. He'll bring it round about ten past twelve.'

'Oh all right, if you prefer Saxon's driving to mine.'

'It isn't that, dear. And I think Saxon really drives quite nicely now.'

'So I should hope, after two cautions, a new mudguard and a fine.'

She went out whistling, and Mrs Wither stooped for the paper, but Mr Wither, as though absently, stretched out his hand for it, and she let him have it.

'Are you going to practise, Tina?' she asked, putting her hand on her daughter's thin shoulder on the way to the door.

'I suppose so.'

'Ought to go out,' pronounced Mr Wither, coming to the surface of his gloom like a seal for air. 'Mooning indoors won't do you any good,' and he submerged again.

Mrs Wither went out.

Tina crossed to the window and stood for a little while, looking up at the brilliantly white clouds behind the black-green branches of the monkey-puzzle. The world looked so young this morning that it made her very skin feel withered; she was conscious of every creamed and massaged wrinkle in her face, and of her hardening bones; and all she longed for, and the only thing she cared to think about on this young, light-flooded earth, was Love.

Mr Wither went out of the room, crossed the cold blue and black tiles of the hall, and shut himself into his own snuffy den, a little room furnished with a worn carpet, a large ugly desk, financial books of reference, and a huge fireplace which gave out a hellish heat when lit, which was not often.

This morning, however, it was lit. Mr Wither had not made up his mind in a hurry about ordering it to be lit; he had thought the matter well over, and decided that the fire would not be wasted, though an alarmingly large quantity of coal must be burned if the hellish one were not to go out about half-past two in the afternoon.

Mr Wither intended to invite Viola into his den after lunch and have a little talk with her, and he thought that she might be easier to talk to if she were warmed. Women were continually grumbling about being cold.

It disturbed Mr Wither to think of a silly young girl like Viola having control of her own money. True, she could not have very much; when the money that her father had left her was added to the money that Teddy had left her, she could not have (thought Mr Wither, sitting upright in his baggy-seated old black leather arm-chair and gazing sadly into the furious fire) more than, say, a hundred and fifty pounds a year. But even a hundred and fifty pounds a year ought to be properly looked after, and Mr Wither and his financial adviser, Major-General E. E. Breis-Cumwitt, DSO, were certainly more fitted to look after it than was Viola.

If Mr Wither had had his way, he would have known how much money Viola possessed, but at the time of his son's death, circumstances had conspired to keep him from finding out.

To begin with, Teddy had always been irritatingly secretive about money (as, indeed, he was about all his affairs) and his father, though he knew how much he earned, did not know how much he saved. Every fortnight or so, during Teddy's lifetime, Mr Wither asked Teddy if he were saving money, and Teddy said, 'Yes, of course, Father,' and changed the subject. He refused to answer direct questions about How Much and What In; he retorted that that was his affair. Nevertheless, his father had assumed that he did save something.

Then, when he died suddenly of pneumonia, Mr Wither had been unable to go to the funeral (which took place in London, at Viola's wish), much less investigate his son's estate and take over its management, as he wanted to do, because he was at the time helpless with a sharp go of lumbago.

But he did know that there had been no Will, and this made him uneasy.

He wrote to Viola; he wrote two longish, earnest letters about the Money. He received in reply one short, vague little note saying that she was 'going to stay with Shirley, a friend,' and giving no address.

Mrs Wither said that Shirley's other name was Davis and that she lived in a place called Golders Green.

Mr Wither went to the trouble of looking up all the Davises in the London Telephone Directory, Golders Green was creeping with them, so that was no use.

He wrote another longish letter, to his son's old address, and at last had a short reply, giving the Davis address, and saying nothing about the Money but vaguely mentioning difficulties about letting the flat.

Then Mr Wither wrote once more, for the last time, saying nothing this time about the money but announcing firmly that his daughter-in-law must come at once to live at The Eagles.

It was the only thing to do. While Viola was in London, there was no hope of his being able to manage her money for her, and the idea of it, knocking about on its own like that, was beginning to get on his nerves. The fact that he did not know how much it was made matters worse. Why, it might be three hundred a year!

He thought Viola a silly, common little girl, but did not actually dislike her. Of course it was a pity, a great pity, that she had been a shopgirl, but after all, her father had owned half the business in which she was employed and it was a solid little business, long established and well patronized. That was all to the good; Mr Wither liked to feel money on all sides of him, like a stout fence; he liked to feel that his remotest cousin four times removed had a bit put by (as, indeed, all the Wither cousins had).

No, he would not mind Viola coming to live at The Eagles. It was a large house; he would not often see her. When he did see her, she could be organized. And then he would be able to manage Teddy's money for her, and see that it did not get spent or otherwise misused. It would make a nice hobby for her, too. She would follow his wise administration of her little income with interest throughout the years, growing wiser and (he hoped) more organizable as she grew older.

She was just the sort of characterless girl that Mr Wither had always expected Teddy to marry. This did not prevent him from being very annoyed when Teddy did. What with Madge and Tina not marrying at all, and Teddy marrying a shopgirl, and Mrs Wither being so disappointed about all three of her children's reactions to marriage, Mr Wither was quite sick of the word.

But Teddy never had been ambitious. Mr Wither had put him into a job, minor but with prospects, in the gas company, when he was twenty-two, and it was understood that he would work his way Up (where to was glossed over).

But there Teddy had stayed for twenty years, his salary rising by five pounds a year because everybody's salary in that company below a certain level did so automatically. It was not as though he had been content, either, with his minor job in which he earned so little money that Mr Wither was quite ashamed to think about it. Mr Wither was frequently told by friends of the family that of course Teddy's real Dream had been of doing architecture or painting or something artistic; and these Dreams, always popping up at Mr Wither, annoyed him very much.

He was sure that his acquaintances said, behind his back, that he ought to pay Teddy more money. But this he would not do, for many good reasons. Teddy did not deserve more money; nobody holding that job ever had had more money and he must not show favouritism to his son; Teddy did not need more money because he was not married, and so on.

When at last Teddy did marry, at the age of forty-one, Mr Wither was in the happy position of not being able to raise his salary, for by that time he had sold out his interest in the company. He gave his son an allowance of eighty pounds a year, saying that this would be a help. But when Teddy had enjoyed the use of this for a year, he died, and Mr Wither was able to take it all back again.

Mr Wither, gazing vaguely into the fire, mused that some fellows were very cut up when their sons died. Now, he had not been very cut up when Teddy died. It was a shock; of course, it was a shock. But it was strange that he had not been more cut up. Never had got on with Teddy, somehow, even when Teddy was a boy. Through his mind drifted the word 'Milksop'. Yet there must have been something in the chap for a girl like Viola, quite a pretty girl, who must have known plenty of chaps and had plenty of choice, to pick him out and marry him.

Not that it wasn't a very fine thing for her; she knew which side her bread was buttered, no doubt, thought Mr Wither, sitting upright, frowning and nodding. And this afternoon he and Viola would have a little talk.

Meanwhile, he must telephone to Major-General Breis-Cumwitt about that dismal piece of news on the City page, which he had carefully encircled with a sable ring.

Not that Major-General Breis-Cumwitt could do anything; no power on earth could stop money when it began to jig about like that, but at least the two of them could confer, and discuss; and condole; and then Mr Wither (despite the one and threepence spent on a telephone call to London) would feel better.

At ten minutes past twelve exactly the car came round the short circular drive, and stopped in front of the house.

The chauffeur sat with his beautiful profile turned carefully from the house; a correct chauffeur does not peer up at the bedroom windows, scan the front door, nor appear aware of anything at all, and Saxon was most correct. The Eagles was a house of dark grey stucco, too tall for the grounds in which it stood, so that it seemed to stoop over them in a frightening way. There were more boring shrubs round the front door, approached by a good many steep steps. The windows on the lower floors were hung with heavy dark curtains; the upper ones had those half-curtains of white material with bits of coarse lace let into them which always suggest the windows of a nursing home, and also that the bedrooms are large and draughty.

Two plaster birds, not badly modelled, sat on the two columns at the entrance to the drive and gave the house its name. These birds got on Mr Wither's nerves for some reason, but he was afraid to ask how much it would cost to have them taken away; also, the house had belonged to his father, and he had a vague feeling that the eagles ought to be left there because his father had approved them, so there they sat.

Saxon knew the exact instant that Mrs Wither appeared at the door, though he was not looking at the house, and he stepped from the car and deftly opened its door for her, touching his cap.

'Good morning, Saxon. Isn't it a beautiful day!'

'Good morning, Madam. Yes, Madam.'

'So nice for Mrs Theodore,' continued Mrs Wither, having her toes muffled by Saxon in a horrid old rug of unknown fur which Mr Wither refused to have put out of commission. 'To come to us on a nice day, I mean.'

'Yes, Madam.'

Mrs Wither, who had once been a woman who enjoyed talking to servants, glanced at him and said no more. Saxon did not seem to like being talked to.

The gentle reader is no doubt wondering why on earth anyone should have married Mr Wither, and must here be told that she had married him for what (it is said) is a common enough reason:

she feared that she would never have the chance to marry anyone else.

And when he was young Mr Wither had not been quite so bad; he had had a bold eye and a semi-dashing manner rather like that of a small bull-dog. He ordered waiters about, elbowed himself into hansom cabs and had a rich father. Mrs Wither, who was not romantic, had thought that a young woman might safely trust herself to Arthur Wither, and she had done so. Their marriage cannot have been so bad as some, for here they were, at seventy and sixty-four, sharing The Eagles, two daughters, the memory of a dead son, and a daughter-in-law.

Mrs Wither was sorry for poor Arthur; he worried so. She wondered and grieved about him in his absence, and though she always enjoyed herself when he was not there and never when he was, she was fond of him; and Mr Wither in his turn disapproved of Mrs Wither less than he did of anybody, though he never showed it.

What exalted lies are told of marriage! but one promise at least can be fulfilled: ye shall be one flesh.

# CHAPTER II

Saxon drove slowly, because Mrs Wither had as usual ordered the car too early, and he disliked what he called to himself 'bloody hanging about' outside Chesterbourne station. The country through which they moved was chiefly grazing land with some under wheat and barley, and it had the unconventional charm of Essex land-scapes; the little hills with oak coppices climbing them, now in early rose-brown leaf, the loops of a river shining in a wide, tree-hidden valley to which all the roads seem to lead, and the near and distant cries of birds, like the country itself singing. The woods and hedges were alive with them; they love a land like this, flat and wooded and watery.

The country about Sible Pelden, the village nearest to The Eagles, was not much spoilt. One main road ran near the village, but not near enough to ruin it. (All the inhabitants wished that it did.) It was a quiet tract of land, with a few shabby villages and one or two big houses belonging to wealthy people who had had connec-tions in the district for well under a hundred years. London was just over an hour away by a good train. The sea was thirty miles away, and there were marshes between it and Sible Pelden where swans nested and rarer birds. In summer the countryside seemed quietly awake under a silvery sun (it was so flat that the sky seemed always full of light, enormously high, and falling almost like a mist) and in the winter it was surprisingly desolate. It had only two places of historical interest and no stunning beauty-spots.

Outside Chesterbourne there were some new bungalows, and Mrs Wither, looking at them, remembered that Teddy and Viola had been talking about renting one, instead of their tiny flat in Greater London, just before Teddy died. At least Teddy had talked of it, and Viola had not said a word. Mrs Wither had gathered from this that Viola had wanted to stay in Greater London. She had also gathered that Viola was a pleasure-loving girl; dances, new frocks, lipstick, perhaps even Cocktail Parties.

Mrs Wither sighed. It was dreadful to feel that her own grief for Teddy was fading. Of course she *had* grieved; his death had been a shock, a great shock. But she had never felt as close to him as she did to Madgie, or even to Tina (though Tina was very difficult sometimes, spoke rudely, and laughed at things that were not funny). Mrs Wither knew that she did not get on well with men; they flustered her, and Teddy had been like all the rest. He had been a stranger to her, even when he was a little boy, though that was a dreadful thing to think. He had always liked talking to other Mothers and Nannies better than to his own; and when he grew into a man he would never tell her anything, and sometimes he was rather unkind.

Here Mrs Wither interrupted her thoughts remorsefully, for she was on her way to meet Teddy's widow, a young girl who (pleasure-loving though she might be) had yet loved Teddy so much that she had chosen him out of all other men (and some of them much younger, no doubt, than poor Teddy) to marry.

There must have been a side to him, thought his mother, that we never knew. Well, of course, that was only natural. Parents cannot expect to know every side of their children.

As for Viola, she may have loved Teddy, but there is no doubt, thought Mrs Wither, that she jumped at the chance of making such a good match, marrying into a comfortably-off family with a big house and a certain position in the countryside. That was a big step up for a little shopgirl in Chesterbourne. It would have been very surprising, even rather shocking, if Viola had refused to marry Teddy.

The car stopped outside the station.

Saxon opened the door for Mrs Wither and handed her attentively out, and she hurried through to the platform, for the train was in.

And there was tall Viola, in one of the newest-shaped hats somehow looking not quite right, with her very pale, soft curls straggling under it. She came down the platform lugging a big suitcase in one hand and holding on to her new hat with the other, peering about for someone to meet her.

'There you are, Viola,' said Mrs Wither encouragingly, catching at her arm, and Viola stooped and gave her a clumsy kiss.

'Hullo, Mrs Wither.'

Her voice was a little deeper than most women's; not much, but enough to make it admired had she moved in circles where such differences are noticed. Nevertheless she was no siren, but a would-be-smart girl of twenty-one, in a cheap black coat and skirt, a pink satin blouse, and gloves with fussy cuffs. She was pale, with narrow eyes of a soft grey, a childish mouth with small full lips half parted, and pretty teeth. She did not look quite a lady, which was natural; as she was not one.

'Did you have a comfortable journey?'

'Oh yes, thanks, ever so comfy.'

'Your trunk has come.'

'Oh, marvellous.'

They walked out to the car, Viola towering a head and shoulders over Mrs Wither, and Saxon, touching his cap, took the suitcase. With lowered eyelids he settled the case beside the driver's seat while the ladies got in at the back: and they were off.

'Ripping the country looks,' said Viola.

'Yes, that's all the rain. As I always say, it *is* tiresome at the time, but, after all, it does bring everything on so.'

'Yes. It's ever so pretty.'

'And how are you, in yourself, I mean?' pursued Mrs Wither dutifully. 'No more colds?'

'Oh no, thanks awfully. I'm quite all right again.'

'And did you manage to settle everything satisfactorily in town – your flat, and the furniture, and the cats?'

'Oh yes, thanks awfully. Geoff did it all for me, you know, Geoff Davis. My friend Shirley's husband.'

Mrs Wither nodded. She felt a little awkward. Not only had she not seen Viola since the funeral, and had therefore had time to let strangeness grow up again between herself and this daughter-in-law whom she had never got to know well, but the flat was an embarrassing subject. It was because Viola had not been able to let the flat that she had not been able to come to The Eagles until more than three months after Teddy's death. She had kept on writing to her in-laws, putting off her arrival because of the flat, until Madge, in her blunt outspoken way, had said that it was as plain as a pikestaff that the girl did not want to come at all.

Then there had been more delay over the cats.

Teddy had been exceedingly fond of the cats, Sentimental Tommy and Valentine Brown (named after characters drawn by his favourite author, Sir J. M. Barrie) and that was why Viola had felt it her duty to find a first-class home for them. This took time, because both were enormous, full of crotchets, set in their ways, and hearty eaters. They also refused to be separated, immediately falling into a rapid decline if anybody tried it on. Viola, with Shirley's help, had at last landed them in a roadhouse near St Albans which believed in the personal touch.

But it had all taken time: and Mrs Wither, catching the note of embarrassment in Viola's voice as well, wondered for the hundredth time if she really did not want to live at The Eagles.

If she did not, it was very wrong and ungrateful of her.

'Shirley Davis? I think I have heard you mention her before, have I not?'

'Oh, hundreds of times, I sh'd think. She's my best friend, you know. She was at my wedding.'

'I remember her perfectly. A very striking-looking girl.'

With dyed hair, thought Mrs Wither, for that shade of red could never be real.

Some uninteresting conversation about the flat followed while the car got slowly through the narrow crowded streets of Chesterbourne. Viola answered Mrs Wither's remarks politely and sensibly, but it was plain that she was thinking about something else; and when at last the car passed a small draper s shop on the corner of the High Street she leaned right out of the window, exclaiming, 'Oh, there's the shop! How lovely to see it again,' and craning still further as the car drew away from Burgess and Thompson, Ladies' Outfitters, 'Oh! there's Catty! At the door, matching something!'

Mrs Wither said nothing, the usual method in the Wither *ménage* of showing someone that they had dropped a brick; and Viola slowly drew herself into the car, leaned back, and rolled the fussily cuffed gloves into a ball. She said nothing, either.

After the little pause, Mrs Wither thought this a good moment to make the speech she had prepared about being glad that Viola was coming to live with them, and how she must try to feel that The Eagles was her real home.

It did not occur to Mrs Wither to apologize for the lack of night-life, or of any life, at The Eagles, because it did not occur to her that a young widow needs life. Mr Wither had said that Viola must come to live with them because, if she did not, she would get into a muddle with Teddy's money. Also, the Wither cousins would Say Things. That was why Viola was coming. Mrs Wither felt that she was doing her duty in making the little speech, but she did not much like Viola (so young, so pleasure-loving, rather common) and was secretly dismayed that she was going to live at The Eagles.

She was trying not to mind Viola's having been a shopgirl. It was not Christian to mind; Tina did not mind. But poor Madgie minded; she demanded what the devil would everyone say up at the Club? and it was for Madgie's sake that Mrs Wither had gently repressed Viola when she stared at the shop out of the car window.

In reply to Mrs Wither's speech, Viola gave her a quick nervous glance and a little smile, and Mrs Wither leaned back more comfortably now that duty was done, and the embarrassing incident over.

Mr Wither was working out figures in his den when they got home, but Tina was on the doorstep, smiling and waving, and she hurried down to kiss Viola as Saxon opened the car's door.

17

'It *is* nice to have you, Vi,' putting her arm about her sister-in-law's waist; 'I am so glad.'

Her eyes filled. She did indeed feel warmly fond of Viola, and grateful to her, because Viola's arrival meant that there would be someone different to look at and think about.

And then Viola was a widow; mysterious, unguessable state! so different from that of all the other women under Mr Wither's thumb at The Eagles.

Perhaps, too, Viola would 'stand up for herself'?

Not that Tina enjoyed scenes; after a stern and scrupulous examination of her feelings about scenes she could look the book on feminine psychology in its eye and swear that scenes made her feel ill; but she felt that someone ought to make a few at The Eagles. They would clear the air.

Tina thought vaguely about scenes as she sat on Viola's bed, watching her comb the untidy curls just touching her shoulders.

'Is your hair naturally curly?'

'Just a bit, but it's permed, of course. Shirley says it's *awful*. It *won't* keep tidy.'

'Isn't hair a nuisance. I'm awfully disgruntled with mine; I tried to change the parting this morning but it looked so woeful that I had to give it up. I ought to go to town, really, and have a new perm. Mine has quite grown out. I used to go up once a fortnight, a few years ago, just for a wash and a set.'

'Don't you now?'

'No.'

'Why not?' asked Viola idly, wondering what was for lunch .

'Haven't the energy.'

This was not true. The answer was Mr Wither; it always was Mr Wither when someone at The Eagles was unable to do what they wanted to do.

'How old are you?' asked Tina abruptly, staring at her sister-in-law as she stood in the white blaze of April sunlight.

'Just twenty-one,' with a shy, cheerful smile. 'Shirley says I'm a regular babe.'

'Is she older than you?'

'Oh, lord, yes; keep it under your hat, but she's getting on for twenty-seven.'

'Dreadful!' said Tina wryly. 'Isn't she married?'

'Oh yes. Been married three years. She's going to have a baby in December.'

'Oh, my dear, how lovely for her! She must be pleased.'

'Well, as a matter of fact she's a bit fed-up. You see, it may mean giving up her job.'

'Oh, she has a job as well?'

'Yes. She's awfully brainy. She's secretary to some old boy. She gets a jolly good salary.'

'And what does her husband do?'

'He sells cars. He works in a car saloon in Golders Green, where they live, and Shirley works down in the City.'

'A husband, a job, *and* a baby,' murmured Tina, staring at the floor. She stood up abruptly. 'Well, I must go and powder my nose for lunch. Got everything you want?'

The gong went while Viola was staring round her room.

It was furnished with large white elephants from the rest of the house, and draughts whistled under the door and between the window sashes and from the cracks in the old boards, but it was so big and the windows showed so much sky that the general effect was pleasing.

Viola could not help wishing that it had been smaller, with pink curtains instead of brown serge ones; in fact, she wished that it looked just like the little room over the shop where she used to sleep before she was married, but as she had been wishing, ever since her marriage, that all her bedrooms were that little pink one, she was used to the wish and took its presence for granted.

If only I had someone to talk to! she thought, running down the stairs.

Mr Wither greeted her with reserve, Madge waved at her boyishly. Mr Wither was afraid that she might begin at any minute to cry about Teddy, and as he did not care to risk this by talking to her, he let Tina chatter to her during lunch.

But afterwards, ah! afterwards! The hellish fire had been banked

19

up just before lunch by Mr Wither's own hands, the prospectuses of several safe and highly recommended investments were arranged neatly upon the desk, a flat, depressed little old cushion had even been found by Mr Wither from somewhere in the den and arranged, how cosily! in the large arm-chair. When Viola sat down, Mr Wither planned to pat the cushion and ask her if she were quite comfortable. And then the little talk would begin.

Mr Wither had been looking forward to it for days. He was so busy planning just what he would say and wondering exactly how much money Viola had that he looked up with a start when asked if he would take cheese, realizing that lunch was over.

He shook his head, waving the cheese away. Now was the moment.

He leaned over the table to Viola (who was, he observed, wastefully putting a whole ball of butter on only a quarter of dry biscuit), fastened his mournful bloodhound's eyes upon her, and breathed in a low mysterious tone,

'You and I must have a little talk.'

Viola was very frightened. When people came at you like that and spoke of a little talk, it always meant something awful about which you had to make up your mind, and which would prevent you from enjoying anything for days because you would be thinking about it. Teddy had been the one for little talks; Viola usually had one from him every ten days, so she knew all about them.

She gave her father-in-law one wide, startled look from her usually half-shut eyes, then gazed down at her plate, muttering, 'Yes, Mr Wither.'

'Soon,' persisted Mr Wither, leaning further over the table. 'No time like the present, eh? and get everything settled.'

She nodded.

'*Now*,' said Mr Wither triumphantly, rising to his feet and beginning to move towards the door. 'In my study.'

But even as he moved, the corner of his eye was caught by an improper gleam of white in the garden, and he turned to look out of the window.

Daisies, eleven of them, in the middle of the lawn, looking untidy. Saxon had been instructed that morning to get them up, but he had not. He ought to have; he must be spoken to again: and Mr Wither, turning round from the window, found that Viola was not there.

Neither was Tina. Neither (oh, base!) was Mrs Wither. Only Madge sprawled at the table, buttering an unnecessarily big wedge of bread.

'Where is Viola?' cried Mr Wither.

'Gone to get a handkerchief.'

'But we were going . . . she did not say . . .'

'Yes she did, only you were looking out of the window and didn't hear.'

'And your mother . . . Christina?'

'Mum's gone to see Saxon about the daisies, she said. Tina wants to wash her hair or something.'

Mr Wither walked in silence from the room. At the door he paused, saying,

'When Viola returns, say that I am waiting for her in my study.'

But Viola, locked in one of The Eagles' three lavatories with a copy of *Home Chat*, did not return until, from its window, she saw Mr Wither set out for a walk, with bowed head, smacking at things with a walking-stick. He wore a little check cap, shrunk in the annual rains, that matched his trousers, and a mackintosh, and he went off towards the wood, where he could be peaceful and think about money undisturbed.

Then Viola went up to her bedroom and spent the afternoon unpacking, with Tina's help.

Tina was awfully kind; she admired all Viola's clothes (though in fact her own were better, because she had a certain choiceness of taste which her sister-in-law lacked) and helped her to re-set her curls. Nevertheless, by teatime Viola felt miserable, because the house was so quiet and everybody in it was so old.

All the afternoon, shadows of the beautiful white clouds floated quickly over rooms filled with well-kept, ugly furniture; at night the rising moon would draw her stealthy, dreary rays slowly across mahogany claw-foot tables and enormous sideboards. It must be awful here at night, thought Viola. So quiet.

Nothing in the house seemed to have changed, or grown, for fifty years. Mr Wither, despite his dislike of spending money, believed in buying The Best when he did spend it, because The Best was the cheapest in The End; but unfortunately The Best lasted such a long time that The End never came, and Mr Wither's furniture, at fifty years old, was as good as the day he bought it, and entirely lacking the personality given to furniture by a busy, vivid family life.

No one scuffed the Wither furniture with their boots when they came home tight from a party, or scratched it during a charade, or used it for making an aeroplane or a cage for bears. No one left cigarettes to burn long scars on its edges or put wet-rimmed glasses down on it. There it stood, superior and glossy, and twelve big rooms full of it weighed upon young and probably silly spirits.

Time seemed slowed to half its usual pace by the heavy ticking of an old clock in an alcove, the faint smell of furniture polish, the meagre clusters of flowers in thin glass vases, and the dull shine on well-polished wood. Three middle-aged religious maids kept all this glory going; with their faith, the wireless, and their disapproval of almost everything, they were well content.

Viola was frightened, as well as depressed. She dreaded to meet Mr Wither at tea after her flight from him at lunch. She did not dare to look at him as the party took their places round a small fire in the huge pallid drawing-room and Mrs Wither began to pour out; she gazed down at her plate, but presently she became aware of a creaking towards her, and Mr Wither saying:

'Did you forget our little talk? I quite wondered where you had run off to.' And Mr Wither laughed, an alarming sound.

She glanced at him and nodded, dumb with nervousness.

'Ah well, another time, perhaps,' creaking back again. 'I expect you will be busy for a few days, settling down, will you not?'

She nodded, and no more was said.

But in Mr Wither's bosom, till now only mildly disapproving of his daughter-in-law, a strong suspicion and disapproval had been planted.

The hellish one had consumed a bucket of coal all for nothing, the arrangement of the prospectuses, the curves of the cushion – all had been wasted. Worse, Mr Wither had been done out of his little talk, and he still did not know how much money Viola had. She had now been under his roof for nearly five hours, and she was the only female in that situation about whose income Mr Wither was ignorant.

It was all most annoying. Mr Wither stared into the smouldering fire, chewed a very small tea cake, and decided that a firm hand must be taken with Viola.

After tea (good lord, was it still so early?) Viola went upstairs again to her room. No one asked her what she was going to do until dinner time. Noises from a bathroom suggested that Tina was washing her head; Mrs Wither and Madge had merely disappeared. She shut her door, crossed the room listlessly, pushed up the heavy window and, balancing herself on the sill, gazed out across the view.

It was a beautiful evening. The wind had fallen and the sun gone down behind coral-red clouds. The air was mild, and scented by new leaves. One star was out; among the woods, already dark, a thrush was singing.

It was all enough to break your heart and Viola began to cry.

Girls of nineteen may be put in two classes: those who assume that they will marry immediately and those who fear that they will never marry at all. Viola Thompson, only daughter of Howard Thompson, part proprietor of Burgess and Thompson, Ladies' Outfitters, had belonged in the latter class.

She had a poor opinion of her own charms, and when Teddy Wither fell in love with her she was more embarrassed and distressed than flattered.

Teddy had gone into Burgess and Thompson's one Saturday morning when he was home from London for one of his rare weekends, to buy himself a handkerchief. He had a cold, and his handkerchief had blown out of his pocket on the drive into Chesterbourne.

It is, of course, nonsense to say that just anyone will fall in love with just anyone else. Teddy had never loved anyone but himself, yet when he saw Viola, smiling with the other shopgirl as she tucked a thick pale curl away, he fell painfully and violently in love with her.

No one else but this tall, very young, not quite ordinary girl would do. He found out her name and besieged her with miserable letters asking her to go out with him. He gave up his room in London and stayed with his family at Sible Pelden in order to be near her. (This was a true sacrifice, for he did not like his family, and did not spend much of his time with them.) He sent her flowers. He took her home to tea at The Eagles, to his family's surprise, annoyance and dismay. At last, trembling with passion, he implored her to marry him.

Viola did not like him very much. She was sorry for him, but she giggled when Shirley Davis called him Mr Therm, and she was never easy in his company; he stared so. She was happy living in three rooms over the shop with her father, a tall irritable man who would interrupt his bursts of bad temper with quotations from Shakespeare, scoop up his daughter, and rush the two of them off to the pictures, so that he could pick the film to pieces afterwards and swear that the Theatre, the Glorious, Ancient and Down-Trodden Theatre, was the only art.

He was an ardent amateur actor and a lover of Shakespeare's plays. 'Viola' was not a sentimental accident but a favourite and familiar name bestowed upon a beloved daughter. Viola's mother had died when she was born, and her father had brought her up, as Prospero did Miranda. When such a father and daughter are happy, it takes a more lovable man than Teddy Wither to lure the daughter willingly away.

But Viola's father was knocked down by a young man driving a car, and died in an hour.

The young man was fined, and had some severe remarks made about him, and drove away from the court faster than ever because he was so cross: and after a while, Viola heard that her father had left her only fifty pounds.

Mr Thompson had often needed money to help the

Chesterbourne Players. He would hire the costumes for a period play, or stage a special effect, or get a professional actor to work for three nights with the amateurs. The hall in which the Players played was old, chilly, and falling down; Mr Thompson put in a stove, and footlights, and had the roof repaired.

This went on for ten busy, happy years; while Mr Thompson's share in Burgess and Thompson slowly passed, in return for ready money, into the hands of Mr Burgess, who was good at business.

And so Viola had only fifty pounds.

Then Shirley Davis (born Cissie Cutter, daughter of the town's most prosperous hotel-keeper and dearest friend of the orphaned and miserable Viola) said that she ought to marry Mr Teddy Therm, it was the sensible thing to do. Viola's two aunts, sisters of her father, said so too, and so did old Miss Cattyman at the shop. Teddy's kindness (a little spoiled by jealousy of her dead father, which she did not then notice) was comforting, so she took the advice of all her friends and married him.

Everyone was relieved that poor Viola was settled except Shirley, that downright girl, who was sorrier for her friend than ever.

On the eve of Viola's wedding Shirley, who was staying with her, had run down into the shop to find some white silk to mend something with. The little rooms over the shop where Viola had lived with her father were brightly lit and full of females, all talking at once and admiring the trousseau, on which some of the fifty pounds had been spent. But down in the shop it was dark, except where the dismal light from a street lamp shone upon dismantled stocking stands and shut drawers, rolls of rayon covered in dust-sheets, and stacks of Cosycurl knitting wool. A faint glazey smell came from a newly opened bale of Horrocks's longcloth, and near it, sitting with her ankles curled round one of the customers' chairs and her head down on the haberdashery counter, was Viola. She was crying.

'Heart alive, girl, what's up with you?'

'Oh, Shirley, I'm so miserable.'

'And I don't blame you,' retorted her friend, hitching herself up on the counter and beginning to swing her beautiful legs. 'So should I be.'

'Well, I do like that, considering it was you made me give in about it,' mopping and sniffing.

'Only because I don't see what else you could do. But I didn't know you'd feel so down in the mouth.'

'Well, I do.'

Shirley did not assume that Viola was crying for her father. Her tears had a frightened sound.

'He makes me feel sick,' she whispered, staring through starry tears at the street lamp.

'What, all the time?'

'No, only when he kisses me. I hate being kissed. It's beastly,' she added.

Shirley stared down at her friend's untidy head, glimmering ashily in the dim light. She was very disturbed and distressed. She said suddenly,

'Look here, Vi, don't go through with it. Chuck it all up and come and live with—' she stopped herself from saying 'Geoff and me', and ended 'near us'. 'I'll find you a room and a job.'

'Oh, Shirley, I'd *love* it!'

'His face – when you don't turn up tomorrow!' giggled Shirley, who did not consider that a short, plump man could suffer.

But the picture of Teddy's face sobered Viola. He had told her so often that she was the only person that he loved in the world, that his life lay in her hands and it would break his heart if she ever let him down.

It would be wicked to let a person down when they felt like that about you: and as she stared longingly up at Shirley, she gently shook her head.

'You aren't thinking of marrying anyone else, are you, for mercy's sake?' inquired Shirley, slithering off the counter and relieved (though she still felt disturbed and distressed) that Vi, after all, was going through with it.

'Me? Good lord, no!'

This was true. Viola had no regular boy when she met Teddy, and few admirers. She was too quiet for local taste, which admired Shirley's thick red curls, clear pink and white skin, and ringing voice; and though she went to dances sometimes and met boys and thoroughly enjoyed such outings, she enjoyed going to the pictures with her father, or watching him act, quite as much. Boys did not notice her much, and she did not notice them. It was quite true that she was not 'thinking' of marrying anyone else.

Nevertheless, at the back of her mind, whenever she retired there for a reverie about a wedding, lingered the day-dream that one day she would marry Victor Spring.

All the girls who had grown up in Chesterbourne – the girls in Woolworth's and the young ladies in Barclay's Bank, the assistants in the two smart hairdressing shops and the tradesmen's daughters, the shopgirls and the typists and secretaries, the young reception-ist at the Miraflor Café and the waitresses therein – they all day-dreamed just a little, when they retired to the back of their own minds for a reverie about a wedding, of marrying Victor Spring.

He was the richest young man in the neighbourhood, he had the biggest car, the smartest house, the gayest parties. He was so good-looking that he made the heart, in that foolish old saying, beat a little faster, and was so charged with controlled energy and health that everyone felt more alive when he had been near.

All these local girls like Viola, who had grown up in Chesterbourne or Sible Pelden and found jobs there, knew all about Victor Spring, his widowed mother and his cousin Hetty Franklin, who lived with them. While the day dreamers were still at school, they used to see Victor, home from Harrow at Christmas, passing through the town in his father's car on the way to some festivity at one of the local big houses. The glimpse of the handsome boy, self-assured, charming in his Etons and the legendary, absurdly becoming topper, went straight into their romantic pigtailed or shingled heads and lingered there for years.

No one remained virgin for his sake, no one drowned herself in the Bourne, they all grew up prepared to marry the publican, the tailor and the chemist as their mothers had done before them; but there was a continual soft current of feminine speculation and comment in Chesterbourne and Sible Pelden about the doings, the income, and possible bride of Victor Spring.

Viola had day-dreamed like the others, although she had never spoken to the young god. Even after she was Mrs Theodore Wither (and was not very happy, because after he was married to her, Teddy discovered that she was not so poetic and marvellous as he had supposed, and naturally this made him less fond of her) she sometimes found herself imagining a wedding in the old church at Sible Pelden, to which she and her father used sometimes to walk on Sundays, with herself in white satin and orange-blossoms; and, waiting for her at the end of the church as she came slowly down on her dear father's arm was Victor Spring.

Then she would wake up with a shock, realizing that she *was* married and would never have a lovely wedding like that, with a handsome young man to look down lovingly at her and tell her that she was beautiful.

And as she was now a widow, moored firmly in the bosom of her late husband's family, it did not seem likely that she would ever marry Victor Spring.

As she leaned against the window frame, crying because she was so lonely and missed her father so much, she could see through her tears and the thinly leaved trees the red brick and white woodwork of the Springs' house, Grassmere, crowning the hill on the other side of the valley.

Between the two hills, each with a house, was a little wood. Its paths were dark with evening now.

She stared at the house, realizing that it was his, yet not actually thinking about him. He was not a real person to her; he was a dream. But he lived, and had lived ever since she had known about him, in a wonderful world where everyone was happy, and wore lovely clothes, and went to dances and shows every night and enjoyed everything.

How she longed to live in that world!

The house looked romantic as a fairy palace to her, as she stared across through half a mile of twilit air. How big and rich it was! There was a light in one of the upper rooms, strong and golden (all the lights at The Eagles were dim; Mr Wither said that bright lights were bad for the eyes).

This is a beastly, miserable hole, she thought, the tears running warmly down, and I've got to live here for *ever*, until I'm as old as Tina. I'll never get away. Never.

Away on the other side of the valley sounded the long arrogant note of a car's horn. It was Victor Spring's great Bentley, bringing him back for the weekend, dashing homeward through the darkening lanes. Like the horn of the Prince who came to awaken the Sleeping Beauty it sounded, a thrilling, imperious call echoing through the little twilit wood.

# CHAPTER III

On the same April morning that Viola came to The Eagles Mrs Spring, of Grassmere, sat in the morning-room glancing through the *Daily Express* and sipping her orange juice.

Victor had already gone to London. The house still quivered with his departure; virtue had gone out of it. It was left to women and servants until his return in the evening.

He had said nothing at breakfast, except that he would be in to dinner, and only once had he glanced out of the window because something, a gleam of improper white, had caught his eye. Daisies, five of them, on the green suede lawn which his gardeners kept perfect.

But he at once looked down at his paper again, without frowning. By ten o'clock the daisies would be gone; the gardeners would have worked round to them in their daily routine.

The house and its grounds resembled the first-act set of an old-fashioned musical comedy. The brickwork was a strong new red, the woodwork, of which there was much, a dazzling white. So soon as either material lost this freshness, Victor had it cleaned and repainted, for he did not so much dislike shabbiness as take it for granted that shabbiness could not exist; and every room in the warm, perfectly equipped mansion went through the same strict treatment.

If gin was spilled upon a cushion of bright plum-red velvet with a heavy silver fringe, then that cushion disappeared and another one, of black satin embroidered heavily with irises in fourteen natural shades and costing 49s. 11d., took its place. Should an ashtray in the shape of a winsomely begging Sealyham fall on the floor and chip an ear, away it went, and another, shaped like a coquettishly imploring Cairn, appeared in its stead, each having cost 37s. 6d.

Baskets of brightly gilded wicker full of seasonal plants in blossom hung above the pleasant veranda which ran the length of the house. A troop of dogs sprawled in the sunlight on the veranda floor, not troubling to glance at the open french windows because all five knew that, if they strayed inside, they would be heartily thrashed.

Below the three tennis courts a shrubbery of rhododendrons sloped to the banks of the Bourne, where Victor had a private landing-stage, and the house for his outboard, punt and little sailing-boat. Every now and then a white sail glided past above the dark green bushes or the patched one of a barge, the colour of a tiger-lily, loomed by on its way up to Chesterbourne.

The house and grounds had that feeling (delightful or not so delightful; that depends upon whether one likes parties) of moving a little faster than other places, as though it were always upon the brink of a party. This was because cheerful, though permissible, noises sounded through the parquet-floored corridors and the luxurious rooms that did not contain a single book. A pretty maid steered the Hoover across a carpet (Mrs Spring hated plain maids; they depressed her), a burst of gay music came from a wireless that was being overhauled in readiness for next weekend's party, a young gardener whistled as he worked, or Mrs Spring sat before her pianola playing the Handkerchief Dance. The telephone rang every half-hour or so. Vans from Harrods, from Fortnum and Mason and Cartier, came up to the house, and out of them came plain, wickedly expensive-looking parcels that were carried triumphantly indoors. These were for Mrs Spring, whose hobby was shopping.

It was money royally spent that flowed through this house like the Gulf Stream; warming the rooms, making the maids smile and the gardeners whistle, luring vans to the door. Victor treated money, not like a tyrant that must be alternately fawned upon and bullied, but as an old pal; he stood it drinks, so to speak, and it stood him more drinks in return. He had a way with it; it came to his whistle.

His father had left him a valley in Kent filled up with soft-fruit beds and a factory for canning their produce, and this brought him a very handsome income; but Victor had used the Sunny Valley Brand as a mere jumping-off point. He had (to speak moderately) extended his interests. He was a rich man, and would be richer.

Despite the lavishness of his establishment, he lived within his income and did not get into debt. Indeed, for such a rich young man, with such golden prospects of being so much richer, he lived rather modestly. His tastes were simple: he liked the best and plenty of it.

Mrs Spring, daughter of a country-town doctor and a social rung or two above her late husband, had a more than comfortable income of her own, left to her by Mr Spring. Some of it went on beauty treatments. But they were useless; her skin knew that it was fifty-two years old and stretched over a body in ill-health, and it refused to look anything but ravaged. She dressed fashionably, without forgetting her age. Her delicacy of body made her often irritable, but in her heart she was content enough. She lived from moment to moment, unharried by imagination, enjoyed entertaining her many friends, was extremely fond of Victor and tried to be patient with her niece Hetty, but did not find this easy.

She was breakfasting earlier than usual because she was going up to London for a day's shopping. She enjoyed such excursions more than anything in the world; her only regret was that she had no daughter to enjoy them with her.

Hetty was no use at shopping. Hetty took no interest, unless Mrs Spring hurried into the book department at Harrods to buy a book of dog and horse pictures, costing 18s., for a friend who was keen on dogs and horses. Then, indeed, Hetty could hardly be dragged away. She was a thoroughly sickening girl. 'Old Het-Up', Victor called her, because she got so excited over poetry and all that sort of thing.

Nevertheless, Hetty was going to town today with her aunt because the fine weather seemed to have set in, and a gay, busy summer with many guests, parties and excursions lay ahead of Grassmere, for which its ladies must have the right clothes and plenty of them.

Mrs Spring compelled herself to relax while she sipped the juice and skimmed the anything-but-relaxing pages of the journal, but she was feeling irritable because Hetty was not there, dressed and ready to start. Hetty had eaten her breakfast and slipped off. She was always slipping off, and it annoyed Mrs Spring very much; she liked to have someone there to ask advice of, and to discuss the day's plans with.

Besides, at the last minute Hetty might be missing; that had happened once, and the train had been missed. Even Victor had been very angry with Hetty about that: he could not believe that anyone could actually miss a train. He was not easy-going.

Today there was plenty of time, but Mrs Spring was uneasy. She rang, and said to the maid who came in, 'Go and see if Miss Hetty is in her room, and ask her to come down.'

The girl, a very pretty little thing from Merionethshire, said, 'Yes, Madam,' and went out. But she did not go upstairs.

Victor's unrelaxing standard of efficiency kept the whole of Grassmere's interior new and spotless, and the grounds as well. But, like a king whose empire is so vast that he cannot find the time to visit certain squalid tribes on its frontiers, Victor never went into the hinterland of the vegetable garden, a desert of dumps, disused frames, manure heaps and a very large water-butt, originally painted a bright turquoise blue.

Time and weather had faded this colour to softness, and it now glowed coolly against the canopy of pale red and white blossoms in the little orchard, where the apple-trees were out. The almond-trees were flowering, and the cherry, and the pear in a waterfall of white stars, and the dark pink crab apple. Hetty sat on three old bricks with her back against the water-butt, a book on her knees, gazing up at the youngest gardener, a comely youth tied up here and there with bast. He was saying:

33

'You see, Miss Hetty, it's Mr Spring. He likes to know every single thing as goes in, Mr Spring does.'

'Yes, I know he does, but surely he'd never notice one more cherry-tree among all the others.'

'He'd be sure to see me puttin' her in, Miss Hetty. 'Sides, it 'ud take me off my reg'lar wuck. Proper lot to do there is, here.'

'I could put it in,' she said eagerly.

'Not right, you couldn't, if you'll excuse me a-sayin' soo, Miss Hetty. Why, even a doddy tree like that un here,' he pointed to a little cherry close by, 'her takes time to put in, an' it moost be done right. If she ain't done right, her might die, and you wouldn't like that, would you?'

His young voice, in which the colourless vowels taught to him at school were gradually being replaced by the natural broad ones of his county, was soft and kind as though he spoke to a child, but it was also amused. Miss Hetty certainly didn't goo on like most young ladies, and her differences were funny.

'No, I shouldn't,' she answered shortly, turning her head quickly away to look at the fairy cloud of flowers. Her small blue eyes were deeply set and slightly misty from too much reading. They had a resentful look which never left them except when she saw a book or the name of a writer.

'You see, Heyrick,' she began again, after a pause, then stopped. Then went on, 'Do you like music?'

'Don't know much about it, Miss Hetty.'

'Well, do you know a song called *In Summertime on Bredon*?'

'Like this, does it goo?' and Heyrick broke into beautiful whistle, strong as a blackbird's.

'That's it – that's it! How on earth did you come to know it?'

'On the wireless last night, Miss Hetty. Proper good 'un, that is.'

'And the words – do you remember the words?'

He grinned widely. 'Count I never noticed 'em, Miss Hetty.'

'Well, never mind, only they're very beautiful and the man who wrote them has just died. That's why I want to plant the cherry-tree, you see. In his memory, sort of.'

Heyrick nodded, his amused look deepening.

'He was a writer – a poet,' she explained, hugging her knees and

34

staring up at the starry white waterfall (*The pear stood high and snowed*). 'A very true poet.'

'Same as Kipling? We larned a piece by Kipling at school. *If*, it were called. Count I've forgotten most of it now.'

'Not a bit like Kipling,' corrected Hetty, 'though Kipling's a marvel. Only he's out of fashion, they say (dunderheads). Oh well,' scrambling up ungracefully and dusting her skirt, 'thanks, Heyrick. It doesn't matter. It's not worth the fuss there'd be. Only I thought as a wild cherry, full standard, only costs seven and sixpence, I could just buy one and stick it in somewhere. I might have known I couldn't . . . though there's room enough.'

'There is soo, Miss Hetty,' said Heyrick with feeling; he was a little lazy.

Hetty grimly pulled her hat over her resentful eyes, and was bending to pick up her expensive handbag from the ground when little Merionethshire came breathlessly round the water-butt.

'Please, Miss Hetty, Madam says will you go in. She wants you.'

'Did she send you out here?'

Hetty's tone was alarmed. The water-butt, in the only untidy corner at Grassmere, was her poetry-reading place.

'Indeed no, Miss Hetty, she said to go up to your room, only I thought as you'd most likely be out here, seeing it's a nice morning and Heyrick said—'

'All right. Thanks,' Hetty interrupted the flow of lilting Welsh. 'Don't tell anyone I come here, will you, please, Davies? It's nice to be quiet sometimes.'

'Indeed and I won't, Miss Hetty,' promised Merionethshire with a trace of condescension but willingly enough, and meant what she said. A secret was a secret, even if it wasn't about Boys. Any secret was better than none.

'Poor Miss Hetty,' said Merionethshire when Hetty had gone, turning a flower-like effect of carnation lips, peony cheeks and pansy-dark eyes on Heyrick. 'She did ought to get married, I think.'

'Count she ain't the only one,' and Heyrick loomed down upon little Merionethshire, who disappeared against the corduroys and bast in a storm of squeaks.

'Where did you get to, Hetty?' fretfully inquired Mrs Spring, pulling on her gloves. 'I do wish you wouldn't sneak off like that just when I want to talk to you.'

'Sorry, Aunt Edna.'

They took their places in the car, which moved off as Mrs Spring began to talk about the day's programme.

Hetty sat silent, in the smart coat and skirt chosen by her aunt, which she wore badly. She was a plump girl of a little over twenty, with dark hair worn in an untidy knob, a bad complexion and small, well-formed features that were unexpectedly attractive.

She was the only daughter of Mrs Spring's only sister; her father and mother were dead, and she had lived, since she was five, with her aunt and her cousin Victor. She had some hundred pounds a year of her own left to her by her mother, but Mrs Spring did not consider this pittance enough for a girl to live on in virtue and comfort, and had insisted upon carrying Hetty off.

Mrs Spring had loved her sister very dearly; their affection had been the deepest experience in her unimaginative life, and she had hoped that Hetty, as that sister's daughter, would be like Winnie come back again.

But Hetty had taken after her father's side; the unsuccessful (that is, poor) Franklins who were all teachers and parsons and librarians, and as dull as ditch-water, with their noses in books, their socks in holes and their finances in muddles. Hetty was a disappointment. All that Mrs Spring could do with Hetty was to let Victor see that her investments did not go down, while she herself chose her clothes and tried to marry her off.

Not that Mrs Spring was a fanatic about girls getting married; a lot of rubbish was talked about marriage, and nowadays a girl could have a really good time (dances riding, shows, flying, parties, yachting and golf) without marriage, especially if she had money.

But Hetty had no money. Mrs Spring did not look upon one hundred pounds a year as money: she would have agreed with those gangsters who refer contemptuously to small amounts as chicken feed. Hetty was also a discontented, queer girl whom nothing pleased but rubbishy books by immoral highbrow authors. So the sooner Hetty married, the better.

As for Hetty, she had not the courage to say so, but she considered the life led at Grassmere to be tedious, futile and coarse. (She was always wondering what Doctor Johnson would have said about it, and inventing Imaginary Conversations with him about the people who came down for weekends – 'Sir, Mr So and So is a fool, and twice a fool, for he is not aware of his folly.') Her aunt's interests bored her, and she found her cousin Victor's lack of imagination unattractive.

What was the use of a man's being handsome if he were also stupid?

She could talk to no one at Grassmere about books.

At Grassmere no one read books. They occasionally read a thriller from the Boots in Chesterbourne, but more often they looked at the *Tatler*, *Vogue*, the *Sunday Pictorial*, *Homes and Gardens*, and journals about cars and outboards. These periodicals had to compete with the wireless, the pianola, the telephone, visitors, gossip and the dogs. Usually they were defeated.

Hetty's passion for poetry (the word, usually too strong for the taste it describes, here falls short of her feelings) had been discovered by her at school, and fostered there. Now it must be indulged in secret; or her aunt and cousin laughed, then spoke sharply. They did not like young girls to be brainy and different. Brainy, different girls, who were yet not brainy enough to have a career, were misfits. When, like Hetty, they were bad at parties, riding, tennis, skiing, flying, yachting and golf, they were a trial, thorns in the Spring flesh.

Hetty turned to stare at The Eagles as the car passed; she always liked to look at that tall dark grey house in which lived Mr Wither and his sad-looking daughter. Hetty had never spoken to any of the Withers, but she liked to muse about the inside of their house and their life; she imagined it full of strange psychological complexities, like a very modern novel.

The house, with its dreary flowerless shrubs and darkly curtained windows, was as full of romance to her as a mansion in a story by Chekov. It was so different from Grassmere, where everything was beastly *new*.

I wish I could get away, thought Hetty wistfully as the car swung into the station yard, and live in a house like The Eagles, where it's peaceful, and life is full of a muted, melancholy beauty.

'Hetty! Your handbag!' exclaimed Mrs Spring.

The chauffeur bent and carefully picked it from the gutter.

# CHAPTER IV

When Viola had been at The Eagles four days, Mr Wither made another attempt to bring off the little talk, and this time he succeeded.

His den commanded a view of the little library across the hall, and by sitting with the door half-open in a ghastly draught he had discovered that Viola went to the library every day after lunch to choose a book.

She made no attempt to organize her days at The Eagles; she went about bored and miserable, and half the time Mr Wither (whose own days were well organized in prowling after his money and bothering Major-General Breis-Cumwitt and wondering how much money other people had and how it was getting on and organizing his wife and daughters and seeing that nothing was wasted) did not know what she did with herself. But for three days now he had seen her go to the library and stand for some time flicking over the pages of books and sometimes making a scornful little face which affronted Mr Wither very much, because it implied that the books in his library were not worth reading.

On the fourth day Mr Wither gave her five minutes to get settled at her flicking and face-making, then he quietly got up from his chair and scuttled across the hall.

'Oh!' cried Viola, dropping *My Dogs and Me* by Millie Countess of Scatterby. 'Oh, Mr Wither, how you made me jump!'

'Choosing a book?' inquired Mr Wither, with the smile he used when he wanted to lure people into doing something that they would dislike. 'Well, there's plenty of choice, plenty of choice. Getting along quite comfortably, eh? Settling down, and feeling quite at home?'

'Yes, thank you, Mr Wither,' muttered Viola, staring at him and desperately remembering how Shirley had warned her not to let Old Therm get her down. Stand up to him, the old heel, had been Shirley's advice.

'Then how about our little talk?' suggested he, moving temptingly towards the door, even as Pan, with one eye on a nervous nymph, might have waved invitingly at the distant woods.

She gulped, muttered something, and followed him.

She had never been in his den. It was frighteningly small, especially after Mr Wither had shut the door. He patted the gloomy arm-chair and apologized for the absence of the hellish one, 'But it was such a warm day that a fire was hardly necessary, was it?'

Viola nodded. To give herself courage she lolled back in the arm-chair, and this annoyed Mr Wither, because no one sprawling like that could possibly give proper attention to what he was going to say.

'I am sure you know what I want to talk to you about,' began Mr Wither in what was meant to be a cheerful tone but which only gave an alarmingly unnatural colour to his voice as though a fit were pending; at the same time he creaked forward and gazed at her with a fixed smile. 'Money.' He spoke the word reverently. 'A little word, but a very important one.'

Viola made a faint sound, gulped, and at last brought out, with her drowsy grey eyes wide as a kitten's with alarm, 'I can pay for myself.'

'Ha! Ha!' cried Mr Wither, patting her knee and shaking his head (though, in fact, why shouldn't she? She ate far too much butter; and he was relieved to learn that she *could* pay for herself. But that could be gone into later.)

'No, no. Of course, there is always a little difference in the housekeeping books when another mouth comes into an establishment, especially when that mouth is a *young* mouth, ha! ha! But the situation is not serious yet, Viola, ha, ha! No (though what you suggest is not at all a bad idea, and we might bear it in mind for the future), I did not want to talk to you about that. It is about your money. Theodore's money.' He lowered his voice and gazed glassily at her, as though at a sacred image. 'How much have you, my dear?'

There was a pause.

'I haven't anything,' giggled Viola, pulling out a Woolworth handkerchief and blowing her nose, while her suddenly brilliant grey eyes laughed at him above the coloured cotton.

She was very frightened: but how Shirley would roar when she heard this story!

'You haven't *anything*?'

Mr Wither was stunned. He gazed at her with his mouth open.

'Yes. No, I mean. Well, I've got—'

'Then what do you mean by saying that you could pay for yourself?' interrupted Mr Wither. Perhaps she was playing a joke; a wicked, senseless joke, but still, a joke. People did, he knew.

'Well, I was going to say that I could pay for myself for a bit.'

'For a bit?' muttered Mr Wither, shaking his head dazedly. 'What bit? What do you mean?'

'For a little while, I mean. Just for a bit. I've got twelve pounds.'

'Eh?'

'I've got twelve pounds,' she repeated, rather sulkily, staring into the huge black grate.

'Is that all?'

'Yes.'

'Where is it?' demanded Mr Wither, for even twelve pounds was something, and it ought to be properly taken care of. A girl like Viola might have left it lying about – in the bathroom, the car, anywhere.

'Upstairs.'

'Where?'

A tiny pause.

'In my bag.'

Mr Wither opened his lips, then pressed them tightly together. Then opened them.

'Do you mean to tell me that twelve pounds is all the money you have left, out of the sum left to you by your father?'

She nodded, still sulkily.

'Yes, but he didn't leave me much'

'How much?'

A longer pause.

'How much did your father leave you, Viola? Come, you must tell me, you know. This is very serious.'

'Fifty pounds.'

'A year, you mean? Fifty pounds a year?'

'No, just fifty pounds.'

'But the – the establishment – the shop,' cried Mr Wither. 'I understood from my son that your father was part proprietor.'

'Oh well, he did used to be, only he sold it to Mr Burgess. You see,' her eyes filled with tears, 'Dad was absolutely mad on amateur theatricals, and he did a lot for the Chesterbourne Players, putting in new lights and all kinds of things he did for them like that, and that's how his money went. It took a long time, of course. Years. When I was a kid we were all right. I went to the High School; I stayed there till I was sixteen. Only I don't think Dad had much head for business, he ought to have gone on the stage, we always said, and Mr Burgess is an old beast, everybody says so. Hard as they make them, Miss Catty – everybody says. And if you ask my opinion, I think he just cheated Dad.'

She wiped her eyes, trembling.

Mr Wither said nothing for a little while. Her tears embarrassed him, but he felt that they were only proper; he gave her time to recover her composure. This concession did not prevent him from being very seriously annoyed with her, and dismayed as well.

Still, there was Teddy's money; he had not yet heard about Teddy's money. All might yet be well. The omens were not good, but Mr Wither thrust the omens from his mind. She might have meant only twelve pounds *in cash*.

Presently he said,

'And Theodore's money? How much did my son leave you?'

'Ninety pounds,' she sighed.

'A year, that is? Ninety pounds a year?'

'No. In the bank, I mean.'

'Is that all?'

'Yes.'

'But,' cried Mr Wither in anguish, 'for twenty years Theodore never earned less than five pounds a week, and I myself, for the past year, allowed him an additional eighty pounds a year! For the last year of his life, when he married you, he was earning seven pounds a week.'

'Did he earn seven pounds a week?' she asked. After a pause, 'I used to wonder how much it was, but I never thought it was as much as that.'

Mr Wither had nothing to say to this: he thought it quite proper that a wife should not know how much her husband earned.

'But where did it all *go*?' he cried, creaking forward and gazing at her with popping eyes. 'What did he spend it on? He ought to have been able to save a hundred pounds a year. He never went any-where. He was not gay, or wild. Surely *you* must know where it all went?'

'Well, there was the rent, that was twenty-eight and sixpence a week, and he gave me thirty shillings for housekeeping, and there was the charwoman, and I had five shillings a week pocket money—'

Too much, thought Mr Wither. Unnecessary.

'. . . and there were his fares and lunches and hair tonics . . .'

'Hair tonics?' exclaimed Mr Wither. Were all his children insane on the subject of hair? Tina was always complaining about *her* hair and wanting to spend money on it, and now Theodore had appar-ently spent about four pounds a week on his.

'Well, lotions, you know, and Rowland's Macassar Oil and things. His hair was . . .'

She stopped. Sometimes she was schoolgirlishly loyal to her hus-band's memory, and such a scruple had overcome her now. It made her feel very sorry to remember that poor Teddy had worried about going bald (though she used to laugh about it with Shirley) and she did not see why his horrid old father should know everything. She was quite serious now; and did not feel like laughing any more.

'And then there were clothes,' she continued faintly. 'He liked to look smart, you know. And – and of course he had to. For Business.'

Mr Wither snorted. He knew all about that particular business.

'And lots of other things . . .' she ended hastily.

Mr Wither nodded glumly, staring at her with his knees a little apart and his short red hands, darkly veined, spread over their caps. She looked quickly down at her shoes.

'And so you haven't anything,' said Mr Wither at length, still glumly staring.

She shook her head.

He continued to gaze at her for a little while longer, shaking his head with compressed lips; then he bent forward abruptly and stood up.

'Well, we shall have to see, that's all,' he observed.

With which comforting remark he opened the door for her, and she escaped.

When she had run quickly upstairs, he returned to the arm-chair and to his thoughts. They were not cheerful.

She had no money, she ate a great deal of butter, she was only twenty-one, and she had come, at his express and urgent request, to reside at The Eagles for life.

Viola ran all the way up to her bedroom, and flomped face downwards on the bed. She lay for a little while staring vacantly at the carpet and slowly clacking her shoes together while she waved her legs in the air. Then she got desperately up, put on her coat, and ran very quietly downstairs again.

She slipped out through the back way by the garage (late stables). She liked this side of the house, which was directly under her bedroom window, because there was always more going on there than elsewhere at The Eagles. The maids did not make much noise, but there was often a comforting smell of cooking, and sometimes Saxon was there, doing things to the car. Viola considered Saxon to be very stuck-up and too handsome for a boy, but she could not help being pleased every time she saw him because he was the only other person at The Eagles who had no wrinkles. His presence made her feel less lost in a sea of ancients.

44

He was there this afternoon, standing with his legs a little apart in shiny black gaiters, and a pair of very white shirt-sleeves rolled up over his arms while he polished the car. The brilliant sunlight of April, that made most faces look old, only increased the youth of his.

He saw her coming through the window of the car, and gave her such a gay, mischievous, impudent smile that she could not believe her eyes. Well! what's up with him this afternoon, she thought, her spirits soaring at the friendliness of it: but when she came round the car, and went past him, he was as correct as though the smile had never been.

'Good afternoon,' she said shyly, slowing her pace a very little. She had not quite the courage to call him Saxon.

'Good afternoon, Madam,' responded he, respectfully.

'Isn't it a lovely day!' she observed, more faintly, almost over her shoulder as she left the yard.

'Yes, Madam, beautiful.' He gave her a direct, respectful look but did not smile.

Feeling snubbed, and cross with him, she stuck her hands into her pockets and set out along the road beside the little wood.

He doesn't half think no small beer of himself; been drinking pearls out of a gold cup, I should think (quoting old Miss Cattyman at the shop). I only said it was a nice day—

> Don't be so disagreeable!
> I've only come to say
> How do you do-dy, do-dy, do-dy
> do-dy, do-dy-day!

That old song of Dad's! I do think death's awful; it's like half of you gone away.

P'raps Saxon's people are rich, and he's doing it for a joke, she mused, swinging along, kicking at little stones. None of the Withers had mentioned Saxon to her since she had been there. She was surprised to see a new chauffeur at the station when Mrs Wither met her; she had not known that they had one. There had

45

not been the usual exchange of small items of family news, which goes on in most families, between Teddy and his wife and the people at The Eagles. Teddy felt that his parents and sisters disapproved of his marriage with a shopgirl, and he had seen even less of them after his marriage, so they were almost strangers to his wife. An ageing chauffeur, to match the ageing maids, had driven Viola on the few occasions when she had been in the Wither car. Saxon was a new one on her.

No, she thought, he can't be doing it for fun. No one 'ud come to live at The Eagles for fun.

She recalled her own disagreeable situation; and sighed.

She now wished with all her heart that she had been brave enough to take Shirley's advice and refuse to live at The Eagles. Good lord, girl, you've had one marvellous escape; don't go and tie yourself up with The Therms *again*, said Shirley. Besides, you know what old Therm is; it's your money he wants. Only in this case want must be his master, because you haven't got any.

But I did have, thought Viola, walking with her head bent and her hair glittering like spun glass, only I spent such a lot. Nearly a hundred pounds. I am *awful*.

It had not been easy to keep from spending money while staying with Shirley; the Davises had such a good time. They ran a little car, and danced a lot, and went to many parties, and gave them, with much drink, in their pretty little house.

All this was done on what Shirley called The Plain Van system. The Plain Van, said Shirley, was the modern Fairy Godmother. You wished: and whoopee! It was at your door.

Viola could not stand outside the parties, nor could she sponge on Shirley; besides, she welcomed this flow of Greater London's gaieties; it took her mind away from her grief over her father (and Teddy, of course; she was sorry about poor Teddy). She paid her share; brought a bottle to this party and stood in with the eats for that, bought a new dress for another. She went often to the hairdresser, because her hair must look immaculate, like the hair of all Shirley's crowd. The Crowd was six or seven young matrons, with jobs, and their husbands; all very smart, all very knowing, all just a little bored with the ones they were married to and wondering just a little what Jim or Roger, Anne or Chrissie, would be like to have a flaming affair with.

In fact, Jim, Roger, Anne and Chrissie would have been exactly like Tom, Archie, Irene and Connie, but as they lived in different bodies, there was at least the promise of Romance. The Crowd, when it spoke of Love over its morning coffee, was cynical. Men – and women, said the husbands over their drinks – were out for what they could get. But in its secret heart, The Crowd was starving for Romance, more and more of it, so that the real world dissolved, and no effort need be made to adjust oneself to the real world. When The Crowd fell, it fell hard.

Viola remained uncorrupted. Was it because, when she was eleven, her father used to declaim to her in his fine voice:

> The moon shines bright: in such a night as this
> When the sweet wind did gently kiss the trees
> And they did make no noise, in such a night
> Troilus methinks mounted the Troyan walls,
> And sighed his soul toward the Grecian tents,
> Where Cressid lay that night.

Probably not. She liked to watch her father as he read, and to listen to the smoothly rolling tones; she felt no curiosity about what the words meant. It was only Shakespeare, and she was used to him.

But she did not like being kissed by Jim and Roger, Tom and Archie. When they whispered that they were crazy about her, she wriggled away and suggested that they should try to get to Paris. The Crowd liked her, summing her up as a funny little thing, under-sexed, but sweet.

She had enjoyed her three months with The Crowd. Now, it seemed impossible that she had ever had such a lovely time.

Yet nearly all her money was gone.

She had been afraid to refuse to live at The Eagles. She felt, strongly if not clearly, that it was up to her to go there because she had not loved Teddy as much as he had loved her. Shirley had

47

promised to find her a job, but Viola had not been sure that she could do the sort of job that Shirley would find; she was not clever.

On the whole, what with being afraid of Mr Wither, and her conscience, and having very little money, and not wanting to sponge on Shirley, and being firmly told to do her duty and be grateful for her luck by old Miss Cattyman and the aunts in Chesterbourne, she had decided that it would be best to go.

Here she looked up, saw a little path going into the wood, and turned down it, still with bowed head and hands in her pockets. She was planning a long letter to Shirley that she would write that evening.

The evenings at The Eagles were almost the worst part of the twenty-four hours, because, outside the house, all was so beautiful. The sunset slowly faded into a tender twilight, the stars shone out, and the young moon, and if anyone glanced up at the tall windows of the drawing-room, a big, slow-flying bird was crossing the flushed sky on its homeward way – a heron, perhaps, or a swan from the marshes.

'What became of that piece of cold pork?' would demand Mr Wither, looking up suddenly from his newspaper.

'It's all right, dear; Cook is making some patties.'

Mr Wither would return to the journal.

Viola would sit with a ten-year-old novel by Berta Ruck (a lovely story, lent to her by Tina, but it only made her feel worse because the young man in it was such a darling), wondering what Shirley and The Crowd were doing, and then at a quarter-past ten it was time to go to bed, and tomorrow evening would be exactly the same, *for ever*, unless some awful old thing about fifty came to dinner and what was the use of that?

So this evening, for a change, she would write to Shirley and tell her how ghastly it was, and how mouldy were all the Therms, except Tina who was really very decent only she got on your nerves because she was simply dying to get married, and not a hope, my dear, she must be forty if she's a day. And I daren't take the bus into Chesterbourne to see Catty and the aunts because the Therms pull such a face if I even mention THE SHOP!

It's funny about being married, she thought, walking deeper into the wood. I didn't *mind* it, but it all seemed so ordinary, somehow, not a bit like what you read in books, and even now I don't feel like Mrs Wither (she smiled), I feel just the same as I did when I was at school, only not so happy. Well, you wouldn't expect a widow and an orphan to be happy, of course.

Here she stopped her soft whistling, realizing how quiet everything was, and stared vaguely about her.

The broad light above the road had gradually gone, veiled away by branch after branch laden with transparent, rosy-dun leaves, stiff and fresh. Young birches, and dark festoons of vigorous ivy matted on the oak trunks, helped to make this gradual veil and seclusion, while a feeling of freshness, solitude and peace told her that she was in the heart of the little wood. She looked up into the delicate shades of a massive bough, thinking, 'It's lovely here.' The path still sloped gently down, and under a hollow made by fern curling over and by hazel thickets, she heard water running.

Down by the hidden stream, so piled over with dried branches that she only noticed it on her second glance, was a little lean-to made of rusty corrugated iron. It stood in a blackened patch of ground, where white ashes were gently spraying under the wind.

As she looked, round the corner of the hut came a head covered to the shoulders with thick grey curls like a cavalier's, and a dirty sturdy old man came out. He stared back at her, and presently called:

''Ullo, ducks,' nodding in a satisfied way. His voice was low, hoarse and cautious, as though he were about to tell a secret, and he wore a coat and trousers of sacking, neatly sewn with little flat pads of dirty newspaper. On his feet were huge broken boots carefully tied together with string.

Viola began to move away. She thought that he was mad. She knew who he was: The Hermit. Occasionally there was a paragraph about him in the *Chesterbourne Record*, but she had not known that he lived in this little wood; she was rather sorry he did.

'Don't you be afraid o' me,' he called, louder. 'I know 'oo you are all right. Young Mrs Wither up The Eagles. Ain't that right?'

She nodded, reassured. His eyes were very small and their brightness made her think of an animal's, but they were sane.

'Knew you was,' said the Hermit, whose conspirator voice and the wild logic of whose dress contrasted curiously with his gossiping tone. 'Knew your Late by sight, too. Fat, weren't 'e?'

This was true; and, like most true remarks, rude. She said nothing.

'You ever 'eard o' me?' he went on. 'Up The Eagles, I mean?'

She shook her head.

'What, not from old Shak-per-swaw?'

'Old *who?*' She moved a little nearer down the slope forgetting her mistrust in curiosity.

'Old Shak-per-Swaw. Your Late's dad. All for Number One, see. Shak-per-Swaw.'

She only saw that he meant Mr Wither.

''E knows me well enough, old Shak-per-Swaw does. Always on about me to the Council 'e is, wanting to 'ave me turned out. But bleshyer, they don' take no notice of 'im. I don't do no 'arm, and Mr Spring puts in a word for me now and again, so I'm all right. Like to come inside?'

He jerked his head at the frowsy hut.

She shook her head, smiling.

'Ain't much doin' up The Eagles, is there?' he asked suddenly, with such a violent wink that she thought it was a spasm of his eye.

She shook her head again, still smiling.

She had never been taught by her father that people must be kept in their places and that because A has enough to eat and enough to wear, B, who has not, must be respectful to him. She had not seriously caught the infection of snobbery from Miss Cattyman and her aunts, who had it chronically. Her father would have called the Hermit 'A wonderful old bit of Shakespearian character, Viola, ripe and rare'; and though she did not like his wink, it did not occur to her to think him over-familiar.

However, she felt an ashamed loyalty to Teddy and his relatives, so she answered with more reserve than was natural to her:

'It's a bit lonely.'

'Ah. Not thinking o' getting married again?'

'No,' laughing.

'Not cold in bed o' nights?' and this time it was clear that the wink was not a spasm.

But at that she really did move on, saying 'Good afternoon' in a prim voice and blushing.

'Goo'-bye, ducks!' called the Hermit, staring yearningly after her; then louder, 'In a bit of a 'urry this afternoon, ain't yer?'

She hurried on, taking no notice though he called after her several times, and climbed the gentle slope until she found another path which led her to the road. The trees here were beeches, shooting up into the fairy blue of the sky and making a murmuring green cavern with their leaves. Here she was near Victor Spring's house; the red and white turrets gleamed through the fence of quick-growing conifers which he had had planted to screen his residence, and presently she passed the white gates of the drive.

She walked slowly, staring, and wondering what the people who lived there were doing. *He* would be in London, of course; but she could hear laughter and cries and the soft energetic thud! of balls on overstrung rackets coming from the tennis courts, the whirr of a mowing-machine and the joyous yelping of a young dog. Happy house! where everyone was busy and entertained all day long!

This road was lonely, but presently she came to a crossroads, one of which led to the main road from Colchester to Bracing Bay, and here there was a settlement of iron shacks, kiosks and a filling-station, with one or two little cottages so plastered with TEA notices and NEW-LAID EGGS notices and CIGARETTE notices and LADIES and GENTLEMEN notices that their formerly decent faces could barely be seen. Two taller cottages, without any notices, standing half-retired in the green shades of the wood, caught her glance, and she sauntered along the path which led to them.

They were joined together, two grey little buildings with peaked roofs and 'St Edmunds Villas 1893' on a scroll across their front. One was empty and falling to ruin, with broken windows and a sealed door round which the spring grass was blowing. The front door of the other stood open before a patch of glowing green grass thinly sown with the cool purple-blue heads of bluebells.

Viola lingered to admire the flowers, and to stare into the house's little parlour. An attempt had been made there at elegance; the walls had recently been re-covered with a cheap buff-coloured paper, and two or three dim old watercolours and photographs were sparsely arranged on them as though someone had just learned that over-crowded walls are unfashionable. A shiny new wireless cabinet, made of cheapest varnished wood, stood in one corner and pieces of bright blue material had been arranged over the shabby seats of the horsehair chairs. Two rugs from Marks and Spencer's, the colour of mud, covered the most worn parts of the carpet.

Even to Viola's casual glance the little parlour looked depressing and mean. The only pretty thing in it was a bunch of Solomon's Seal stuffed into a Woolworth vase on the round Victorian table, and even the long leaves and thick white bells of these were limp, as though dying for water.

As she lingered staring, the door into the parlour was jerked open. Someone came in, glanced sharply at her and slammed the front door. Embarrassed, she walked on.

The woman who had slammed the door hurried back into the scullery, whence came a cloud of smelly steam; and presently a low dismal sound began, which gradually increased until words were distinguishable. Even at this stage the noise could hardly be called talking; it was rather a sort of grizzling through parted lips while the hands of the grizzler were hard at work.

It was Mrs Caker, complaining about everything.

'. . . proper mucky, they are, worse'n worse every week. If I weren't afeared o' losin' the work, I'd speak to she. Aye, mingy owd cat, she is, sendin' blankets out ter wash 'stead o' to the larndry, and her dog's pillow-covers . . . disgrace, that's what they are, disgrace. Aye, if it weren't for the money, that's what I'd do, for sure, on'y how'm I ter know he won't walk out of the house one day and leave maye wi' on'y the washin', an' where'll I be then? Proper hard he is, an' cunnin'. Wish I know'd what he gets . . . ah, wish I knew! The maids up there might know; count I might ask 'em, on'y they're soo high an' mighty. He might tell maye, his own mother, aye, he might. 'Tis his dooty, for sure, to tell maye.'

She stood upright, straightening her back with a little moan.

A green woodland light fell through the dirty window of the scullery, and gave a ghostly look to her face as she glanced up. She had been a very pretty woman, and her large blue eyes, delightfully set in her head with an attractive slant, were still beautiful; her little nose was pretty too. But she had hardly any teeth; dirt was grimed into her skin, and her expression was discontented. She had thick brown hair, badly cut in a bush and caught with a pink mother-o'-pearl slide; a dirty blouse was pulled tightly over her bosom, and the hem of an old-fashioned skirt made of very good but very dirty cloth dipped in pools of water on the stone floor. This was Me Skirt; she had worn it for twenty years, and hoarded it for years before that. It had the rounded hips and braided hem of the early 1900s.

The deep blue eyes, swelling bosom, and a hint of laughter in her look, shining through the discontent, made her a woman that men would always want to talk to. She looked as though she would griz-zle but take nothing seriously.

'Nothen to him, it isn't,' she went on, bending again over the tin bath. '"*Why don't you get up earlier*," says he (mimicking). 'Cause I don't care to trouble, mie lad, that's why. When I am up, there's no comfort, no prosperity nowhere. Never thinks I might like a drink up The Arms, never takes maye to the Pictures—'

Slam! A bowl of steaming clothes went down on the greasy flag-stones.

'. . . aye, he's ashamed o' maye, that's what it is. Maybe I have got a bit slumocky, had enough to make maye, t'ain't as though I were old yet. I'm not old, nay, I'm not. If t'weren't for the old man, where'd I be for a bit o' company? Aye, much he cares. A bad son he is, bad and cunnin'. And who'd wash his seven shirts a week if I died! Seven shirts a week to wash 'n iron for him, and no prosper-ity nowhere.'

While she wrung the last drops from a cheap shirt of pale blue cotton, the scullery door opened and a man, outlined against the bright forest landscape, stood looking into the little cell.

'Mother, is my shirt ready?' he asked crisply.

'Aye,' she answered, not looking round.

It was the beautiful young chauffeur.

# CHAPTER V

For a fortnight nothing interesting happened.

The weather, the sky and woods, grew steadily more lovely as the spring deepened, with its exciting feeling of promise that ends in the black-green trees and almost silent birds of August. But none of the people in this story could be satisfied with perfect weather and landscape; they wanted other things.

Mr Wither said not a word more to Viola about their little talk. When she thought about this silence of his, she was disturbed for her future, and wondered if he would turn her out of The Eagles, and almost hoped that he would, because then she would have to go and live with Shirley; or go back to work in the shop and live with Catty or one of the aunts. She would not mind doing that, if she could go to town sometimes and see Shirley and The Crowd.

Mr Wither, however, was not going to turn his daughter-in-law out. He did not think it necessary to tell her this, because he had never threatened to turn her out, and therefore did not consider that she needed reassuring; but his mind was made up. There she was; there she would have to stay. Mrs Wither had made it up for him. She agreed with him that Viola was a silly, extravagant and rather deceitful girl, but she gave a number of reasons why she should be allowed to stay. All the cousins would Say Things if she went, she did not really cost much to keep if one thought of their income (though I know that we are not rich, said Mrs Wither hastily) and she was, after all, their dead son's wife. Also, she was company for Tina.

Madge ought to be enough company for Tina, objected Mr Wither. Her own sister.

Madge has her golf and tennis, dear, said Mrs Wither. She is not really much company for Tina. Tina is very fond of Viola, she said so the other day.

Oh well, then. Mr Wither supposed that Viola must stay. After all, he seldom saw her except at meals, and though he would never forgive her for having deceived him about the money, she now gave him no active trouble. She was a woman. She could always be organized.

It did not occur to Mr Wither that Viola had already on several occasions shown that she would not be organized.

As for Viola, she had settled down. The Withers did not often make a remark which drew attention to the depths hidden under the surface of daily life, because their attention was fixed upon its details, and when the depths insisted upon being noticed, the Withers ran away; but Mrs Wither did once remark to Madge that Viola seemed to have quite settled down.

'H'n'h,' retorted Madge, with a contemptuous expression.

Like her father, she mistrusted Viola because Viola was so young and rather pretty; she suspected that Viola had 'caught' Teddy. 'Caught' was not clearly defined in Madge's mind, but it meant that Teddy had been bamboozled into marrying Viola by wiles, possibly 'beastly' ones.

Madge described all the natural development of love between men and women, when its expression passed beyond the handshake, as beastliness. It was possible, of course, to have a man pal without any slop. In moments of emotion, when he had just done something pretty super at some game, you might bang him on the back; in return, he might slap you between the shoulder blades. That was all right; that was the decent friendly expression of deeply felt emotion. There were one or two young men up at the Club whom Madge enjoyed banging on the back on somewhat slight excuses. A very hard handgrip was all right, too, when saying goodbye to a soldier who was sailing next week for India with a young wife. Such a grip showed him that, though he had chosen to be sloppy over a fool, there was still a sensible woman left in the world who could give a man the unsloppy palship that he really needed – as he would no doubt realize jolly soon and be pretty fed-up.

But kisses were sloppy, unless accompanied by scuffles and shrieks under the mistletoe in front of a tolerant Christmas crowd, and all stronger manifestations of love were beastly.

Madge's ideal was simple: it was decency, just common decency, but surprisingly few people managed to come up to it. If one looked, it was pretty sickening how much beastliness one could see in a week, even round a tiny place like Sible Pelden, especially in the spring.

Dogs, of course, were decent, more decent than human beings. Also, they could be controlled. But Mr Wither would not let Madge keep a dog. They had fought that battle out many times during the last ten years; and now Madge never suggested that she should have a dog. But she went on wanting one, 'pretty badly', as she once blurted out to Tina.


Cautiously as a sea-anemone, as any apparently fragile growth that must adapt itself to its world or die, Viola had been making little pockets of fun and comfort for herself during her first weeks at The Eagles.

Tina was an unexpected help. She was old, of course, but she was so *awfully* kind, and together they discovered the joy of laughter over incidents that did not amuse other people. Viola had a little humour, Tina had a little too, and when these came together they fed one another and grew.

It made life at The Eagles less depressing, less like a frightening marking-time that would go on for ever, until one was old, if two people could see that it was all rather funny, really. And perhaps, after all, something would happen.

The worst part of life at The Eagles, Viola and Tina decided, was the constant *wanting something to happen*; one did not know what, not necessarily something wonderful, but just something. This desire, and the illogical feeling that it would be fulfilled, haunted their days like a perfume or a tune. It made them restless, glancing at their watches to see how long it was until a meal, then wishing that it was time for the next one as soon as that one was over, wishing that it was time to go up to bed, to get up, to go down to breakfast, glance over the paper . . . the days and nights glided into one another like a long dull dream, and the weeks. It was May.

Once Viola took the bus into Chesterbourne and had a lovely afternoon with Catty and the Aunts. Her happiness came mostly from sticking it on to Catty and the Aunts, and pretending that she was perfectly happy in a gay, luxurious home surrounded by adoring in-laws, but this she did not realize. She only felt the pleasure of being once more in places she knew, smelling the familiar lineny odours in the shop, patronizing the two latest little 'prentice girls in their shabby frocks, with their big alarmed eyes; and drinking in Miss Cattyman's mixture of affection and disapproval, and watching the tears come into her ageing eyes when she spoke of 'your father, Vi. Your dear father.'

This slow gathering of tears while Miss Cattyman spoke of Howard Thompson was one of the earliest things that Viola could remember; when she was a little girl she used to watch for it, fascinated, as Miss Cattyman knelt before her, circling Viola's small velvet waist with her two hands, seamed by countless tiny work-lines. Miss Cattyman, and two recurring shrimps of 'prentices with popping eyes and sudden fits of impertinence, were like the foundations of Burgess and Thompson's: it was impossible to think of the shop without them.

The Aunts were Howard Thompson's sisters, two kind, small, fattish, stupid women, solemnly anxious that Viola should do her duty and be a good girl. One was a district nurse, the other kept house for her. They were devoted to one another, and found their busy life, darkened by small cares and lit by small escapes from care, well worth the living.

But Viola rather spoiled her chances with Catty and the Aunts by pretending that she was so happy at The Eagles.

Before they saw her, so cheerful in a new hat bought that day in

Chesterbourne, they had been prepared to offer her comfort, advice, and even a home for life if she needed one. But she made it so clear that she had a pleasant home already, and did not need advice or comfort, that the Aunts and Catty lost a little of their interest in her. Happiness can never hope to command so much interest as distress.

She's all right, thank goodness, thought the three old women, a little relieved at not having to give up what spare rooms they had, but also a little disappointed because now none of them would be able to say '. . . and so I gave the poor child a home; what else could I do?' And Viola, riding home in the bus, felt depression creeping over her as she realized that now it would be difficult to go to the Aunts or Catty and ask to be given a home in return for fifteen shillings a week out of a salary earned at Burgess and Thompson's. What had made her pretend that she was quite happy at The Eagles? She was bored, depressed, haunted by a feeling that the months were flying and she would soon be old.

I am a silly ass, she thought; she seldom discovered her true motives for her behaviour. Actually, it was her loyalty to the dead Teddy, whom she had not loved, that made her pretend she was so happy with his family.

Also, like most very young people, she found it difficult, almost impossible, to admit that she was unhappy to somebody old. Old people (she dimly felt) were so beastly *pleased* when you said you were fed-up. Ah, their faces said, so life isn't all roses and honey, after all, you see! Just because you're twenty-one, you needn't think you'll escape. You'll learn. You just wait.

That was what Mr and Mrs Wither's faces had said only yesterday about Saxon, when they saw him walk past the window on his afternoon off, wearing a grey suit in which he looked as beautiful as he did in his dark uniform (differing therein from many chauffeurs, whose appearance when in mufti suggests that of escaped convicts).

Not that Viola was interested, now, in Saxon. He was only a local boy whose people had come down in the world, whose services Mr Wither had got cheap because he had picked up his knowledge of driving at the cross-roads service station and this was his first job.

He used to mess about at the station doing odd jobs for the proprietor, and when Mr Wither's own chauffeur left him to get married, Saxon had applied for the post. His mother lived over on the other side of the wood in a dirty little cottage, and they had no money except what Mrs Caker made by taking in washing and the two pounds a week that Saxon earned by driving the car and looking after the garden.

His father had been a prosperous miller, who drank away every penny he earned; ten years ago, one snowy Christmas morning, he had been found drowned under his own mill-wheel.

'. . . fell in when he was drunk,' ended Tina, with a spiteful note in her voice, as she finished telling Viola Saxon's story. They were sitting in Viola's bedroom with the big window open to the lovely afternoon, mending their stockings and gossiping, a day or two after Viola's visit to Chesterbourne.

'Isn't his name really Saxon, then?'

'Oh yes, but when he asked Father for the job he said could he drop the Caker and just be called Saxon and Father said yes. It's such an ugly name. Caker, I mean.' Tina sharply bit off her silk.

'He's rather conceited, isn't he?'

'Oh, that's just his manner. He's very keen on being the perfect chauffeur nowadays, but he wasn't always such a model, I can tell you. When I was a kid about your age, up at the Art School in London and coming home for weekends, I used to see him leading a gang of his own age all over the neighbourhood, trespassing, and robbing orchards.' Her hands sank in her lap, the needle poised over the grey silk, and she stared through the open window at the light-filled sky with an absent expression. 'He was always in some kind of a mess, and as cool as a cucumber, never lost his head, and used to make people laugh when they wanted to be angry with him. He had an old red jersey full of holes, I remember, and such bright eyes. I used to think he looked like a young wolf – sort of silky and dangerous.'

'Good lord!' said Viola mildly, opening her own narrow grey eyes with a cheerful smile. 'As bad as all that?' This was her usual comment on any flight of fancy.

Tina laughed, but she looked a little annoyed, and ashamed, too. No, it had not been as bad as all that. The book on feminine psychology was teaching her to try to be honest with herself; and she had to admit that her comparison of Saxon with a young wolf had been made, not twelve years ago, but last week. The truth was not 'I used to think that he looked like a young wolf,' but 'Now, remembering how he looked, I think he was like a young wolf.'

And *had* he looked so like a young wolf? Why dangerous?

Damn the book; damn trying to be honest with oneself. How unhealthy introspection is!

'He's not much good, anyway,' she ended crisply. 'Out for what he can get, I should imagine.'

'What's his mother like?'

'Oh, an awful old slut. At least, she's not so old really, I suppose, but she's had a lot of trouble, and that class,' she bit off her silk sharply again, 'ages so quickly. Mother has some old story about Mrs Caker being the Belle of Sible Pelden umpteen years ago, and driving to church with her father every Sunday in a pony-trap and a white dress, with a big hat all over poppies. It's difficult to imagine her now, anyway. They've just gone down and down.'

'You don't like Saxon, do you?'

'My dear child, he's only the chauffeur,' quickly, with such hauteur in her voice that Viola looked up, surprised. 'One doesn't like or dislike servants. As a matter of fact I'm rather sorry for him. He's had a rotten time since he grew up; country people won't let you forget, you know, when there's been a mess-up in your family, and I think he feels it more than most boys in his position would. Or perhaps he doesn't. I really don't know. Anyway, he's quite a good chauffeur now, and Father gets him cheap, so we're all happy. What about a walk before tea?'

Tea that afternoon was to be graced by the presence of a visitor, one Mr Spurrey, an old friend of Mr Wither.

Mr Wither honoured so few people with his friendship that those he did honour were invested with an awful importance, which made their visits resemble a Personal Appearance of the Dalai Lama. For days after Mr Wither had announced, from a letter read at breakfast, that Gideon Spurrey was visiting in the neighbourhood and would come to see them all at The Eagles on Friday afternoon, a vibration of solemn excitement was felt throughout the house. The maids were instructed to prepare Mr Spurrey's favourite sandwich and cake, Saxon was detailed to call for Mr Spurrey at the house where he was staying with the car, and all the womenfolk were warned by Mr Wither that tea would be at a quarter-past four, not a moment before, not a moment after. Tina and Viola must have their hair properly arranged (or whatever it was that made them so frequently late for meals), Madge must cut short whatever game she happened to be charging about in that afternoon, and Mrs Wither must forgo her nap. By four o'clock four women and Mr Wither must be seated in the drawing-room to receive Mr Spurrey.

So when Tina, at a quarter to three, suggested going out for a walk, Viola said,

'But what about Mr Spurrey? Will there be time?'

'Oh heavens, yes, of course there'll be time. We'll only go a little way. What are you going to wear?'

'This.'

'So am I; I changed after lunch on purpose. All we need do when we get back is our faces. Come along, for heaven's sake; I want some air.'

Viola was used to these desperate little fits of air-wanting on Tina's part; they blew up like typhoons on a smooth sea, out of hungry depths. She docilely put on a pair of clean gloves (Shirley had taught her, on some unknown authority, that it is smarter to wear gloves and no hat than it is to wear hat and no gloves) and they set off, proposing to return in an hour.

The energy and beauty of the spring afternoon, the fact that each was wearing a new and becoming dress, and the prospect of a ramble on the fresh edge of the wood before the ordeal of tea with Mr Spurrey raised their spirits to gaiety. Also, after Mr Spurrey had gone, he could be giggled over; and they giggled in anticipation. They walked along by the wood talking loudly, swinging their arms and kicking at bits of stick, picking a bluebell here and pulling a spray of young leaf there, and deciding that they would just have comfortable time to walk to the cross-roads before turning back. They meant to go round by the road, as they had not been that way for some time.

Moments passed so pleasantly that they did not notice the stealthy packing of clouds across the brilliant sky, and they were a good mile from The Eagles when a voice hailed them, in a warning tone touched with complacence—

'Goin' ter rain. Spoil them pretty frocks o' yourn.'

Startled, they looked up, and saw the Hermit standing on a rabbit-bank beside the wood's edge, gazing fondly down upon them. The Hermit liked female society, of which he did not get enough. He spent many hours in each week with Mrs Caker. Her draggle-tail dignity, and her memories of former Caker glories, at first made her almost unable to see the sturdy form of the Hermit in her very front-garden, but under the fire of his flattery she soon melted. She loved talking, and so did he; they would sit in the scullery (Mrs Caker would not at first have him in the parlour) engaged upon some pithering and unnecessary task such as sorting old newspapers or scraping the labels off jam-jars (which the Hermit collected) and talking themselves weak and hoarse.

'Come out without yer 'ats, ain't yer,' continued the Hermit. 'Sensible girls. Good for the 'air, that is. Makes it 'ealthy, like mine.' He shook his grey curls. 'Keeps yer from looking yer age, thick 'air does. Now 'ow old,' to Viola, 'would you say I was?'

It was starting to rain.

Tina and Viola ran to the edge of the wood and stood, as far from the Hermit as possible, under the thin canopy of beech-leaves. They looked up anxiously, the clouds hung low and thick.

'Eh?' demanded the Hermit. ' 'Ow old would yer say I was?'

Viola glanced sideways at Tina, who shook her head. They both stared aloofly in front of them. Viola's dress was darkly marked by raindrops and Tina's ruffles were already limp.

''OW OLD WOULD YER SAY I WAS?' suddenly roared the Hermit through his hollowed hands, standing on tiptoe.

'Oh good heavens, how should we know? About sixty, I suppose,' said Tina, jumping violently and giving him a distracted look. 'Vi,

63

do you think we'd better run for it? We can't get more soaked than we're getting here, and it's nearly twenty to four.'

'Seventy-six,' nodded the Hermit triumphantly, standing on the rabbit-bank with his curls streaming rainwater. 'But like a young man, I am. Like a young man. And why, you asks, am I like a young man? (in all sorts o' ways, mind you, not only me 'air). Because I lives a natchral, 'ealthy, out o' doors life like Gawd meant us to live. That's Why.'

'I really think we'd better run,' said Viola, also giving the Hermit a rather distracted look; one never knew what he would say next but one could always guess. 'I say, will there be an awful row, do you think?'

'I'm sure,' said her sister-in-law grimly.

It was nothing, really, it was only being late for tea, but Mr Wither had such a way of making nothings seem awful; and there was no doubt that they were going to be very late indeed, for when they did get to the house they would have to change all their clothes. Water was running off their faces, and their shoes and stockings were spattered. What sights we must look, thought Tina dismally, but Viola was too alarmed to think about how she looked. She had only nine pounds left: would her father-in-law turn her out because she was late for tea?

'Better lay up in my place for a bit,' advised the Hermit. 'My little grey home in the west, as they say. Plenty of room. Yer could dry yer cloes. I wouldn't mind if yer took 'em all off and warmed yer little selves by my fire, not me. Bleshyer. Eh? What about it?'

Tina, biting her lip deeply, stared down at her shoes. Rain rolled slowly off the ends of her hair.

'Tina!' urgently, 'I really think we'd better make a dash for it. It's nearly ten to four.'

Tina looked up; and at the instant there sounded the long, arrogant horn that Viola had heard across the darkening wood on her first evening at The Eagles, and round the curve of the road dashed a very large dark red car of the type best described as semi-sporting, its windscreen-wiper working accurately yet with an impression of fury, its lamps and nose tearing ahead of itself as though wild to go.

Viola, awed, did not even think of raising her hand for help; besides, the car was not going their way. Tina, knowing to whom it belonged, felt that it would be folly to signal, and the Hermit had suddenly gone away. However, as they automatically turned to watch the car out of sight, it slowed down and began to back neatly and swiftly towards them, while a female head, wearing a smart and unbecoming hat, suddenly poked out from a lowered window, calling,

'I say, would you like a lift?'

'Well, it's most awfully kind of you,' cried Tina, plashing down the bank into the full flood of the rain, 'but I don't think you're going our way. We want to get back to the Chesterbourne road.'

'Oh, that's all right, we can turn,' said Miss Franklin of Grassmere, confidently, and she added, to the person who sat in the driver's seat, slewed sideways with a hand in a thick, pale glove flung across the wheel, 'Can't we, Victor?'

'Of course,' said Victor Spring politely, and he smiled.

It was clear, despite the smile, that he did not want to turn.

'But we really can't . . .' dithered Tina. 'It's most awfully good of you . . .' She was strongly conscious of her own sopping rats'-tails, of Viola's splashed shoes (which somehow looked even cheaper than they were because they were wet), of the elegance of the car and its occupants, and, most of all, of a pair of cool yet bright dark eyes regarding her derisively from the back of the car.

'Get in, do,' said Victor, showing very white teeth again and speaking just a little more quickly. 'You're getting so wet.'

They bowed their heads and climbed meekly into the back of the car, which was not quite large enough to hold three people in comfort when, as in this case, some expensive suitcases were piled on the floor; and arranged themselves so that they did not drip upon the third passenger, a girl of about twenty-five whose whole presence, perfectly produced in a yellow coat and skirt with a dark fur, glowed with a subdued yet striking smartness.

Tina, smiling nervously at this vision, was so impressed by the beautiful dark skin of which her gloves, shoes and handbag were made that for days afterwards, whenever Viola mentioned the incident, she saw in memory the dull lustre on the young lady's toecaps and smelled the faintest breath of a perfume, hitherto unknown to her, not unlike Russia leather.

'Were you out for a walk?' asked Hetty, leaning back from her seat next to Victor and speaking to Tina but including the sopping Viola in her friendly smile.

'Yes, it was such a lovely day, we never thought it would rain . . .'

'Yes, it came up so suddenly.'

There was a faint movement and a murmur from Viola, who was dripping over one of the vision's ankles. The vision, smiling kindly, pulled her ankle out of the way.

She could afford to be kind. Tina's quiet choiceness of dress, Viola's bloom of youth, Hetty's touch of studentish distinction, were eclipsed utterly by the perfect grooming and poise of the dark stranger. They were just three dowdy females.

Hetty was the only one who did not mind this. The vision was only Phyl Barlow, without two ideas in her head. She carried on a determined conversation with Tina, while the car dashed along the wet mile to The Eagles, discovering some mutual acquaintances in the neighbourhood and recalling that her aunt, Mrs Spring, had met Mrs Wither last year on the Committee for the Chesterbourne Infirmary Ball.

She was not going to lose this opportunity of scraping acquaintance with the sad-looking younger Miss Wither, who might be most interesting psychologically, and whom she had more than once seen in the bookshop in Chesterbourne, browsing.

'My sister-in-law,' murmured Tina, remembering her duty and indicating Viola as the car drew up outside The Eagles. There was no sign of the Wither car, with Saxon and Mr Spurrey. Horror upon horror! he must have arrived early.

Viola, who had been stealing a good look at the young god who was driving (to Miss Barlow's amusement), glanced round at Hetty with her cheerful smile and said, clambering out of the car:

'Thanks awfully for the lift.'

'Not at all,' replied Victor, supposing that she was speaking to him when in fact she was far too impressed to dare. 'Hope you won't both catch cold.' He raised his hat, indicating by his 'both' that he had at least taken in the fact that there were two of them, though he had not once glanced round or spoken during the drive.

Viola, running shivering into the house, carried away a picture of so much masculine elegance that it quite overwhelmed her. Such a width of shoulder, such becoming sunburn on a hard, clear profile that was faintly military, such a tiny fair moustache and bright hazel eyes! with a quick, summing-up look under their short thick lashes.

He's the most marvellous-looking man I've ever seen, she thought, peeling off her wet clothes in the big chilly bedroom, and he does remind me of someone, now who is it? (oh dear, we're going to be so late, I do hope it won't be very awful, how I *hate* living here).

She ran downstairs buttoning her frock, and as she turned the handle of the drawing-room door, whence came the dirge-like soughing of voices, she remembered who it was he reminded her of. The young man they always draw to advertise Llama-Pyjamas, of course, that's who it is!

Quite pleased, she went in.

# CHAPTER VI

'Now what did you want to do that for, Het?' interestedly inquired Victor, as the car rushed gladly away from The Eagles. 'You are an extraordinary woman.'

'Well, poor creatures, they were getting wet.'

When Hetty talked to her social equals she was careful to keep her speech free from slang, for she enjoyed the touch of pedantry thus given to her sentences, and the contrast between her diction and that of the Springs' friends, especially Miss Barlow's. But when Hetty talked to Heyrick or to little Merionethshire she talked in an ordinary way: she did not want the servants to think her stuck-up, as well as queer.

'We shall not be late for tea,' she added mildly.

Her cousin accelerated, saying nothing more. She had asked him to pull up when she caught sight of the two Miss Who-ever-they-weres sheltering under the trees, and he had done so, partly because of his slight but steady curiosity about all her actions, and partly from a less good-natured reason.

He always liked to see what old Het-Up would do next. All the people round him behaved, as he did, in an ordinary manner; and he took it for granted that sensible people everywhere behaved like this. But Hetty often behaved oddly and she was interesting to watch; it was like having a mongrel dog about the house, without breeding but with plenty of character. Sometimes her oddities annoyed him but usually he was only amused, for he was fond of old

Het-Up, who took herself so seriously; they had, after all, grown up together and she took the place of a sister.

Miss Barlow said nothing, either. She was irritated. She knew why Victor had stopped the car; it was because she had exclaimed impatiently, 'Oh, do let's get on, Victor, I've hung about enough for one afternoon.' He had wanted to show her that her wishes, her impatience, had no power over him and that he was not sorry for having kept her waiting three and a half minutes at the station.

It appeared that he had stopped at a shop in the town because Hetty wanted to fetch a book she had ordered. He had told Hetty that she could stay in the bookshop for ten minutes, but Hetty had stayed twelve, and that had made them late.

Twice, in half an hour, Hetty had held up Miss Barlow's plans, and prevented her from moving as quickly as possible on to the next pleasure. Miss Barlow liked her life to be a steady movement towards pleasure. While she was having one, she was thinking about the next and what she should wear while she had that.

What a little beast she is, thought the elder girl coldly, looking at the bun of hair sticking out untidily under Hetty's hat. Thoroughly selfish, unattractive, and spoilt. I think, as soon as Victor and I are married, a good long cruise would be the best thing for Miss Hetty, since she's so fond of travel books. She might pick up a husband that way – though I doubt it, she's so affected. There's nothing men hate so much as affectation.

Miss Barlow's own success with men (eight full-blown offers of heart, hand and fortune in five years, and numberless hints at undying devotion repressed by loyalty to marriage vows or lack of money; storeful of flowers, sweets, jewellery and minor articles of clothing, to say nothing about a ceaseless stream of invitations to dances, races, and shows) was due, she thought, chiefly to her lack of affectation.

The word had a special meaning for her, wide enough to cover all behaviour different from her own. Thus it was affected to love reading, to like being alone, to play games professionally, to dress in the extreme of fashion. The steady pursuit of conventional pleasures, none of them lasting very long and all of them costing a good deal of money, was Phyllis's ideal of how life should be lived.

It was taken for granted by the Springs and by Phyllis's family, a nest of rich stockbrokers, that she and Victor would one day marry, for they had kept up a half-attracted, half-irritated friendship since their Harrow and Roedean days, but each was always so busy making money or pursuing pleasure that so far they had had neither the time nor the inclination to undertake the bother of getting married.

There was also the question of children. Phyllis, at fifteen, had decided that she would never have children. Children, both before and after, made one look a sight. Victor wanted children. They had never talked about this, but each had gathered the other's views. There would be all the bore of threshing that out, too. In short, the longer they put off getting formally engaged, the pleasanter life would be. Meanwhile, they saw each other often at the flat of Phyllis's parents in London, where there was much entertaining all the year round, and every summer Phyllis came for many weekends to Grassmere, where the Springs usually had friends staying.

Mrs Spring liked Phyllis's company, for they had the same interests and the same solemnity about the details of entertaining, house-decorating, and dress; but it cannot be said that Mrs Spring was fond of Miss Barlow. She felt in the younger woman's apparently candid nature a desire to boss, and to excel, that she did not like. If any woman had to boss and excel at Grassmere it should be Mrs Spring, not Miss Barlow. Victor did both, of course, but his mother did not mind that. Victor was a man, and one did not mind being outshone by a man.

Nevertheless, Phyllis would make a handsome, wealthy and suitable wife for Victor, and after she was married she would probably change her mind about children: girls often did. A handsome grandson, just like Victor, would be delightful!

Mrs Spring was lying on a long chair on the veranda under a light rug, watching the sudden rainstorm beating on the pewter-coloured river at the bottom of the lawns. There were some other people staying in the house but they were out motoring. She did not feel well today, and was trying to be sensible about it, but this was difficult, for she had so much that she felt good health might just as well have been thrown in. Hetty, now, and Phyl, and Victor, they were all three as strong as horses, and took their health for granted.

'Hullo, Phyllis,' she said, looking up as the three came towards her. 'How nice you look. (Hetty! Your hair!) I expected you half an hour ago; was the train late?'

'The train was all right,' Miss Barlow unslung the fox from her neck, smiling down at Mrs Spring, 'but Victor was late.'

'Three minutes.' He said it over his shoulder; he was fiddling with the wireless.

'And on the top of that,' continued Miss Barlow, cautiously pressing the waves on her dark head, 'he stopped to give some people a lift.'

'Oh? Anyone we know?'

'The Withers,' put in Hetty, who had slumped into a chair.

'The—? Oh, those people at The Eagles.'

'We had to turn the car round,' went on Phyllis lightly, 'and take them *right* back to their front door!'

'Whatever for?'

'It was raining,' drawled Hetty. 'I asked Vic to stop. The younger Miss Wither and her sister-in-law had gone out for a walk and the rain came upon them unexpectedly, I gathered.'

'The sister-in-law?' interrupted Mrs Spring. 'That's the brother's widow. He died about a year ago. She was in a shop.'

'The sister-in-law was?' asked Hetty.

'Yes. Some place in the town – Thompson and something. What's she like?'

Mrs Spring, though now a wealthy woman with the interests of her type, had been born in a small town in Hampshire, and had the small-town woman's interest in a local personality, however unimportant.

'If she were groomed,' said Hetty slowly, pensively staring down at her shoes, 'she would be a beauty. She is the ethereal type, like one of Greuze's girls, with that fine-textured skin and silky hair that men always admire.'

'One of whose girls?' said her aunt fretfully. 'I wish you would pay more attention to your own grooming, never mind other people's.'

She stood up, with determination, for she refused to play the invalid in front of guests unless they were old acquaintances like Phyllis Barlow, and at any moment the Randalls would come in.

Phyllis said nothing. When tactless men asked her if she did not think Rosemary or Diana a swell doll, Phyllis said heartily that she did, though she did not. But she never on the other hand made the mistake of over-praising women to men, because she knew that men saw through that game: they were not so stupid as they were supposed to be. Victor went out of the room.

'You've got your old room, Phyllis,' said Mrs Spring. 'It's just been done up.'

'Oh good!'

'The wallpaper's a sort of pale Futurist, all mixed, you know, and there's a Hunting Scenes chintz,' continued Mrs Spring.

'It sounds marvellous; I think I'll go up and look at it.'

'There'll be a drink when you come down. Some people are coming in. Now, Hetty,' as Phyllis went out, 'that's how I want you to look one day. Phyllis has perfect taste and wears her things beautifully.'

'Why?' droned Hetty.

Mrs Spring stared at her.

'Why? What do you mean, why?'

'Why does she wear them beautifully?'

'How on earth should I know? Because she does, I suppose. It's a gift . . . and you haven't got it.'

'Oh.' Hetty was eating, rather than reading, large slabs of a very thin book of contemporary verse each page having a thick wodge of print, without capital letters, starting at the top and running nearly to the bottom. Her eyes were very close to the book and she frowned with concentration.

'Hetty! Do put that down and go and make yourself fit to be seen. The Randalls will be back at any minute. Your stockings are twisted and your hat's on straight; it ought to be right over one eye. What have you got hold of there, for pity's sake?'

'*Ashes of Iron*.' Hetty began to bite a finger-nail, absently but with the ghost of a malicious smile turning up the corners of her mouth.

'What?'

'*Ashes of Iron*. It's the name of a book. Poems.'

'Rubbish,' muttered her aunt, moving uneasily across the room to the wireless, making a little face of weariness and pain. 'What on earth does it mean?'

'I don't know, but one has to read it and try to find out,' said her niece sternly, going towards the door with the book carefully cradled in one hand.

Mrs Spring switched on the wireless and music, of a sort, slowly grew in the big luxurious room.

I don't want to write, of course, mused Hetty, running upstairs two at a time, and anyway I know I can't, but really, if one was a genius (as I suspect this *Ashes of Iron* man is) one could be it here without a soul (I err; I should say, without a body, for souls they have none) suspecting. Never heard of Greuze, never heard of Donat Mulqueen and *Ashes of Iron*! I might be Donat Mulqueen myself, for all they realize.

She went into her bedroom and shut the door.

She had a sitting-room too, but she liked her bedroom better because from it she could see the river. Not a corner of the orchard could be seen, and of course the waste land at the back of the vegetable garden was tucked well away at the side of the house, but the river had poetry; it was better than the unshadowed lawns, the neat beds of blazing flowers.

Her room was big, light and pleasant, with conventionally charming furnishings that had been transformed by Hetty's own odd, vivid and sure taste. Watts's *The Minotaur*, Van Gogh's *Cornfield with Cypresses*, a group of natives by Gauguin, looked strange but attractive against the pale pink wallpaper considered suitable for a virgin's sleeping-place by Mrs Spring.

Bookshelves stood against the four walls. They were shapely and well made, but were all second-hand; Hetty had picked them up on visits to Chesterbourne. She liked her shelves to have personality, as well as the books on them, and though it would have been simpler to order shelves to be fitted round the room, or to buy those book-cases that grow with the growth of their library, she had stood firm against the amusement of Victor and the irritation of her aunt, and had the shelves she wanted.

She let down her thick lank hair and began to brush it, standing in front of the mirror and gazing dejectedly across the now sunlit lawns. The world was so beautiful! so crammed with romance, excitement, horror, irony! In every part of it, except at Grassmere near Sible Pelden in Essex, there were to be found truths that were stranger than fiction, and more satisfying. There were causes to live for, work to be done, philosophies to be examined, religions to be inquired into and rejected, and an ocean, a bottomless ether, of talk to be poured out at somebody – no matter who; someone else young, preferably, who would argue and know a little more than oneself but have the same kind of searching, eager mind. There were people to be taught, wrongs to be righted, there were politics and history and economics . . .

I know just how Florence Nightingale felt.

Why won't they let me go to college, and then try to get a job?

What's the use of a finishing-school, full of useless lilies of the field in crepe-de-chine underclothing, who've never heard of Donat Mulqueen?

Swiiiish! went the stiff brush, down the thick locks. Wait till I'm twenty-one! Only another year.

There was a sharp tap at the door, which opened before she could say anything and admitted Miss Barlow.

'What do you want?' demanded Hetty. She casually put on a dressing-gown, for she still had the fierce modesty of extreme youth, and she hated the fastidious glance that Phyllis had given at her neglected, schoolgirlish underclothing.

'Just want to see if you've got anything new and interesting to read,' said Miss Barlow lightly, 'and we haven't seen each other for such ages that I wondered how you've been getting on all this time.' She began to wander round the room, humming. 'Not engaged yet?'

'Go to hell.' Hetty went on with her brushing.

'You don't mean to say that you've *read* all these?'

No answer.

'Come on, Hetty, don't try it on with me. I've known you since you were twelve. You don't really read all this stuff, you know, and understand it. Why, there are things here that Victor wouldn't understand.'

'Quite.'

'It's just affectation. Pose.'

Hetty went on brushing with longer and longer sweeps. Her scalp tingled from the force of the brushing.

'Poetry . . .' Phyllis pulled out a book roughly, and opened it. Her heart was beating a little quicker than usual, not unpleasantly. She liked excitement, especially when it came from baiting somebody.

She began to read dramatically:

> No truce with the I, the ravener,
> eater of bare nobility—

'What *utter* rot! Why, it doesn't even make – here – shut up, you little beast!'

Hetty, hairbrush raised, charged at her, seized her by the shoulders and, with the full force of a sturdy body superior in weight if not in strength, barged her out of the room and, after a scuffle in the passage, slammed the door.

'Bitch!' observed Hetty, resuming her hairbrushing with a trembling hand. She murmured after a moment:

> No truce with the I, the ravener,
> eater of bare nobility, big-mouth—

then shook her head impatiently, broke off, and began again in a low dreamy tone, gazing out across the green lawns:

> I rode one evening with Count Maddalo
> Upon the bank of land which breaks the flow
> Of Adria towards Venice . . .

Gradually, as the words left her lips, her expression grew calm, save for the old resentful look in the blue eyes, and when she went down a little later she was as usual.

There were eight or nine people in the drawing-room, talking loudly in a haze of sunlit cigarette smoke through the noise of the wireless. Victor was making drinks for one group, and two pretty maids, one of whom was little Merionethshire with all her flowers on show, moved about with trays of delicious and carefully chosen food. There was the thick rich smell of good cigarettes, alcohol, scent, and well-washed people that Hetty called the Smell of Progress. She went and sat in a corner.

Presently a very young man came over and sat down next to her.

'Think we've met before, haven't we?' said the very young man. 'At the Phillipses' tennis party. Seem to remember your face. My name's Anderson. We came over with the Randalls. Friends of yours, aren't they?'

'Yes.'

'Had any more tennis lately?'

'Yes. Yesterday.'

'Weather's been good, hasn't it. Don't like playing in the heat.'

'No.'

'You going to the Infernal Ball?'

'Yes.'

'Ghastly show, isn't it. But my mother *will* go, and my sister and I have to do our duty. I say, will you smoke?'

'Thank you.'

'I say, who's that?'

'To whom do you refer?'

'I say! The tall dark girl with the marvellous figure.'

'That is Miss Barlow.'

'Isn't she engaged to your cousin?'

'I believe so.'

'Marvellous-looking girl, isn't she.'

Hetty slowly turned her head, looked full at him and said in a low, melancholy voice:

> Alas! I have nor hope nor health,
> Nor peace within nor calm around,
> Nor that content surpassing wealth

The sage in meditation found,
And walked with inward glory crowned—
Nor fame, nor power, nor love, nor leisure,
Others I see whom these surround—
Smiling they live, and call life pleasure;
To me that cup has been dealt in another measure.

She stopped, struck by the look of rapt attention and admiration on the young, spotty face turned to her own.

'I say! Do go on. That's marvellous; it's just how I feel sometimes. Who wrote it? You?'

'Shelley.'

'He did, did he? Well, he knew it all and then some. I say, do let me get you something.'

This unexpected reaction to the *Stanzas Written in Dejection Near Naples* annoyed Hetty, but it made her think. She had wished to alarm and embarrass the very young man; she had only put words to his private discontents. Was it possible that others, as well as herself, found their lot imperfect?

When the young man came back with something, she had slipped away.

Old Phyl looks marvellous today, thought Victor, looking over at her as she stood in a group on the other side of the room. He thought, with pleasure, that he would take her out into the rhododendron shrubbery after dinner and kiss her – if she did not want to make up a four for bridge. And perhaps, even if she did want to, he would take her out there and kiss her just the same. She really must learn that he was master; she was too fond of her own way.

Nevertheless, as he looked at her, he felt both affection and pride.

She was not beautiful, but she had so many good points that nine men out of ten preferred her looks to those of beautiful women. Her figure was very pretty, her dark head, perfectly shingled, was a fine shape, with its severe line broken near the forehead by some tidy, feminine little curls. Her delicate nose and well-modelled mouth would wear well, and so would her fine clear skin, of which she took great care. Her slightly aquiline features contrasted oddly with her eyes, which should have been long-shaped in her type of face, but they were round, darkest brown, and sparkling. All her pleasure in dancing, in tennis and golf, in dress and motoring, shone in her eyes.

She was smart, she was a good sport, and she would never let you down.

Clothes do make a difference to women, mused Victor, who occasionally made discoveries of this kind. Hetty, now (the bunchy form of his cousin was just sidling out of the room), it was a pity old Het-Up dressed so badly.

As for the two Miss Whoever-they-weres, the Withers, he did not think of them at all.

# CHAPTER VII

Mr Wither, having seen Mr Spurrey off in the car, went into his den and was seen no more before dinner.

This secluding of himself, like a witch-doctor before practising some rite, was intended to alarm the females, and did it so thoroughly that by the time they were sitting at table, everyone except Mr Wither himself was slightly hysterical.

Even Madge was subdued. It was a Wither tradition that Madge Never Howled; had it not been a tradition, her mother and sister would have sworn that she had been. She spent the afternoon up at the Club, returned in a very silent mood, and sat slumped in a far corner of the drawing-room for the rest of the time before dinner, staring at an article on military life in India in the *Illustrated Fortnightly*.

Before going down to dinner, Viola and Tina told each other that it was absurd to get so worked up simply because they were going to be rowed for being late for tea.

They said indignantly that they were twenty-two and thirty-five (at least, Viola said that she was twenty-two and Tina said that she, Tina, was no longer a schoolgirl) and that the whole thing was simply ludicrous.

Tina looked up the chapter on Fathers and Daughters in the book on feminine psychology, but the things it said (after a bit at the beginning of the chapter warning you not to be shocked) did not seem to have much bearing upon her case. What they warned you against was getting too fond of your father and letting him get too fond of you. As there seemed small danger of this situation arising between Mr Wither and herself, Tina put down the book with a little sigh; and Viola picked it up.

'Good lord,' said she, with a pink face, after a pause.

'What've you found?' laughing.

'I say – who wrote this rot?' She glanced at the cover. 'Doctor Irene Hartmüller. Oh, a *German*.'

'Viennese. Quite young, and brilliantly clever.'

'Well, I think it's bosh,' but she continued to turn the pages gingerly. 'Why – I *say*! – good *lord*! *What* a mind the woman's got! Just like a German.'

'Oh, Viola!'

'What's up?'

'You don't really think that Germans have got a worse sort of mind than other people, do you?'

'Of course I do. Everybody knows they have.'

Tina sighed. She occasionally came across broad bands of sheer stupidity in her sister-in-law's character which reminded her sharply that Viola had been educated at an inferior school which she had left when she was sixteen.

'Well, they made the War, anyway,' said Viola sulkily, dropping the book on the bed.

Tina said nothing.

'And all those Atrocities,' persisted Viola, 'and boiling down dead bodies for soup. Why, it's well known. There are books about it. If they didn't, why are they called Huns?'

The gong interrupted her revelations; but each went downstairs feeling a little ruffled with the other.

When Mr Wither was deeply annoyed with anybody he seldom made a direct attack upon them. He opened fire upon some other object, remote from his true one, and worked round to the latter, suddenly pouncing upon it when the culprit thought the danger past.

This evening, in the quiet room with its handsome dull furniture, while the spring afterglow lit the black Persian boughs of the monkey-puzzle tree, Mr Wither broke his heavy silence thus:

'I had to write to Jameson about that fellow again today.'

Mr Jameson, an old acquaintance of the Withers, was Mayor of Chesterbourne.

Mr Wither's head was bent, showing its two wide bands of thin hair, over a plate of nasty blobby cod covered in white paste.

'The Hermit, dear, do you mean?' Mrs Wither knew all Mr Wither's worries by heart.

'No more a hermit than I am,' intoned Mr Wither, breaking off a very small piece of bread. 'The fellow's a fraud. Spends most of his time in that public house at the cross-roads – what is it? The Lion. The Green Lion. Saw him there myself this morning, drinking with a lot of hobbledehoys. He had the insolence' – Mr Wither took a little sip of tonic water – 'had the insolence to make a remark about my walking-stick.

'Shouted at me,' added Mr Wither, drearily.

'Oh, what did he say?' irrepressibly exclaimed Tina.

'I did not wait to hear,' loftily responded Mr Wither, having raised everybody's curiosity to screeching point. 'I took no notice. I walked on my way.'

Pause. Mr Wither passed his plate for more blob and paste. He had not looked at Tina and Viola, and though they knew his little ways, their fears were gradually being lulled. Perhaps the Hermit really had served as a red-herring . . .'

'I don't know how he manages to live, I'm sure,' contributed Mrs Wither, nervously moving her eyelids. She knew very well what storm was brooding.

'Imposes on fools,' droned Mr Wither, chewing.

'He does a bit of digging for Colonel Phillips now and then,' said Madge, looking up under her pink eyelids and speaking for the first time.

'What have *you* been crying about?' suddenly demanded her father, bending forward and staring at her.

'Me?' said Madge loudly, going brick-red. 'Howling? What do you mean? You know I Never Howl. What on earth should I want to howl for?'

'Don't know, but your eyes are red,' retorted her parent.

'It's the wind, I expect. There was a jolly nippy wind—'

'Nonsense,' interrupted Mr Wither. 'Excuses.'

'And suppose I *have* been howling,' suddenly sobbed Madge, her face contorting like a baby's while two huge tears broke cover and rolled down her face. She dashed down her table-napkin. 'I don't have much to keep me from howling, do I? You won't even let me have a dog.' Sob.

Appalled faces stared at her from three sides.

Mr Wither, however, remained unmoved, only bending more attentively over his cod.

'Colonel Phillips has just got three ripping Sealyham pups,' she continued shakily. 'Thoroughbreds. He's letting them go for two and a half guineas each. They're a dead bargain. Do let me get one, Father. Please. I'll keep it outside in the yard, honour bright I will. I won't let it sleep on my bed' – sob – 'if you'll only let me have it, Father. Please say yes.'

Mr Wither continued to chew an almost non-existent fragment of cod with no change of expression.

'Come on, Father, be a sport.' Tina rushed recklessly in with an hysterical giggle, causing the frozen gazes of Mrs Wither and Viola to flicker across to her quivering face and remain there, fixed.

'Madge is nearly forty, you know; old enough to know how to keep a dog in order. I'm glad she's broken the ice, because,' her voice quavered on shrilly in the dead silence, 'I'm going to ask you to let me have something, too. I want to learn to drive the car.'

Mr Wither gave a slight start, as though struck by a poisoned arrow, but still he said nothing.

'It can't do any harm,' Tina went on resolutely, in a calmer tone, two red spots on her thin cheeks. 'Saxon can teach me in his spare time. He seems to have plenty,' bitterly, 'and if you ask me, I don't think Master Saxon quite earns his hundred a year.'

'Tina, you beast,' quavered Madge, blowing her nose. 'You know I've always wanted to have proper lessons. I do think you're a rotter, cutting in in front of me like that . . . if you let her, Father, you'll let me have the dog, won't you? It wouldn't be fair to let her learn to drive, and me—'

'And Tina and I are frightfully sorry we were late for tea this afternoon,' cut in Viola, gaspingly, leaning across and smiling at him with eyes wide open in alarm. 'Truly, it wasn't our fault; you see, we got caught in the rain and we had to get a lift home in someone's car. Now if we'd had the car ourselves, and Tina had been driving—'

'Shut up, Vi,' muttered Tina. 'Father, you might let Madge have her blessed dog, you'll never see it if she keeps it out in the yard. As for me, I'm not so keen as all that on learning to drive, only it makes me rather sick to see Saxon idling about with so much spare time on his hands . . . it would kill two birds with one stone . . . give me something useful to do, and keep him busy . . .'

'Why are we waiting for our pudding?' demanded Mr Wither, lifting his head and gazing past the sea of tear-stained and agitated faces to that of Mrs Wither, who jumped three inches. 'Or perhaps there is no pudding tonight?'

'Yes, dear, of course, ground rice.' Mrs Wither pressed the bell.

Complete silence for three minutes while the stout parlourmaid arranged the paraphernalia for pudding. Madge tried to speak, but only made a strange noise, causing Viola to give an hysterical snort. Mr Wither, as the parlourmaid left the room, for the first time darted his daughter-in-law one dreadful glance. So, it said, *you* are the one who blows up the whole works in front of the servants. That is exactly what I should have expected you would do.

'Ground rice, dear?' inquired Mrs Wither of Madge, glancing tenderly, nervously, at the big, tear-stained face. Madgie was her favourite, and always had been, though it was wrong to have favourites, she knew.

'No thanks.'

'Tina?'

A shake of the head.

Mrs Wither glanced coldly at Viola (really, that noise she had made was too bad, quite uncontrolled, what would Fawcuss think?). 'Will you have some ground rice pudding, Viola?'

'Please,' muttered Viola, her eyes suddenly swimming in tears. Oh! supper with Dad at home, after the shop was shut in the evening, frying tomatoes on the gas-stove while he read bits to her out of the paper, and the room was full of golden light, and laughter, and the warmness of love! She stared away, out of the window, at the mean garden where shadows were lengthening.

Madge gulped.

'Well, Father, will you let me have the dog, please? You might say one way or the other.'

Her tone was calmer now; the shadow of disappointment at the refusal which she saw shaping itself upon her father's lips lay over her blubbered face.

Mr Wither looked up. With a shock of immense surprise, felt through their individual agitations, three of the women realized that he looked both tired and upset. Mrs Wither had observed this from the first, but then (as the reader shall hear) she had been prepared for it.

'We've talked all this over before, Madge. No.'

He pushed away his half-emptied plate, and got up.

'Father! Aren't you going to finish your pudding?' breathed his wife, gazing at him anxiously.

He shook his head, moving towards the door.

'And what about my driving lessons, Father?' Tina spoke firmly, raising her voice a little. 'There's no reason why I shouldn't have them, is there?'

'Please yourself,' he said heavily, and shut the door behind him.

Tina burst out crying.

'Tina! What on earth's up?' But Tina shook off her sister-in-law's protective young arm, and rushed out of the other door, slamming it, and leaving the other three gasping.

The door of her father's study was shut. It loomed black and square across the hall, where dusk was beginning to fill the tall well of the staircase. She ran lightly upstairs, crying into her cupped hands, rushed into her bedroom, and collapsed on the bed, shaking in a hysteria which was caused partly by relief, partly by an obscure feeling of shame.

Doctor Irene Hartmüller told her readers authoritatively that the only way to get mental harmony was to face one's desires (however degrading they might be) and, when it was possible without doing too much damage to one's fellow-creatures, have them.

For weeks Tina had been facing her degrading desire to sit next to Saxon in the car while they drove alone down an endless road lined by the flowering trees of summer. Now that her desire was apparently about to be gratified, without much damage to Mr Wither, she wondered that she had made such a fuss about it to herself. It was a simple enough thing to want . . . only it was rather an odd one.

And it had not grown up without encouragement from him. Why had he looked at her once, so fully, with such candid friendly mischief, the chauffeur's mask completely dropped, as though it were twelve years ago, and she were again the dainty little art student, home from London for the weekend, and he a wild boy in a ragged red jersey?

If he had not looked at her like that, only once, as she crossed the yard one day on her way back from a walk in the little wood, she would never have let his image grow to such a height in her mind.

No woman with a proper self-respect (thought Tina bitterly, lying on her bed with wet eyelashes), no woman who's been decently brought up gets sentimental about her father's chauffeur without any encouragement . . . even if she has known him for twelve years.

It's not having anyone to love, too.

Oh, I know quite well what's the matter with me.

All the more reason why I should get these lessons over quickly, and as soon as I hear his Essex drawl and see that his finger-nails aren't quite clean . . . *his hands are beautiful*, said a clear little voice in her head, *I should like to walk with him hand in hand*.

She sprang up, flushing and terrified, and, walking firmly to the window, leaned out into the evening. What a sudden burst of song down there in the darkening wood! And again! so strong and clear; then silence.

As soon as Tina had gone, Mrs Wither got up, went over to Madge, and patted her shoulder.

'Mum,' said Madge miserably, looking, despite her prowess at golf and her twelve stone, about fifteen years old.

'There, there, dear. You mustn't upset Father, you know.'

'Yes, but, Mum, why won't he let me have a dog? I promise I'll keep it out of his way, and I know all about taking care of them, you know; I had that year at Roxbourne. They're such jolly little beggars; I wish you could see them.'

Mrs Wither patted her again, sighed, and stood gazing down at the floor.

Viola, who was rather embarrassed by this family interlude, sat with her arms resting on the table, staring in a vacant and irritating way at her mother- and sister-in-law.

'If you have finished, Viola, please press the bell,' said Mrs Wither tartly; then she went out as well.

'It's rotten about your dog, Madge,' said Viola's soft, deep voice after a minute.

'Oh, that's all right. Sorry I made an ass of myself,' and Madge got up, and shouldered her way out of the room as the parlourmaid came into it.

Viola still sat over the table. She did not move until Fawcuss came at her with the crumb-brush and tray, then she stood up, yawning and stretching her slender arms. Faint music came in at the window, under the fading sunset. It was a quarter-past eight.

'Is that your wireless, Fawcuss?'

'No, Madam,' said Fawcuss, after a pause intended to show Mrs Theodore that maids also have their souls and their privacies, as well as have shopgirls living on their betters' charity even though they had caught Mr Theodore, not that he was much catch.

'Where is it, then?'

'It's over at Grassmere, Madam. Mr Spring has a party there to-night, Saxon said.'

'Lovely,' murmured Viola.

'They've got the wireless out on the water, Saxon said,' volunteered Fawcuss disapprovingly; like most women born in a tidy-sized river town she had only once been on what she called The Water and regarded it as dangerous and rather low to do so.

'Boats, do you mean?'

'Yes, Madam, so Saxon says.'

That was why the music echoed so over the wide calm river, through the little wood in its valley, wandering about in the tranquil evening air.

Viola went slowly upstairs.

Mooning . . . the soft, long, languishing word exactly describes her state of mind as she gazed across the miniature valley, thinking of Victor Spring.

She was not so romantic, so lacking in common sense and in experience, that she could imagine herself in love with a man seen once, for five minutes. But he had deeply printed such imagination as she had, already warmed by the legends about him that she had heard since her childhood. His good looks, the solid elegance of his car and clothes, the decisive, impatient quality of his voice, now came to dress the dream of him that she, in common with the other Chesterbourne girls, had had at the back of her mind for years.

Below in the wood, whose tree-tops were now a warm rosy-green in the afterglow, there came a loud, sweet, strange burst of sound. What bird is that? she wondered, gazing down into the shadowy maze of branches. And again! so clear and strong; then silence.

Mrs Wither, meanwhile, went across the hall, where the blue tiles were no longer distinguishable from black in the dusk, and tapped upon the door of Mr Wither's study. There was no reply, so after a pause she tapped again, then firmly opened the door and went in.

It was nearly dark in the little room; the only light was that of the dying sunset falling through the one very tall window, looped with heavy curtains. Mr Wither was sitting back in his arm-chair, with hands crossed over his stomach, and as she came in he turned his head wearily, saying:

'Is that you, Emmie,' in such a low, discouraged voice that her alarm deepened.

'Wouldn't you like the light, dear?' She stood, hesitating, with the door half-open.

'No, no. Plenty of light,' he said impatiently. 'Come in, do, and shut the door.'

She did so, and sat down upon an uncomfortable little chair opposite his big one. There was silence for a while.

'Don't you feel well, dear?'

Mrs Wither guessed what was the matter; her alarm was not because she had never seen him like this before. She had: but she had never before seen him leave his pudding unfinished in front of the girls. He would show his depression by scolding them, or by silence, but he would never break away from his usual behaviour. Pudding must be finished, though stocks fell like ninepins.

'Would you like some bicarbonate, dear?' suggested Mrs Wither at length, dutifully giving him the chance to say that he was suffering from indigestion, and thus save his pride.

He shook his head. Mrs Wither sat patiently on, in the deepening dusk. Presently he would begin to talk about what that old Mr Spurrey had been saying.

He was usually like this after he had been with Mr Spurrey. Mrs Wither had been prepared for the mood, and had planned to deal with it as she usually did, but she had not been prepared for Mr Wither not to finish his pudding.

He can't stand shocks, and bad news, and quarrels, like he used to, poor Arthur, thought Mrs Wither, sighing inside herself. It *was* unlucky that the girls should have chosen this evening to upset him so.

But it's all Mr Spurrey's fault though, really. It's too bad of him, really it is; too bad.

It is difficult to decide just what use Mr Spurrey was in this world, but no one had ever asked themselves this question, because in the respectable and wealthy circles in which Mr Spurrey revolved, people do not ask themselves what is the use of a rich bachelor aged seventy-five, of quiet habit, occupying a house in Buckingham Square and waited upon by five servants.

True, Mr Spurrey's name appeared upon the prospectus sheets of a number of rich and reputable companies, but for all the work that Mr Spurrey did for those companies, he might as well have been dead. He had no living relatives; he was the only son of an only son, and his more distant connections had gone long ago. He had no active hobbies. He pottered about. People were nice to him. Had he lived in a savage tribe, Mr Spurrey would have been buried up to his neck in earth and left to die. Savages, we are told, are logical creatures except when dealing with their own taboos. But people were nice to Mr Spurrey.

The world is thronged with such old creatures, without beauty, character, brains, who do not breed, who are not angels nor monsters nor even warmly human. Yet when we hear that one of these old things has a cold, we observe, 'Poor old chap. It's this ghastly weather,' and when we next meet the old body, we ask it how it does, and say that we are sorry to hear it has been ill.

This is one of the unobtrusive gifts to mankind of civilization, gentlest of the sciences. It seems small: yet if we started to be logical about the uses of the Mr Spurreys, civilization would quietly die.

And it was not easy to be nice to Mr Spurrey because he had a disturbing habit: what he liked best of all was frightening people, and when he got alone with someone, that was what he always did.

No sooner had the door closed upon the butler, when the liqueurs glowed upon the board or the muffin oozed upon its dish, when the fat ash tilted from the cigar or the tea was lifted to the eager lip – then did Mr Spurrey, having first seen to it that the fire was drawing nicely and there were no disturbing draughts, lean forward and, fixing upon his victim an eye surprisingly like that of a parrot, lower his chin funereally and intone in a low, hoarse voice:

'Heard a shockin' thing this morning.'

'Indeed,' or 'Is that so?' would feebly reply the victim, helpless under the eye, probably with their mouth full of muffin.

'Shockin',' would repeat Mr Spurrey. 'When I heard it – well! Give you my word I could hardly believe it, for a minute or two.'

But he always did believe it; and so, in the end, did the victim. For though people under forty might laugh ringingly at the shocking things heard by Mr Spurrey about Abyssinia and the Means Test, about Hitler and Mussolini, and Armaments and Fascism, about Abdication and Spain, and the Special Areas and Air Defence – in the end, these very scoffers had to recall one morning on seeing the newspaper placards or opening their own journal, that Mr Spurrey had been right. Shocking, so shocking that when first you heard it you could not believe it was true . . . but it was.

By George, old Spurrey told me that, weeks ago, and I laughed at him!

But old Spurrey did not care whether you laughed at him or not; what he liked was frightening people, and by the time the nasty thing had happened and the scoffer was convinced, old Spurrey was busy frightening someone else.

That is what he had been doing to poor Mr Wither, with the result which the gentle reader hath seen.

'Was it Mr Spurrey, dear?' at last inquired Mrs Wither, giving up pretence.

'Awful things, he told me,' said Mr Wither hoarsely. 'Really appalling. I haven't been to town for some months, you know, Emmie, and I had no idea . . .'

'I don't expect it's true, dear,' said Mrs Wither. 'Shall I draw the curtains?'

She did not ask what the things were: there was the Infirmary Ball coming off the week after next, and she did not want her anticipatory pleasure spoilt.

'Oh, yes it is,' said Mr Wither gloomily. 'What Spurrey says is always true. Uncanny. Quite uncanny, the way he always knows what's going to happen.'

'Well, I shouldn't worry about it if I were you, dear,' said Mrs Wither, who would have advanced this remedy from sheer habit if someone had just swallowed poison. 'I don't want to bother you when you're so upset and worried, Arthur, but I do wish you could see your way to letting Madgie have a dog, dear. It would give her so much pleasure, and she wouldn't worry you any more about it if she had one.'

'It would get distemper.'

'They don't have distemper now, dear, Madge says; they get canine hysteria, I think she called it, instead.'

'Worse,' muttered Mr Wither. 'Much worse.'

'Oh no, dear. Not so infectious – and Saxon could nurse it if it did.'

'Spurrey was much impressed with Saxon.' Mr Wither roused himself, speaking a shade less gloomily. 'Said what a smart boy he was, and how well he drove. He's very dissatisfied with his own man. Says he's getting old.'

'Well, so is Mr Spurrey; I thought he looked *very* old this afternoon,' said Mrs Wither spitefully, 'and I should think his memory's failing and he imagines things.'

'Nonsense. Sound as I am.'

'Well, dear . . . about Madgie's dog. Don't you think you could let her have it? She's such a good girl.'

Silence. Mr Wither gazed gloomily at his feet, which he could not see because the room was in darkness.

'Couldn't you, Arthur?'

'Madge has everything she wants,' he said at last. 'A good home, pocket money, liberty. I never interfere with her playing all those games, though I'm sure they can't be good for her.'

Mrs Wither sighed. She knew, as a woman and a mother, that the splendours enumerated by Mr Wither were not enough. What Madge needed was something to love. But it never entered her head to tell her husband so. Not only would he not have understood, but it would have been the kind of thing that one does not say. There were ever so many things like that; most things, in fact.

There was another long pause. The sound of gay distant music somewhere across the valley floated into the dark room, making Mrs Wither feel depressed. She shivered.

'I suppose she can have it,' said Mr wither grudgingly, 'but tell her that the first time I find it in the house it must be destroyed.'

'Yes, of course, dear; I will make that quite clear to Madge, and I am sure that she will see it never does come in.'

But she did not feel at all sure.

Her heart sank at the prospect of agitating scenes, with Madge rushing the dog out through the french windows as Mr Wither came in through the door, of the dog being smuggled up to Madge's bedroom, and Mr Wither tripping over gnawed bones in the bathroom, of slippers destroyed and pools in prominent positions where Mr Wither would be sure to see them on his way to luncheon, of vets' bills and bills for dead chickens, of Madge in hysterics because her father had decreed that the dog must die, of barking fits at three in the morning, and possibly batches of puppies twice a year.

'It *is* good of you, dear; I do appreciate it so. And now do come into the drawing-room; it's quite chilly in here. I shall tell Fawcuss to bring you a glass of port.'

'I'm just coming; only going to draw the curtains. I don't want anything.'

Nevertheless, as he moved slowly into the drawing-room he thought with pleasure of the taste of port, and when the surprised Fawcuss brought some in, on an old glass tray that had belonged to his father, he said, 'Ah, thank you, Fawcuss,' and sipped it with an increase of comfort.

Emmie's a good wife to me, a very good wife, suddenly thought Mr Wither. And then, like a cold wind – What shall I do when she's gone?

# CHAPTER VIII

Saxon slept at his home. It was only a twenty-minute walk through the wood from the cross-roads to The Eagles, and Mr Wither saw no reason why Saxon should occupy a good bedroom, burning good electric light and eating a good breakfast under his employer's roof in addition to earning a hundred pounds a year. A few days after Tina had got her father's permission to have driving lessons Saxon was lying awake in the early morning, in his room.

It looked over the wood: he could see the tops of the beeches from where he lay, his arms behind his head, covered in coarse and worn but very clean bed linen. He wore flannel pyjamas in the same state as the bedclothes; the whole room had this look of poverty and fierce cleanliness: even the windows flung back the early sunlight like sheets of crystal.

He never slept well; he had not done so since he was a little boy. Too much (he supposed) went on in his head. People whom he called Fatbottoms slept all night, without ever planning what they were going to do the next day, and deciding the most efficient and quickest way to do it. At present he was sleeping worse than usual because he was worried. He was beginning to get sick of his job at The Eagles, and wanting to leave it, yet he had no prospect of any other. If he left The Eagles it must be to go to a better job, even if it was only a little better. He would not take a worse one; he would sooner stay where he was. Yet he was nearly twenty-three and he had been at The Eagles six months; it was high time that he made a move. He had learned everything that there was to be learned about driving and repairing Mr Wither's make of car; now he needed more difficult, responsible, and better-paid work.

The men at the filling-station where he had picked up his knowledge of cars and learned to drive had often asked him why he did not try for a job in Stanton, the fashionable and exclusive seaside town some twenty miles from Chesterbourne. There were lots of rich people there with cars who might give him a trial, the men said. Even Chesterbourne, one-horse hole though it was, had a professional and prosperous class that ran cars and chauffeurs; surely anything would be better than working for old Wither, a smart young feller like you.

But Saxon did not want to leave Sible Pelden; he wanted to show all the people there, who remembered him as a ragged boy running about the countryside with a dirty home and a drunken father, that he was getting along fine these days, in a smart uniform, earning a good salary and putting a bit by for a rainy day. If he went even so far as Stanton to look for another job, no one would know him, or see that he was making good; if he went to London, he would be just about lost, like a pin in the gutter; London was such a huge great place. He had driven the old boy up to London once or twice; and though he knew how big London was, and could even remember figures (for he read his newspaper every day with serious concentration) about its population and growth, it had proper surprised him; it went on for such a long time, and that time was only a little bit of it. No, he wouldn't try London just yet. Later on, perhaps. First he would show all the Fatbottoms who had been at school with him that he was going right ahead, and getting a better job each time he changed.

But there were no better jobs to be had round Sible Pelden. Mr Spring's chauffeur, Colonel Phillips's chauffeur, Sir Henry Maxwell's chauffeur were all married men with families, well dug in, who dared not die or try to get work elsewhere.

There's nothing doing round here, he thought, staring up at the still, hazy sky of early morning, with his cool grey eyes.

Tina's imagination and senses had not been seduced by a pair of fine shoulders on a lout. Saxon was that rarity, a beautiful young man without a trace of effeminacy. Beauty in peasants is usually spoiled, in the judgment of non-peasants, by coarseness of texture in hair and skin, but Saxon's hair and skin were fine, like those of the mother who had passed them on to him, and neither his manners nor voice were coarse. His ambition and his impatient hatred of his dirty home and sodden father seemed to have given a fineness to his nature that showed in his body. His beauty first struck the glance, but what held it, so that it returned again to his face with pleasure, was his air of confidence, of knowing what he wanted and being sure of the way to get it; in short, character. His mind moved in one piece, practically and realistically, and this gave him a look of calm that was attractive. Men said he was a cool hand, and women, after the talkies had been for some years in Chesterbourne, said that he was fresh. Cool and fresh: the adjectives apply to so few human beings that it is not surprising Tina found his image haunting her heart.

His good looks, and the memory that his father had once been a respectable, comfortably-off miller with land, gave him a feeling of superiority towards the hobbledehoys he led as a youth; he despised them while he ran with them, and this made his father's gradual decline from decency and his beastly death sink the deeper into his son's mind. Saxon had never been popular in the village; and when his father died and there was no money to pay the debts and the Cakers had had to move into a squalid cottage, the Sible Pelden people were more interested and I-told-you-soish than kind. Mrs Caker alternately grumbled and joked about her miserable poverty, and Sible Pelden did not like either attitude. The decent country women suspected her for being pretty, for being dirty, for buying diamond hairslides, for reminding them that her husband used to have his own mill; and the men, while they admitted that Saxon was deft, intelligent and hard-working, disliked his stuck-up ways. Some people said that it was a credit the way he had got himself on, dropped his loutish hangings-about at the cross-roads and found a job, but these were not many. Most of Sible Pelden said that he was a proper swell-head, adding that he would leave his mother next

95

thing, as sure as they were standing there, because she shamed him with her slumocky ways.

These were the Fatbottoms, the people Saxon wanted to 'show', by getting better and better jobs.

But he was so much a country boy, so soaked and coloured by the atmosphere of those few square miles of Essex wherein he had always lived, that he could not strongly feel the pull of a wider world. He read about it in his newspaper and saw it on the pictures, but he had not yet felt it as a real place. His real place was Sible Pelden. He knew, with his cool common sense, that if he really wanted to get on he must leave the place and try for work where work was to be had, but there was a part of his nature that was not cool, and was still so young that it wanted to show off in front of old, contemptuous neighbours. This joined with his unconscious feeling that Sible Pelden was home, and kept him there.

He knew that he had this narrow streak of imprudence: he called it 'letting go' and blamed his dead father for it. It made him do silly things sometimes; like smiling at girls in the street or at Miss Tina, or at Mrs Theodore, as he had smiled the other day, out in the yard.

Bang! on his door.

'Saxon! Here's yer tea.'

'Thanks, Mum.'

He got out of bed and took in the tea; his mother was already half-way down the narrow stairs. No tea was slopped in the saucer. So she had come to her senses about that, had she? He, who was neat as a cat, had once ticked her off for bringing up his tea slopped in the saucer, and ever since that day, weeks ago, it had come up with the cup swimming.

Now she had come round; so she could have that half-crown put back on her week's money.

She don't like me much, he thought, pulling off his pyjamas and putting them over the bed to air. She liked Cis best.

Cis had died during their third horrible winter in the cottage, at eight years old, because she could not get enough warmth and food; and because Mrs Caker, telling the more prosperous neighbours about Cis's illness in her grumbling voice with her eyes touched by laughter, did not make Cis sound as ill as she really was. Cis was a great one for a joke too; she was laughing a few hours before she died, while the doctor, fetched by Saxon, bent over her and said something funny.

Bad to remember. I'll show them. He began to splash in cold water; he would shave downstairs.

His mother was proud of his good looks, because he got them from her, and she grumblingly admired the way he had got on, telling him that he was a proper comic and as artful as a wagon-load of monkeys, but they sometimes had terrible rows because he hated her dirty ways. He hated, too, with the distaste of the unawakened, her easy attraction for every man she met. It made him embarrassed and ashamed.

He sometimes took a Chesterbourne girl to the pictures and kissed her good night for a quarter of an hour, but he had no regular girl, and had never got beyond kissing his irregular ones. What he liked was ladies; not ladies like Mrs Theodore who had worked in a shop and was therefore not a lady at all, but ladies like those who stayed over at Spring's, who filled their lives with unknown and therefore romantic activities. He admired them because they had no need to work, and because they had a good time. He was not envious of them nor of the wealthy people in the neighbourhood, because he was coolly determined that he would one day be wealthy himself. He had not yet planned in detail how this wealth was to be gained but his whole nature was set upon gaining it; and showing it, when he had got it, to the Fatbottoms of Sible Pelden.

Meanwhile it was a satisfactory start to have learned to keep himself and his room clean, to read the papers, steer clear of tarts, not talk Essex, and thoroughly understand the management and running repairs of a 1930 Austin saloon.

All the same (fastening a suspender) I wish I'd got a man-sized job. This one's getting me down, and I'm starting to let go. That smiling at Miss Tina, the other day, that was a fair let-go and a damn silly one too. Might have got me the sack, if she'd taken it the wrong way, and I only did it because it was a lovely morning, and I felt good, and she used to be such a pretty little thing. As for Mrs

Theodore, she's only a kid. That wasn't like giving a lady the come-hither. She wouldn't say anything, Mrs Theodore wouldn't. Besides, she's been married. She's a pretty little thing, too. Must be dull for her, up there. Dull – Jeeze! Is it dull or is it dull!

The young men of Chesterbourne had taken this rhetorical demand to their hearts, as had the young women; it would not be too much to say that it was heard everywhere. Am I hot or am I hot? Do I want a coffee or do I want a coffee? Was that rain or was it rain? Their elders said that they could not see anything in this silly way of talking. It didn't, said the elders pathetically, make sense.

*I must get a better job*, thought Saxon, running lightly downstairs with his waisted jacket over one arm, but he did not think it dramatically or tragically; he thought it with impatient common sense. Neither he nor his mother were tragic people; tragedy overtook them, but it did not deepen their natures, because it found no answer therein. The long-drawn tragedy of his father's life had made Saxon, not bitter and humiliated, but self-respecting and ambitious.

It would seem that Tina's good taste in dress extended to her taste in young men, though it is doubtful if this would have been Mr Wither's first thought, had someone said to him, 'Your youngest daughter is falling in love with the chauffeur.'

She herself thought that she was interested in Saxon only because there were no young men of her own class and fortune in the neighbourhood with whom to fall in love. If there had been a flock of nice, good, comely bachelors earning enough to keep a wife, with whom she could have danced and played tennis, Tina (who was rather a coward, though she was trying hard not to be, with the help of *Selene's Daughters*) told herself that she would never have been so reckless as to be attracted by the portionless and peasant Saxon. Her senses might have been stirred by his beauty, but her common sense and her self-respect would have soon sat on *that*.

But there were no men: there were just no what-you-would-call-really men at all, and her common sense, like all her other senses, was silently starving. Much chance it has of sitting on the others! she thought bitterly.

There were men, of course, but they were darkly thought of by

Tina as *No Use*. Colonel Phillips was sixty-odd and very married, Sir Henry Maxwell was fifty-odd and run by his mother, the rabble of three or four boys just down from, or going up to, the universities never stopped zooming past in noisy sports cars, so that it was impossible to imagine any of them troubling to climb out of the car and propose; and to them Tina seemed very old; she was not the type boys fall in love with.

There was Victor Spring, of course, dazzlingly eligible: too eligible. It was hideously clear that the first thought of any unmarried woman on meeting Victor Spring must be, in the old song's words:

Oh, what a prize you are,
Oh, if I only had you!

And that was enough to make any sensitive woman shrink from Victor Spring as though he were the local leper. Not that they got much chance to shrink, for he seldom saw any of them. When he took women about, they were Phyllis Barlow or other stunners from London, who shot like stars down the humble familiar lanes by his side in his big car. He used Sible Pelden, it was dimly felt, like an hotel. Bed, breakfast; but out and away all day on exciting and expensive activities at which the neighbourhood could only guess.

And even now, as Victor Spring lay in bed at a quarter to eight on this May morning, propped on his elbow while he sleepily gulped very hot tea, he was planning to see even less of Sible Pelden. He had a service-room in town where he could change and sleep if, as he often did, he wanted to spend a night in London; and he thought it would be a good idea if he had a whole flat. He was getting dissatisfied with Grassmere. The old place was all right, he supposed, pretty good in the summer when he could use the river and get his tennis; but it was a long way from London. It tied him. His mother, of course, never asked him about his movements unless they had people staying there; it was not she who tied him, but the thought at the back of his mind that he lived in the country. It was a nuisance. After all, they had lived at Grassmere for nearly thirty years; it was time they made a move.

One of those new flats in Buckingham Square that were running up on the site of Buckingham House would be the thing; they were not finished yet, but three-quarters of them were already let. They were expensive. Let them be; something must be done with the money his interests were coining; and a man must have a place he could ask people to; people must be entertained and impressed.

Grassmere, though large and comfortable, was not impressive to the moneyed eye, and Victor vaguely felt it. A family cannot live in a house for thirty years, even if that house is kept in perfect repair and solid luxury, without giving to their mansion an air of domestic comfort and stability which is not found impressive by the moneyed eye.

What the M.E. likes is something very new, staggeringly expensive and just a shade precarious; not enough to scare off the M.E., but enough to hint that here is so much money that it must have been raked off a dirty deal into which the M.E. may have a chance of muscling. The M.E. prefers a place to look like a blend of a bar and a luxury liner, and that was the sort of a place Victor was thinking about having.

But the disappointing truth is that this young god's own tastes were not exotic. The very fact that he was only now planning to live in chromium luxury in London, at the age of twenty-nine and after some five years of enjoying a steadily increasing income, proves how well content he was with old Grassmere. He liked all the things his City friends liked; speed, women, spirits, golf, tips, scandal and smut, but he liked them in a non-flashy way because there was no flash in his nature. His father had been born in Derbyshire and his mother in Hampshire, and from both those places the Levant is a long, long way.

He now began leisurely to get up, while his thoughts walked practically about in his head. He outlined some letters that he would dictate that morning; and felt irritation against General Franco and the Spanish Government because their civil war was hitting some interests that he had in a new line of small ships built for luxury cruising; then he wondered if he should advise his fellow-directors to lend money to a dubious company that wanted (ignoring the shrieks of the helpless residents) to build a pier and Amusement Park on to a seaside town in Dorset. He reminded himself to tell his secretary to change the two biscuits provided every day for his tea because he disliked coconut; and decided he would drive out that afternoon to look at a Victorian mansion near Hatfield, which his co-directors wanted to buy and pull down. On the site they would build a swimming-pool. When in doubt, build a swimming-pool, was their motto. But he must see the site for himself.

It is no wonder that Victor had at the back of his mind a vague irritation about the inconveniences of living in the country, for the Spring Developments Association Ltd was gaily destroying the country, at the rate of some square miles a month; his irritation may have been the country getting back at him. He had no conscious scruples about the way he made his money; when artists and ancientry with one foot in the furnace attacked his company and others like it by threatening him with the dreaded secret police of the S.P.R.E. and the National Trust gang, he retorted that business was business and meant it. Yet he came of country stock, he was country born and bred, and perhaps his discontent with life in the country was actually a dim sense of guilt. If he went to live in London, he would not see the bungalows built by his company outside Bracing Bay creeping across the quiet and beautiful lands between Sible Pelden and the sea.

Anyhow, I'll drop in at Buckingham Square and look at those flats on the way back from Hatfield, he thought, knotting a thick pale grey tie.

All his clothes were carefully thought out and perfectly executed, and gave the impression that it was not possible for any sane person to dress in any other way. He spent a good deal of money on his clothes, because he had so many activities and it was necessary to wear the correct clothes while doing any one of them, even while doing nothing, and none of the clothes, of course, were interfusable. It was not possible to wear the golfing clothes for walking, or the punting clothes for tennis.

His clothes gave him quite two-thirds of his efficient, sophisticated and summing-up manner, which some people found alarming and women found attractive. No one saw Victor naked, except the masseur at his Turkish baths and certain obscure persons upon whom he chose to bestow that honour; and the masseur had no thoughts except that Mr Spring was in very good shape, while the thoughts of the other persons are not relevant to this story; but it may be said that Victor, naked, looked simple, warm-natured and kind, which (except when anyone missed a train or neglected to prune the roses) is exactly what he was.

The idea of a flat in town made him think of Phyl as he stood staring out of the window, softly whistling and clappering his hair with two brushes.

Old Phyl. What a dazzler she was, easy on the eye, the top, the smoothest thing yet. He reminded himself how much he liked kissing her, firmly pushing to the back of his mind a suspicion that she did not quite so much like kissing him. She was a sport, who never whined if she lost a game. But dammit, she hardly ever did lose. At least, she lost quite often to him but he had to go all out to prevent her winning. He did not like that. He liked a good fight with a man, but that was different. Phyl never seemed to tire, she might be made of steel. A woman oughtn't to be like that. It was unfem— no, that's absurd of course: sounds like old Phillips. But a man doesn't like a woman to – oh well, I suppose some men don't mind it, but I do, and she isn't going to wear me for a mascot when we're married, so the sooner that gets home the better.

I suppose we'd better get things fixed up definitely this summer. There'll be the Bracing Bay business to get going in the autumn and I shan't have time for that *and* getting married. Get engaged in July, and married early in September.

Through his mind drifted the phrase, 'Oh, God, the whole ruddy works,' but it never occurred to him that a wedding need not have the whole ruddy works. All his friends had groaned; but their weddings had been huge, gorgeous, reverberating, barbaric feasts. That was the only way of getting married. Besides, Phyl would expect it.

None of Victor's set said that so-and-so was 'in love'; they said he was crazy about, had fallen for, or was making heavy passes at, someone. He vaguely supposed that he felt like that about Phyl, but what he felt when with her was that mingling of irritation, admiration, and determination that she should not master him, that he had felt when he was sixteen and she a composed, elegant, dark child of eleven.

Oh, it'll be all right when we're married.

He slowly pulled on his jacket.

All I know is, I keep on putting off this business with Phyl, and that isn't like me; I might try to get things fixed up with her when she comes down for the Infernal Ball (this was the name given by the local frivols to the Infirmary's yearly benefit). She's starting to get under my skin.

He went downstairs whistling.

She got under his skin like a spike of summer grass, he compared her to steel, and swore that he would not be her mascot. Admirable antagonism! Just what the late D. H. Lawrence, of whom Victor had not heard, would have ordered.

Half a mile away across the valley, Tina lay musing with arms behind her head, her large sad brown eyes staring through the open window. She looked prettier in bed than she did when dressed, because her nightgowns were softer in design than she permitted her day clothes to be; they were always white, decorated with narrow red or green ribbons. No one cared much how Tina looked, so she dressed to please herself.

Thoughts, quietly sad as she imagined the thoughts of the old must be, rose uselessly in her mind. They were all familiar to her, like worn paths; she experienced anger and boredom even while the well-known train unfolded. For so many years she had lain awake on spring mornings, while tea cooled on her little black lacquer bedside table, gazing through the curtains the maid had just pulled apart at the changing sky! Ten years ago there had been painful weeks when she waited in hope, her heart banging violently, for letters; and when they came she read into their friendly sentences meanings that were not there, and she had known, with her common sense, that they were not there, but had tried to deceive herself because she was so hungry to feel!

Other women – (oh, that path! it was very worn) – other women loved their families, or had their work. I did try to have a career; but a career just wouldn't have me. And I don't really see (another very worn path) why one should love one's relations just because they are one's relations.

We've never been a united family, that's all. I suppose Mother and Father didn't love each other properly or something; there doesn't seem to be much love between all of us, anyway. I wish there was.

We don't attract people, either.

For a little while her thoughts played with the half-forgotten pictures of men she had known at the Art School, who had told her she was charming or kissed her. Five times. Five men had kissed her. Well, six; only young Farquhar was drunk: I suppose that doesn't really count, if one's honest.

I wonder why (this path was so worn that she turned from it, in sick impatience, even as the thought came up) I've never had anyone in love with me? Other women do, not half as nice-looking as I am.

Of course, I've always wanted love very much; real love, for keeps, not just an affair, and I'm sure that puts men off. They hate you to be serious.

While she lay there with these old worn thoughts coming obediently into her mind, called there by habit and the familiar quiet of early morning, she was aware that at the back of her mind there was another thought that was not at all stale, but so fresh that it was nearly a feeling, with all a feeling's delicious power to kill thought. She had not yet told Saxon that he was to teach her driving, and this morning she would speak to him about it.

Tina had stopped trying to be honest with herself, put *Selene's Daughters* away in a drawer, and decided to be – not honest perhaps – but certainly sensible. Goodness and Doctor Irene Hartmüller only knew where she would end up, if she went on trying to be honest. Besides, there is a point at which honesty with oneself can become the mother to a wish; and she dimly felt this.

I've been too heavy, as usual, about the whole thing, she decided, sitting up in bed with soft lifeless brown hair falling against her thin cheeks. Just take it as a matter of course. Naturally I find him good to look at – stuck down here (thought Tina, vigorously common-sensible) without a man in sight for miles. She yawned, stretching.

Probably when I start the actual driving it'll be such fun that I'll stop being thrilled (deliberately she used the cheapened word, because she wanted to cheapen her emotion) about Saxon, and turn into a car-maniac.

She got energetically out of bed, ignoring the little voice inside her head that suddenly, with the driest possible intonation, observed, *But I think not.*

# CHAPTER IX

What a scene of unharnessed *libido* there was in the courtyard of The Eagles about eleven o'clock that morning! Tina, sauntering out to have her little talk with Saxon, met Madge coming back from Colonel Phillips's, followed by a fat, big-pawed, panting lump with a fondant-pink tongue; the Sealyham puppy. Madge's face was shining with pleasure and excitement, but she was trying to look severe because the dog must be made to realize, from her first hour as its owner, that she meant what she said; and she was now trying to make him follow her across the yard.

'Is that him? What a pet!' exclaimed Tina, her own eyes bright with happiness. It was such an exquisite morning! She wanted to be off, away, flying through the thin blue air: and round at the side of the car, cleaning it after a dismal expedition yesterday with Mr Wither into Chesterbourne, was Saxon, smiling at the puppy and trying to look correct and get on with his work all at once.

'Don't talk to him now, please,' said Madge quickly, as Tina stopped and held out a finger which the puppy was only too delighted to bite. 'It's frightfully important to begin training them from the very first moment you have them, and I do want him to be decently trained; a badly behaved dog is ghastly, I think.'

She rammed her fists deeper into her tweed pockets and, standing with her legs slightly apart, called in a low, carefully controlled voice: 'Come here.'

The puppy lumbered off and smelled Saxon.

'Come here,' repeated Madge. The puppy lumbered off and smelled Tina.

'Come here.'

'Bless him! He's nothing but a wuzzer,' protested Tina, laughing. 'Come and kiss your Aunt Tina, then.' She lifted him up.

'Oh, don't do that, please, Tina,' said her sister urgently, 'he *must* learn to come when I call, and he'll never get the idea if you keep on distracting his attention. Put him down, please.'

Tina put him down.

'Come here,' said Madge, in the same quiet, firm tone, and this time the puppy strolled over to her and smelled her brogues.

'There!' radiantly. 'He'll soon learn. It does pay to persevere with them.' She bent and gave the puppy one short, controlled pat. 'Good dog.'

'What are you going to call him?'

'Polo.'

'What?'

'Polo.'

'Polo the Game, or just Polo?'

'Don't be an ass, Tina,' laughed Madge good-naturedly, 'you couldn't call a dog Polo the Game. Just Polo, of course. I think it's rather neat myself. One gets so sick of Jerrys and Whiskys and Pats.'

She went off to Polo's large new kennel, standing as near to the back door as she could put it, and began to instruct him how to get into it, in what Tina foresaw was going to be her Polo-voice.

Nice to see poor old Madge so happy, thought Tina, strolling over to the car. It's pathetic, of course, that a puppy can make her look ten years younger and as pleased as a child, but she doesn't know it's pathetic, so that doesn't matter.

She herself felt easy and cheerful; her intense mood of the early morning had vanished. When Saxon stopped polishing as she approached, and stood upright, respectful and inquiring, she looked at him without even the faintest shock of emotion and said pleasantly,

'Oh, good morning, Saxon. I want you to teach me to drive. Can you fit that in, do you think, with your work and the garden and everything?'

'Oh yes, Madam,' said he, looking nothing but correct. His voice was pleasing; he neither spoke Essex nor tried to talk like gentry. It was just a naturally nice voice that would have been attractive in any young man, and Tina did not realize how anxiously she had been waiting to see if it really were as nice as she, in one or two humiliating reveries, had believed it to be.

'Good. Well, can we have the first lesson soon, please? It's such lovely weather now, and later on it may get hot and dusty and I hate motoring in the dust.'

How true all this was, how sensible and practical! Things were going quite normally; they could not be going better. *My true love hath my heart and I have his*, suddenly said that little voice in her head, as she looked calmly into Saxon's calm grey eyes. *Shut up*, Tina told it fiercely, *that's pure hysteria and doesn't mean a thing*.

'Yes, Madam, it does get dusty later on. Would you like a lesson this morning, Madam? I've nearly finished cleaning the car, and perhaps I could just show you how it works.'

His respectful but easy voice was quietly taking charge of the situation, and Tina did not like that much, because she wanted to feel that *she* was managing the affair, but she could not bear, after this little talk with him, to re-enter the chilly quiet house and watch the cloud shadows for the rest of the day while she buffed her nails and wondered what in heaven she should do about that little voice in her head, so she answered:

'Yes, that's a good idea. I'll come back in fifteen minutes, then.'

'Very good, Madam.'

Tina walked competently across the yard and into the house, feeling efficient and briskly serious. It would be useful to know how to drive, one never knew when a knowledge of driving might come in handy. It's high time I did learn, really, she thought as she went upstairs to her room. I ought to have learned years ago, only somehow – (no . . . her thoughts sheered away like a flock of frightened sheep) I was just lazy, I suppose.

Downstairs, dawdling through the sunlight and looking only half-awake came another lazy one, her silly but rather sweet sister-in-law, with an open novel in her hand. A pang went through Tina; dawdle, idle, be silly as she might, how young she was!

'Where are you flying off to?' inquired Viola, rather sulkily; few sights are more annoying when we feel lazy than that of somebody bounding upstairs.

'Just going to have a driving lesson,' over her shoulder as she went into her room.

'Oh, who with? Saxon?' Viola followed her in and plomped on the bed, a habit of hers that Tina disliked. She nodded. She knew, in a fury of impatience and dismay, that Viola would say, 'Oo, can I come too?'

'Oo, can I come, too?' said Viola.

'No, you can't,' pronounced her sister-in-law lightly, summoning her extra fifteen years of experience and firmly grasping the situation. 'I'm serious about it; I really do want to learn, and if you're at the back, breathing down my neck and giving me advice, I shan't be able to concentrate.'

Pause. Tina put on her beret.

'Oh, all right,' said Viola amiably, getting up. She added, going slap into the heart of the situation with devastating simplicity, 'I don't want to butt in.'

'Butt in?' repeated Tina, pulling on her gloves, and trying to be haughty. 'My dear child, it isn't a question of—'

But the mildly inquiring look on Viola's face, with just the hint of a laugh in the eyes, defeated her. She giggled angrily, shook her fist, and went quickly out of the room,

It was delightful to be teased about Saxon! She ran downstairs singing. How easy life was if you took it lightly!

Viola stood by the bed, a little forlornly.

It did not occur to her primitive mind that Tina could want to learn to drive the car for any other reason than to be near Saxon. No one had taught Viola that ladies did not fall in love with chauffeurs. Had she asked Miss Cattyman, Miss Cattyman would have said that some ladies did; there was that awful case in the papers; and the aunts would have said that of course ladies, real ladies, didn't. But her father, that romantic whose irritable yet rose-coloured view of life had coloured her own childish outlook, would have pointed out what a lot of ladies in Shakespeare's plays had fallen in love, quite uninvited, with the most unsuitable and surprising people: and Viola went by what her father would have said. It seemed to her quite funny, natural and exciting that Tina should be keen on Saxon.

She had felt, for weeks, Tina's interest in Saxon floating between herself and her sister-in-law every time his name was mentioned. Her feeling was vague but strong: when Tina admitted, by her laugh and her shaken fist, that she wanted to be alone with Saxon, Viola experienced no surprise; she felt that she had known for weeks how Tina felt.

But Tina's happiness made her feel both lonely and sad.

After all, she thought, going slowly downstairs, she has got Saxon on the spot, and she can see him and be with him and that's something; it isn't like having absolutely *no one*, and the only person you're at all keen on being frightfully rich and having a gorgeous time and engaged, I expect, to someone simply marvellous, like a film star.

She stopped at the back staircase that led down into the yard.

'Come here,' floated up a low, controlled voice. 'Polo. Polo, come here.'

This glided off Viola's mind without interesting her: she was not inquisitive. I'll go out the front way, she thought, in case Tina's down there with him. I don't want to make her laugh.

Love, in Viola's opinion, was a matter for giggles. Her practical experience of it had never made her want to giggle, but it made Shirley giggle, and The Crowd (in public, at least), and here was Tina, giggling like the rest. It was a matter of pride to giggle. Don't let it Get You Down, The Crowd earnestly advised any one of its members who might be in love – rather as though Love were an all-in wrestler with a lot of patent holds which it was the victim's job to dodge.

But Viola herself did not feel like giggling.

'I'll go for a walk in the wood,' she decided, and tiptoed past Mr Wither's den and out through the front door.

She saw the car's glossy backside just dwindling down the road, and waited until it was out of sight; then she wandered off into the wood with her hands in her pockets, thinking that she only had five pounds of her money left and wondering if, when that should be gone, she dare ask Mr Wither for some more.

Tina sat beside Saxon in silence. She was having her desire. On either side the blossoming trees went by, and the road ran ahead, and she breathed the air of late spring, while she saw, without looking, his hands on the wheel and his profile against the green woods. She felt so peaceful and content that she did not want to begin the driving lesson; she wanted to move like this for ever, as though he and she were two lovers in a gondola. I'm glad I've known him for such a long time; it's not like being with a stranger; after all, it's only little Saxon who I used to see swinging on gates and forgetting to shut them on purpose; and I've lived here for so long, too . . . that's why everything's so peaceful. I'm sure love is calm, not violent and frightening. Like a dove there sailed into her mind:

> And with the morn those Angel faces smile,
> That I have loved long since, and lost awhile.

Doctor Irene would have a lot to say about that, I'm sure.
People are so clever.
Saxon slowed the car, braked, and turned respectfully to her. The lane was very quiet, as the nasty noise of the engine died away.
'Would you like me to explain how it works, Madam?'
'Please.' Tina leaned back comfortably and turned upon him an alert, intelligent expression, but he was not looking at her. If there was the dimmest feeling at the back of his mind that Miss Tina did not seriously want to learn how the Austin worked, he repressed that feeling and set himself to show her; for he might be mistaken, and that would be a nice letting-go, that would, getting fresh with Miss Tina. The Push with no reference, that's what that would mean.

All the same, he was flattered that she wanted him to teach

her. The Old Boy could have done it just as well, really . . . only no one in their right mind 'ud want to learn anything off – from – him.

So he began to explain very clearly how the Austin worked, beginning with the bit about the gears, for he took it for granted that his pupil only wanted to know how to make the thing move, not how it was that it moved at all. When he said, 'How it works,' he meant 'How you work it.' He decided that she could be told about the engine later on.

'There's a lot to remember, isn't there?' said Tina, presently, but more for something to say than because she meant it.

'There is at first, Madam, but you'll find it comes suddenly. They say learning the piano's just the same, and the typewriter.'

In fact, she found little difficulty in concentrating on what he was saying and remembering it, so that when he mentioned third gear she knew, without stopping to think, what he meant. Her brain as a young woman had been quick and intelligent and a good memory had helped it. She was not a fuzzy person like Viola; had she been, she might have married, for the distressing truth is that the fuzzies usually do; men like them. She had kept her brain exercised by reading heavyish books, which might not always be truly wise but at least were not those meringues of the intellect, those mental brandies-and-sodas – *novels*.

And she tried hard now to concentrate upon what he said, because she was frightened by the mood of dreamy contentment that had fallen over her like the rays of the sun, shining high, so high that it was lost in its own light above the summer landscape of Essex. She could feel magic in the quiet spring day, like a sorcerer's far-off voice, and lines of poetry floated over her mind as if they were strands of spider-web.

'Now,' she suddenly interrupted him, 'I want to go through what you've told me and see how much I remember before I actually take the wheel.'

'Very good, Madam.' He took his own hands off the wheel and turned attentively towards her. His look, so serious that she knew it only just controlled amusement, yet suddenly human again and different from the look he gave to a gear-box, gave her a shock. The ground seemed to go noiselessly from under her feet.

'There are four gears and a reverse gear,' she began, speaking more quickly than she had meant to. 'You start in neutral, let out the clutch by pressing down your left foot . . .' She continued the boring recital to an end, then looked at him questioningly, smiling.

'That's right,' smiling too, 'you're getting along fine – Madam. Now see if you can remember which gear is which.'

She remembered without a fault, and while she was running through her lesson the second time, the bell in Sible Pelden church struck half-past twelve, reminding her that The Eagles was still there, with lunch simmering inside it, and that there would just be time to drive home and get her nose powdered before she sat down to that meal. No one ever missed a meal at The Eagles unless they had warned everyone, days ahead, that they were going to. If you missed a meal, you were ill or some accident had leapt upon you; you never forewent one on purpose.

'There won't be time for any more today,' she said, giving a little sigh and leaning back. 'Will you drive home now, please; and I'll watch carefully and try to follow what you're doing.'

Saxon sent the car slowly along the narrow lane, where the young hedge-growth was still a distinct and delicate labyrinth of differing greens, and the small white or purple flowers glowed vividly against thin Maytide leaves, because there was as yet no dust to dim them. Like any lonely lane, this one seemed the end of the world, with the sunny, misty blue sky at its end and bird song scattered all over it, and if there were spirits, here they might be. Ah! the sorcerer's far-off voice! We can come here tomorrow, thought Tina, not taking in what Saxon was doing with the car. This is all I want; just this lane, and the sunlight and the noise of the engine, and Saxon beside me and neither of us saying a word.

I darsent ask him for pocket-money, thought Viola, going down into the wood, but that's what I'd really like. Five shillings a week, like Teddy gave me, then I could save up for anything I really wanted. Dad used to give me some too, I could say. Mr Wither, my father

113

hadn't much, but he gave his girl what he could. How much? Seven and sixpence, Mr Wither. That isn't very much; I will give you seventeen and sixpence. Oh, what a beast I am, thinking that seven and sixpence wasn't much! It was all Dad *could* do, anyway, towards the end, and I had my salary. Twenty-five shillings . . . and where it goes I *don't* know. Well, Catty, I had to have some stockings and there was five shillings I lent Shirley and that blouse . . .

It's three months since I had a new frock.

'There y'are, ducks,' called the Hermit, who was sitting among the fern beside his smouldering fire, carving something with a bright-bladed knife. Opposite him, on a tree-stump with her elbows on her knees and her chin in her hands, sat Hetty; a book had slid off her lap and lay face downwards among the fern stalks. She looked up at the Hermit's shout, and waved.

Viola, wondering who she was, waved back and went on towards the fire, for she was not afraid of the Hermit's roving eye when someone else was there.

Hetty was pleased to see her, because she looked neither rich nor smart; indeed, with her shabby tweed coat, untidy heavy fair curls and sleepy expression, she suggested that she was not only poor, but stupid in a way that might, because Hetty was not used to it, prove interesting.

'You don't remember me, do you?' said Hetty, louder than usual because Viola looked such a half-wit. Viola shook her head, smiling, though she had now recognized her as Victor Spring's cousin without a hat, and felt very embarrassed and shy.

'You're Mrs Wither, aren't you?' pursued Miss Franklin. (So I am, thought Viola, surprised: doesn't it sound awful!) 'Don't you remember? We gave you a lift the other day in that thunderstorm. I hope that neither of you caught cold?'

'Oh no, thanks ever so; it was awfully kind of you.' Viola hopped across the half-drowned plank that bridged the stream, and came slowly up to Hetty, smiling.

'And were you very late for tea? I seem to remember that Miss Wither said something about being late for tea.'

'Oh yes, we were rather, but it wasn't so bad as it might have been – at least' – remembering what dinner on that evening had been like – 'there wasn't a row about *that*.'

'Come a bit nearer, ducks,' invited the Hermit, putting wood on the fire. 'Take yer shoes orf and warm yer feet.'

'Our feet are not cold, thank you,' said Hetty, half-turning her head to look at him.

'I won't mind if yer *'ave* got 'oles in yer stockings,' persisted the Hermit. 'Come on – come up closer and let's be cosy, eh? Wot say?'

He did not seem to expect an answer, but bent again over his carving.

'What's he doing?' muttered Viola.

'Making a walking-stick. He hopes (vainly, I fear) to sell it to your father-in-law.'

Viola stared. 'To Mr Wither?'

'That's 'im. Old Shak-per-Swaw in person,' said the Hermit, looking up.

'What's that on the end of it?' Viola craned her long neck and tried to see.

'Bear with Cubs,' said the Hermit, holding up the stick with a shapeless lump at one end. 'Just 'ollering between the bear's legs. Cor! it don't 'alf take some doing, too. Four legs and a 'ole between each: one 'ole between each of the three cubs, another 'ole between the group of cubs an' their dam, and little 'oles between all the legs of the three cubs. There's a lot of work in this 'ere, ducks. Not to mention their ears. Eight ears, all 'ollow. I reckon this'll take me every bit of May – 'alfway through June, I reckon.'

'It is an ambitious subject,' said Hetty musingly, in a lowered tone, gazing with misty blue eyes at the Hermit sitting cross-legged in the fern. 'He only began it this morning. I suggested a less complicated subject, an apple, for instance, or an orange, but he said no, he had promised to carve old Shak-per-swaw a smarter walking-stick than the one he usually carries, and he is going to keep his word. What is your father-in-law's daily walking-stick like?'

'Oh, it's got a sort of Indian's head on it or something, I think,' said Viola vaguely, but laughing because Hetty was laughing and it was so nice to be with somebody young, even if you were scared stiff of them because they were His cousin and talked like a book.

'What a funny thing to want to do. Carve, I mean,' she said. 'I mean, carving a walking-stick – it's jolly difficult.'

'Oh, he actually sells his carvings sometimes to motorists, so it is not so funny as it appears. He stands at the cross-roads on Sundays with a tray from Woolworth's round his neck and the carvings on it, and the motorists, lured by his unusual appearance, pause, and are betrayed by what is false within – namely, their own taste.'

'But they aren't very good, are they?' in a whisper.

'They are more bad than the eye inexperienced in bad carvings would conceive it possible for carvings to be,' drawled Hetty, 'but I imagine that the motorists are amazed that an object can be made by the hands alone, because all the objects which they encounter in their daily lives are made by a machine or emerge from a tin. They are so amazed that they assume that an object made by the hand alone is necessarily worth having, and so they buy it.'

'Oh,' said Viola. After a pause, 'But how did he learn carving?'

'He says that he used to be a model at Carlotti's.'

'Where's that?' demanded Viola simply, who was never afraid of showing ignorance and did not know how rare this fearlessness is.

'It's a famous art school in London,' explained Hetty, looking at her kindly and speaking less artificially because she saw that she was bewildering Viola and making her uneasy. 'I think your sister-in-law used to go to an art school, did she not? My aunt says so. I expect she knows Carlotti's – you ask her when you get home.'

'That's right,' nodded the Hermit. 'Carlotti's in the King's Road, Chelsea. Sat to all the big men, too, I did. Mr Whistler, Mr Alma Tadema, Mr Holman Hunt. All the big men. Beautiful, I used to be, a fair treat. Am still, come to that. Now don't think I mean no 'arm by this, ducks, 'cos I don't. I ain't that sort, and I know young ladies when I see 'em, though, mind you, nowadays it ain't so easy to tell a young lady from a you-know-what as it was when I was a lad. All the same, I don't mean nothin' you wouldn't like yer mas to know about, see? That's straight, that is. It's Art, and that makes all the difference. *When it ain't Art it's dirt, but if it's Art it's all right, see?*

Well, wot I was going to say was if you was to happen to be down 'ere some morning when I'm 'aving me dip, you could see me. Beautiful – muscles, proportions, everythink. Even me feet – and that's most unusual, that is. I remember Mr Le Strange, the Great Le Strange, they used to call 'im, sayin' to me, "Ah, Falger," 'e says, "there's ten pairs o' good shoulders about for one pair o' good feet." Very fond of drorin' my feet, Mr Le Strange was. I remember one picture of 'is, "Morning" it was called, me in a sort of a tunic, runnin' up a 'ill after a goat. Very pretty, it was. Large pitcher. It's in the Westwater Art Gallery.'

'And he picked up carving from watching the students, or so he says,' murmured Hetty.

'That's right,' affirmed the Hermit whose hearing seemed to be better than that of people who live in houses. He held up Bear with Cubs, and surveyed it, not critically but with a look of quiet approval, then muttering, 'Cor, 'Ot. 'Ow about a drop of Rosie,' he put the carving carefully down on a piece of newspaper and crawled into his lean-to.

'Are you going to the Infirmary Ball?' next inquired Hetty, glancing at her wrist-watch.

'I don't know. Tina (my sister-in-law, the one I was with that day, you know) she did say something about it, but I don't know if they'll take me too.'

Hetty resisted the temptation to say 'Never mind, Cinderella,' and went on:

'It will be next week – yes, a week today. How the year flies!' and a sullen look came over her face as she imagined those flying years, wasting her impatient youth in their flight.

'Will – are you going?' blurted Viola, timidly, longing to ask if *He*, Mr Spring, your cousin was going, and thinking that this was the best way of finding out.

'Unfortunately, yes, I am.'

'Why, don't you like dancing?'

'No.'

'How funny! I adore it; I'm simply *crazy* about it,' and indeed she looked it, with her eyes open very wide and a caterpillar swinging in the fine fuzz of her hair. 'Oh, I do hope they take me! Will you go alone?'

'No, I shall go with my aunt and a party,' said Hetty dejectedly.

She was clever and sensitive; her imagination held the wood and its subtlest shades of beauty, as well as the psychological shades in the characters of three human beings in the wood, as though in a fine-meshed net. Yet she did not guess that Viola wanted to know if Victor would be at the ball. Truth, the simple fish, did not even slip through the subtle net; he just never went near it.

'A big party, will it be?' pursued Viola faintly.

'No. Quite small, yet large enough to be tedious. My aunt, my cousin Victor, a Miss Barlow who will be staying with us for the event, a young man of ample fortune and no conversation, and myself.'

'Lovely,' murmured Viola; then added, starting out of her thoughts, 'I'm awfully sorry you don't want to go though.' She added kindly, 'Buck up; I don't expect it'll be so bad when you get there; things often aren't. Often when I've been simply dreading going to a place, I've quite enjoyed it when I got there.'

She no longer felt shy of Victor Spring's cousin, because Hetty was friendly and kind. Also, they had exchanged grins over the Hermit's remark about holey stockings, and this made Viola feel friendly towards Hetty, as we always do towards a stranger with whom we have shared a joke. As for Hetty, she was wondering if she should ask Viola what it was like to live at The Eagles, but she decided not to, because it was plain that although Viola was a girl with much natural charm, she was also a girl with much natural silliness, who would think The Eagles a boring place and be quite unconscious of the subtle, Chekhovian currents that moved sluggishly through its dark silent rooms. I expect she would love the kind of existence we lead at home, which is about as subtle as a pie-dish and far less useful, thought Hetty. Not that I ought to grumble. I have money of my own, a luxurious home in excruciating taste, and all the clothes I want. All that is lacking is liberty, an aim to work for, and the conviction that my life is worth living. I am a most fortunate young woman.

'Was it a nice party you had the other night?' asked Viola wistfully.

'It was not so bad as our parties usually are,' began Hetty, then she glanced at Viola's face and her imagination took a quite remarkable leap, right over into the gaiety-starved mind of the other girl. She realized how entrancing the idea of that party was to Viola and how much she would have loved to be there. She went on, in a different tone:

'Yes, it was rather nice, really, because it was such a beautiful evening and my cousin had all the boats – the punt, and the outboard and the little sailing-boat (she's called *Marlene*) out on the river and we had supper down there.' She went on slowly, choosing her words and watching the audience, 'The sky was gold, and then it was violet, and there was a smell of syringa—'

'And did you have cocktails?' interrupted Viola.

'Yes,' said Hetty, laughing.

'And what to eat?'

'Salmon mayonnaise and chicken and soup and ices,' answered she, inventing. What had they had to eat? All their food, eaten in circumstances unheightened by the imagination, was excellent, and all of it tasted the same to her. Food only became interesting when it was symbolic, or when it was eaten to the music of witty talk, or by brave men in danger, by true poets who were starving.

'Lovely,' sighed Viola.

'You must come to one of our parties one day,' said Hetty impulsively.

'Me?' Viola went bright pink. 'Oh, I say, how marvellous! But I haven't – you don't – I mean, wouldn't your aunt mind?'

'She would be delighted,' said Hetty firmly. She had gone too far; she knew it. Mrs Spring seldom invited people to the house unless they were wealthy, ordinary, and conventional. Viola was none of these things, and no pleasure or profit could come to Mrs Spring from inviting her.

'I am sure she would,' added Hetty.

The words sounded weak and untrue as they fell on the warm spring air. They seemed to go into a silence, and quietly disappear.

'That would be lovely: thanks ever so,' muttered Viola, thinking: I haven't got a proper frock.

Hetty stood up awkwardly and brushed bits off her skirt while Viola, picking up the book from among the fern, glanced at its title.

'*Collected Poems of Robert Frost*,' she read. 'Poetry. Good lord. What a funny name, Frost.'

'Thank you,' said Hetty a little stiffly, taking it from her and wishing that she could meet someone who did not think it a symptom of insanity to read poetry for pleasure. 'Are you going now, or shall you stay here?'

'Oh, I must be getting along, or I'll be late for lunch.' She got up.

There was a sort of commotion in the hut, and the Hermit reappeared, with no boots on. He lifted a large bare horny foot, which may have looked pretty good to the 'nineties, but which had depreciated with the remorseless march of time, and said proudly:

'There. Perfect. Every bone.'

Hetty and Viola, trying not to laugh, gave polite exclamations of interest and admiration and he sat down to his carving again, while the two girls stood looking at each other rather shyly.

'Well, goodbye,' said Hetty at last. 'I hope we shall meet again. I often come down here.'

'Yes, I hope so too. Thanks ever so. Goodbye.'

Each walked away up her side of the little valley while the Hermit waved first to one and then the other, calling affectionately, 'Goo'-bye, ducks, goo'-bye,' and whittling busily away at the Bear with Cubs. The truth always sounds fantastic. The Hermit, with his lack of responsibilities, his interest in everyone's affairs, and his admiration of himself, was the happiest person in the neighbourhood. If only it weren't for them bloody birds. 'Ow they did go on, waking you up at five o'clock in the morning, shrieking and hollering after dinner when you wanted a doss. Then there was that one that went on 'alf the night, as though all day wasn't enough. Skizz! He viciously whizzed a stone in the direction of a dazzling song among the water-rooted hazels, and out darted a small brown bird, singing as he flew away.

'Gar,' muttered the Hermit. 'Shut up.'

# CHAPTER X

No sooner did Viola enter the dining-room than she saw that some-thing was up, and her spirits, raised by her chat with Hetty and the brightness of the morning, slid gently down again. Tina and Madge, who were already at the table, looked cheerful enough, but Mrs Wither was flustered and Mr Wither looked cross.

'Sorry I'm late,' muttered Viola.

'No. Oh no. It's only just one o'clock. We are a little early today,' answered Mrs Wither, absently and coldly.

They began to eat. Mr Wither kept his eyelids lowered in the way they all knew meant that trouble was brewing. What shall I do this afternoon? thought Viola. How long the days are. It's awful. I wonder what's up?

'How did you get on with your lesson?' she asked Tina, presently, too nervous to sit in silence.

'Not badly, I think. It isn't so difficult as I thought it would be. I quite enjoyed it. I'm having another one at eleven tomorrow . . . if you can spare Saxon, that is, of course, Father.'

Mr Wither said nothing.

'It's the Infirmary Ball next week, isn't it?' observed Madge, after a pause. 'Have the tickets come yet? They're dashed late with them this year, they're usually here by the twenty-sixth. I suppose that's because there was all that fuss about Lady Dovewood changing the date.'

Mr Wither looked up, fixing a bleared eye upon Viola.

'Someone called to see you this morning,' said Mr Wither. 'On a bicycle.'

He paused. Everyone felt that Viola's visitor ought to have come in a Rolls.

'Me?' stammered Viola, going pink. 'Who?'

'Your aunt, I believe. In a nurse's uniform.'

Pause. Mr Wither ate a forkful of pickle.

'That's right.' Viola was relieved, and she smiled. 'She is a nurse. My Auntie Lizzie, that would be. Was she all right? Fancy her coming right out here on the bike! She doesn't cover Sible Pelden, only New Chesterbourne, where the slums are. Did she say anything?'

'She was selling tickets for the Infirmary Ball, I understood her to say,' droned Mr Wither, eating more pickle. 'Naturally, I could not buy them from her. I had to explain to her (at some length) that we have always procured our tickets direct from Lady Dovewood. By the way,' he laid down his knife and fork, put two fingers into his waistcoat pocket and brought out a bunch of pink cardboard slips, 'here are the tickets, Emmie. They came this morning. You had better take care of them.'

'Yes, dear.' Mrs Wither took the slips, counted them, then looked up.

'They've sent one too many, dear. There are five here. Now isn't that silly of them? Have you paid for them yet, Arthur?'

Mr Wither nodded and jerked his head at his daughter-in-law, who was sitting very upright, with her cheeks once more pink and her eyes bright with an incredulous hope.

'For me? Oh, I say, thanks most awfully, Mr Wither, it *is* kind of you!' stammering rapturously. 'How lovely! How much is it?'

'Eh?' said Mr Wither, startled. 'What? Nonsense! Everyone goes to the Infirmary Ball. Only once a year.'

'Yes, but I *want* to pay for myself,' persisted Viola, insincerely, 'I shall enjoy it *ever* so much more if you'll only let me.'

Silence.

'I mean,' she stammered, scarlet, 'I mean it's so awfully kind of you, I don't like to think of you wasting your money on me, you know.'

Silence. Mrs Wither slowly tinkled the little bell to summon Fawcuss, and while Fawcuss was removing plates, Viola regained her composure.

But it was difficult for her to be composed when she was so very happy! The room seemed full of brilliant sunlight and the song of the blackbirds in the garden sounded so loud and sweet that she wanted to sing too. She was going to the Ball! and He would be there! She would wear her silver dancing shoes again and have her hair waved, and get some new pearl ear-rings from Woolworths (no one would know they came from Woolworth's. Of course, you always knew when other people's ear-rings came from Woolworth's but they never guessed about yours). Perhaps he would dance with her; a waltz, slow and dreamy, or quick and exciting. She could still see the enormous white crinolines looped with flowers floating round the ballroom in that film about some Austrian queen, 'Empress of Hearts' it was called, and the young officers with their jackets slung over one shoulder and their shiny high boots. She saw herself in a white crinoline, waltzing with Victor Spring and looking up into his eyes.

'Viola . . . shape?'

'No thanks,' she murmured. 'Yes, please, I mean.'

The shape was eaten in silence. Tina, too, looked dreamily happy. Things are getting better, thought Viola. Madge has got her puppy, and Tina's got Saxon (well, she hasn't exactly got him yet but I expect she will) and I've been talking to His cousin only this morning and she said I must go to one of their parties one day (and perhaps if I meet him at the Ball he'll introduce me to his mother and perhaps she'll invite me too, and then everything'll be all right). *And I'm going to the Ball! I'm going! I'm going!*

Saxon will drive us there, thought Tina. I wonder if he dances, and if he likes it . . . if he takes girls to those dances at the Baths one sees advertised in Chesterbourne . . . I know absolutely nothing about his life, and yet I feel that I know *him*. I wonder if he's got a girl? This thought had not occurred before to her, and she was dismayed, even amidst her dreamlike content, to discover how much it agitated her.

After the shape, there was cheese. Cheese over, these three infatuated women were free to go away and dream as much as they liked; Tina went slowly out into the garden with a novel under her arm, and Madge hastened away to see how Polo had enjoyed his dinner, and Viola was going quickly out of the room to overhaul her wardrobe in preparation for the Ball, when Mrs Wither gently stopped her.

'Viola dear,' began Mrs Wither, in a frighteningly kind voice, 'there is something I want to talk to you about. Come into the morning-room for a moment, will you?'

Oh, please God, don't let her say I can't go to the Ball after all. Amen.

'Righto, Mrs Wither. All right, I mean.'

Mrs Wither, having mysteriously shut the morning-room door, sat down and patted a chair facing her, on which Viola miserably seated herself.

They seemed very alone. Not a sound broke the morning-room's quiet, except the slow tick-tock of an old clock in a corner.

'Now, dear, Mr Wither is not *angry* with you about what happened this morning,' began Mrs Wither, opening her pale eyes wide and convincing Viola that Mr Wither was very angry indeed, 'but he was very much upset by your aunt's visit. Coming like that on a bicycle, without letting us know or anything. And you were out, of course; you had just run off somewhere in the way you often do – Oh, I know it does not *matter*, you were not doing any harm, but your aunt must have thought it very strange that you were not here to welcome her. And there was another thing that upset Mr Wither very much. Your aunt had a little accident as she went off; the bicycle caught against a stone or something, and your aunt had to jump off very quickly; she almost fell, in fact, and Mr Wither happened to be looking out of the window at the time and it agitated him very much. It gave him quite a shock, he nearly went out to see if she were hurt. So next time, dear, if you will just tell your aunt to *let us know* when she is coming, everything will be all right. We do not mind your friends coming here, dear, of course; we are glad to welcome them for your sake, but we *like to know*.'

The door opened and Fawcuss looked in.

'What is it, Fawcuss?' inquired Mrs Wither, patiently.

'Mrs Theodore is wanted on the telephone, Madam. It's a call from London.'

'Oh, I bet it's Shirley! – sorry, Mrs Wither,' cried Viola, and ran out of the room'.

'Hullo, darling,' called Shirley's clear voice, sounding strong and full of life though it was speaking so many miles away. 'How's things? How are all the Therms?'

'Oh, all right, thanks,' answered Viola, glowing. 'I *am* glad you phoned. Is it anything special or did you just—'

'Listen, darling – is the ancestral mansion creeping with Therms or are you alone?'

'Yes. Yes I am, I mean.'

'Good. Well, just make sure no one's got their ear pasted at the keyhole.'

'They can't. It's in the hall.'

'So useful, of course. No one can fix up a dirty weekend without everyone else getting wise to it. Listen, darling, can you come up to town tomorrow and meet me at the Oxford Street Lyons Corner House at eleven? Main entrance. I've got the day off for shopping. Decent of the Death's Head, was not it?'

'Oh, Shirley, I'd love to!'

'What's to stop you?'

'Well, I must just ask, of course.'

'Oh God. All right. Run along. I'll hang on. Tell them I keep a bad house and we want new blood.'

Viola ran back to Mrs Wither, who was sitting exactly as she had left her, looking patient and affronted.

'Oh, I say, Mrs Wither, I'm awfully sorry I had to dash off like that, but it's Shirley. My friend, Shirley Davis, you know. She's got the day off tomorrow to do some shopping and she wants me to go with her. May I go, please? I could catch the early bus and I'd be back in time for supper – dinner, I mean.'

'You must please yourself, dear,' said Mrs Wither disapprovingly. 'You are your own mistress, you know. It is rather short notice, is it not?'

'Yes, that's what makes it so ripping. It's such a surprise. Can I go then, please, Mrs Wither?'

'Of course, dear. And I think you had better try to call me Mother; it sounds better.'

'Yes, Mrs Wither – Mother, I mean. Thanks awfully.'

She darted away, leaving Mrs Wither sighing. Common, pleasure-loving, discontented with home life, extravagant, not behaving at all as a widow should. Ah well, no cross, no crown, thought Mrs Wither, straightening a mat.

'It's all right, Shirley! I can come!'

'Good. I hope no one flew asunder with the effort. Well, you be outside the main entrance at the Oxford Street Lyons Corner House tomorrow at eleven o'clock. (You can get the tube straight through from Liverpool Street to Tottenham Court Road.) Goodbye till then.'

'Goodbye, Shirley, and thanks *awfully*.'

'Vi – here – hi – are you there?'

'Yes?'

'Got any money?'

'Five.'

'Shillings or pounds?'

'P.'

'Good! We'll get through some of it tomorrow.'

'Lovely. Goodbye, darling.'

Viola hung up, and raced upstairs to her room with a head full of delightful fancies. As though the Ball were not enough, now there was this! It never rains but it pours, she thought, standing in front of the wardrobe and looking, without really seeing them, at two limp and faded evening-frocks. What shall I wear tomorrow? . . . I've got no clean gloves . . . I must wash them . . . oh . . . aren't my shoes awful?

Suddenly coming out of her dream she realized how worn were her silver slippers, tarnished, stubbed at the toes, a button missing. I can t wear those, she thought. I must get some new ones.

But the thought did not really worry her, because she knew that she would be able to buy a pretty, fashionable and comfortable pair for less than a pound.

Civilization as we know it is corrupt. It may be doomed; there are plenty of omens. Its foundations are rat-eaten, its towers go up unsteadily into lowering clouds where drone the hidden battle-planes. But it can, and does, supply its young daughters with luxuries at prices they can afford. No woman need be dowdy, or shabbily genteel. While she has a few shillings to spend on clothes, she can buy something pretty and cheerful. This may not be much, but it is something. Tomorrow we die; but at least we danced in silver shoes.

Saxon put his head round the kitchen door and told Cook that he was going home for lunch today. Cook nodded. The three elderly maids at The Eagles, all Chesterbourne women, approved on the whole of the young chauffeur, because he was polite and hard-working and so far they had not been able to find out anything against his character. They felt that he ought not to have been so good-looking, but after all that was hardly his fault, and no doubt as he got older he would get uglier and that would be all right; it was more natural, the maids felt, for everyone to be plain. They were all three plain, and they looked rather like three elderly fat pebbles which have been quietly rolling round in a pocket in the bed of a stream for so many years that all their corners have worn away and they resemble each other.

But despite their virtue and the fact that they never gossiped about their betters in front of him, Saxon was not going to give their six gimlet-eyes a chance to fasten on him when he was feeling bucked and flattered by Miss Tina's interest, so he went off through the wood, whistling. He would get some bread and cheese and beer at the cross-roads pub.

'Mornin', son,' called the Hermit, waving at him a can – presumably full of Rosie.

Saxon took no notice. He hated the lousy old bastard, always jawing and making an exhibition of himself down at the pub, a dirty, half-mad liar, sponging on fools who ought to know better than to give him anything. How could a chap keep himself respectable when there were people like that hanging round him, who ought to be in prison or the asylum? And he had good reasons for hating to hear himself called 'son' by the Hermit.

I wish Mr Spring 'ud turn him out of the wood. He could, if he wanted to. The Council 'ud listen to him. If the Old Boy (this was Mr Wither) had *his* way, the dirty old devil 'ud have been kicked out long ago.

But as he climbed the opposite hill where the beech-trees began, he started to whistle again, because he was so bucked about Miss Tina. Half-way through the lesson he had given up trying to pretend, for prudence's sake, that he thought she really wanted to learn driving. She wanted to be with him. He was sure of it. He grinned and sent a shower of brilliant whistling notes up to join the whistles of the birds as he walked vigorously up the hill. That's one up to me, he thought. He was not flattered because Tina, an individual, liked him (women always liked him, he was used to that); but because she was a lady and the daughter of a comfortably-off father. She was Gentry; not high-up Gentry like Lady Dovewood, of course, nor such smart Gentry as the Springs, but Gentry all right. Educated, nothing to do, coming into a bit of money when the Old Boy hands in his dinner-pail, I expect.

Might be worth my while staying on there for a bit, after all, he thought, grinning as he went into the pub. You never know your luck.

In fact, he had not the vaguest idea as to what luck might come from Miss Tina's interest in him, but his masculine vanity was so tickled by her attention that he felt on top of the world, like a young rooster bugling away, feathers spread and scarlet comb glowing, in the early morning sunrays.

'Well—' said Saxon, lifting his glass. He shifted his elbow to avoid a slop of beer on the bar, and nodded at the barman.

The barman, a realist, nodded back.

Saxon looked in at the cottage before going back to work because there was something he wanted to say to his mother. This new business with Miss Tina made him feel he must stop the way she carried on with old Falger (of whom Saxon refused to think as the Hermit). What was the use of him, Saxon, being taken up by Gentry if his mother was going to disgrace them both by letting that dirty old devil have the run of their place? He had ticked her off more than once about it, and this time he was going to put a stop to the whole business.

'Mum,' he said, walking into the sitting-room where she sat sluttishly over a cup of tea and the newspaper with her arms on the table, and going straight to the point, 'I don't want you to have old Falger round here. Understand? Never again.'

Mrs Caker looked up in angry surprise, her blue eyes without their glint of laughter.

'Deary me! And who're you, givin' orders ter maye about who I'll have in the place, I'd like to know! You mind your business, and I'll mind mine, see?'

'It's my business, all right. It's a disgrace, that's what it is, having a beggar round the place, and I won't stand for it. The next time he comes up here I'll kick him out.'

'You'd better try,' she jeered, putting her arms behind her head so that her jumper was pulled tightly over her full bosom. 'He's a proper match fer you, any day, though he is old enough fer yer grandad.'

'Well, you mind what I say, that's all. I mean it. It's a disgrace.'

'Proper worked up, aren't 'ee?' she said, looking at him curiously. 'What's Falger been a-sayin' ter you? I haven't seen him up here ter-daye, come ter that. And if I do, where's the harm? It's company fer maye; it's lonely up here, day in day out, no one ter talk to or have a bit of fun with.'

'That's not all,' he said, going red, 'not by a long chalk.' He was half-way out of the door, looking down at her with mingled embarrassment and disgust.

Mrs Caker burst into a loud laugh.

'Ah, wait till yer grown up! You don't know half yet, little boy. Then yer won't be so down on the old 'uns.'

'You shut your gab,' he muttered, the Essex drawl strong in his low angry voice. 'And mind what I say. If he shows up here he'll get my boot up his backside, and you can tell him I said so.'

He strode into the wood, dragging off his cap to let the wind cool his forehead. His mother called angrily, staring after him with a red hand shading the sunlight from her eyes:

'I'll do as I please. You go to hell!'

When Viola was very happy, which had not happened many times since her father died, she always thought about her childhood and the delightful times he and she had had together, in the three little rooms above the shop. It was as though her present happiness, so rare and so quickly gone, sent her mind back to the years when she had been happy all the time, even when she was asleep.

She was very happy the next morning as the train carried her, past woods covered in freshest green and hedges white with may, to London. She sat in a corner warm with sunlight, a copy of *Home Notes* open unread upon her knee, and watched the green meadows flying past while the business men in the carriage talked about the news in the papers – awful, as usual – their golf, their gardens, and the detective stories they were reading.

She was in a waking dream, staring out of the window without seeing the buttercup-fields floating by, or a sudden silver swirl of moon-daisies on the bank near a tunnel. She was remembering, for no apparent reason, the tattered old volume of Shakespeare's plays with no cover that Dad used to read to her when she was a little girl. She liked to get hold of the book after he had hurried downstairs again into the shop, and sit in front of the fire looking at the pictures in the book, while Catty cleared away the tea-things, with her mouth full of a last radish or a knob of crusty bread.

The book was illustrated with paintings by famous artists of the best-known scenes from the plays. There was a slender Hamlet with fair hair floating on his shoulders, dressed all in black and wearing wrinkly stockings that fascinated the little Viola (whose own socks were so firmly hauled up by Catty). He stood under a cedar-tree with a skull in his hands, while in the dim background whispered a group of his friends, looking sadly at him. There was a gipsy Cleopatra too, with bare chest and a crown made of feathers, holding the little snake to her heart while a black man, waving a mighty fan of palm-leaves, stood behind her couch. And lastly there was the picture which Viola felt was her own special picture, because (so her father said) this was the girl she was named after.

Underneath the picture (she could remember the words, all these years afterwards, and said them over to herself as she sat in the railway-carriage staring out unseeingly at the flying fields) there was some poetry. It said:

> . . . She never told her love,
> But let concealment, like a worm i' th' bud
> Feed on her damask cheek.

Viola had never been quite sure what this meant, and later on, when she was at school, the girls always made a joke about it and said *damaged* instead of *damask*, which, of course, made it funny, and you laughed.

But she had liked the picture better than the poetry: and she could remember that, too, so clearly. There was a beautiful young man with a long drooping moustache and a hat with a plume in it, sitting in a chair with a high carved back, and a big dog resting its head lovingly, as though in sympathy, on his knee and gazing up into his face. He looked very sad. Standing in front of him, with her arm raised as though she were saying the piece of poetry under the picture, was the girl, Viola, that our Viola's father had called her after. She was tall, and dressed prettily as a page in long stockings, full breeches that came far above her knees, a tight-fitting jacket with big buttons, and a jaunty little cap. But what Viola had liked best of all was her hair, cut short like a boy's and curling prettily all over her head. Viola never tired of looking at those boyish-girlish, gallant curls. They had spelled all romance for her, all adventure, and escape from her own soft floppy mane of hair that would never keep tidy.

Fancy my remembering all that, she thought, impatiently pushing up a soft unmanageable curl. It must be fifteen years ago. And the train slowly drew into Liverpool Street.

Because she did remember it, the whole pattern of her life was changed that day.

Victor Spring, driving home in the evening from Bracing Bay where he had been inspecting the site for the new housing scheme, saw a very pretty girl getting on to the Sible Pelden bus. That was not unusual; there are thousands of very pretty girls in England and some of them lived in Chesterbourne. But this girl was different . . . that word, that danger-signal Victor had often guffawed over when he heard it used by an infatuated acquaintance. But this girl, she really *was* different. She was taller than most girls and she wore no hat, she was swinging it in one hand while in the other she carried a load of parcels. She was pale, with a pretty pink mouth, and seemed rather sleepy and bewildered as though the traffic in Chesterbourne High Street were too much for her.

He did not notice much what she had on: black, he thought; anyway, she was very well dressed. But what was really striking about her, what made him turn round to stare after the Sible Pelden bus while he slowed the car a little, was her hair. It was ash-pale and cut very short in big soft curls all over her head. The curls rolled and tugged in the breeze, and the very pretty girl tossed them as though she liked the feeling.

That's a swell bit of goods, thought Victor, accelerating. Ve-e-ery nice, I call that. Now I wonder, would that be local produce?

It would.

# CHAPTER XI

There was a tradition about the Infirmary Ball. It was always a roaring success, not only in raising money for the Infirmary (which was perpetually at its last gasp and flopping hysterically on everybody for succour) but in the number of guests, the decorations, band and refreshments. The Ball was under the personal supervision of Lord and Lady Dovewood. Lord Dovewood's great-grandmother had started the original Infirmary in a disused shed in 1846, helped by a band of devoted ladies brave as buffaloes, who did not care what people said about them; and hence his family was Patron to the present Infirmary. It was Lord Dovewood who saw to the refreshments, and very good they were, for they included dishes made from old family recipes, while Lady Dovewood saw to the decorations which had to be better every year. The young Dovewoods acted as unofficial Masters of the Ceremonies, and saw that the parents did not pick on too leprous a band.

Envious souls had been heard to mutter that there was a sight too much Dovewood about the Infirmary Ball, but there were not many of these. Most people, being warmly natural snobs, enjoyed the feeling (which the Dovewoods managed so well to convey) that, even though they had paid for their tickets, they were the guests of a Lord. They enjoyed mingling with the gentry and noticing what they wore and how they behaved; and as the common herd usually made itself up into parties and arrived like that, few people at the Ball went partnerless or felt out of things.

This year they had proposed to have Ray and His Five Demons for the band, but two days before the Ball an awful event occurred. Ray and His Five Demons betrayed the Infirmary and the Dovewoods by coolly accepting an engagement to play at a much higher fee for a private dance in Stanton. This was felt to be all the baser because Ray was actually one Stanley Burbett, a Chesterbourne boy who had made good, and he knew well how important the Infirmary Ball was to the district and the tradition that it was always a blazing and cloudless success. Many harsh remarks were made about Ray and His Five Demons, and discontented local boys were told that Getting On and making money did not always mean an improvement in the character.

'Oh, Mr Spring,' said Lady Dovewood, on the telephone, 'I do hope I'm not interrupting you . . .'

'Not at all, Lady Dovewood. Anything I can do for you . . . only too happy.'

'. . . but I wonder if you know of a really good, *reliable* band? I expect you've heard about those disgusting Five Demons letting us down . . .'

'Yes, of course. Too bad . . . bad show . . .'

'. . . and there's so little time. It must be *reliable* but *snappy*. The children want what they call a Swing band . . . Do *you* know anything about Swing, Mr Spring?' ended Lady Dovewood plaintively, who liked to pretend that she lagged behind fashion.

Yes, Victor knew all about Swing, and he thought that Joe Knoedler's Boys would fill the bill nicely if they were not booked. Would Lady Dovewood like him to fix things with Joe Knoedler's agent? He would be in the West End that morning; and Lady Dovewood was not to bother about Knoedler being expensive. He (Victor) would be delighted to see to that.

Lady Dovewood was more than grateful to Mr Spring, and it was *most* generous of him.

'Blast,' said Victor, hanging up. Now he would have to go to the Infernal Ball, out of which he and Phyl had decided to wriggle. He got more bored with it every year, seeing the same faces above the same dresses, eating the same ham stuck with the same cloves from the Dovewood herb-garden, shivering in the same draughts that had moaned through the Assembly Rooms for a hundred years. The whole thing was most dreary.

But if he secured Joe Knoedler's Boys, he supposed that he would have to turn up to see that they were doing their stuff properly, and not tight or ravishing the ladies or anything; and be thanked by Lady Dovewood. He had planned to stay up in town on the evening of the Ball with Phyl's people, telephoning his decision to his mother at the last minute, but now he would have, he supposed, to go. It was a bore, a ruddy bore. He opened the *Daily Telegraph* and forgot it.

Though it would be more interesting, and easier, to say that the countryside was in a fever of excitement as the night of the Ball approached, it would not be true. The movies, the dog-racing track built by the Spring Developments Association outside Bracing Bay, the wireless and the fortnightly dances at the Chesterbourne Public Baths had robbed the Ball of much of its pre-War glamour. Now it was possible to be a bit gay all the year round, instead of only once a year about 14th June, and the Chesterbourne district preferred to do the former.

Nevertheless, the Ball remained firmly fixed in the affections of these country-living people who had heard their grandparents speak of it; and as the night drew near, hairdressers in Chesterbourne were busy, a good many bottles of coloured nail varnish were sold at Woolworth's, and Thompson and Burgess sold a large number of their fine-gauge silk stockings.

There were four prices for the tickets; three-and-six, five shillings, seven-and-sixpence and half a guinea. No one got a whiff of extra food or decoration for the extra money which went direct to the Cause, the gasping, only-just-kept-alive Infirmary; but it was a point of honour to give as much for tickets as possible. Every year Lady Dovewood proudly gave a statement to the *Chesterbourne Echo* that 'only so-and-so many of the cheapest tickets were sold this year' and there was a tradition that the number grew less every year. If it did not, Lady Dovewood made it, for her politics were Machiavellian.

The gentry, of course, bought the most expensive tickets. Sometimes they doubled the price. Mr Wither always did, and Mrs Spring, who had a habit of dashing off impulsive cheques to hospitals and lying-in homes, trebled it.

The weather was very hot during the two days before the Ball, with a huge moon showering her light over the massive heads of trees in opulent summer leaf. All night the countryside did not seem to go to sleep, for the roads were busy with the tiny jewelled beetles of cars racing their owners down to the sea for a moonlit bathe, and all along the shore for miles, bungalows and beach-huts were full of golden light and laughing voices, and damp towels dragging vigorously across wet bodies. Don't often get this kind of thing; may as well make the most of it. Unbelievably beautiful, the long silver waves rolled in, over the dark rocks of Cornwall, the white rocks of Sussex, the flat firm sands of Northumberland and the rounded baylets of Wales. Even the bathers, running screaming and splashing into the milk-warm water, felt the beauty of the sea rolling under that green magian-light.

'Good to be alive, eh?' they said to each other, with characteristic English unreserve. 'Glad to be alive on a night like this, eh?' – in a world toppling with monster guns and violent death.

Tina had given up trying to be sensible about Saxon. She was in love with him; she faced the fact and did not want it to be otherwise. For the first time in what seemed to her a very long and half-starved life she was feeling an emotion, strong as wine, satisfying as the warmth of sunrays. She did not know it, but her love was like that of earliest youth, asking nothing in return but a smile, a gentle word, and the presence of the beloved. So long as she could have her hour's lesson every day and exchange demure little jokes with Saxon, she was completely happy, and she did not feel miserable because he did not love her. She seldom thought about his side of the affair, because she was so absorbed in romantically loving his beauty, his youth, the sound of his voice and the colour of his eyes. She wanted life to go on like this for always, in the dreamy hot weeks of early summer, seeing Saxon every day.

In the evening she would lean from her window for long spells of time, staring across the darkening wood in the valley, whence sometimes came that song! like the very voice of Love. If he ever walked the earth thousands of years ago, given form by the passionate dreams of lovers in the Ancient World, that was how his voice had sounded. He was hidden, and winged, and he sang.

Saxon was still much flattered by Miss Tina's interest in him, but by now he was also a little disturbed. She never said anything outright, of course, or did anything, but she looked at him in a way that he found most embarrassing, though he quite liked it. What could a chap do? What *could* he do? There wasn't any harm in it, only he did wonder what the Old Boy would say if he knew. The Sack.

Well, he'd been planning to leave, anyway, at the end of the summer. Only The Sack would mean no reference; and besides, he was not so sure that he wanted to leave now, not since this business with Miss Tina. It might be worth his while to stay on. He still did not clearly see why it might be worth his while, for his imagination was timid, and at present he saw no other way of securing that fairy money of which he day-dreamed than by working very hard for it, but he no longer felt restless and discontented at The Eagles.

There were Miss Tina's feelings, too. He supposed (this was when the dismay crept into his mind) that she would be cut up if he left. And he would quite miss her. She was a nice little thing, even if she was a bit older than he was. Gentle, quiet, sweet little thing, with her big brown eyes and pretty smile. He began to look forward to the daily lesson. He also began to flirt with Miss Tina. Demurely, in perfect taste, he flirted just a very little. Forgotten art! pushed into the lumber-room since the psychologists told us how dreadfully dangerous it is to repress our passions, and how much healthier it is to book a double-bed at the Three Feathers and get it over. How they despise the prolonged handclasp, the lingering glance, the double meaning, and the compliment, all the old, old moves in the Prettiest Art! Poor psychologists, how solemn they are, how well they mean, and what a lot they miss.

So Saxon and Tina drifted; Tina completely happy and Saxon a little dismayed, wondering what was going to happen, and wondering too, with his cautious self-improving streak, just how he could best use the situation to his advantage.

Two of the chief female protagonists in this story had fusses made about their evening-frocks on the morning of the Ball.

At Grassmere, Mrs Spring came grumbling into Hetty's bedroom, where her niece was on her knees in front of a bookshelf, and asked her rather sharply what she was going to wear that night.

'I hadn't thought. My purple, I suppose,' said Hetty vaguely. 'It's got hock on it, but Davies can get that out, I suppose, can't she?'

'Hock?' snapped Mrs Spring. 'When was that? How clumsy you are, Hetty . . . a new frock, only worn once.'

'It wasn't me. It was Phyl. She knocked me.'

'Nonsense. Phyl is never awkward.'

'Oh yes she is, when she wants to be.'

'Do you mean she did it on purpose?'

Hetty nodded.

Instead of looking incredulous and angry, Mrs Spring stared thoughtfully at the floor. There it was again, that disagreeable side of Phyl's nature which would make her a trying daughter-in-law and possibly a bad wife. Mrs Spring thought Hetty a trying girl, too, but she was not a liar. If Hetty said that Phyl had purposely knocked against her to make her spill wine on a new dress, then Phyl had. Mrs Spring trusted her niece, though she disapproved of her.

(Actually Hetty was a finished liar; she had to be, or she would have had to give up her private life and be a Spring. But she never lied unnecessarily or from malice, and this time she was speaking the truth.)

The fact is (thought Mrs Spring) though Phyl is so suitable for Victor in many ways, I don't like her much. Oh dear, why can't girls be like men? I never had an hour's worry with poor Harry (her husband) and Victor is just the same. They *are* much nicer than women, people can say what they like. Now here's Hetty and Phyl, both very tiresome in different ways, when they both ought to be a comfort to me.

'Yes, well, never mind that now . . .'

'I don't. It wasn't a book. If she'd ruined my *Seven Pillars of Wisdom* now, I might have.'

'. . . you'd better wear the white.'

'It wants cleaning.'

'Oh, *Hetty*! I told you to give it to Davies.'

'I forgot.'

'The blue, then? Is that all right?'

'Yes, I think so. Part of it has burst out, I think.'

Mrs Spring, in silence, switched open Hetty's wardrobe and took down the dress from its place in a row.

'Where? Just show me.'

Hetty pointed to a minute split under one arm.

Mrs Spring shook her head. 'No, that will spread. You can't wear this again, you must give it to Davies.'

'Oh, can I? Excellent.' Hetty looked pleased. 'She wants a new frock, she's going to the Baths with Heyrick next week.'

'Is she?' Mrs Spring was interested, for she was a good mistress to her maids. She looked over her shoulder, while her hands were busily rummaging among the dresses. 'Is she going to marry him, do you think?'

'Oh, I would hardly say that they have got as far as that. She is always careful to tell me that he is not her Regular.'

'Here . . . what about this?' Mrs Spring pulled out a salmon-pink one. 'Has she got a Regular?'

'No. She says she is still turning them over. She has Heyrick, and a policeman, and the new young postman.'

'The red-haired one? Hetty, this will do. Just slip it on, will you, and we'll see how it looks. I think it will do very well when it's pressed.'

Hetty listlessly peeled off her dress and wriggled into the cloud of salmon-pink frills.

'Do stand up, child, and don't look as though you were going to a funeral. Don't you want to go tonight?'

Hetty shook her head. Her arms hung slackly at her sides, she stooped, and her whole posture expressed a lugubrious indifference to her fate.

'Why not?'

'It will be so tedious, and I dislike Bunny Andrews.'

'Rubbish. He's a charming boy. It's just like you to take a dislike to one of the few really nice boys in the neighbourhood, for no reason. I suppose you would rather sit at home all evening, and frowst with a book.'

'Indeed I would.'

'Hetty, you're a very discontented, ungrateful, tiresome girl, and very selfish too. Do you ever think that you might make life much pleasanter for me if you tried to be more like an ordinary girl? What do you expect to be like when you're my age, if you're so odd and unnatural now? You'll never attract men, you know, or get a good time while you go on like this.'

'I don't want what you call a good time, thank you, nor do I wish to marry.'

'What do you want to do then? – and don't talk in that stupid drawl, it's affected.'

'I want to go to College. I want to be educated. I want to meet interesting people. And I want a job,' said Hetty, in a savagely careful voice as though she were repeating a lesson. 'And I see no reason – absolutely no reason at all, Aunt Edna, why I should not do those four things. That is why I don't care for dancing or the Bunny Andrews of this world. But there is no point in prolonging this argument, is there? Shall I wear the gold shoes or the brown satin?'

'The gold. No, you are not going to College; it's a waste of time and you'd never pass the exams. You aren't clever, like your mother was. One day you'll thank me for having stopped you from wasting your time and money. Get Heyrick to cut you some of those Los Angeles roses; they'll just match your dress.'

She hurried away, anxious not to quarrel further with Hetty, for the mention of her dead sister made her sad. This was not one of her good days, which was a nuisance, for she was looking forward to the Ball, where she would meet old acquaintances and show off her clothes and her good-looking son.

Meanwhile, at The Eagles, Mrs Wither was slowly climbing to

Viola's room, her hand dragging along the polished mahogany stair-rail and upon her face the expression worn by one who does an unpleasant duty.

She was going to find out if Viola had The Proper Clothes.

The idea that Viola might not have them had been put into her head, surprisingly, by Mr Wither. Usually Mr Wither took no interest in the wardrobe of his womenfolk, beyond telling them that they spent too much money on it; but ever since Viola had come back from London with her hair cut in that untidy, vulgar mop, Mrs Wither had noticed him keeping a very watchful eye upon his daughter-in-law. Mrs Wither knew how he felt; she felt like it, too. They could not be sure what Viola would do next; they could only be sure that they would not like it. Who would have thought that she would come back from London with her hair like that, so conspicuous, so common-looking, so unlike the hair of all the nice girls living round about? It made her look a different person. Before she had it done, when she came into the room no one noticed her, which was as it should be. Now everyone stared at her, which was very annoying. Even nowadays, when apparently all the old nice ways had gone for ever, a widow should not be conspicuous. And Viola's manner was different, too. She laughed more often, she seemed more *self-confident*. Mr and Mrs Wither did not think this a change for the better.

So, with all these ominous changes in mind, Mrs Wither quite agreed with Mr Wither when he said that it might be a good idea just to find out what Viola was going to wear that night, in case it was 'unsuitable'. By unsuitable, Mr Wither meant likely to be stared at, cut very low with a very short skirt, red velvet with a lot of poppies on it, or something of that sort.

Mrs Wither knocked at Viola's door.

'Hullo?' said her rather muffled voice. 'Come in.'

She was washing stockings in her basin, a habit of hers that Mrs Wither much disliked; a row of them was hanging half-way out of the window and two pairs of gloves were pinned to the curtains.

She looked up and smiled. She had been crying.

Mrs Wither knew why. It was the anniversary of her father's

death, Tina had said yesterday. Mrs Wither thought it wiser not to refer to this. She began:

'There you are, dear. I just wanted to have a little talk with you about tonight. (Those could always go to the laundry, you know . . . they take such a long time to dry here . . . Oh dear! they are dripping on the floor.')

'I'll put down a newspaper,' said Viola, and did.

'Well, dear, now about tonight. What are you going to wear? I just want to make sure that our colour-schemes will not clash. Tina is wearing her brown, as you know, and Madge will be in green, and I shall be in wine-colour.'

'Oh yes,' said Viola, in that new cool tone she seemed to have acquired with the loss of her hair. She went rather pink but said no more. A bagful of advice from Shirley, and the knowledge that her new haircut was fashionable as well as startlingly distinguished, had hardened our Viola surprisingly. Inwardly, she might be the same girl; but outwardly she was not.

'And what will you wear, dear?' pursued Mrs Wither.

'A frock,' giggled Viola. 'At least, it would look rather odd if I didn't, wouldn't it?'

Mrs Wither smiled painfully.

'What colour?'

'Well . . .' Viola was wringing out a pair of stockings and sending splashes over the wall-paper. 'As a matter of fact, it's a surprise, so I hope you won't think me an awful pig if I don't tell you. I don't want anyone to see it until tonight.'

'A surprise! That sounds very exciting,' said Mrs Wither gloomily. (Red. It was sure to be bright red, with a lot of spangles and cut disgracefully low).

'Yes, it is,' said Viola, smiling with happiness at the very thought of her frock.

'Don't you think, dear, you had better give me just a hint about the colour? Then the girls and I can be quite sure that we shan't clash.'

'Oh? that'll be all right,' off-handedly.

'It is white, then? Or black?'

A smiling shake of the head.

'Well, I must just possess my soul in patience,' said Mrs Wither, getting up, with a tight smile. 'I am quite longing to see this wonderful frock.'

'Oh it's *lovely*,' said Viola, earnestly. 'It's a – no, I won't tell you! You wait till tonight.'

Alone, she went over to the glass and began to comb the famous curls. She never tired of doing this, nor of studying her transformed face. Her chin was more pointed, her mouth pinker and prettier, her eyes and eyebrows darker below their ash-blonde crown. She had small shapely ears; now they showed. Her head was a good shape; that was displayed too. Her neck was longer and whiter than most girls'; that had an innings as well. Best of all, she no longer looked what Shirley called moist. She was demure yet gay, like a cherub on its night out.

And all because she had said casually to Shirley, as they sat finishing their black-currant jelly sundaes at the Corner House, *I must do something about my hair. I'm awfully fed up with it. Funny, only this morning, coming up in the train, I was thinking about that picture in Dad's old Shakespeare I used to love when I was a kid, the one he always said I was called after, you know, the girl dressed like a boy with her hair in curls all over her head. That's how I'd love to have mine done.* And Shirley had said, as casually, *Well, why don't you? You've got a natural kink, haven't you, and you could have it permed to help it. Let's go and get it done after lunch.*

And after lunch they found a hairdresser with three hours to spare, off Oxford Street, and got it done.

Oh, please, *please*, let Him be there, and let Him dance with me.

Miss Barlow, thoughtfully rubbing a quiet but expensive toilet-water over her smooth arms at a quarter to eight that evening, in front of her mirror at Grassmere, thought what a bore this Ball was, and congratulated herself on having brought down for it a dress she had worn several times, which was not one of her favourites. There was no point in wasting a good dress on these people. No one would be there. Essex was a dowdy county; and the Dovewoods were frumps. Not an old title, six plain clever children, not much money, religious, a large, ugly, inadequately heated house. Who were the Dovewoods, that Miss Barlow should shine for them?

Bang! on her door.

'Phyl! Can you do something to this tie for me? I've slaughtered two already.'

'Of course.' She unhurriedly put on a house coat, and opened the door to Victor.

He was in shirt sleeves and dress trousers, with a fresh white tie in one hand, and looked attractive, as a handsome man does in undress. There was an intimacy in the competent wifely way she took possession of the tie and began to adjust it that showed how old their friendship was and how naturally it would develop into marriage; anyone, seeing them thus, would have said that they were married already.

'Keep still.'

'You're tickling.'

'Sorry.'

'What's that stuff you've got on? It's good.'

'My perfume, do you mean? *English April.* I'm glad you like it.'

Her brown smooth fingers moved deftly, switching the white strip into a correct butterfly of a bow.

'There. How amusing – your still not being able to cope with a tie.'

'I can usually; only tonight, lady, I'm kinda noivous.'

He gave her a lightning kiss and went back laughing to his room. Phyllis was smiling, too, as she took off her coat and re-painted her lips. Victor was nice tonight. Sometimes he bored her, and sometimes he irritated her by coming the he-man, but tonight he was definitely attractive. As he laughed down at her, she was warmed by a sudden glow of feeling. She had been fixing ties for Victor since he was eighteen, and tonight she felt willing, even eager, to go on fixing them for him until he was sixty-eight. Good old boy; nice-looking, rich, go-ahead, first-class at his job and likely to get even better (and richer) as he got older. True, she had known him for so long that he was more like a brother than a possible husband, but at least she knew him thoroughly, and they liked the same things, the same sort of life. There would be no fear of their ending up after three years with a divorce. Phyllis took divorces for granted, of course; if a thing wouldn't work, it wouldn't; but she did not want her own marriage to end in one. Divorces were rather bad style, really; it was smarter and newer to have one husband for a long time and be seen about with him. Children were smart, too: but there were limits. I don't spoil my figure for anyone, thank you.

All the same, it would be fun, being married to Victor.

The Ball began at eight o'clock, and the common herd, determined to have its money's worth, was there on the tick; but the quality never arrived until nine or even later, thereby creating the impression that their lives were such a dervish whirl of gaiety that what was the Infirmary Ball to them?

To Viola, in a fever of impatience to get there and begin dancing, the Withers seemed to crawl through dinner (lighter than usual, because of the Refreshments they would take at the Ball); but at last it was over, and they all went out into the splendid light of evening, where the car waited with Saxon holding open the door. The green heads of the oaks on the other side of the road glowed above dark bushes in the drive, the sky was peaceful gold, the air smelled of wild flowers and dust. A cloud of gnats moved up and down, up and down. The ghostly moon was rising, huge in the east over the far-off sea.

The ladies settled themselves, Viola wrapped from neck to toes in a large old velvet cloak that had been Shirley's which successfully hid the surprise dress. There had been a number of sour jokes because she wore the cloak during dinner. Mr Wither, exhaling a strong odour of moth-balls, seated himself with creaks, posed his hands upon his knees and counted the flock.

'Where is Madge?' demanded Mr Wither, resignedly.

'She won't be long, dear.'

'She's just saying good night to Polo,' said Viola, and even as she spoke, a voice could be heard crying heartily: 'Good dog! Good dog! Lie down, sir. Back soon,' which manly words did not at all conceal the emotion in the speaker's tone. Then Madge appeared at the double, looking enormous in bright green.

Tina made room for her. Tina was trying not to look at Saxon; and wondering if he thought she looked pretty in her chiffon dress of silver, brown and grey, like a moth.

'Now, if we are all here, we may as well go,' said Mr Wither awfully, putting back his watch into his pocket.

'The Assembly Rooms.' The car moved off.

'Good heavens, it's still afternoon! Are you sure it's really nine, Victor? Hetty, is that bit of hair meant?' Two cool fingers sharply pulled Hetty's rat's-tail. 'That's a good dress; I've seen it before, haven't I?'

'So have I yours; you had it last year,' retorted Hetty, stooping into the car and raising her voice as Miss Barlow disappeared into the other with Victor. Hetty looked despairingly at the two faces confronting her: her aunt's delicately painted, middle-aged, cheerful and tired; young Mr Andrew's, a mere vacuity, so many insignificant features grouped meaninglessly upon a frame of bones. She wondered if his own mother would know him in a crowd. Then she wondered what would Dr Johnson have said of a face like that? The corners of her mouth went up and she felt better.

'The Assembly Rooms,' said Mrs Spring.

With Victor driving his own, the two cars moved off.

# CHAPTER XII

When the Springs' party arrived, the Ball was well away, and the rooms were full. Three hundred laughing, chattering people in their best clothes were there, exhilarated by swift movement to music and by the Dovewood Cup, which had been tasted by Mr Joe Knoedler and the Boys and pronounced, in amazed voices, to be not so bad. (Alcohol, in short, could be detected therein.)

The ladies went at once to the cloakroom to repair the ravages caused by the drive, while Victor and Mr Andrews, having parked the cars, awaited them in the vestibule.

The vestibule had yellow stucco columns, a shabby red carpet with settees to match, and busts of musicians all over it; the Rooms had been locally famous for a series of concerts during the 1880s. Behind the tall swing doors, Victor could see the dancers and hear the music swell and die as the doors swung open; and as he was staring idly, wondering if Knoedler's Boys were coming up to scratch and how soon he could go home, he saw something familiar drifting past the glass panels. It was a girl's head, covered with short fair curls.

There she is! he thought, recognizing her with an excitement that amused him. So she *is* local produce! Who's that with her? No one I know. Rather a tick. Not tall enough for her. She looks a bit down. What a peach. I wonder who she's staying with?

Viola was, in fact, a bit down. She had arrived at the Ball on tip-toe, quivering with happiness and excitement and longing to dance. The long wall-mirrors told her that she was transformed into a tall, silver-headed belle in a floating dress of palest blue pleated chiffon, with a dark-red sash like a little girl's. Everyone was staring at her; lots of people had waved and said, 'Hullo, Vi! I didn't recognize you. I like your hair!' and gone on staring at her as they danced away.

And Mrs Wither had approved her frock, after all, though she did say that it must be rather chilly, with no sleeves and no back and not much front, and even Mr Wither, revolving slowly in a corner with Mrs Wither on a square foot of floor, had said that it was pretty (he was so relieved that it was not red and very short and all over spangles, that he was prepared to like anything) and Tina had opened her big eyes exceedingly wide and said, 'Hul-lo! and where did *that* come from? If that isn't a Rose-Berthe, I don't know anything about clothes,' and Viola, hopping with glee, had said triumphantly that it *was* a Rose-Berthe, reduced in successive sales and sold at last to Shirley by a friend who kept a dress shop, and Shirley had sold it to Viola for – 'Well, I haven't any money left now, but never mind!' and away Viola had skimmed, like a pale blue angel, and dived into the heart of the Ball . . . where there was no one romantic to dance with her.

There were only local boys, red-handed and would-be funny, or Doctor Parsham, sixty and stout, who said that such a lovely lady must spare him a dance, only the son of the chemist whose family had kept shop in the Market Place for two hundred years, who was contemptuous about the Infirmary Ball and well informed about slums in Glasgow, only a spotty young house-agent whose father had known Viola's father, and a number of other persons of that sort.

The Withers did not at all like Viola dancing with these people, but they kept on coming up on the slightest excuses and asking her for dances and the music was so enticing, the floor so good, that she could not bear to sit out most of the dances, as Tina and Madge were doing; and as the Withers knew so few young men, they could not blame Viola if she found her own partners.

There was a number of young male gentry there, but, like Victor, they had come with their own parties and had to look after the girls in them. It was many years since local young men had occasionally cultivated the acquaintance of the Withers because of Tina, and now there was no reason why the Withers should know any young men so they did not. Viola was a widow; widows should not need young men, thought Mr and Mrs Wither, though it was true that no one would think Viola a widow, from the way she behaved.

So Viola's excitement slowly died away, and she began to feel sad as she bumped round in the grasp of the young house-agent. Mr Spring (she now thought of him, in her subdued mood, as Mr Spring) had not come. She was taller than most of the women there, she could see, as she was bumped round the four corners of the large room and the glass door leading into the vestibule, but there was no handsome head of bright brown hair like a young soldier's, no wide shoulders and white tie.

Her gaze moved mournfully to the buffet in the next room. No, he was not there, either.

'Cheer up,' said a low masculine voice, and there was Mr Knoedler himself, gazing immovably up at her while he blew down some instrument belonging to one of the Boys. 'Hasn't he shown up?'

Viola went very pink, and laughed.

'Now, isn't that just too bad,' murmured he, blowing softly into the instrument, then handing it back to the Boy, and going up again on to the conductor's little platform. He put on a silly hat, and the young house-agent whirled Viola away.

This incident was observed by Mr Wither, where he revolved in his corner, this time with Mrs Colonel Phillips. Smiling at the Band. Very bad form; all of a piece, though. Shopgirl. Breeding would out. Round and round went Mr Wither, quite enjoying himself. Catchy tune, that. Tum-te-tum, tum-te-tum-tum.

Suddenly – there he was! Bright brown head, wide shoulders, hazel eyes with their quick summing-up look, just moving into the dance with – oh lord! – the marvellous girl who had been in the car that day. Viola's heart soared then sank. Of course. She ought to have known that he would come with a partner, and dance with her most of the evening. Had Miss Franklin come too? She was Viola's only hope. If she came up and spoke to Viola, and the two parties mingled, then there was just a chance . . .

Meanwhile she had come round to the Band again, and to her horror Mr Knoedler, looking very solemn, jerked a thumb at Victor, then slowly winked.

Nearly sinking through the floor (horrid, beastly little man, how did he know?) she haughtily turned her head away, instead (as she instantly realized she should have done) of smilingly shaking it, but out of the corner of her eye she could see Mr Knoedler laughing as he put on another silly hat.

Victor was also glancing round casually as she turned (she had a faint impression that he was looking for someone and trying not to show it) and their eyes met. For the first time, they looked full at one another; for so long that their locked glance grew into a steady gaze. His expression was cool and steady, taking in every detail of her face and dress. Under her alarm and pleasure because he was looking at her at all, she had a dim feeling that she did not like his look. It was sort of . . . she did not know what, but she did not quite like it.

They moved away in the mazes of the dance, which almost immediately ended, and while Viola stood dutifully clapping beside the house-agent, she felt, with that unease we have all at some time experienced, that someone else was staring at her, and turned to see whom it might be.

She encountered – though it was immediately removed from her – the gaze of the bright dark eyes she had first met in the car that stormy afternoon. Victor's girl (for thus unwillingly she thought of her) had been stealthily but avidly taking in her person, from sandals to curls. As Viola watched, she said something to her partner, and they moved over to the band and began talking to Joe and the Boys, who seemed pleased to see them.

The house-agent escorted Viola back to her party, which seemed to have made a sort of Wither-den for itself on a settee under a dusty palm in a corner. However, they were cheerful enough. Tina had been dancing with Giles Bellamy, the eldest Dovewood boy, and Madge had been secured for supper by Colonel Phillips, to whom she could talk about Polo and Polo's parents. Mr Wither was to take Mrs Colonel Phillips to supper, Mrs Wither was going in with Sir Henry Maxwell (whose mother was mercifully prevented by age from being there) and Tina with the Dovewood boy. Only Viola was partnerless for the supper dance. This was generally felt to be a shame. Why had Viola let the house-agent slip away? Viola sat on the settee, staring among the groups in hope of seeing Hetty Franklin, and catching her eye.

'Het,' said Victor in a low tone, as he stood with his cousin at the far end of the room, 'do you know the girl with the red belt?'

Hetty silently pointed, four times, to four girls with red belts within a few feet of them.

'Not like that – a wide thing – sort of a sash, I suppose you'd call it. Blue dress. Short curly hair. Fair.'

'No,' said his cousin helpfully, 'I cannot say that I do.'

'I want an introduction,' grinning.

She looked at him pensively. It would relieve the tedium of the evening if Victor flirted with someone and annoyed Miss Barlow.

'Show her to me and I will see what can be done. I might pretend we were at school together, if that would gratify you?'

'I can't see her just for . . . yes, there she is. Right over there under that palm, with some other people . . . a fat woman in green . . .'

Hetty peered short-sightedly but could see nothing but a pale blur on a darker ground.

'I will go and investigate,' she announced, beginning to move across the room. 'Where's Aunt Edna? Oh – with the Dovewoods . . . you come slowly behind me and oblige me, please, by not *pouncing*, as you invariably do when I do this kind of thing for you . . . where's Phyl?'

'Over there with Andrews. Get a move on, she's looking this way.'

> The snow leopard stared from her narrow head,
> Neglecting for the prey that onward sped
> The prey beneath her talon, not yet dead,

muttered Hetty. 'Hurry, do.'

They moved quickly across the room, and the crowd closed on them, shutting them from Miss Barlow's view. She saw where they were going, but she was not seriously concerned. Victor might stare at a young and very pretty girl without injuring Phyllis's position or making her jealous, because she considered her position so secure that Victor might be allowed a little rope.

All the same, when Victor stared at a girl, Phyllis liked to know what there was to stare at; and she admitted to herself that Viola was stareworthy. That was a *very* good dress; and the hair was good too. She had distinction, and the soft, childish charm that big men found enchanting. It soon goes, thought Miss Barlow coldly, watching Victor and Hetty.

'No.' Hetty shook her head as she approached the girl on the sofa, and spoke over her shoulder to her cousin. 'I don't, Victor. It will have to be reminiscences of the fifth form, I fear.'

'Well, she knows you, anyway. She's smiling at you,' muttered he, thinking what a pretty smile it was.

'Indeed?' Hetty peered closer, and suddenly said, 'Of course.'

She went up to Viola with her hand held out. 'Mrs Wither. How nice to see you here. You know my cousin, do you not?' standing a little aside so that he could come forward. 'Victor, you remember Mrs Wither? We gave her a lift, some weeks ago, on that stormy afternoon. We did not quite recognize you at first,' smiling and glancing at Viola's head.

'Of course,' Victor said easily, looking down into Viola's eyes and feeling a little disappointed because she was a girl he had already met, transformed by a new frock and a new way of doing her hair, 'I remembered you, but I couldn't be sure where we'd met.'

Viola said nothing. She was overwhelmed. She gave him her hand, smiled, looked down at her sandals, and was mute. She could not have done a wiser thing; his touch of disillusion faded under the charm of her silence and he looked at her with renewed interest.

Hetty meanwhile was talking to Tina, being presented to Mr Wither (whom she regarded as the most interesting person at the Ball, an alluringly neurotic blend of old Mr Barrett, late of Wimpole

Street, and old Mr Gosse, the father of Edmund) and his wife, and being asked by Madge if she were fond of dogs.

'Do you dance much?' asked Victor, lounging by Viola's side, scarcely troubling to talk to her as though she were an adult. As well as being a shopgirl, and the widow of a chap like Wither, she seemed to have no conversation and to be overwhelmed by his, Victor's, glory. Yet in spite of behaving like a kid of fifteen, there was something taking about that little face on top of that long slender body. He stared approvingly at her very white arms, which had the texture of a child's. And he liked her being overwhelmed by his glory; it amused him, but it also flattered him. Women who were awed by masculine splendour were not found at every dance nowadays. He did not think all this out clearly; he was only aware that he rather enjoyed sitting next to her and making her blush.

'Not very much, but I'm simply crazy about it.' She then went pink in a panic because he might think she wanted him to dance with her.

'You're enjoying yourself tonight then, I expect,' indulgently.

'Oh yes, *very* much. I've been looking forward to it for *ages*. Well . . . that is, I *hoped* I was coming, only I didn't know until a few days ago that Mr Wither (that's my father-in-law, over there with Miss – your cousin) had got me a ticket, and ever since then I've been looking forward to it.'

Yes . . . of course, she was a widow. He had forgotten that. She looked the very image of innocence, she talked like a schoolgirl, but widows were not innocent. However young and simple a widow might seem, you could not get away from the fact that widows, presumably, were not . . . Well, this girl was actually more experienced than old Phyl.

And she had been a shopgirl, married Wither for his money, and knew how to dress.

Victor gave up trying to make conversation, bent his head a little lower as he leaned against the red plush of the settee and murmured:

'I like the way you've done your hair. New, isn't it?'

She did not answer, but her hands moved nervously, and as she stared down at the tip of her sandal, there slowly grew on her mouth a proud, shy little smile. It was so enchanting that Victor, to his own amazement, experienced a strong wave of desire. He moved a little nearer to her and muttered:

'Will you give me the next dance?'

'But it's the supper dance?' Narrow grey eyes glanced at him, wide with alarm and hope.

'Oh . . . is it . . .?' a little disconcerted. He had that with Phyl.

She nodded seriously. The supper dance – everyone knew that the supper dance was the most important one of the evening, because one was taken in to supper with the person one danced it with, and had them to oneself all through the supper.

'Oh . . . well, I'm booked for that, I'm afraid. But what about – here, let me see your programme.'

She gave it to him obediently. The last part of it was almost empty.

'How about seventeen? That's the first dance after supper. It's a waltz.'

(A waltz!)

'Oh yes, thank you.'

'Thank *you*.' He scribbled V.S. against the number, not foreseeing that the little white and gold programme would some hours later accompany Mrs Wither to bed.

'Now I must get back, I'm afraid.' His hand squeezed hers for an unbelievable second, he smiled at her, got up and looked round for his cousin.

'Your house must be very quiet, lying off the main road,' Hetty was observing to Mr Wither. They were discussing the conveniences and inconveniences of living in the country and in town; and Hetty was hoping to lure Mr Wither into making some Gosse-Barrett remark on the lines of 'all-the-quieter-to-beat-my-daughters-in.' But Mr Wither (like too many other persons who are supposed, by romantics, to be romantic) was not coming up to scratch.

'Yes, very quiet,' droned Mr Wither.

'But I suppose,' pursued Hetty, not supposing anything of the sort, 'that you often have friends to stay. We do. It makes a pleasant change.'

'Yes,' said Mr Wither. 'No; that is, no. No, we do not often have people to stay with us. It upsets things.' And Mr Wither gave a short, disagreeable laugh. 'Not like you young people, always wanting Change and Excitement.'

'Oh no . . . I prefer a quiet life,' protested Hetty. 'I am devoted to reading. Do you read much, Mr Wither?' For she was always interested to know what people read, supposing erroneously that their books were a pointer to their characters.

Mr Wither reflected for a little while. Then he said, 'No.'

'Oh . . . what do you read then, when you do?'

'Detective stories,' said Mr Wither. 'Very good story I read the other day by that chap – can't think of his name for the minute. Always writes about the same detective. Cripple. Pushed along in a chair by a nigger boxer. Very far-fetched, but it makes good reading. Light, y'know. Don't want anything heavy when you settle down after dinner.'

'No,' said Hetty, dreamily. Nothing heavy. Not Shelley, with wings and bright mist; not Shakespeare, mossy Greek columns in an English wood; not Keats, a wreath of peonies on Midsummer Eve . . .

'Het, we'd better be getting back,' said Victor. 'How do you do,' to Mr Wither.

Mr Wither nodded, almost affably. Young Spring must be worth a very pretty penny indeed. Mr Wither hoped that Viola had not been taking up young Spring's time with silly gossip. He sat gazing complacently as young Spring and his cousin walked away. Mr Wither was not envious of those who were richer than he; he liked people to have a great deal of money because it gave him a warm, safe, respectable feeling. Surely, where there was money, nothing very bad could happen. Death seemed far away tonight to Mr Wither. He was enjoying the ball; he wondered what there would be for supper.

'I suppose we *must* stay and eat?' said Phyllis to Victor, as they moved round in the supper dance. 'Surely we've been here long enough. It seems like five hours.'

'Oh, I m rather enjoying it.' He smiled impudently down at her, for he knew exactly why her tone was petulant.

She had to laugh, but she was annoyed as well as bored.

'Oh, of course, if it's like that. I should hate to take the Great Lover off the trail. I'll stay exactly half an hour more, and then I shall get Andrews or Bill Courtney to take me home.' Bill was an old acquaintance of the Springs who lived just outside Chesterbourne.

'Just as you like,' he said easily. He did not mind what she did. They were not engaged yet; and he had always resented her attempts to appropriate him. She might as well put 'Reserved' on him, and be done with it.

As for the little widow, she must know what she was up to, and she had a grand technique that was a new one on him. And all that had been wasted on Wither! who wouldn't know what to do with it when he got it.

Viola went in to supper with the chemist's disagreeable son, and sat in a dream while he told her about a fascinating scheme the Government had for preventing drains from smelling. The smell would still be there but it would be used to turn electric fans or something so as to blow itself away. Every fragment of smell would be used up. A scientist had worked it all out, with charts, said the chemist's son, glowing. It was called the Principle of Self-consumption, or words to that effect.

Viola nodded, staring at him and not hearing a word.

Tina sat listening intelligently to Giles Bellamy's monologue, which was interesting, and longed for the time to go home, when she would leave the hot noisy ballroom and go out into the summer night, to find Saxon waiting in the car, and he would drive her home through the dark lanes smelling of dew. She wondered, too, how he was spending his evening. There would hardly be time to drive home to the cottage at the cross-roads and then come back to the Assembly Rooms; besides, her father would have forbidden such a waste of petrol. He had probably gone to the pictures, alone. Her imagination refused to show her Saxon in a dark hall with a girl's head on his shoulder.

The lights and the smiling, flushed faces all around made her eyes ache, and Giles Bellamy's pleasant voice, telling her an amusing story about Wengen, jarred on her nerves like a slight but noticeable pain. She compared him with Saxon, and found him unmasculine and insipid. For the first time she felt the disadvantage of loving a common man, a servant. He had driven them to the Ball; and vanished back into his own life of which she knew nothing, and when he reappeared to drive them home, she would not be able to guess how he had spent the hours of his absence, because all the men she knew were gentlemen, whose ways of passing the time she knew about, or could guess at with a chance of being right. But of common men she knew nothing; and she began to feel unhappy.

In fact, Saxon was at a near-by pub, innocently employed in playing snooker.

'And how is Hugh liking India?' asked Madge of Colonel Phillips. Now that one had Polo waiting at home, safe in his kennel, growing daily larger, more obedient, and more satisfactory in every possible way, things were so much jollier that one could ask Colonel Phillips quite cheerfully and naturally how Hugh was liking India, and hear without making an ass of oneself (or at least, not so much of an ass as one used to) that, apart from the niggers and the climate, Hugh seemed to be having a very good time. He'd got his tennis and his swimming and his cricket and his polo, and in his last letter he said that there was just a chance of his regiment getting a look-in at the Waziristan show, if all went well. Here Mrs Colonel Phillips confided to Madge that she, Mrs Colonel Phillips, hoped to hear in Hugh's next letter that she was a grandmother.

Madge expressed delight, only just refraining from slapping Mrs Colonel Phillips on the back.

(I wonder if Polo'll be awake when we get in? Perhaps he'll bark. Father oughtn't to mind if he does; it'll show he's going to be a good house-dog. Who'd want a baby when they could have a dog?)

Supper was over. People began to move back to the ballroom, and Viola glanced round to see if she could find Victor. Yes, there he was, talking to the marvellous girl, who was standing in the doorway with a young man.

In a minute, thought Viola, I shall be dancing with him.

'Can I have this one?' said the chemist's well-informed son, morosely.

'Thanks, awfully, but I've got it with Mr Spring.' She made this sound like a line of poetry. 'Perhaps—' but she stopped. Perhaps Victor would want the next dance, as well; it would never do to promise it away.

'I shan't be five minutes, Phyl; you might just as well wait,' Victor was saying irritably. 'You don't want to go, do you, Bill?'

'Oh rather, if Phyl does.'

'Well, I must go, or my partner'll think I'm going to cut it. Good night, Bill – thanks very much.'

Thanks very much for taking Phyl off my hands. Thanks for putting up with her bad temper on the way home, for soothing her in the car, for lighting her a cigarette and mixing her a drink and sitting with her in the moonlight until I get back.

Where's my Merry Widow?

She was standing a little forlornly against the wall looking his way. He waved and nodded reassuringly as he went over to Joe Knoedler, and said something which Mr Knoedler, standing on his little platform, inclined his head to hear. Then Victor came down towards Viola, smiling

Thank God Phyl had cleared out. He had done his duty by asking her to stop, but now if he wanted to hold the Merry Widow close as they danced, no one would care. They might stare, but they would not care. His mother had gone into a huddle with Lady Dovewood, he could not see Hetty, and young Andrews was well away with some girl or other. He did not care in the least what they all thought, but somehow he found himself looking to see what they were all doing before he put his arm round Viola and they moved away into the dance.

It was an exciting melody, slow and dreamy and strong, with the swaying rhythm beating through it like the sea under showers of foam. Round and round they swung, Viola's flying sandals obediently following his lead the fraction of an instant after it. She had no will, no thoughts, she knew no past and no future, going with him as lightly as a flower, her sash fluttering out and the pleats of her frock flying, her eyes half-shut and her lips parted in a little smile of happiness. He held her very close and looked down at her, but she did not once look up at him. The exquisite pleasure of swift movement to music was like a drug, and though she felt his arm holding her ever closer, and saw the firm line of his chin and mouth just above the level of her eyes, she was so lost in delight that she did not realize she was waltzing with Victor Spring. It only seemed that she had been waiting, all her life, for this moment.

The tune swayed on, pulling the dancers irresistibly like the moon dragging the tides of spring. People glanced at one another and laughed, and waded into the ocean of music as the moonlit bathers had gone out into the silver-green sea. Round and round, white crinolines swaying like the bells of flowers, cloaks swinging gallantly from young shoulders. The music swelled and fell as the waves of warm, moon-swayed water rolled round and round, and the dancers dreamed that life was beautiful, in a world toppling with monster guns and violent death.

The white crinolines whirled and the music grew faster: she spun in his arms with closed eyes, clinging to him in the dragging waves of the moon-moved sea in which she was drowning. Oh let this go on for ever – but the music clashed to its close.

'Thank you,' muttered Victor, wiping his forehead, staring at her ecstatic face.

'Oh, that was *lovely*!' she cried, eagerly joining in the clapping that broke out on all sides. 'How *beautifully* you dance . . .'

'Just thinking the same about you . . .'

'I've never enjoyed *anything* so much . . .'

People were clapping louder. ' 'Core! 'Core!' they shouted impatiently.

'Oh, let's have it again,' cried Viola, clapping until her hands stung and standing on tiptoe to shout ' 'Core! 'Core!' at Mr Knoedler.

But Mr Knoedler, that dedicated artist, did not personally care for waltzes. When asked to play a certain waltz by a rich young man like Mr Spring, who was a patron of the Cardinal Club where Mr Knoedler and the Boys mostly worked, Mr Knoedler obliged. But Mr

Knoedler's own taste was for Swing, and whacky at that, and into Swing he now burst, hauling the Boys along with him.

'Oh . . .' said Viola, disappointed; and at that very moment, like the stroke of twelve in the bemused ears of Cinderella, there sounded in her ear the voice of Mrs Wither.

'Viola, dear,' said Mrs Wither, standing disapprovingly at her elbow and putting two fingers on her arm. 'Mr Wither would like to speak to you for a moment.'

Aw, scram, you old prune, thought Mr Knoedler, scowling at Mrs Wither, for he had fallen heavily for Viola, and he conducted harder than ever, hoping that the violence of Swing would drive Mrs Wither away.

But Mrs Wither stayed, her fingers upon Viola's arm, smiling dimly upon young Mr Spring, who being also much moved by the dance and desiring to dance again, was wishing her in the hottest nook in hell.

'Oh . . .' said Viola, dismayed, glancing at Victor. 'But . . .'

They were in grave danger, by this time, of being knocked end-ways-up by the Swing addicts (Chesterbourne had flown straight for Swing like a homing bird) so they edged their way to the wall, and into the arms of Mrs Spring and Hetty, who had been trying to get to Victor but were afraid of Swing.

'Victor, I'm so sorry, but I shall have to go home,' said his mother quickly in a low tone, smiling and bowing pleasantly to Mrs Wither. ('How do you do; we haven't met since our Committee days, have we?') 'Can you come at once? I really do feel rather seedy.'

'Of course,' he said, instantly suppressing irritation and desire, and moving towards his mother to his arm. 'You've got your things – that's right. Will you be all right with Het while I get the car?'

'Of course. *Good* night, Mrs Wither,' shouting courteously across the heads of two or three Swing-ites, 'so nice to have seen you again. We must . . .'

The dancers shut them off.

Victor turned to smile at Viola, but she had turned away. He looked back over his shoulder long enough, however, to see her turn again and to smile at her, and give her an impudent *heil*-flick with his hand. At that, Viola's face brightened, too, in a smile; and then they were both (in spite of the ruthless selfishness of contemporary youth) borne away by old women to whom they owed affection and duty.

'Mr Wither is not *cross* with you, dear, about dancing to that tune,' began Mrs Wither gently, as Viola steered her across the floor, 'but he just wants you to come and sit quietly with us for the next two or three dances. You look so hot.'

'What tune?' asked Viola, still dazed by the strong magic of the waltz.

'The waltz, dear; It was not – well, a very wise thing to do, Mr Wither thinks. Of course, we quite understand that it was difficult for you to refuse to dance when Mr Spring asked you, but that tune—'

'*What* tune?' demanded Viola, quite crossly for her. 'The waltz, do you mean? Why shouldn't I dance to it? Is there something wrong with it?'

She was trying to remember the name of the waltz, but there were two waltzes whose titles she always confused. One was the *Beautiful Blue Danube*.

'Didn't you know, dear? But you must have, Viola. Everybody knows *The Merry Widow*. That's why Mr Wither thinks you'd better come for a little while and sit quietly with us.'

# CHAPTER XIII

It was all over and everybody was going home. It had been, as usual, a huge success: and Lady Dovewood was telling everyone so, thereby increasing their content and softening the regret naturally felt at the end of a delightful evening.

But the choicest wine can contain bits of cork, and some of the local crab-apples were departing sourly. The chemist's son thought the whole affair a sinful waste of money and time. Why had he been fool enough to go? Women never liked him. Roll on, the Revolution. And Mrs Wither was seriously displeased with Viola, who had made herself doubly conspicuous by her hair and by waltzing in that way, to that tune, with Mr Spring; while Tina and Madge had their own reasons for being glad that the evening was ended.

But Mr Wither was sorry. Mr Wither had enjoyed the Ball, and as he stepped creakingly into the car, helped respectfully by Saxon, he was actually humming a tune, and it was not until his glance fell upon Viola, wrapped in her big cloak, and looking dreamy, that he realized what tune it was, and stopped.

Yes, of course, Viola had been very indiscreet, very unwise to dance like that. Drawing attention to herself, making herself conspicuous. So Common. Vulgar, even. Throwing herself at young Spring's head. But there, what else could be expected? Poor Theodore; perhaps it was as well he went when he did.

Viola, brought back to this world as violently as a suddenly aroused sleepwalker, sat staring out at the streets of Chesterbourne, moving noiselessly past the windows of the car. Mean cottages made into garages, thin, shaky Queen Anne houses, stucco villas, the gold and crimson of Woolworth's were washed into beauty and mystery by blue-pouring moonlight. Dad died two years ago today; I oughtn't to be so happy. It was heavenly. If I shut my eyes (she did so, turning her face to the blanched streets so that no one might see) I can feel it all again.

I wonder if I'll ever see him again – to talk to, I mean?

Victor, having a last drink with Phyl and Hetty in the drawing-room before going up to bed, was thinking, among other things, that he wanted very much to see her again, but that it would be wiser not to, especially as he intended to get formally engaged to Phyl next month. No girl had made him feel as Viola had done since that Welsh girl four years ago. That affair had come to an inevitable and satisfying climax, because the Welsh girl was a rover without background, who knew her way about, but a young widow, living half a mile away with her husband's people, was a very different matter.

No, it won't do, thought Victor twenty minutes later, pulling off the tie that Phyllis had arranged for him, and wishing that it would.

That was very rude of Phyllis, going off like that with Bill, thought Mrs Spring, lying in bed with her face thinly covered by a nourishing cream costing twelve and sixpence a pot and wishing that she did not feel so ill. Even if she was bored, and annoyed with Victor for dancing with that pretty girl in pale blue, she ought not to have gone. I couldn't say anything, of course, but I think she saw I didn't like it. Even with such old friends as we are, she ought not to have done it. It's no use; she wears her things very well, of course, but I can't really like her at all.

In fact, Phyllis was also regretting that she had given way to her boredom and irritation by going home. The rest of the party had returned to Grassmere only half an hour after she had, which had not only robbed her gesture of its effect but had done poor Bill, who was in love with her, out of an hour or two alone with her. She might just as well have stayed at the Ball.

It had been silly, too, to let Victor see that she minded his making a dead set at that girl with the curly hair. I ought to know by this time (thought Phyllis, covering her face with a thin layer of cream costing six and sixpence a pot) that Victor loathes me to behave as though we are married. But he needn't think I'm going to stand for curly-haired lovelies when we are. Oh no. It makes me look a fool, and I won't stand for that from anyone.

He'll get over it. I can always tell when old Victorious is in a state; he tries so hard not to let one see! Shouldn't think it'll come to an affair; he surely wouldn't start anything with a common little thing like that, living practically next door?

Anyway, he'd better not.

She got into bed and snapped off the light.


When the party arrived at The Eagles, the maids (with Mrs Wither's permission) had gone to bed, but they had left a cool drink and sandwiches in the morning-room, whither everybody would repair to take a little something and discuss the evening's events.

'Good night, Saxon.'

'Good night, sir; good night, Madam.'

He stood correctly by the door, holding it open as they came out one by one. Mr Wither, Mrs Wither, Madge, Viola, Tina.

'Good night, Saxon.'

'Good night, Miss Tina.'

She did not look at him. The moonlight, the stillness of the woods, the solemn glimmer of tiny stars, acted powerfully upon her senses. How pure the moonlit air smelled! moving very slowly across miles of country where hawthorn and bean-blossom, orchards and gardens, could yet out-perfume the towns and garages, as they had conquered the middens of Charles II's day. The old earth keeps her sweetness. And I have to go indoors, to bed, thought Tina, with all this beauty outside. I should like to drive all night, away to the sea. She could hear, in fancy, the long waves rolling in.

Mr Wither shut the front door.

'Oh dear, I *am* so tired.' Mrs Wither patted away a yawn and rue-fully bent to rub her evening shoe, wherein a faithful corn was undergoing martyrdom.

'Polo didn't bark,' announced Madge wistfully, beginning on the egg sandwiches. 'I expect he's asleep. I wonder if I just ought to run down—'

'Nonsense,' said Mr Wither austerely, with his mouth full. 'What do you want to do that for? Waking the dog up at one in the morning; you'd never get him to sleep again.'

There was a sleepy pause while everyone ate. Even Viola ate, for enjoyment had made her hungry; but Tina felt the sandwiches going down in dry lumps, and at last she put a half-finished one on her plate, murmured something about '. . . my bag . . .' and slipped from the room.

I can't go to sleep without seeing him. It won't do any harm – just to go out into that light again, and see him, and say good night. It's a perfectly good excuse – where is my bag, by the way – oh, on the hall seat—

She had heard the noise of the car's engine retreat as Saxon drove it round to the side of the house where the garage was; he would be there now, putting it away.

She ran lightly down the old kitchen stairs that creaked where her feet touched their worn hollows; it was dark, but she knew them so well that she remembered the fifth one had the loudest creak, and stepped on the side instead of the middle. She used to climb down them laboriously when she was a baby girl to ask Cook for a piece of dough to make little men; and run down them when she was a schoolgirl to visit her dog (poor old King, dead these fifteen years) in the yard.

She hurried across the stone floor, shudderingly hoping that there were no cockroaches, and trying to silence the little voice in her head that insisted she was about to do a silly, undignified action. Giving yourself away, said the little voice. Nonsense, it isn't as though I hadn't got an excuse . . . and it's so lovely out there, that blue light on the blue-green woods.

She stooped to unbolt the yard door. Through its frosted pane she could see the pale glow of moonlight, and hear muffled noises; the car's engine running, the yapping of Polo, then Saxon's voice reassuring the dog.

She got the door open and stood on the step, looking down at Saxon.

He was stooping to pat Polo, who looked very white in the moon-rays, as he lay on his back with his legs in the air.

Saxon glanced up. He was laughing, but his face went serious at the sight of her.

'Miss Tina! Is anything wrong?' He stood up, and his long shadow ran across the yard.

'No.' Tina's heart was banging against her side but she spoke coolly. 'Nothing much, that is . . . only my bag. I just wondered if you'd seen it?'

She stepped down on to the dusty cobblestones, a bunch of brown and silver dress gleaming as she held it up in one hand. Her feet looked very small, dark in their satin slippers, on the moon-whitened stone.

Saxon went towards the open door and she strolled after him. How still the night was! The moon poured her rays from a remote height with an enormous brown moonbow round herself, and not a star within the circle.

Saxon opened the car and put on the light. She slowly approached the shed.

'It's not here, Miss Tina.'

She could see his face, serious and a little concerned, as he lifted up cushions, peered into cubby-holes full of dusters and maps.

'Was there much in it?'

'Oh no, only about five shillings. A silver bag with a tortoiseshell handle,' in a murmur, standing by the open door, 'and a lipstick I'm rather fond of.'

'Nice find for some lady,' said Saxon, turning to smile at her. 'Perhaps you left it at the Rooms? I can run down there tomorrow morning, I've got to go into town for Mr Wither, and ask, if you'd like me to.'

'Yes, thank you,' faintly.

Saxon shut the door, the light went out. He turned, and Tina moved towards him with a breath of sweet scent.

'Oh, Saxon, about tomorrow—' she was beginning in a quick,

shaky voice, when her perfume, the look on her face and the note in her voice went straight to Saxon's head. He smiled, put his arms round her even as she drew back, and took a long kiss.

She heard a muttered 'dear little thing' or 'little Tina' before his mouth pressed hers, but she thought nothing clearly. She only struggled violently to get away from the body of a stranger who frightened her, yet even while she battled, saw with a pang of tenderness how youthful was the line of his cheek.

'What's the matter?' he whispered, the Essex lilt strong in his voice. 'Don't you like me?'

'Don't, don't,' turning her head distractedly from side to side, 'oh please, *please* let me go. *Please*, Saxon, let me go.' She was weeping.

He let her go, and stood looking down, slowly jerking the cuffs of his jacket while she tidied her hair with shaking hands. He seemed neither sulky nor disconcerted, only thoughtful.

In the silence a bird began to sing in the wood across the road. The wild, sharply sweet notes made Tina feel unbearably miserable. She was glad when it stopped abruptly.

'I must go,' she said at last. She could not leave him like that; she must say something.

He looked up.

'If you won't tell your father about this, I'll give in my notice tomorrow,' he said. 'I'd be . . . obliged' (she saw him struggling with *grateful* and decide not to use it) 'if you wouldn't. If you do, I shan't get a reference, and I'll have to have one, to get another job.' He spoke to her, for the first time, as to an equal.

Her heart seemed to turn over.

'Oh, but . . .' she began.

He misunderstood.

'All right, if you must, you must. I got what was coming to me, that's all. It was mostly your fault, though. Coming down here' (the Essex lilt again) 'at this time o' night, dressed like that, and expecting me not to think you wanted . . . me to do something about it.'

'I know. I'm sorry. I did want you to,' said Tina, while a burning blush began to creep from the top of her head slowly down to the tips of her slippers, 'only somehow when you did, it was so different . . . I . . .'

'Didn't like it, eh?'

She shook her head.

'Maybe I was a bit sudden,' said Saxon, with a quick delightful smile. 'I knocked the breath out o' you, is that it?'

Nod.

'Not used to it, are you?'

She shook her head.

'That's funny. You're nice to kiss,' watching her under his eyelashes.

'Am I?' A murmur.

'Yes. You're so . . . kind of small.'

(And not old? thought Tina, desperately. You didn't feel, when you were holding me, that you were holding someone much older than you are?) She did not at all like his suggesting that she was unused to kisses, but of course she could not register indignation about that.

'I was going to say,' she began, trying to recover a cool, light, friendly but ladylike tone, 'that I won't tell my father. You see, as it was partly my fault . . . I mean, I suppose I felt silly or it was the moonlight or something,' laughing in a most unconvincing manner, 'I feel that you ought not to take all the blame.'

'That's only fair,' said Saxon, making, at a single stroke, the conversation again one between equals.

'Yes,' said Tina, dropping the ladylike voice and realizing with alarm that Saxon had the situation perfectly in hand, 'yes, I suppose it is.'

He knows I love him, of course. That's why he's being so bossy, and laughing, though he's pretending not to. How awful. Now he thinks he can do anything he likes, because I love him. He thinks he's only got to say he'll leave, and I'll implore Father to ask him to stay, and raise his salary. It's horrible, it's an impossible situation, and I won't put up with it. What I must do (trying to plan coolly) is to say that I won't have any more lessons, as I'm going away soon, and tomorrow I'll write and ask Joyce if I can go to her for a week or two.

But when I come home, he'll be here and things'll be as bad as ever. Oh what *shall* I do? Why did I ever let myself get into this mess? Who'd have thought, when I used to see him rushing around in his old red jersey, that I'd ever feel like this about him?

'Better shut the door,' said Saxon, moving, and deftly slid it to. A quarter past one struck muffledly from within the house. Their whole conversation had taken less than ten minutes.

Of course, I ought to have gone in the minute he let me go, thought Tina desolately, bunching up her draperies again.

'What about your lesson tomorrow?' inquired the young man, in a calm friendly voice. No 'Miss Tina' now; no subtle inflection of respect. Will he talk like that in front of other people? Surely he won't dare!

'Oh, I don't know. I think perhaps I won't—'

'I think you'd better, don't you? You're getting along so nicely now, it 'ud be a pity to stop half-way.' (Was this an unpardonable double-meaning?)

'Oh, very well then,' sighed Tina tiredly. 'Eleven o'clock, as usual.'

'I'll be there,' said he cheerfully. They had crossed the moonlit yard, and now stood by the open door leading into the dark house.

Polo came out, inspected their shoes, and waddled in again.

Beauty isn't fair, thought poor Tina, looking at Saxon. It gives people such an advantage.

'Good night,' she said distantly, turning to go in; but he took her hand in his, pulled her unwilling face towards him, and dropped the gentlest of kisses on her cheek.

'Good night, you funny little thing,' whispered Saxon: and went home whistling through the moonlight.

Tina crept rather than walked up to bed, so tired that she could think of nothing. She could still feel the warm soft touch of his lips on her cheek. Oh, where is this going to end, she thought, her hand on the knob of her door.

'Tina!' Madge's cropped head was poking urgently half-way out of her room. 'Where on earth have you been?'

'Hunting in the car for my bag.'

'But it's on the hall chair.'

'I know.'

'But – oh well, so long as you've got it. Did Polo come out?'

'Yes.'

'How did he seem?'

'Oh God, Madge, he seemed all right. How could he seem? You've got that dog on the brain.'

'Well, I only wondered. He's just at a critical age, of course; growing so fast, and learning—'

'Yes. Good night.'

Tina went into her room and shut the door. As she opened a jar of cream costing two and sixpence, she felt so wretched that she was surprised to see in her mirror that she looked pretty. Her eyes were very bright, her face had an alive, transparent look. She turned away angrily.

Just before she dropped asleep it occurred to her that she had at least fallen in love with a young man of character.

A floor higher up, Viola was already dreaming, with her face covered with a cream at sixpence a tube and a dance programme under her pillow.

# CHAPTER XIV

The blankness and boredom that fell upon Viola after the Ball was over were very hard to endure, and she therefore made no attempt to endure them, but grew more depressed and discontented as the hours drew into days, the days into a week, a fortnight. She had been so sure, in spite of her small knowledge of men, that Victor was strongly attracted to her that she expected him to telephone to her or write on the day after the Ball; and when he did not, she was as puzzled as she was miserable.

Her guess was true. He was most strongly attracted to her, but not romantically. The intentions of the Prince towards Cinderella were, in short, not honourable: and as we have seen, he thought it the prudent thing not to see her. He did not wonder how she felt about him. He assumed that a widow like that would have plenty of men and plenty to do with them. He knew nothing about the dullness of life at The Eagles. He only just knew Mr Wither by sight. For all he knew to the contrary, life at The Eagles might have been a whirl of gaiety, and he purposely did not ask Hetty any questions about Viola because he did not want to be mocked at.

Hetty saw quite plainly, in fact, that he was attracted to Viola, but the situation made her so impatient and irritated that she would not think about it. How petty men and women were! getting attracted to each other, fussing over new frocks, planning parties, while the human race was living through perhaps one of the most repulsive yet interesting eras it had yet known! And Hetty took the bus to Chesterbourne to inquire if her German grammar had arrived.

At the back of Victor's mind was a feeling that sooner or later he was bound to run into the Merry Widow again. Couldn't help it, surely, as she lived so near; and then, if he had a good excuse for seeing her, no one could say that he had looked her up on purpose, and things must just . . . work themselves out. That was how Victor put the situation to himself, when he occasionally thought about Viola in the intervals of working hard and seriously playing a lot of games.

But Viola believed that he felt about her as she felt about him; and therefore, she could not, though she thought of every possible and impossible reason, imagine why she did not hear from him.

She knew that he was not officially engaged to that marvellous girl; but presently the thought occurred to her that he might be unofficially engaged to her. If he is, thought Viola indignantly, then he oughtn't to have squeezed my hand.

Here she hit on just the sober truth; but she did not for an instant accept it as such, because it was sober.

She did not dare to telephone him. Even Shirley, whose methods with men were unorthodox and successful, said that it was a dam' silly thing to do to phone a man you'd only met once, unless you had a cast-iron excuse like a cinch for the Derby or the news he was a father, and even then, better not. *So we can't do anything*, Viola had said dejectedly and Shirley had replied, *That's about the ticket, darling. Vote, Marie, perms, and all, we can't do anything.*

Proper pride, of which Viola had a larger share than the better-educated and more intelligent Tina, prevented her from going near Grassmere when she went for her walks, and as she did not have the luck to meet Hetty again in the wood, she had no news of Victor, as well as no glimpse of him; and the lowness of her spirits was increased by the fact that she now had five shillings and three halfpence in the world.

She would very much have liked a confidante; but she was shy of writing a long letter about Victor to Shirley. She did not know why, but the feeling was strong enough to prevent her from writing. Tina was the obvious person in whom to confide, and on the day after the Ball gave her an opening by saying, casually, 'You made rather a hit with young Spring, didn't you? What do you think of him?' but she had seemed so low-spirited herself, and so uninterested in her own question, that Viola had only replied hastily that he danced marvellously and was awfully good-looking, wasn't he? but that she hadn't really thought much about him; they had only danced once. Tina had replied rather snappily that she supposed he was good-looking but he wasn't her type, and no more was said.

Viola never thought of analysing her own feelings, and if she had tried, she would have done it incorrectly. For the first days after the Ball she lived in a romantic, dreamy, hopeful excitement that made time fly and every-day matters delightful. She did not say to herself: *I love Victor Spring*, but thought about him constantly with glowing admiration; every object connected with him became dear to her and interesting, apart from the glamour of his position.

She was full of innocent snobbery. It never entered her head to fall in love with Saxon, who was better-looking than Victor and nearer her own social and economic position. No, Saxon worked with his hands; one did not fall for someone who worked with their hands. One went up and up and on and on. Even had Saxon not been working in her father-in-law's establishment, Viola could never have fallen in love with him, because he was a chauffeur.

Hail, Snobbery, by mink and broadtail bounded,
On whom the English hierarchy is founded.

It was Tina, the would-be realist, who discerned beneath Saxon's dangerous beauty and his low birth a quality that drew forth Love and Love's despised elderly sister, Respect.

The dim youthful day-dream of marrying Victor never occurred to her nowadays. She was so busy wondering if she should encounter him by chance whenever she went out, or whether that was him on the telephone, that she had no time for picture-making.

Tina had no time for it, either. She had never much indulged herself in dreaming since she left her late twenties, because all the psychological handbooks, in one great bellow like the trumpets outside Jericho, said that day-dreaming was Pernicious; and Tina, having no religion and no husband and children, had to hang on to something and tried to hang on to Psychology. As a girl she used to day-dream, but after she took to Psychology she tried not to, and partly succeeded. She had not day-dreamed about Saxon. She had only wanted to be with him and breathe the quiet, enchanted air that his presence made for her. When she was away from him, she longed to be with him again, but she never let her fancy off the lead. She did not want to. When some women fall in love their thoughts do not go beyond the present (though it is very difficult to make men believe this) and Tina was one of them.

On the morning after the Ball she lay, as usual, staring out of her open window, arms behind her head, while her tea cooled on the little black lacquer table. She was in a painfully agitated state, for shame, anger, love, alarm and a great many minor but disagreeable emotions were running across her nerves in exhausting waves, and she wished with all her heart that she had not told Saxon she would have her lesson that morning.

Yet she must go, or he would think his kisses had meant more to her than a piece of moonlit impudence.

Besides, she wanted to see him. Yet she dreaded to see him. How *unpleasant* violent feeling is, thought Tina angrily, forgetting for how many mornings in the past she had lain in that same position, staring at the sky as it changed with the changing seasons, and longing to *feel*.

Suddenly there slid into her mind the memory of a forgotten friend, *Selene's Daughters*, thrust contemptuously to the back of her stocking drawer. What would Doctor Hartmüller say about the exhausting, humiliating situation she had blundered into? I made a mess of things because I tried to mix psychology and common-sense, thought Tina. I gave way to my desire, but I tried to be 'sensible' as well. I ought to have been all one thing or all the other. Mixing them's fatal. If I'm to get out of this without more misery, I must make up my mind what I want, and go all out for it, clearly, using my intelligence, not getting in a state.

What do I want?

She lay there, trying to get out of a state.

It was not easy. Emotions crowded in upon her mind, and she was also rather shocked. It seemed so cold and calculating to decide what one wanted, and go all out for it. Yet one did that when one was matching embroidery silks. Why should not one do it with one's feelings?

Well, do I want to be sensible, or not sensible?

Both.

But which do I want *most*?

Ah! I want to be not-sensible.

How not sensible?

I want . . . this took some thinking out. Tina frowned with the effort.

I want to be with Saxon. I want him to kiss me (gently, *not* all crushed up. Oh well, I suppose I may want him to kiss me all crushed up subconsciously, but certainly not consciously, not at all). Do I want to marry him? No! no, I certainly don't want to marry him, that would be a disaster; it always is when a woman marries 'beneath' her – though men seem able to do it successfully for some reason. Do I want to have an affair (beastly word!) with him, then? No, I don't; I should hate it, it would be vulgar and horrible and spoil everything, all that feeling of his being part of my youth.

I think – why – she sat up in bed in her excitement – I think I want to be friends with him. That's it! I've got it. I want to be friends with him and have jokes, and go for walks and talk, as though he was a boy again in his old red jersey and I was the same age.

Only (she fell back on the pillows) when he really was a boy, I was a girl of twenty-two.

The thought sobered her, but not for long. Now that she knew she wanted Saxon's friendship, there was no harm in going coolly ahead to get it. Of course, I expect he'll think it rather peculiar at first; he may not even believe that's all I want, but I can make him see, I'm sure I can, if I always keep the same honest, friendly attitude. I don't see why we shouldn't be friends. Of course, it will be difficult . . .

*If Father sees him kissing me, it certainly will,* coarsely observed the little voice in her head. Well yes, it will, admitted Tina, glowing with will power and mental hygiene. Very difficult.

I never thought that it wouldn't. But surely it's worth a bit of difficulty to begin with to get the whole thing straightened out.

Eight o'clock. Time to get up.

She got out of bed, calmed, strengthened and refreshed because she had faced the situation; and very determined to work coolly to win Saxon's friendship.

How brutal and numerous are the defeats sustained by applied psychology! It is more like a ninepin than a science.

When she came out into the yard (pale gold in the sunlight now!) Annie was chaffering with the butcher at the back door, Madge was watering Polo, and a man had arrived to put a washer on a tap; the place, in short, was seething with people.

And there stood Saxon by the car, his eyes wrinkled up against the morning sunlight, smiling at Polo's antics.

People ought to be surprised if I didn't love him (not that I do) thought Tina, confusedly, but advancing with a friendly smile. She had on a new frock; she thought she looked rather attractive.

'Good morning,' she began, kindly.

'Good morning, Miss Tina,' returned Saxon, standing to attention, touching his cap, and using his chill, correct chauffeur's voice.

Tina's smile grew mechanical, her heart seemed to be sliding away down miles of a dark shaft towards her shoes . . . but perhaps it's just that he doesn't want to flaunt things in front of other people . . . only I *don't mind* if people *do* see we're friends, I must make him see that.

But as the car moved out of the yard and the expression on his fine profile did not change, and he did not speak, her courage died. I did try to show him I want to be friends, and apparently he doesn't want to. I can't—

'Where would you like to go, Miss Tina?'

She nearly said, Anywhere, I don't care, but controlled herself and replied briskly that she thought it might be a good idea to have a little practice with traffic in Chesterbourne this morning (no more lanes at the end of the world, where sounded the enchanter's far-off voice).

'Very good, Miss Tina.'

Alert and efficient, he watched her hands on the wheel, her footwork, while she drove steadily through the summer lanes towards the town. Once he lightly and quite impersonally dropped his hand over hers to make some change in the car's direction, at the same time explaining why he did so. Never once, by any note in his voice, or any glance, did he remind her that eleven hours ago she had been in his arms.

This was most calming. When the car turned back into the yard at half-past twelve Tina felt that she would just be able to get upstairs to her room before she began to cry.

'Shall I come at the same time tomorrow, Miss Tina?'

'Please, if you will.' (*Oh, how can you be so brutal to me? You must know almost anything would be better than pretending nothing's happened . . . and yet he's perfectly right, this is the only way to take it.*)

'Good morning, Miss Tina.'

'Good morning, Saxon, thank you.'

Saxon put the car away and went into the kitchen to take the small glass of beer with bread and cheese provided for him on the days he worked in the garden; he exchanged two decorous jokes with Annie, Fawcuss and Cook, then went out to the tennis court. As he cut the grass, he whistled blithely as a blackbird.

Tina, powdering her pink nose in her room, heard him and swallowed a fresh gush of tears.

Saxon felt blithe. He had done a good morning's work, carrying out to the letter the plans he had made while walking home through the wood last night. He had then made up his mind to let Miss Tina make all the running, with no encouragement from him, until they were well away. Then he would go to Mr Wither, and threaten to tell the whole neighbourhood what was going on unless Mr Wither paid him not to.

Some people might say that's a dirty trick, thought Saxon, deftly guiding the old mowing-machine over bumps, with his handsome, serious face looking quietly absorbed over the job, but if you don't make up your mind what you want in this world and go all out for it, you'll never make good.

I want enough money to get started in a filling-station of my own; and I don't see why little Tina shouldn't help me get it.

A few more lessons like this morning, and she'll be asking me to kiss her again. And I don't mind if I do.

He smiled a little as he turned the mower and began on the return trip over the thick glossy grass. Sweet and careless, the whistle broke out again, a rival to the courting-notes of the birds.

Unfamiliar longings were stirring in the bosom of Mr Wither. If this were a realistic story they would be both familiar and nasty; as we are all out to enjoy ourselves, however, it must be said at once that they were innocent, nay, that they did him credit.

Mr Wither was going to give a garden party.

The fact was that Mr Wither had enjoyed the Infirmary Ball (despite Viola's unbecoming behaviour) very much indeed. His gay doggishness was giving a final wag before he settled down into being really old. It will be recalled that Mr Wither in his youth had been definitely dashing, recognizing the various brands of oysters at sight and possessing many picture post cards of Edna May, Camille Clifford and other lovelies.

It was many years since he had enjoyed the Ball or anything else, but this year's Ball had been different because it had left a hangover in the shape of a wish for more gaiety – but this time gaiety at home, gaiety under his own roof, where he could regulate it and see that it was gaiety of the proper kind.

Accordingly, to the almost hysterical amazement of his family, Mr Wither proposed to give a garden party on the twelfth of July, some three weeks from now, and preparations for the same were at once put in hand.

Invitations were sent to some friends and acquaintances, including the Dovewoods, the Colonel Phillipses, Doctor Parsham, and others who had contributed to Mr Wither's pleasure at the Ball;

Saxon was instructed to pep up the tennis court; and chairs and tables, together with three dozen cakes and the same number of Kool Kups, were ordered from a caterer's in Chesterbourne. The Eagles then settled down to wait for 12th July, hoping to goodness that it would be a fine day.

Viola heard with feelings of delight and alarm that the Springs had been invited, 'though I hardly expect young Spring will turn up; he's a coming man, you know, and has his hands pretty full these days, he may not be able to get away,' warned Mr Wither complacently; he liked to think of anyone being so busy making money that they could not spare the time to go to a garden party, even if it were his garden party.

Indeed, when Mrs Spring telephoned to accept for Hetty and herself, she thanked Mrs Wither for Victor, but said that he might not be able to get down from London on that Saturday, as he was so busy.

Victor had told her to say this. Nothing was going to keep him from that garden party; but he did not want his mother and cousin to suspect it. There was no one else to suspect; Phyl was going away for a fortnight to play in some tennis tournament, as she did at intervals throughout every summer, and she would not be down at Grassmere for another month. He felt at ease, without her eye on him. He was strongly tempted to see Viola again, and the garden party would give him the perfect opportunity, as casual as it was conventional. He would be there.

Viola had no coherent plans, except that she must have a new frock and that it must not cost more than four shillings.

The weather continued fine; Mr Wither's money, exhausted by its gyrations in April, lay on the floor, so to speak, panting quietly, temporarily at rest. Major-General Breis-Cumwitt hung over it like a devoted aunt, Mr Wither like a mother. They could do no more, only watch and pray. Presently their prayers were heard; the money sat up and breathed less painfully; soon its pulse was normal.

Mr Wither's heart was fairly light as he set out for a walk in the little wood that morning, with Major-General Breis-Cumwitt's comforting letter in his pocket. It was a fine day, the money was better, the garden party was coming along. Mr Wither breathed the wood-land air with feelings not unlike pleasure. Of course, the day might cloud over, the money might relapse, some catastrophe might prevent the garden party; but for the moment, all went well.

The Hermit was happy too; but then he always was. He had no inhibitions, and a sense of his own importance that was never shaken no matter what anyone said or did to him. Small wonder he was happy.

He sat in front of his shack, working on Bear with Cubs. He had spent an idyllic hour potting at birds with a catapult and had bumped off a pigeon which he proposed to have for lunch; it was stewing, with four large potatoes stolen from Colonel Phillips's vegetable garden, in a tin over the fire. He had spent the previous evening with Mrs Caker, while Saxon was in Chesterbourne. As he worked on Bear with Cubs, he sang a hymn and wondered what he should have for supper.

He glanced up.

'Good mornin', guv'nor,' he called, in a respectful yet friendly tone. 'Nice mornin'.'

Mr Wither, moving aloofly along the skyline in his constitutional, took no notice.

'Nice day, I said (*oo's been at my Eno's?*),' repeated the Hermit, louder.

Mr Wither, walking a bit faster, still took no notice.

'NI SDAY, NI SDAY!' bellowed the hermit, and the wood rang: 'I SAID IT'S A NI SDAY, AIN'T IT?' he added, more quietly, 'Guv'nor.'

Mr Wither, starting violently, glanced about him as though to discover whence came the bellowing, at last happened to look in the Hermit's direction, and loftily inclined his head.

''Avin' a breather?' pursued the Hermit chattily. 'Does yer good, don't it? Ah, when yer gets to our age, guv'nor, there's only one thing to do.'

Mr Wither could not bring himself to speak to the Hermit, but assumed an expression of condescending interest. Anything was better than having the fellow make that noise. Noises, especially when made by semi-lunatics, agitated Mr Wither more than they used to do; Mrs Wither had been right when she said that he could no longer stand excitement.

'Live regular,' nodded the Hermit. 'Plenny er fresh air, plenny er sleep, no booze, well, say 'ardly any booze, no you-know-what unless you feels up to it.'

Mr Wither, looking uneasily at a tree over the Hermit's shoulder, gave a very slight tremor of his neck.

'That's the way to live to be a 'undred,' ended the Hermit. He held up Bear with Cubs. 'Gettin' on, ain't it?'

Though Bear with Cubs did not look like anything definite, it had ceased to look like a lump of wood. It was meant to be something: but what, it was not possible to deduce.

Again Mr Wither tremored. He had no idea what the Hermit meant.

'I been thinkin'. I'll let you 'ave it for twenty-five,' went on the Hermit.

Mr Wither found his voice. 'Twenty-five what? What do you mean?' demanded Mr Wither, startled.

'Bob.'

'What are you talking about? What for? Why should you let me have it for twenty-five bob? What is all this nonsense?' said Mr Wither wildly, advancing upon the Hermit with an alarming feeling that some devilish plot, which would end in his having to hand over one-pound-five, had burst upon him like fiery hail out of a clear sky. 'I don't want anything from you; I don't know what you're talking about.'

'Walking-stick. Commission.' The Hermit held up Bear with Cubs. 'Don't say you don't remember you an' me 'aving a talk outside the Green Lion the other day? And you a-saying to me as how you wasn't satisfied with your walking-stick, and me a-saying to you as I'd do you a better one for thirty shillin's? You remember; 'course you remember.'

'No, I do *not* remember,' said Mr Wither, very angrily indeed. 'I did nothing of the sort; I never said anything at all, it's a pack of lies. I shall speak to the Council about you, Falger. This time you've gone too far.'

' 'Ope it keeps fine for your party,' shouted the Hermit, as Mr Wither strutted off in considerable agitation. Then louder, as Mr Wither got further away, ' 'Ow's your youngest gettin' on with 'er moter-car lessons, eh? MOTERCAR MY AUNT'S CAT!' (in a bellow that made the leaves quiver).

Mr Wither did not clearly hear the first part of this remark, and if he had he would have thought it no more than a piece of impertinence. Now if it had been a hint about Viola – you never knew what she might be up to; but although Tina and Madge might be very unsatisfactory in many ways, they would never get into mischief. He knew them too well.

The Hermit's other remark irritated him much more. How did the fellow know they were going to give a garden party? Had Saxon been gossiping? No, Mr Wither seemed to remember overhearing Saxon say to one of the maids that old Falger was a disgrace. Saxon would not gossip with a disgrace. Besides, Saxon did not gossip; he was a good servant, shaping very well nowadays.

Despite his annoyance with the Hermit, Mr Wither re-entered The Eagles musing upon this pleasanter note.

# CHAPTER XV

The day of the garden party dawned bright and fair but by eleven o'clock it had clouded over and the wind had got up. Mr and Mrs Wither were much annoyed. Mrs Wither said that It Might have kept off, It Might, and went down into the kitchen to upset Fawcuss, Annie and Cook by warning them that they might have to help Saxon move the tables from the garden into the drawing-room in a hurry if it came on to rain just before tea.

As they were already rather upstage because some of the refreshments had been ordered from a caterer instead of Cook making them all, they were quite ready to be upset. They moved slowly about the large, tidy kitchen like a cageful of offended elephants, saying Yes, m'm, no, m'm, and very well, m'm, carefully avoiding bumping into Mrs Wither, who stood forlornly in their midst, with their large print-covered persons. Excuse me, m'm, thank you, m'm, beg pardon, m'm. After three times repeating her instructions and thoroughly rounding off the good work she had started, Mrs Wither returned to the morning-room to find Mr Wither sunk in despair. The money had had a relapse.

'What'd I better do with Polo this afternoon, Mum?' Madge looked round the door. 'Shall I just let him run about? He'd enjoy that; he loves a crowd.'

'Good heavens, no,' exclaimed Mr Wither, roused from his anguish for an instant, looking up with a dejected face. 'Nobody wants a dog all over the place at a garden party.'

'Well,' said Madge, defiantly, 'Doctor Parsham's bringing Chappy.'

Exclamations of horror from Mr and Mrs Wither.

'Bringing Chappy? Who said so?'

'He did. I met him out this morning. He said he thought you wouldn't mind, as Mrs Parsham's away and Chappy doesn't like their new domestic. I said I thought it would be all right. He can be tied up in the yard. That's why Polo must be in the garden. They might go for each other.'

'Chappy!' repeated Mrs Wither, despairingly. She added feebly, 'I won't have him.'

'Oh, Mum, you can't do anything about it now. I told Doctor Parsham he could bring him along, you wouldn't mind.'

'Chappy,' muttered Mrs Wither. A gust of wind sent a little branch sailing past the windows. The sky was covered by hurrying grey clouds. 'And he's bound to get loose, you know he always does. Oh dear, it is *too* bad.'

Chappy was an enormous great dog, of extraverted temperament and seething energy, disliked by the entire neighbourhood. He was not vicious: everyone wished that he were, and then there might have been a chance of getting rid of him. He was only too much; too large, too friendly, too energetic. He was also a barker, delighted with any excuse – or without any excuse – to bark for an hour or more. He liked galloping round with a gang of small boys. He liked a crowd, preferably a well-dressed crowd, but any crowd was better than none. He had dozens of acquaintances but no friends except the Parshams, who were very fond of him.

Colonel Phillips hated and despised him. Ill-trained, a mongrel, uncontrolled – Chappy, in the eyes of Colonel Phillips, was hardly recognizable as a dog.

It was a pity that he was coming to the garden party. His presence could be counted upon to spoil Colonel Phillips's afternoon.

But nothing could be done about it now that Madge had said her mother would not mind his coming.

'Well . . .' Mrs Wither got up, sighing, lingered a minute looking in distress at Mr Wither, then said: 'I'm so sorry, Arthur, I suppose you don't want me for anything just now, do you, dear? I've got such a lot to see to.'

Mr Wither, staring lugubriously out of the window at the lowering sky, waved her away, and she went.

What a mockery it is, thought Tina, looking out of her window at the tables on the scanty lawn below. Nobody wants to come, the food's thoroughly unexciting, and it's going to rain. There's no point in doing this sort of thing at all unless you do it often and well. The Springs do it properly, with marvellous food and coloured umbrellas . . . I wish Saxon hadn't got to wait at tea, I know he's hating the idea of it and I shan't be able to help looking at him. I shall be glad when the whole stupid affair's over.

For days she had got no further towards winning Saxon's friendship. She had kept up a pleasant, kindly manner in face of his over-correct one, but it was clear that he did not want to be her friend, and for pride's sake she could not go on giving him opportunities, however slight, that he would not take.

She had begun to lose hope, and had been on the point of giving up her lessons, when she noticed the faintest change in his manner. He became just a shade less formal; he commented upon the size of a pig which they passed on the road without Tina saying something about it first. Twice he smiled at some remark of hers. It was these feeble signals of spring that made her decide to keep on with the lessons for a little longer, though she had long since ceased to enjoy them.

(P'raps I'd better give her a hint, had thought Saxon, as bored as she was by their dull, instructive excursions. We don't seem to be getting anywhere at this rate . . . *and it gives me the jitters to see her looking like that, poor kid.* He thought fiercely about the filling station; and then made the comment upon the pig's girth.)

But neither felt that their separate schemes were going well.

Viola was dejectedly turning over her clothes and deciding that not one of them would do. She pulled some in pieces: then wished that she hadn't, as they were not improved, and finally decided, as it was a chilly day, to wear her old black suit, put on a lot of lipstick, and hope for the best. She felt shy, frightened, ashamed of her shabbiness, and rather hoped that Victor would not come.

Cook burned the dinner, and a cold wind moaned round the house, rattling the windows in a putting-off manner. Mr Wither was very depressed about the money. The cakes had not come. Half-past two struck; and still the cakes had not come. Ah, said Annie and Fawcuss, if She'd let Cook make everything nice and fresh the day before, *this* wouldn't have happened. The rain did not fall and the wind dropped a little but the sky was still sullen.

'Good gracious, dear, you look very *wintry*,' said Mrs Wither, giving Viola a disapproving smile as they met on the stairs. The cakes had still not come. 'Haven't you got a nice summery afternoon frock, something pretty, instead of that costume?'

'Only my green.'

'Well, do put on the green, dear. That looks so unsuitable.'

Viola went up and put on the green. It had an ice-cream blob on its front, over which she pinned a bunch of artificial poppies.

'Good heavens, Viola, do take that off,' said Tina, crossly, meeting her sister-in-law on the stairs. 'It looks perfectly awful.'

'What does?'

'Those roses or whatever they are,' waspishly. Saxon, his dark head bent against the wind, was carrying crockery out into the garden.

'I can't. It's got ice-cream on it. Have the cakes come?'

'No. Your petticoat's showing.'

Elegant in dark blue, she hurried downstairs. The first guest was at the front door.

('Very sorry, Madam, but the van's broken down. Yes, Madam. Yes, I'll tell the manager, Madam. We'll do our best, Madam. I'm very sorry.')

Exhausted, Mrs Wither hung up the receiver.

'Cook, will you make some small cakes please, at once? Those wretched cake people's van has broken down.'

'I doubt if there'd be time, m'm,' said Cook, in a remote, holy voice. 'Now if everything had been made yesterday—'

'Yes, I know, but I thought we should have the cakes. Scones, then, if there's no time for anything else.'

'Mother, they've got two kinds of sandwiches and jam and those

186

two big cakes . . . can't we manage with that?' said Tina, suddenly sorry for her mother, whose poor little party was sliding to disaster. 'Don't worry, dear: there's a nice fire in the drawing-room and the Phillipses are well away with Madge about Polo. I'm sure it's going to be all right. Cheer up.'

Mrs Wither shook her head, and went smiling into the drawing-room where Madge and the Phillipses, hugging the fire, were trying to ignore the steady gale that sighed through the open french windows and made the fire puff smoke into the room. The cloths on the tables, pinned down by the crockery, tugged in the wind with a noise like little flags.

'Too bad the sun couldn't shine for you,' said Mrs Colonel Phillips. 'Isn't it always the way, though? Any other day . . .'

Surely we aren't going to have tea in that tornado? thought Tina, stealing a glance through the french windows at Saxon, who was arranging cups with a face like a thundercloud. There's wind enough to blow the milk out o' yer tea, as the country people say.

At that instant there struck upon the air a familiar sound. Many a night, when sunk in well-deserved rest, had the residents of Sible Pelden been aroused by it, and thrown things at it out of their windows. Everyone looked up, aghast, unwilling to believe their own ears as it came nearer. It came very near. It was in the hall, mingled with the hearty notes of a man's voice. It receded, growing louder and protesting as it was led away.

Colonel Phillips spoke first.

'Surely that isn't that beastly brute of Parsham's?' said Colonel Phillips remorselessly, looking very straight at Mrs Wither.

'Only in the yard . . . no trouble,' said Mrs Wither, faintly.

The drawing-room door swung slowly open and in bounded Polo.

'Go away! Outside! Bad dog! Off!' cried Mr Wither, flapping at Polo. 'Madge, you know I don't allow . . . be off, sir! Down, down!'

'Never allow a dog in the house. Bad, very bad,' said Colonel Phillips stonily, ignoring the passionate laving of his boots by Polo.

'Yes, of course. Polo, come here,' said Madge, much embarrassed. Polo took no notice, but displayed a pink stomach at Colonel Phillips. Take me, I am thine, said his attitude.

'*Polo*,' repeated Madge, in the voice.

Polo took no notice.

'He's showing off,' said Madge, brick-red, laughing heartily. 'Just like kids, always show off in front of a crowd.'

'Ought to be thrashed,' said Colonel Phillips.

'I never hit Polo,' began Madge.

'Outside, sir! *Will* you go outside! Madge, put him out *at once*. Saxon!'

Saxon took four strides through the french windows, snatched up the yelping Polo, and went out in another four strides, holding Polo at arm's length. A minute later he came back with a cloth. While he was on his knees the door opened and Annie announced:

'Mrs Spring, Miss Franklin, Mr Spring, Doctor Parsham, Lady Dovewood.'

He'll never forgive me for seeing that, thought Tina, going smilingly forward at her mother's side. What snobs and fools and cowards we all are. If we were real people, we'd have roared with laughter. One day I'll make it up to you, my darling.

'How do you do . . . Yes, isn't it? . . . Well, I thought it was going to before lunch but it's kept off . . . Too bad of it, isn't it . . . Oh, I am sorry, nothing serious, I hope . . . I'm so glad you managed to get away, Mr Spring . . . oh, he'll be no trouble out there, none at all, I'm sure . . .'

In the pauses of the talk, the chilly, smoky drawing-room echoed with the noise of Chappy's barking.

'Oh, he's all right,' said Doctor Parsham heartily, in answer to an inquiry from Colonel Phillips. 'It's a habit, that's all. He enjoys it. There's nothing wrong with him.'

If I had my way, thought Colonel Phillips, he would no longer be there for there to be anything wrong with. Beastly great brute.

It's exactly like I thought it would be, thought Hetty, sitting beside Tina and carrying on a jerky conversation which was broken by long pauses. The mud-coloured curtains and those enormous seascapes in heavy gilt frames and the chairs covered with faded chintz, and all those photographs, and the white bearskin rug, and the smell of oldness. Amazing atmosphere. It's a mixture of

Chekhov and Proust with a dash of Jane Austen. It's too good to be true.

On seeing the Springs arrive, Viola had retired into a far corner by the piano, and begun to turn over some music in an old rosewood case with a dutiful, absorbed expression as though someone had told her to. Tina darted glances in her direction, trying to lure her out from her corner to do her part as hostess; she would not see, but continued to turn the pages of *I Hear You Calling Me, Thora, Our Miss Gibbs,* and *The Trumpeter.*

'Are you going to sing to us?'

She looked up, startled, into Victor's laughing eyes. He had crossed over to her so quickly that she had not even seen him before he was in front of her, shutting out the rest of the room.

She shook her head, letting *I Love the Moon* fall at her side. She could not speak. Go on, ass, say something, she thought angrily; but it was useless.

'Don't you think you must be a very attractive person?' he went on in the same low voice, pleased by her apparent confusion. 'I cut two Board Meetings and a trip to the North to come here this afternoon.' (This was not true.)

'Did you really?' she murmured.

It was no more than the silliest bleat; but Victor took it – so firmly fixed was his judgment of her character – as a soft ironical drawl, a sort of amorous oh yeah?

'Yes, I really did. Garden parties' (his tone said *this sort of garden party, anyway*) 'aren't much in my line.'

'Oh, aren't they?'

'But I wanted to see you again,' he went on coolly, staring full at her, 'and I thought this would be a good excuse.'

'But you could have—'

'Could have what?'

'Well, phoned or written or something,' she blurted, in a soft indignant rush of words. She remembered how unhappy he had made her and looked at him with a mingled shyness and severity. He took her look for one of challenge.

'Did you want me to?'

'Well – not exactly – but I thought you might have.'

'Why?' in a still lower tone, staring at her with half-shut eyes. She looked down at the song she held, for she had a momentary disagreeable impression that he did not quite know what he was saying.

'Oh . . . I don't know,' she muttered feebly. Then, 'Hadn't you better go and talk to someone else? It looks so funny.'

'I don't want to,' still staring at her.

'Well, never mind that, but *please* do, it looks so awfully queer, us staying in this corner like this.'

As he heard the distressed tone and schoolgirlish words, for the first time a faint suspicion crossed his mind that the little Wither was less forthcoming than she looked. But he dismissed the suspicion. He himself, though he would have been horrified to hear it, was neither sophisticated nor a judge of women; and as for his opinion of Viola, his wish was certainly father to his thought.

'All right,' he muttered, 'but I must see you alone some time. Can't we do a show in town, soon?'

'I'd *love* it,' almost whispered Viola, glowing, earnest-eyed.

'Good. I'll write to you.'

And he melted back into the crowd so easily that only Mrs Wither, Mrs Colonel Phillips, Lady Dovewood, Tina and his mother noticed what he had been up to.

The party, so far as Viola was concerned, was now a riot; but no one else was enjoying it at all. True, they were sustained by the thought that they could pick it all to pieces on their way home, but this scarcely made up for two or three hours' boredom. The smoke got in people's eyes, for the fire had been upset by an attack made upon it with the poker by Mr Wither. Chappy barked hoarsely and without stopping, and though the sun had now come out, the wind was still high, and the gale continued to sough round people's legs.

One or two hardy spirits went into the garden, but were driven indoors again by Polo, who escaped a second time and rushed all over their skirts with his very muddy feet. Madge surmised that he had been down to the duckpond. No one cared at all where he had been, so long as he did not get into the garden again, and said as much among themselves.

Mr Wither was not enjoying the party. The relapse of the money, the inclement weather, Polo, Chappy, and the non-arrival of the cakes, had broken his nerve; and he crawled among his guests without sensibly enlivening their spirits. Every ten minutes Madge disappeared to look at Polo, every twenty minutes Doctor Parsham went round to the yard to comfort Chappy and tell him that his master would not be long, saying: 'Will you forgive me if I have another look at the old chap?'

Really, I am quite glad we came, this will be a lesson for Hetty, thought Mrs Spring, quietly studying Viola's radiant face and dreamy manner and the deplorable poppies. Perhaps she will appreciate our parties more, now that she has seen how dreadful a badly-run one can be. Poor Mrs Wither; I really feel for her, but *what* a stupid woman, why didn't she let Lyons do everything? That pretty little thing is in love with Vic; it's too bad of him, naughty boy.

Everyone was relieved when tea was announced, though their spirits were dashed again on seeing Mrs Wither at the french windows, firmly waving people into the garden, which seemed peculiarly uninviting. Everything was blowing about, and Saxon, Annie and Fawcuss looked furious as they stood behind the tables. The monkey puzzle cut off what sun there was, and the wind sent bits of twig and dust down into people's cups.

A mild scene was created by Doctor Parsham who firmly refused to go into the garden to have his tea but insisted upon having it brought to him by the fire. Doctor Parsham said that his life, as a medical man, was of more value to the community than that of any lay life; and therefore he was not going to risk it by sitting about in that gale. Other people could please themselves: he was going to keep the fire warm; and Doctor Parsham roared with laughter, while everyone else looked wistfully at the fire but had not the courage to follow his example.

Fortunately, the sun came out quite strongly during tea, and people's teeth stopped chattering. Someone round in the yard put a bone or something in Chappy's mouth and shut him up; Polo was again seized by Saxon and firmly tied up in a far, sheltered corner of the garden with a lump of cake, so that he could not make a nuisance of himself a third time; and spirits began to rise as the refreshments circulated.

Tina's, indeed, rose dizzily. As Saxon handed her a cup of tea, coming for a moment between her and her companion (for Saxon had not been trained as a waiter), he had given her, with the cup, a slow, tiny wink; a wink of unutterable boredom, sophistication and friendliness. Really, as one intelligent person to another – said the wink. Recklessly Tina returned it, lowering her long lashes. Oh, he's not angry with me! sang her heart. He's forgiven me. Everything's going to be all right, I'm sure . . .

It was at precisely this idyllic moment that there burst upon the air an uproar from the yard, in which Chappy's barking, the outraged voice of Cook, and a man's loud deep tones were mingled.

Mr Wither, appalled, half-rose from his chair with a cucumber sandwich in one hand, and gazed at Mrs Wither. What has gone wrong *now*, said his look? The money, Chappy, Polo, the cakes, the weather – what further thunderbolt had Fate in store?

'MISHTER WITHER!' roared an enormous, a fatally familiar voice. 'MISHTER WITHER! YER WALKING STICK'S DONE! I'VE GOT IT 'ERE. BETTER COME AND FETCH IT. LET YOU 'AVE IT FOR FIFTEEN BOB. MISHTER WITHER!'

The roar stopped abruptly.

'What are you a-doin' 'ere?' demanded the voice, more quietly, but in the same carrying tone. 'Go 'ome.'

'Go home yourself, Dick Falger,' said a woman's voice, shrilly (Tina, watching Saxon, saw him start, and move forward, then stop himself). 'Proper drunk, you are.'

'So are you,' retorted the Hermit. 'Both of ush. Nev' min'! MISTER WITHER! MISTER WITHER!—'

It was impossible to ignore the deafening noise. The guests gave it up. With cups and food suspended in mid-air, they gazed in the direction of the yard, concealed from the garden by a screen of limes in blossom and thick shrubs. In the pause Chappy began to bark furiously.

No one said anything. No one moved. Mr Wither gazed helplessly at Mrs Wither, everyone gazed inquiringly at everyone else.

Finally Colonel Phillips, staring straight ahead of him, said curtly:

'No business of mine, but can I be of any use?'

'Oh no, no, I don't think so, thank you, very good of you,' stammered Mr Wither. 'It's only that fellow who lives in the wood across the road, you know, he – Saxon, go and see what's the matter, will you? Turn the fellow out . . . disgraceful . . .'

He bent forward and began to tell Colonel Phillips about the Hermit, while everyone else, revived by this incident, fell upon their tea with renewed appetite.

Saxon went off quickly, looking rather pale.

Tina, forgetting that her companion was waiting to be informed about the Hermit, stared after him, her heart beating faster. Suppose there was a fight?

For a few minutes there was silence. Everyone ate, talked, asked for more, with their ears pricked.

Suddenly the uproar broke out again, louder than ever. Bellows, screams, scuffling, shrieks, cries of pain and the furious barking of Chappy, suddenly changing to an agonized yelping, rang behind the screen of trees.

'Chappy! Chappy!' roared Doctor Parsham, streaking out through the french windows and rushing across the lawn. 'Leave my dog alone, damn you!'

Colonel Phillips, Victor, Mr Wither and all the other men were on their feet.

Polo began to yap. Madge darted to his side.

'MISHTER WITHER!' bellowed the voice.

A piercing shriek.

'Come on!' cried Colonel Phillips, and everyone, yielding to temptation, hurried across the lawn in the direction of the trees. The noises were so alarming that even Mrs Spring, usually correct in her behaviour, felt it her duty to investigate, while Lady Dovewood, as the mother of two sons whose hobby was boxing, felt a semi-professional interest in any fight. Besides, the party was such a boring one.

Viola found Victor by her side. He took her hand, and pulled her back so that they dropped behind the others, darted into a little old summer-house in a sheltered part of the garden, and dragged her in after him.

'There!' he said coolly, shutting the door. 'Now we . . .'

It was almost dark in the summer-house, save for a shady, moving summer light coming through the window, dimmed by some evergreens. Viola, lost in a trance of pleasure and happiness, ardently returned his kisses, both arms round his neck, her eyes shut, her breath coming fast. Neither spoke.

They forgot where they were. Everything was silent, except the rush of the wind through the glittering laurels outside, whose lights danced over the cobwebbed ceiling.

At last Victor muttered, 'This won't do. They'll be wondering where we are.'

She sighed, and slowly opened her eyes. The pupils had spread velvet black over the grey; they looked up at him solemnly.

'Wake up!' He gave her a little shake. 'Pull yourself together.'

It would never do to have her reappear with that look on her face. She might as well wear a placard round her neck.

'What's your name?' he asked gently, looking at her over his shoulder as he opened the door.

'Viola,' almost in a whisper.

'Pretty . . . like you. Now look here . . .' he was cautiously yet casually looking round the garden; it was deserted, but confused sounds still came from the yard, 'not a word about this to anyone, do you understand?'

'Of course not,' she said, going very pink. 'I shouldn't dream of it.'

'Well . . . mind you don't. Because . . .' They were walking quickly across to the screen of trees. Viola shivered a little in the cool wind; she still felt dazed: '. . . if you do, it may land us in all kinds of a mess.'

He gave her a caressing smile which she faintly returned. She was completely happy, walking over the grass in a dream of delight. He had kissed her, he loved her. He would take her to the theatre, and while they were there, he would ask her to marry him. It was wonderful; it was like a fairy story, but it was true.

'The battle seems to be over,' said Victor cheerfully, as they stepped round the lime-trees, 'Mrs Wither turned her ankle, and I stopped to look after her,' smiling impudently at Mrs Wither senior, whose distressed yet sharp eyes were turned suspiciously upon Viola. 'Have you got rid of the Hermit?'

'Yes, Colonel Phillips and Saxon had to run him out of the yard,' said Mrs Wither, who was so much embarrassed by the events of the afternoon and so overwhelmed by the calamities that had befallen her garden party that she was nearly crying. 'Here they come now . . . oh, Colonel Phillips, how good of you! I do hope you're not hurt? I can't tell you how sorry we are . . .'

'Nonsense, nonsense. Not your fault. No harm done,' said Colonel Phillips, grimly (he was limping). 'Your chauffeur got the worse of it, I'm afraid. The fellow got him down before I could stop him. Gave his head a nasty crack. Your good Cook is attending to him. Parsham! your beastly dog got loose and legged it up the road . . . bowled me over, confound it. He's half-way home now, I should think.'

'Is Saxon much hurt, Annie?' asked Tina, with trembling lips, as the party slowly went back into the garden, all talking at once and agreeing that the Hermit was a disgrace, Mrs Caker a great pity, and their association a scandal. A beautiful evening was setting in, the wind had fallen at last. Little gold clouds were spread over the sky.

'Not much, Miss Tina; he's got a nasty bruise. But, Miss,' Annie lowered her voice, staring down respectfully at her large feet, 'he's so upset. His mother being there, you know, Miss. With that man. The worse for drink. Isn't it dreadful, Miss, a nice respectable boy like Saxon. In front of everyone. Calling him names, Miss. Cook and me didn't know where to look.'

'I'll come down and see him,' said Tina suddenly, turning her back on the garden party (which was now going like a house on fire, since something nasty had happened and given everyone a subject for talk. There is nothing like something nasty for bringing people together).

'I'm so sorry about it all, Annie,' went on Tina, as they walked quickly back to the house. 'He *is* a nice respectable boy, and I should like him to know that we're not angry with him because his mother came here like that.'

There was an indescribable comfort in talking thus to Annie, who had been with them for fifteen years and known Tina as a girl, in the shadow of the ugly, staid house where she had been born. Though she did not love the house nor the people in it, though she took them for granted and longed to get away from the life she lived there with them, she felt that by talking about Saxon like this she was drawing him into the circle of her own life and surrounding him with comfort and warmth. Tina wanted to show Annie, Saxon himself, everyone, that The Eagles cared for him, and supported him against the grossness of his mother and her life.

The hush that had fallen with evening, the calm golden light on the house, the cobblestones and the half-open garage door, seemed beautiful to her. She felt happy yet sad, as though she were listening to music.

'Is he in your parlour?'

'Yes, Miss Tina.'

The servants' parlour was on the other side of the house and had a view of the road and the oak wood. The room was full of reflected sunbeams thrown up from the white lane, and in this strange shimmer of light, Saxon looked very pale. He was sitting in Cook's own wicker-chair while Cook herself carefully bathed an ugly bruise at the back of his head with warm water and boracic. He was very quiet. Tina saw at once that he was blinded by rage. He looked up at her as though he did not know her.

'There – here's Miss Tina come to see you,' said Cook, in as soothing a voice as her austere nature could manage; she spoke as though he were seven years old.

'Is it bad?' asked Tina, quietly.

'Oh no, Miss; Doctor Parsham said I could do all that was necessary. But it's made him feel sick like, for the minute.'

'Of course,' nodded Annie, importantly. (Fawcuss was upstairs helping to usher out the visitors.) 'Falling like that. Bound to.'

Saxon said nothing, but stared at his boots.

I *must* say something to comfort him, thought Tina. It's horrible to see all his courage gone. What can I say? Nothing patronizing; nothing soft or 'cheery'. Difficult.

But as she looked at his dark lowered head and the line of eye-lashes lying obstinately on his pale cheek, she suddenly found herself speaking from her heart, as though he and she were alone.

'You mustn't mind about it,' she said, gently yet with authority, bending a little towards him. 'It's horrible, I know, but it doesn't make any difference to *you*, Saxon. A person's self-respect isn't hurt by what other people do to them. Only you can hurt your own self-respect. So you mustn't mind.'

Cook and Annie, standing apart, seemed a little surprised, but Cook nodded approvingly. The three women looked gently at him, as though he were a child; and Tina's honesty and tenderness, the dour goodness of the ageing servants, seemed to surround him like a wall, reminding him that other people also cared about Virtue in her myriad forms, that his battle was not fought without allies.

He did not look up, but said in a very low, yet distinct, tone: 'Thank you, Miss Tina.'

When she got up to her room that evening about ten o'clock she found on the black lacquer table a little bunch of pink roses, their stems neatly tied with bast. None grew in the Withers' own garden; the nearest came from a cottage on the other side of the wood near the cross-roads, where the children stood on Sundays and offered them to passing motorists. He must have walked all the way back with them, made some excuse to get into the house, and found his way, while the family were at dinner, to her room.

A sweet breath came hauntingly from them and scented the air about her all night while she slept.

About half-past eight that evening, as the servants were settling down to listen-in, a van rushed into the yard, dusty and triumphant, driven by an old man. Out of it hopped a little boy, and flew up to the back door with a huge package.

It was the cakes.

# CHAPTER XVI

How happily three summer days flew past! Viola shone with her secret; she played with Polo, picked out tunes on the piano with one finger, sang last year's songs up and downstairs, tried to help everyone and made rather a nuisance of herself. She wrote Mrs Victor Spring, Viola Spring, Yours sincerely Mrs V. Spring, all over her writing-block, repaired her small store of clothes with a vague idea of being ready for a sudden departure, and kissed the dance programme every night before she went to sleep. It has been hinted that her nature was affectionate; now that it had received encouragement there was no holding it; she was in love, so much in love that she did not realize that it was Wednesday morning and the letter had not come; and that the man she was in love with was the legendary Victor Spring. Victor had now become Him. He was less of a real person than ever. She never once thought about his character or his income or his mother. She was drunk. She wandered about like a dazzled moth, smiling dreamily, and running downstairs when the postman came, crying:

'Anything for me?'

He had said: 'Good. I'll write to you,' so of course he would. It was not like last time when he had not said anything.

When Friday morning came and there was no letter, she could still find satisfying reasons why there should not be, for she remembered Mr Wither saying that Victor was very busy just now; and had not Victor himself told her that he had cut two Board meetings and a trip to the North to come to the garden party? Having made this excuse for him, she happily resumed her waiting for the letter, living on memories and hardly aware of the days as they flew, nor of the fact that the atmosphere of The Eagles was much pleasanter than was usual.

Tina had fresh liveliness in her manner and colour in her cheeks, Madge was always good humoured and made a lot of jokes, which pleased Mrs Wither and kept her from disapproving of everything as much as usual, and Mr Wither, because the money had again rallied, was on top of the world. He showed it by suddenly giving the four women a pound each.

Fawcuss, Annie and Cook were kept busy and contented about the annual Summer Fête given by the Vicar of Sible Pelden; they were knitting, baking and sewing things for the Give What You Like stall. Saxon's whistle, cheerful and sweet even when it was rendering: 'Whaddam I Gonta Do?' was heard all day round the mansion and in the yard like the voice of an invisible house-spirit. Polo learned to do Trust and Paid For. Mr Spurrey wrote that his rheumatism was better. The weather was beautiful, and everything too pleasant to last.

The general contentment was increased on Monday morning by the arrival of an elegant printed invitation, to the entire household, to attend a garden party at Grassmere on the following Saturday!

Mrs Wither studied the card, printed in white on scarlet with a tiny sailing-boat in one corner. It had that air of just having been thought of and rushed off in hundreds by an up-to-date and expensive printing firm that marked all the Spring stationery. It looked exciting. It made you think 'Now why didn't we splash a bit and have our cards done like that?' It was only later that you realized that the party itself, the house it was given in, the food and the drink, would have to be even more exciting than the card, in order to justify the excitement the card had raised. Then, of course, you gave up the whole idea and bought ordinary cards as usual.

'It says "Staff too, please!" on the back,' said Tina, craning.

'So it does,' murmured Mrs Wither, turning the card round. It was pretty, it was exciting. All the same, she did not quite approve of it.

'It must be going to be a jolly big party,' said Madge.

I'll wear my pink, thought Viola, her happiness mounting because she would see Victor again, in the sunny gardens of his own home, and hear from him why he had not had time to write and fix up definitely about the theatre. She wandered off into delightful thoughts about Victor and clothes.

'Did you see this, m'm?' inquired Cook, primly, but looking rather pleased, when Mrs Wither went down later to see her about some domestic matter. It was another card, addressed to The Staff, The Eagles, printed in white on dark blue with a lawn-umbrella in one corner. 'From the staff at Grassmere, m'm. It's a garden party they're giving next Saturday. Quite a big affair, I should think, m'm.'

Cook then shut her lips, lowered her lids, and gazed modestly at the floor. The next move was Mrs Wither's.

'Oh yes. Yes. We have had one too, Cook. We are *all* invited, it seems. Very kind of Mrs Spring,' said Mrs Wither, who thought it very odd and ostentatious of Mrs Spring, but felt that she, as gentry, must back up other gentry, even in their eccentricities.

'Will it be convenient for me and Fawcuss and Annie to go, m'm?' pursued Cook, firmly.

'Oh yes, Cook, by all means. We will all go. We will have a cold, early lunch,' went on Mrs Wither, a faint eagerness invading her voice, 'and lock up the house—'

'I suppose that would include Saxon, m'm?'

'Oh yes, certainly, by all means. Saxon, of course.'

And they went on to work out plans for Saturday in detail, enjoying the party a week before the party was due. This is one of the many advantages of leading a quiet life.

'Well, I'm sure I hope they have better weather than we had, m'm,' said Fawcuss, coming leisurely in to fetch a new tin of Vim from a cupboard. 'I'm sure everything was against us the day we had our garden party, m'm, of course,' said Fawcuss, stooping slowly to get the Vim out of its dungeon, 'weather makes such a difference; all the difference, you may say. It's easy enough to make a show, isn't it, m'm, if everything goes right. But what with the weather, and that dreadful man, and that woman, and the Doctor's dog, and them cakes—'

By this time a sobriety had fallen upon the kitchen. Murmuring yes, it had all been most unfortunate, Mrs Wither retreated.

As they drove through the lanes to Grassmere on the day of the garden party, Viola was happier than she had ever been in her life. Her own feelings, the flowers and trees, the sun high in the blue sky, seemed slowly rising, rising towards some wonderful moment. The whole of life was moving upwards, like music, or a wave before it breaks. At any moment now – as they drew nearer to Grassmere – the marvellous thing would happen, and nothing would ever be the same. She did not think clearly about her feelings, but sat quite still in the heart of happiness with eyes half closed and parted lips. Bright pink roses glowed in the dusty hedges. Summer heat came up from the glaring road and fell from the darkening elms. The day, and Viola, were wonderfully, triumphantly happy.

When Grassmere came in sight they all exclaimed, for the trees were looped with white and scarlet bunting, and there was an awning in those colours over the gates. Music drifted through the trees and they could see light dresses moving across the lawns.

'Quite gay. Must have cost young Spring a pretty penny.' Mr Wither's tone expressed approval, and some awe at the temperament which could spend a pretty penny on a festival so at the mercy of chance as a garden party.

Mr Wither was mistaken. Victor never took chances. If he saw his plans were about to be upset by God, he altered them before God had time to act. Had he not been sure of perfect weather, that garden party would have been turned at the last minute into another sort of party, suitable for indoors.

Saxon, giving Tina a faint smile, drove off to fetch the three maids from The Eagles, and the party moved slowly in through the gates.

It was a far bigger affair than they had expected. There must have been over a hundred people, walking leisurely about, playing tennis, listening to the string band, reclining in deck-chairs and lying on swing-seats, stepping out of the drawing-room french windows with drinks in their hands and exclaiming: 'Isn't it scorching! Couldn't have had a better day for it! Just Vic's luck, of course.' Laughter and the low roar of voices almost drowned the music. White-jacketed waiters moved deftly in and out, feeding and oiling the crowd, popping piles of exotic sandwiches under people's noses, saying: 'Certainly, sir. Very good, sir. Excuse me. Pardon, sir. Pardon, Madam . . . pardon . . .'

The party from The Eagles felt quite bewildered. They could not see one person they knew; the host and hostess were not to be detected, and they did not know where to look for them. The party was so much larger and more luxurious than they had expected that they were almost shocked. It was like finding themselves at the Royal Garden Party in a nightmare.

But after they had all found deck-chairs, and been fed and given tea by the waiters, and recognized one or two people, they began to enjoy the party, though they were content merely to sit and watch. Mrs Wither did say once that they really ought to go and find Mrs Spring, but the chairs were so comfortable, the tea so delicious, and the afternoon so hot that they lingered on, under their rose-pink umbrella, without making a move.

People were still arriving, fashionable strangers, presumably from London, or from Stanton where the Springs had many friends. Viola was quite content, studying the clothes of the women and wondering who they were. She was not jealous of them, because Victor had kissed her. He would not have kissed her unless he liked her better than all these beautifully dressed girls. Presently she would see him.

'Hullo – good afternoon! Have you had tea and everything? Yes – good. Unpleasantly hot, d'you not think? I am so glad that you could come.'

It was Hetty sauntering up to them, pallid with the heat and looking bored, a tail of hair poking out under her shady hat.

'How do you do . . . oh, not too hot, surely? We were just saying what a perfect afternoon it is – provided that one can sit still, of course . . . ! and a *delightful* party, really delightful, so original, and it was so kind of your aunt to ask the maids, too. Are they having their party—?'

'Oh yes, at the other side of the house. May I sit here?' pulling up a chair. Mr Wither, who ought to have bounded to do this for her, slept.

'Do.'

'I am relieved to hear that you are not finding the entertainment too deplorable,' went on Hetty, drearily.

'My dear! Of course not. What a strange thing to say!' Mrs Wither gave a shocked little laugh; what a peculiar girl Miss Franklin was. 'How could anyone not enjoy it? And the maids were so pleased to come – of course, that class doesn't get much pleasure, does it? Perhaps that's all for the best, really, for pleasure seems to have a bad effect on them, doesn't it, though one ought not to say so in these "Socialist" days, I suppose.'

Mrs Wither would have been surprised to learn how much pleasure the Hermit and Mrs Caker had.

'Does it?' said Hetty vaguely, who did not think much about the lack of pleasure among the English working classes. 'Does it not, I mean?'

Her voice went off into silence, and she fell into a reverie about the staff at Grassmere and decided that they had a good deal of pleasure, what with their wireless, separate bedrooms, good table and servants' hall. But it was too hot to argue. She stared dreamily through half-shut lids at the bright dresses floating over green lawns, the pink lively faces with open laughing mouths, the heavy boughs of the trees hanging down.

'Where is your aunt?' inquired Mrs Wither, after a sleepy pause. 'I have not seen her yet, nor your cousin.'

'She is in the drawing-room, I imagine, with Vic and Phyl. They are still being congratulated,' replied Hetty; and then, with a disagreeable shock of dismay, realized what she had said.

'Congratulated?' exclaimed Mrs Wither, animatedly, sitting up. 'What for? Is your cousin—?'

'Yes, engaged. Yes,' stammered Hetty, aware from the corner of her eye that young Mrs Wither was staring at her with a face going ever paler, even under the glow shed by the rosy lawn-umbrella, while her eyes were widening as though she saw a blow coming.

'Yes, it was in the *Daily Telegraph* yesterday, but perhaps you do not take the *Telegraph*' (Mr Wither woke up and shook his head, muttering, 'No, *Morning Post*') 'and this party is really to celebrate the engagement, you see.'

(I must keep on talking, so they won't notice her . . . fancy looking like *that* over a sunburnt void like Vic, indeed and indeed, tastes do differ . . .)

'Oh yes,' she drawled on, not giving Mrs Wither a chance to speak, 'he's been unofficially engaged to Phyl for two years but they only affixed the ring (platinum, I need hardly say, and inevitably, three very large diamonds) this morning; they've known each other since they were at school . . .'

'A boy-and-girl affair! How romantic!' exclaimed Mrs Wither, feeling envious. Why did none of her children get engaged properly? Victor Spring had, as usual, done the correct thing. He would never have blundered into marrying a shopgirl.

'Was that the pretty dark girl in your party at the Infernal Ball?' inquired Tina, feeling warmly generous towards the world and showing her mood in her voice.

'That would be she. She is generally admired, I believe.' (No, she's not going to faint, she's going to cry; I must get her out of this; it wouldn't be civilized to let her see Vic and Phyl with that look on her face, poor little idiot. What has he been doing to her? But how tiresome and unnecessary all these emotions are. Thank heaven for books.) 'But I think her looks are dull,' she ended calmly. She sometimes made these candid avowals, which went rushing off over the idle plains of gossip and returned like boomerangs to stun her aunt by their indiscreetness. (That will show her I am no friend of the immaculate Phyl's – but heaven forbid that I should have to take sides. Nothing so tedious.)

'Well, after that, I must certainly go *at once* and offer my congratulations,' announced Mrs Wither. 'Madge – Tina?'

Everyone stood up and began to move towards the house; but though Viola got up with the others, she did so without knowing what she was doing and made no movement to follow them, but stood there, staring at the blurred colours of the crowd through thick tears, a lump aching in her throat, lost.

'Would you care to come down to the river? It is quieter there. I will take you.'

A cool plump arm came through her own and Hetty led her away.

Down in the shrubbery on the river bank, a few chairs had been arranged for those older guests who liked shade, solitude and the smell of rhododendrons, and it was into one of these temporary bowers that Hetty steered Viola, who was now crying freely, with her head bent and sharp little gasps escaping now and again from between her bitten lips. She sat down on the very edge of the chair, upright, and cried into a pair of crumpled yellowish-white gloves, while Hetty, leaning back in the other, glanced uneasily round to make sure that no other guest was near, and wondered what on earth to say. She felt sorry for the other girl but also scornful and impatient. No one but a person without taste could be so infatuated with Victor, and only a person without courage and reserve would so display their feelings.

How I wish that I had been anywhere but with the Withers when she heard the news, thought Hetty. And how hard she is taking it! I had a suspicion, ever since the Ball, that Victor was attracted, but I had no idea it had gone so far. And I must go and blurt out the one thing I did not mean to. Oh well. Heat-waves always rob me of intelligence.

'Have you no handkerchief?' she inquired, at last, brusquely; and when Viola shook her head, brought out an inky one of her own from the top of her stocking and worked it between the mourner's hands.

'Thank you.' Viola's voice was hoarse and exhausted. With bent head she scrubbed at her eyes, blew her nose, which was pink as an end-of-season gooseberry, then carefully rolled the handkerchief into a ball and stared down at her shoes.

'Awfully sorry to be such an ass,' she said at last.

'That's all right.' Hetty was staring down between the dark leaves at the blue river where the boats swayed at anchor.

'Only, you see, I had a bit of a shock. I'm all right now.'

'That's good.' Miss Franklin's tone was not encouraging. She relished morbid psychology; but she preferred to observe it from a distance; when it came close, it embarrassed her.

'You see' (Viola never had much reserve and now what she had was in ruins, and she was longing to pour out her misery to someone) 'promise honour bright, you won't tell anyone.'

'My patience, yes,' exclaimed Hetty, amused and softened by the schoolgirlish nature of Viola's oath, 'I only wish to mind my own business, I assure you. Pray do not tell me anything you would rather keep to yourself.'

'Oh, I'd like to tell someone,' said Viola, watering at the eyes again. 'It's only that – oh, I suppose I'm an ass. Only I did think He – Mr Spring – your cousin – was rather, well, a bit keen on me, you know; he did make a dead set at me, at that dance, you know, and he was going to take me out to a show in town, he promised to write to me, and I was so looking forward to it, and I was so awfully happy coming along here today and then when I – when I heard he wh – wh—' her voice fluttered, and up went the handkerchief-ball again, '– was engaged, it was such a shock, I couldn't help crying. You see, that isn't everything – dancing with me, I mean, and saying he'd write. He – kissed me, as a matter of fact. Quite a lot.'

'Never!' cried Hetty.

Viola's narrow, wet grey eyes looked at her in mournful suspicion. 'Do you mean he often kisses people? Like that, I mean?'

'About five people a week, I should think,' retorted Hetty, brutally. There was only one course to take: crush this infatuation at once, by any means.

'Really and truly, does he? Didn't it mean *anything*, don't you think?'

'Not one thing. He is a great flirt. He cannot resist any face that is not definitely Epstein-ish.'

Viola only looked bewildered; and Hetty saw that she was unconvinced.

'Honour bright,' she finished, dryly.

'Well, I don't believe it,' said Viola, sulkily. 'Kissing someone like that, and saying he'd write. Why did he say he was going to, unless he was? There wouldn't be any sense in it, would there?'

(There is none in you, thought Miss Franklin.) She said:

'Well, I have told you what he is like, and it is true. If you choose not to believe me, that is not my fault.'

'Oh, I didn't mean you're telling fibs or anything.'

'Fibs? Oh . . . lies. All right. I didn't think that you did—' (how confusing the grammar does become in these emotional situations).

'I only meant you don't understand,' ended Viola, gently.

'Don't understand Victor?'

Viola shook her head bewilderedly. It ached, and her eyes smarted. She found Hetty difficult to talk to and not very comforting.

But there was no comfort anywhere now.

'Never mind,' said Hetty, more kindly. She saw Viola's ignorant, childish, shallow nature spread before her like a little map, and it was not fair to use irony on so much simplicity; it was in rather bad taste, she felt. One was not ironical with dogs and children.

'Have you any powder?'

Viola nodded.

'Then put some on and we'll go and congratulate the happy pair.'

'Oh, I couldn't!' It was a cry.

'Nonsense, you must. You don't want everyone to see that you've been crying, and notice that you didn't congratulate them, do you? Why,' explained Hetty, 'everyone will guess what has happened.'

'Will they?'

'Of course they will, and laugh at you.'

'Beasts,' said Viola, going red, and getting out her powder. 'All right then, I'll come, but I don't want to a bit and I wish I was dead.'

'Well, one day you will be, and so shall I; but meanwhile we may as well behave with courage and common sense. Now come along, and do try to look more cheerful. You are prettier than Phyl, you know; she is only a type. You are an individual.'

'Am I?' murmured Viola, as they slowly walked out of the shrubbery towards the glowing lawns again.

'Certainly you are. Let that be a comfort to you.'

But as Viola was not quite sure what an individual was, she did not find it very comforting.

Phyllis was thoroughly enjoying her afternoon. She was the most important person there, and her dress fitted to perfection. She stood before the flower-concealed fireplace, laughing, flashing her ring, giving one man after another, as they came up to congratulate her, a mischievous look that said 'Better luck next time!' and feeling pleased with Victor, who not only looked very handsome in a new light suit but wore exactly the correct air of deference, smiling embarrassment, and awe at his own good fortune that ought to stamp the betrothed of Miss Barlow. Really, I think we shall make a go of it, thought Phyllis, showing her white teeth, darting smiling sparkles from her round dark eyes throughout the afternoon, and feeling pleased that everything was settled. It would be fun to be a young-married, have a smart flat, and begin to entertain.

Towards five o'clock, as the crowd in the drawing-room lessened, there trailed in Hetty, followed by that curly-haired Wither girl in pink. Phyllis studied her with an almost kindly condescension, for there was nothing now to be feared in that quarter. She knew Vic; he would not start anything now that they were officially engaged.

'I don't think you have met, have you,' intoned Hetty, stopping in front of Phyl. 'Miss Barlow – Mrs Wither.'

'How do you do,' smiled Phyllis, dazzlingly, looking through Mrs Wither.

'Pleased to meet you,' muttered Mrs Wither, studying Phyllis's dress and face with intensity. 'I-hear-we-have-to-congratulate-you,' she added, in the tone of one who quotes a proverb. Hetty had told her to say this, on their walk from the shrubbery.

'Thank you so much,' said Phyllis, sweetly. 'Victor . . . here's someone you know.'

(Oh you double-dyed witch, thought Hetty. Can't you leave anything alone?)

Victor turned from the man he was talking to, with a polite, expectant smile, and looked straight into the grey eyes that had last met his own in the summer-house.

Now they were so unhappy that he could hardly bear to meet them. He said something kind and pleasant – afterwards he could not remember what – and smiled at her, and turned away. Poor little girl, it's a damned shame, was his thought as he took up his conversation again; and for same moments, so disturbed was he by her look, her presence, that he did not hear a word the other man said.

But when she had gone, and the memory of her look was fading, he told himself that he had done the only possible thing. The frank pleasure with which she had returned his kisses had startled him. The next time I get that girl alone we shall lose our heads completely, he had thought. There just mustn't be a next time. And so he had let the whole thing drop, thinking that the little Wither could look after herself and would soon find someone else to kiss (though that wasn't such a good thought, either, as thoughts go) while he was lawfully kissing Phyl.

Now he was wondering, as he talked, if the little Wither – Violet, that was it – was as hard-boiled as he had supposed? Her kisses had been frank, but not practised. Had he been trifling with a village maiden? How Phyl would shout at that! But he would never let Phyl get wise to this little affair or there would probably be hell.

And anyway, I prefer kissing little Violet to Phyl, any day.

Nice state of mind for a newly engaged man, I will admit.

# CHAPTER XVII

After the Springs' garden party, dullness fell upon Sible Pelden. No one invited anyone anywhere, the weather was insufferably hot and heavy; and most of the gentry shut up their houses and rushed off on holiday. The days yawned like hot caverns filled with motionless black leaves, the stream in the wood dried up and the Hermit was obliged to go to Cakers' twice a day to fetch cans of water and tickle Mrs Caker's neck, the birds were silent, and the young people of Chesterbourne hurried out after their day's work to bathe in the Bourne. Viola Wither shed two pounds in weight, Tina Wither put on three and lost the hollows in her cheeks.

Grassmere was empty save for the head gardener and his wife. The Springs, it was said, were abroad.

Saxon's blackbird whistle was not heard so much around the house in this hot lifeless season. He was too worried to whistle; for when he brought the roses for Tina, walking with them through the oak wood in the twilight, bruised and still full of anger and shame, he had lost the power to direct his own life: and he knew it.

It had seemed so easy to let Tina make the running and then blackmail Mr Wither; a sensible man who knew how to look after Number One would never have hesitated, and Saxon had always taken it for granted that he was a sensible man.

But he had calculated without his better nature; and it was just this, which with the help of his will had hauled him out of his squalid home, that now prevented him from exploiting Tina's fondness for him.

Her words in the kitchen that evening had moved him as deeply as his cautious nature could be moved. They embarrassed him because they were what he called creeping-jesusish, and he hated Tina being in the position to say them, but their bravery and candour had impressed him: and when he gave her the roses, he gave her his ruthlessness with them.

Also, he wanted more than ever now to be respectable and as unlike his mother and old Falger as possible. It was certainly not respectable to seduce one of the local gentry and then blackmail her father. If I do that, thought Saxon, I'll be as bad as those two and worse, because they're ignorant, like animals, but I'm not. I know better.

Besides, I don't believe the old boy 'ud shell out all that (he had planned to ask Mr Wither for a thousand pounds) just to shut my mouth. He'd probably kick her out with me, and that would be a nice state of affairs; no reference, no job, no cash, and perhaps a kid on the way. And I shouldn't think she's got a bit put away, or she'd have cleared out long ago.

Fact is, decided Saxon, it was a bloody silly idea.

Far-fetched. Like what you see on the movies. I'll have to think of something else. Only what? Things can't go on like this. I'm getting fond of her, too. May as well face up to it. She's a sweet little thing; got her head screwed on the right way, too. I shouldn't half miss her if I left.

His growing pleasure in her company puzzled him a little, because it never occurred to him that, before he knew Tina, he had been lonely. He had purposely made himself so by dropping his hobbledehoy friends and offending the Sible Peldenites with his standoffish ways, but that did not make the loneliness any pleasanter. He had, without knowing it, wanted the friendship of an intelligent person; and though their conversations were not highbrow, Tina supplied that want.

He also liked being with her because she was so unlike his mother. The girls in Chesterbourne were younger and prettier, but when they were older they might get like his mother, because they were uneducated. Tina would never get dirty, loud voiced, and what Saxon (who retained that simple faith in Education which his betters have lost) thought of as Ignorant. Old educated ladies were all right; there were a lot of them round Sible Pelden, and though they bellyached a bit (or so their gardeners and chauffeurs affirmed) they bellyached in an educated way, not in an ignorant one. He felt so grateful to Tina for liking him, for her words to him in the servants' parlour, and for being gentry, that he could not keep up his coolness towards her, and those roses made it harder still. When they met for the lesson on the morning after the fight, he was as friendly, without overdoing things, as Tina could desire.

As the days of August passed, she seemed to hold her breath lest her delicate happiness should be spoiled. Each morning brought them into a deeper intimacy, but so gently that she could only just be sure, by pausing to think, that it was on Tuesday, and not on Wednesday, that he first put his arm round her. But he first kissed her on Saturday the 19th, when they said goodbye at the end of the lesson. She did remember that; how could she forget?

If their embraces remained gentle, their friendship grew strong. Saxon had never talked to anyone about his ambitions, but he talked to Tina; off-handedly yet seriously, dropping a hint here and a comment there. He asked her if she would correct his grammar, and Tina, wanting to laugh and cry, said that of course she would . . . if he meant what he said? and if her corrections would not offend him. Oh no, he wouldn't be offended; he got over all that sort of thing four years ago, when he decided to better himself. 'It's best to have things straight, that's what I think,' he added, unconsciously praising the candour that he admired in her. 'Say what you mean, right out. Then you can't go far wrong.'

'Yes,' Tina agreed doubtfully, 'but there's a wrong and a right way of doing it. One doesn't want to hurt people. Besides, it's ill-bred to do that.'

He nodded; but she could see the unfamiliar idea, that kindness and education were somehow connected, grinding in his head, much as the wheat had ground in his father's mill. It gave her the keenest pleasure thus to educate him. She had not suspected, when she romantically longed to drive with Saxon along summer lanes, that some of her happiness would come from telling him not to say 'shouldn't half'. Her motherly instincts, her touch of pedantry, and her feelings as a woman who had been compelled to make advances to a young man, were all satisfied by gently telling Saxon not to say 'shouldn't half'. Love has the oddest by-products.

She had never imagined that so much happiness existed. No wonder I used to feel half alive, she thought; I must have known, subconsciously, how much I was missing. It's like having a brother, a child and someone to play with, all in one person.

I suppose a happy marriage is like that.

She refused to think about the future.

Every morning they drove away into the hushed, lonely lanes where blackberry and honeysuckle bloomed and the dusty holly-trees looked over the hedges. Then, when she had dutifully practised reversing, changing gears, and backing out through an opened gate where cows stared with comely lowered heads, Saxon would brake, shut off the engine, push his cap to the back of his head, take out a packet of Gold Flake and silently offer her one. He would shade a match for her while she lit up, still in friendly quiet. Then they would lean back, drawing in smoke, looking dreamily at the cloudless sky. Neither spoke. One of the qualities she liked in Saxon was his silence. He never chattered, although she knew his country-boy's eyes noticed every bird, car, and beast that they passed.

When the cigarette was a third smoked, his arm would go round her waist and he would pull her gently to his side, so that her cheek felt the sun-hot metal of the buttons on his jacket. Sometimes the shadow of his head came between her and the sun as he bent and gently kissed her. They would talk a little, but never about their feelings for one another; they played a game of not noticing the kisses and the arm round her waist.

Towards the end of August they were so peacefully happy that they forgot to be discreet. If a lane was pretty, but also near The Eagles, they pulled up there for the cigarette and the kisses; and often Tina's head reclined upon Saxon's shoulder less than half a mile from Mr Wither's study.

'You know,' said Saxon one morning as they lingered in one of these dangerous lanes, the car turned in at an open meadow gate, 'I never thought you could be friends with a woman.'

'Didn't you?' Tina managed to sound only casually interested.

'No. Not – well, friends, like – I mean, with the others I always had to be talking a lot of – b— a lot of rubbish. Sorry.'

Oh, so there were others, she thought, not noticing the slip and the apology. I wonder.

She tried, without success, not to wonder.

'Well, they weren't anything, really,' he went on, smiling at her. 'Chesterbourne kids, mostly, out for a bit of fun.'

She said nothing. She almost held her breath.

It was at this moment that a loud lip-smacking noise sounded through the peaceful silence, while a voice, apparently from nowhere, announced complacently—

'Yum-yum! Naughty-naughty! I spy you hiding there!'

Tina and Saxon sprang apart, looking wildly round, but there was no one to be seen. The lane was closed by thick hedges, and on the left, the oak-trees of the little wood began.

'Peek-abo!' sang the voice. '*Oh, they were enjoying it so! When one of them said, you saucy old crow, now just you be off with your peek-abo!*'

The sound came from above. Saxon looked up, and saw something unnaturally big and dark lodged in one of the oak-trees. It craned forward and gracefully waved. It was the Hermit.

The Hermit was not at all bitter about his defeat at the garden party, because his superb health and his vanity made for him an armour so thick that it did not occur to him that he could be defeated. If people did not like him, that was their loss, and if anyone got so far as hitting him, he hit back, and usually won. When he lost, he forgot that he had. When threatened, he took no notice, and when reproved, he took it for granted that the mentor was mistaken; so there was really not much to be done about the Hermit, except offer him as a mascot to an inferiority complex clinic. He was not so much hard as rubbery, a ball of springy bounce, a tough Victorian individual lingering on into the mass-produced twilight of a softer age. The London slums of the sixties were a merciless breeding-ground; if a spirit and body survived them, it was tough indeed. Also, all the Hermit's glands worked properly, which gave him an unfair advantage.

He bore no malice towards Saxon, who had helped Colonel Phillips to run him out of the yard, for he had floored Saxon. The Hermit had been drunk, but he remembered flooring Saxon, for whom he felt a large good-humoured contempt, such as any man of the world would feel for a provincial boy.

But though the Hermit was not malicious he had a strong sense of poetic justice; and that sense was satisfied when he beheld Saxon, that nice respectable boy, that interferer with the doings of his elders and betters, that pokenose, that (here the Hermit, fishing in his memories of Seven Dials in 1868, brought up some mammoth bones of Victorian slang) that greenlander and teakettle coachman, with his arm round the waist of his employer's daughter. The Hermit had shouted to Mr Wither that something of the kind was going on; and lo! he was right. In his triumph, he sang *Peek-abo*.

But when he saw their pale startled faces, he suddenly had a good idea. He looked smilingly down on them between the leaves of the thick bough across which he straddled, and waited for them to speak.

'Better take no notice,' muttered Saxon, starting up the car. 'It's all right . . . don't worry, Miss – please don't mind, Tina. The old – (sorry), he ought to be shot. If we get off at once—'

But the Hermit, shinning down the tree like a squirrel, was already standing across the narrow lane in front of the car.

'No 'urry,' said the Hermit mildly. 'I can take my time. I ain't busy this morning.'

'Get out of the way,' called Saxon, in a low tone. He had gone white. The car began to move.

'Saxon! Don't! Everything'll have to come out if you hurt him. Stop . . . *please*.'

He braked just as the car touched the Hermit's legs.

'Temper,' observed the Hermit. 'Narsty temper. No call for it. Bleshyer, I won't tell nobody. Why should I? Wot's it got to do with me if you like to 'ave a bit of slap and tickle on the q.t.? We're only young once. You le' me alone, I'll le' you alone, see? That's fair enough, ain't it?'

Tina nodded with a weak, frightened smile, glancing at Saxon's angry face.

'Hadn't we better be getting on?' she remarked conversationally. Her knees were trembling.

'I will when he lets me.' Saxon raised his voice. 'Stand clear, will you? We're late now.' He tried to speak civilly but his tone only sounded contemptuous.

'Oh, there's no 'urry. You ain't so far from 'ome as all that. What did the young lady say about everything coming out, eh? Wot 'ave you two been up to? Nothin' old Shak-per-Swaw wouldn't like, I 'ope? Upsets very easy, old Shak-per-Swaw does. Sensitive as a 'arp, as they say. I'm sure you wouldn't like to upset 'im, would yer?'

'Saxon,' whispered Tina, her head bent, opening her handbag, 'it's no use, we'll have to give him something.' She was folding up a ten-shilling note.

'Don't be a fool,' Saxon's sharp whisper came oddly from one side of his mouth, convict-fashion. 'Give him half a crown – if you like – but much better not. He'll only come back for more, though. Blast him . . . he's got us where he wants us. Here . . .' one hand came down on hers, and pushed the note back into her handbag; the other felt in his pocket. He brought out a shilling.

'Have a drink with us,' he called, and spun the coin across to the Hermit, who caught it.

The old man's dirty grin, Saxon's slight, knowing smile, sickened Tina. *Common men are horrible* flashed through her head. If I'd been with Giles Bellamy he'd have managed things somehow and got me out of it without coming down to the old man's level and making a joke out of it in that beastly way.

She felt dirtied: and very angry with Saxon. The fact that a shilling meant something to Saxon, and nothing to her, made her angrier still. It did not occur to her that if she had been with Giles Bellamy the situation would never have arisen.

'That'll do to get on with,' shouted the Hermit, crawling through a hole in the hedge. 'I won't say nothing, don't you worry. Course I won't.' Then, more faintly as he went down into the wood, 'You le' me alone and I'll le' you alone, see.'

After his voice had faded, there was a long silence.

Both felt angry, frightened and vaguely miserable, as though they had lost something beautiful, and did not know what was going to happen to them.

Something will have to be done now, I suppose, curse it, they thought.

He had left the car halfway across the lane at an odd angle as though there had been an accident, and though he knew that he must move it because a farm cart might come along at any minute, he felt too irritable, hot and depressed to start.

At last Tina said coldly,

'We'd better get on, hadn't we?'

He started up the engine without answering. She needn't take that tone about it. She'd started it. If they landed in a hell of a muck, whose fault would it be?

He got the car straight and moved quickly down the lane, making for the main road where there was a bit of traffic and he would have to keep his eye on the driving. He got angrier with himself every minute, and cursed his fatal habit of 'letting go'. Here he was, tangled up with her, not wanting to let her down, likely to be bled by old Falger instead of himself bleeding old Wither, likely to get the sack without a reference – all because he had bloody well been soft.

The path of the Super-Man is even harder than sub-men suppose.

Out on the main road to Bracing Bay dust hung thickly, sent up by lorries and cars on their way to the sea; but the roar of heavy engines was unnoticed by the contented-looking women hanging up wet clothes in the gardens, glowing with flowers, that surrounded hideous bungalows. It is fortunate that such a few people mind ugliness and noise.

'Hadn't we better be getting back?' suggested Tina, coughing.

He took no notice: and she was thrilled (the exact word).

She had read that women were men's equals and she believed it, although her own experiences had never proved it. Now Saxon was treating her as an inferior. It was exciting to see the books caught out. The car fairly flew along the noisy dusty road! They would be simply frightfully late for lunch!

'Saxon.'

'What?'

A gentleman would have said Well? reflected Tina. Saxon was certainly not at his best this morning; he kept doing things that reminded her he was common.

'Do stop a minute. We must talk.'

He began to slow the car.

'Down there.' She pointed to another of those beguiling lanes, greeny-white with meadowsweet, and the car turned and bumped slowly down it. Saxon looked sullen and bored.

'What did he mean – you leave me alone and I'll leave you alone?' she inquired, when the engine had stopped and all was quiet. She knew what the Hermit had meant, but she was still angry with Saxon for not being a gentleman and wanted to hurt him.

He went red. Then he said in a surly voice,

'He goes with my mother. You know that as well as I do.'

'Yes. I'm sorry.'

'What do you want to ask me for, then, if you know already?'

'I'm sorry, Saxon, really I am. I'm a brute. You see – oh, it's all so *difficult*,' ended Tina affectedly, but her eyes filled.

He was staring away down the lane, misty with nodding white lacy plates of flowers on either side, scented with a muzzy-sweet smell. Never had he looked to her so young, sulky, and ill-bred, like a farm boy in a scrape.

There then happened a commonplace miracle. At the same instant that Tina, miserable and angry, leant towards Saxon, angry and alarmed, he turned towards her, put his arms round her and passionately kissed her.

'Don't let's quarrel,' he muttered, between kisses. 'I don't know what the hell's up with me.'

Pause.

'Darling, you love me, that's it. Don't you? You love me. Do say it. That's what . . . say it, darling.'

'I love you,' he mumbled bashfully, reddening furiously. Then he suddenly drew away from her, and she caught her breath, inwardly, as she saw him rein in his flying feelings, hold them, and look them over.

'Count I do love you, too,' he said, looking full at her. 'Sweet little thing, you are,' diving at her again.

'Saxon,' holding him off with a small hand spread on his chest, 'I'm thirty-five. How old are you?'

'Twenty-three in December.'

'Then I'm twelve years older than you are,' forcing out the wretched words, hateful as only truth can be. 'You knew I was much older than you, didn't you?'

'Yes,' tranquilly, studying her delicate face, flushed and pretty, her big shining eyes, 'but not so old as that. You didn't look that old. Educated ladies don't. You've never had to work; that's what makes women like my – ignorant women look old.'

'Then you don't mind my being so much older than you?' she persisted.

'It's no good minding,' he answered, with the harsh working-class common-sense that she would have to get used to. 'You can't help your age. I don't mind if you don't,' bending towards her. He did not seem very interested.

'I do, but it's no use . . .' the words were lost.

When she sat up again, tidying her hair, she said practically,

'What are we going to do about this?'

'Plenty more where that came from,' drawled Saxon, smiling, pushing his cap to the back of his head. The sun beat warmly on their faces, the very leather of the car's seat where her hand rested was summer hot.

'No,' laughing, 'no, but it's serious. We can't go on like this, Saxon, because that horrible old man is bound to come for more money, and the more we give him the more he'll want, and I've only got about seventy pounds.'

'I've got twenty-one. And I'll see him somewhere before he gets any of it. But I don't think he'll do much. It's just talk. If I leave him alone and don't say much about him and my mother, he'll leave us alone, the old bastard.'

This time he did not apologize for the word. He dropped his cap on the seat, leaned back, and took out a cheap cigarette case, staring down the road with half-shut eyes. That was a bit of a shock, hearing seventy pounds was all she'd got. Part of his mind was disappointed, another part of it swore that he would never take a penny of her money, because a man can't.

'The point is . . . do you want to go on seeing me?'

He laughed at her, nodding.

'Oh well . . . kissing me, if you like. Yes, well, if you do we must think of some safe place to meet and I must stop having lessons like this, it won't be safe while that old man's about.'

'All right. I'll think of somewhere.' He sat up and put on his cap. 'Time we were getting along.'

He added in an experimental tone 'Darling,' then repeated emphatically, 'Darling. Sounds kind of funny, doesn't it?'

'It sounds sweet,' said Tina absently, leaning back as the car began to move. She was thinking that although the affair had leapt forward that morning into a new warmth, it was as far as ever from being 'settled'. No plans had been made: yet now they would never be happy unless they were kissing each other.

What would Doctor Hartmüller suggest?

Plainly, too plainly, there rushed into her mind what Doctor Hartmüller would most certainly suggest; but she shrank, shocked, from the thought. Oh no, that's out of the question, she told herself decidedly. Her education, the traditions by which she ruled her life, her common-sense and her modesty were all agreed that Doctor Hartmüller's remedy was an impossible one.

But she had forgotten that by her side was a young man, also moved by the morning's kisses, inexperienced, more fastidious than most youths of his class, and strongly attracted by her.

As they drew near to The Eagles, Saxon said quietly,

'When are you going away?'

'Oh!' She turned, startled. 'I'd forgotten that. I don't know; soon, I suppose. It depends on what Doctor Parsham says about my father. A whole month! You won't stay here all that time, will you? I mean, won't you go away, too? You went to Bracing Bay last year, for a fortnight, didn't you?'

He nodded, turning the car into the drive.

'I haven't the money to go away for long,' he said, looking at the road ahead, 'but I was thinking – it's a pity you can't get away somewhere by yourself this time. Without any of them, I mean. Then . . . I could come too, perhaps.'

'*Saxon*,' she murmured, staring at him, while her heart began to beat strongly.

'Yes.'

He braked.

'Then we could have a nice little holiday together,' he ended. 'Darling,' he added, as an afterthought.

'Do you mean . . . in the same hotel?'

'I mean in the same . . .'

He let the last word come almost in a whisper, and gave her a country lad's smile that went straight back into the sturdy green woodland of England's unwritten love history; a hind lying under the oaks in Windsor Great Park might have smiled at a girl like that, four hundred years ago when the trees were young.

'Wouldn't you like that?'

'Better than anything,' she nodded, dazed but honest. It was surprising how quickly education, modesty, common-sense and tradition could swallow a shocking idea.

'Same here,' and as he leant across to open the door for her he broke into his delightful gay whistle; then stopped long enough to say, 'That's settled, then.'

He had taken charge of things now; and he felt utterly self-confident and cheerful. His gaiety spread to Tina; as she ran up the steps she was laughing, the sunrays warm on her lifted face.

Neither of them looked beyond the thought of a weekend's pleasure.

# CHAPTER XVIII

Stanton, most exclusive resort on the coast of Essex, is so well organized in its business of supplying pleasure to wealthy people that melancholy is never permitted to creep over its neat grounds and gay little pavilions even at the dangerous hour of twilight, when any coast town has a habit of looking sea-grey and sad. The red, green and yellow fairy lights twinkle out along the promenade at Stanton a full half-hour before the twilight begins, and all the well-kept, expensive hotels put up their fat gold lights as well, to keep the sea-dusk at bay; while the streets of pretty villas in their luxuriant gardens are so full of young people in white hurrying back from tennis and of groups laughing over pleasant plans for the evening or tomorrow, that the little town seems in the midst of a never-ending party into which melancholy cannot imaginably intrude.

It is a clean, well-planned place with no buildings earlier than 1900, and no slums. The shops are small, dear, and excellent; many exclusive London firms have branches down here. The air is superb, as only East Coast air can be. Some people swear that the air of Bracing Bay (née Clackwell, but the Mayor and Chamber of Commerce got that changed on the grounds that it was vulgar and did not describe the place and would not attract desirable visitors) is even better. But then the air of Bracing Bay, eight miles down the coast, sometimes smells of winkles and shrimps, which the Stanton air does not; Stanton has no pier, and Bracing Bay has two, and piers, as any seasider knows, do encourage winkles. A gay, prosperous, snobby little place is Stanton, with an atmosphere of expensive games hovering over it. Hetty Franklin disliked it more than any place she knew because it has no extremes.

A little girl in well-cut grey flannel shorts and the blazer of an expensive school (no one was shabby in Stanton) was all alone on half a mile of sand newly smoothed by the waves, absorbed in a search for one particular kind of pale pink shell that is found at Stanton and Bracing Bay – and no doubt at other places also, but somehow it seems to belong especially to these two resorts, the refined and the common, lying some eight miles apart on the Essex coast.

'Looking for shells?' inquired Viola, sauntering along the sands in her usual before dinner walk, feeling bored and sad.

'Yes,' replied the little girl cautiously, nodding without looking up. She had been warned not to talk to strangers.

She went slowly hopping on, making the most of the last fifteen minutes before bedtime, and every now and then pouncing on one of the precious shells.

This place is a bit too posh for me, thought Viola. We've been here nearly three weeks now and I don't know anybody. Except that it's marvellous changing for dinner every night, I shan't be sorry to go home.

Doctor Parsham's verdict upon Mr Wither had not been alarming, but he had explained that the liver was disordered and had recommended that, instead of going as usual to Stanton for a month, the family should go this year to the Lakes, where the softer yet bracing air would benefit the liver more than would the strong breezes of the coast. Of course there had been indescribable uproar over this proposal, which had been debated from every conceivable angle until everybody was exhausted and almost in tears, but at last a plan had emerged, and been carried out. Mr and Mrs Wither and Madge had gone for the month to Derwentwater, whence they could take motor-excursions to what was left of the local beauty-spots; while Tina and Viola repaired for a month to the White Rock Hotel, Stanton, where the family usually stayed.

Tina had entreated her father that she might go to Stanton as usual, declaring that she would die if she did not smell the sea, though as for dying she had been looking noticeably well lately, had put on weight, and so on. But Mr Wither was feeling so out of sorts and so wearied by the discussions about the holiday that he had allowed Tina to have her way, only insisting that Viola should go with her, as the proprietor and staff of the White Rock, where the Withers were known and revered, would think it peculiar if she went alone. Polo was boarded out with Colonel Phillips, the car was put away and Saxon turned loose with a month's wages, the maids were given permission to ask friends to the house in the family's absence; and off everybody went.

Tina is a beast, mused Tina's sister-in-law, turning away from the darkening sea and beginning to walk slowly across the sands towards the twinkling lights of the promenade. Even if she didn't want me to come (and she looked simply furious when Mr Wither said I was to) she needn't be so beastly to me, going off all day to see her beastly Elenor Lacey and never saying a word to me when she is here. She used to be so nice; I don't know what's up with her lately. She needn't think I like being here – except the changing for dinner.

At the thought of changing for dinner she looked more cheerful, and turned, as she came to the little water-worn wooden steps leading down to the sands, for a last look at the sea. How big and sad it was! her own face grew sad as she gazed. I wonder if you flew straight across there you'd get to France? I wonder if He's in France and what He's doing? Kissing her, I suppose. I wish I was dead. Well, not exactly dead, but I wish I was a nun or something, or something simply marvellous would happen tomorrow.

The reader will by now have divined that Viola's nature was neither passionate nor deep; nevertheless, its sweet shallows had received from Victor as deep a wound as they could carry. She was so miserable that she was surprised by her symptoms; the way she cried at the least thing, grew thinner, and experienced all kinds of unfamiliar heart-beating and blushings. She honestly endeavoured to control her feelings, saying to herself, Good Lord, girl, pull yourself together for heaven's sake. Get a Grip of Your Guts, as Shirley would say; but it was useless; all her affection, her youthful healthy senses and her romantic dreams flew constantly back to those moments in the summer-house and fluttered about Victor Spring.

The miserable part was that she could not make herself believe that all was over, and that he would soon be married to someone else. She spun day-dreams through the long hours that she sat on the promenade in the sunshine with a novel by Denise Robins, her white shoes crossed, her curly head resting on the sun-warmed canvas, staring dreamily and unhappily at the cheerful well-dressed crowds, and the worst of these dreams (or silly thoughts, as Viola sternly called them) was that she felt so bad when it was time to stop thinking them and go in to lunch; and Tina was no help, on the days when she was in to lunch, for she only sat with a soppy look on her face, silently eating a good deal and saying over the pudding that she was going over to Elenor's again that afternoon, if Viola did not mind; and of course Viola could not say that she did.

This Elenor lived about two miles outside Stanton by bus, in a village called Rackwater, and she had an invalid husband who had been in the war. Elenor and Tina had been at school together, and as she had a boring, hard time of it with the invalid husband (she was very fond of him, of course, but he was a great worry to her) she liked Tina to go over there as often as she could and sit in the garden and talk to the invalid husband while she, Elenor, got on with things. When Viola (who would try anything once and liked going to new places even if they sounded boring) asked if she could go too and help to cheer the invalid husband, Tina said no, it was very kind of Viola but Adrian Lacey mustn't have any excitement or see any strangers or anything.

Viola knew quite well what was up with Tina. She was in love with the invalid husband, and that was why she liked to go over there every day and sometimes in the evenings as well, when the moon was sailing over the mysterious sea. It must be awful for Elenor, thought Viola. I wonder she has her there, I'm blowed if I would. And I thought she was so crazy about Saxon? Some people haven't any deep feelings. Lucky for them they haven't.

She went slowly up the magnificent steps of the White Rock, which was one of the largest and most expensive hotels in Stanton.

'Evening, Mrs Wither. Been having the old constitutional?'

That was Mr Brodhurst. He was the only person in the hotel who took any notice of her. He was a funny man; he always called her walk the old constitutional, and pretended she was in training for some important race that was coming off in the autumn, and they made jokes about it together; but Viola thought that Mrs Brodhurst did not like her very much.

'Yes.' She stopped for a moment to smile at him and have the daily joke, standing at the top of the steps with her small white-shod feet a little apart, hands in the pockets of a tough white coat, her curls blowing about.

'Record time tonight, I hope?'

'Oh yes . . . there and back in twenty seconds! . . . just to see how far it was, you know.'

'That's the stuff! Better and better. Ah, you wait till the autumn! We'll show 'em.'

'Felix,' observed Mrs Brodhurst in a low, nasal, mysterious voice, emerging for an instant from behind the *Daily Telegraph*.

'Yes, dear?' Mr Brodhurst skipped into the Palm Lounge, where the *Daily Telegraph* swallowed him and Viola saw him no more.

She went on, up the impressive stairs covered with dark-red, non-smelling, noiseless rubber. All along the wide window-sills were cacti in pots. The White Rock kept up with the times. If fashion said that ferns were out and cacti in, then into the White Rock came cacti. It was a luxurious, gay, smart place, and Viola was glad that she had been able to buy some marvellous clothes with that thirty pounds.

That thirty pounds had been sent to her just before she came away by Geoff Davis, Shirley's husband, with a letter explaining that he had succeeded in selling, though at a considerable loss, some shares belonging to Teddy that she had handed over to him at Teddy's death. The shares had actually been bought for Viola; so now the money was hers, too. She had forgotten to tell Mr Wither about the shares when they had had their little talk about money;

and now she decided that she would not tell him about the thirty pounds, either.

If was lovely to have all that money. She had bought some really marvellous clothes in her usual slapdash taste from which the pale blue ball-dress had been a miraculous exception, and these had cheered her up for a little while.

Oh, there was the sea again, almost invisible behind the tiny bright lamps along the promenade, looking in at her bedroom window. A maid was pulling the curtains, shutting out the early autumn evening.

This is the nicest time of the day, thought Viola, as the girl went out and shut the door. She pulled off her coat and carefully put it away; then began solemnly, like a child playing a well-loved game, to dress for dinner.

She laid out her dress, shoes and stockings, put some fine oatmeal in the washing basin, smothered her face with cream and patted it carefully round her eyes with the tips of her fingers; then she brushed her hair and began to change her stockings.

This half-hour before dinner was the only time in the long day when she almost forgot Victor, for then all the little rites she so much enjoyed helped to soothe and occupy her mind, driving unhappiness into the background. She was comforted each evening, too, by a dim hope that something marvellous might happen after dinner, and it was to welcome this event that she dressed so carefully. It never did happen, of course; but she enjoyed the vague feeling that it might; and she was therefore rather annoyed when Tina suddenly came in, after a hasty knock, looking agitated and dreamy, and at once driving Viola's own peace away. She was in her outdoor clothes, and Viola supposed that she had just come in from her visit to Elenor.

'Vi,' she began, sitting down on the bed and absently pushing Viola's dress out of the way, 'can you spare a minute?'

'Of course.' Viola rather carefully moved the dress to the other side of the bed. 'What's up?'

She never felt cross with anyone for long; her deplorably weak nature hardly seemed capable of sustaining a healthy indignation;

and this was quite natural to her; she never had to tell herself to forgive people; she just did it without thinking.

'Oh nothing much . . . it's only that Adrian's very bad and Elenor wants me to go over there for the whole weekend.'

She stopped abruptly, staring down at the bed, fiddling with the eiderdown.

'You look swell tonight,' remarked Viola irrelevantly, lifting her wet face from the oatmeal-water and gazing at her sister-in-law's reflection in the mirror over the basin. 'I like that way of doing your hair.'

'Do I? Do I really, Vi?' Tina got up and went across to the mirror, peered eagerly at her face. 'Yes, I do look better,' she murmured, 'I've put on weight.'

She turned away, sighing.

'Is he awfully bad?' asked Viola, her soft deep voice funereally subdued.

'Who?' staring. 'Oh – Adrian. Oh – yes, he is rather. Poor old Elenor.'

'I'm awfully sorry. It must be ghastly.'

'Yes. Yes, it is. Awful – when you remember someone when they were fit.'

'Is he nice looking?' sentimentally.

'Adrian? Oh no – very thin, and he looks very ill now, of course. He used to be, quite.

'Well,' turning restlessly from the dressing-table where she had been fidgeting with Viola's shabby brush and comb, 'I just thought I'd tell you. I'll be back on Monday to lunch.'

'I say, you aren't going now, are you?'

'Yes. Why not?'

'Oh, nothing, only it's so funny – just before dinner and everything.'

'I don't see why. I had a phone message from Elenor about fifteen minutes ago and I said I'd go at once.'

'But you'd only just got back from there, hadn't you?'

'Yes.' Tina's hand was on the door.

'Was he all right this afternoon?'

'What? Oh yes. No, I mean. No, I thought I might have to go

back; he was very much worse before I left. Look here, Vi, I must dash or I'll miss the bus.'

'Oh lord, don't do that. Fly . . . here, half-a-motor-car, though; suppose I want to get hold of you, what's their address?'

'Oh, send it Poste Restante, Rackwater; that'll find me. Elenor won't want Adrian disturbed with a lot of letters, and they aren't on the phone.'

'What's Poste . . . what did you say?'

'Oh, *Vi!* Here . . . have you got a pencil?'

After a hunt Viola found one and the back of a stocking bill, and Tina scrawled the Poste Restante address.

Viola watched her seriously. She knew quite well what Tina was going to do; she was going to spend the weekend with this Adrian Lacey because Elenor had gone off on a visit or something, and that would be a darned silly thing to do.

'Look here, Tina; it's none of my business and I don't want to butt in, so shut me up if you don't want any, but do you want any – you know – information?' austerely inquired Viola, going very pink.

'Oh, good heavens, no!' exclaimed Tina, going bright pink in her turn and suddenly surprising her sister-in-law with a hasty but warm kiss. 'What on earth do you mean? Take care of yourself. Oh, Viola,' she suddenly whispered, turning back for an instant in the dusk of the corridor, where the dark line of the sea looked in through a far window, 'I'm so happy, I can hardly bear it,' and she ran off, snatching up a little suitcase in her flight.

Well, that's a nice state of affairs, I must say, mused Mrs Wither severely, going back into her room and shutting the door. Fancy Tina. She ought to have told me all about it and asked my advice; after all, I am a widow. Now if there's an awful row later on, I shall get the blame because I didn't stop her going. But how could I? You can't stop a person when they really mean to do a thing. I should hate to kiss somebody who was all thin and ill and somebody else's husband. She is funny.

The faint sound of the White Rock dance band drifted up to her from the Palm Lounge. They were not playing the Merry Widow, but her eyes overflowed with tears.

It has no doubt struck the sensitive and intelligent reader as peculiar that so pretty and friendly a girl as Viola should not have attracted a court of admiring men at the White Rock, or perhaps a bevy of cheerful young persons like herself. There were, however, a number of good reasons why she had not. Firstly, all the men at the White Rock were attached to women of some kind; and even when their women were sisters or mothers, the men hesitated to approach Viola because her prettiness, her sad expression and her solitude (for Tina spent most of her time with Elenor Lacey) made her conspicuous; and there is no quality in a woman, we are told, that the average man dislikes more than conspicuousness. No doubt if the average man were given the chance and the income to run a famous film star for a week, nine average men out of ten would refuse, bluffly.

When it is recollected that Viola wore clothes that were subtly incorrect, played no expensive games, and was not quite a lady, her solitude at the White Rock Hotel is explained.

Though she enjoyed watching all these smart cheerful people from the table that she shared with novels by Berta Ruck, Renée Shann and other spinners of romantic stories, and never wearied of noticing what clothes the women wore and of wondering about their lives, she never deceived herself into thinking that she was enjoying the holiday. Young, silly, ill-bred as she was, she had yet learned to distinguish delight from its counterfeits, and she had already written to Shirley that the White Rock is a marvellous place but I'm having a rather mouldy time, really.

This evening she went down to the dining-room in her usual mood of subdued hope, with a novel under her arm called *Time's Fool*.

The dining-room at the White Rock was designed to resemble the deck of a luxury liner, and the waiters were condemned to dress like stewards. There were stylized waves and seagulls on the walls, narrow waxed blocks of parquet that suggested deckboards on the floor, and a bevy of sea gods, dolphins and contemporary bathing beauties wallowing on the ceiling. The spiritless energy of these frescoes was much admired, and people came from far and near, so to speak, to look at the place.

The big room was only a third full, and flooded by the devitalizing silvery glow of concealed lighting. Viola went to her corner, sat down and propped up her book, but before beginning to read, she glanced round the room to see who was there; and the first person she saw was Victor Spring.

Her heart leaped to an enormous height; then began rolling dizzily over and over. The marvellous thing had happened. He was here, sitting at a table quite close to hers, the bright brown head like a young soldier's bent over a menu. He was in day clothes, and looked bored. As she stared, he glanced up to give his order to the waiter, and saw her.

Recognition, pleasure, embarrassment, went quickly over his handsome face. He said something to the waiter, got up, and came over to her table.

'Here's a bit of luck! You expecting anyone, or may I come and have dinner with you?'

'Yes please. No,' she murmured, shutting up *Time's Fool* and pushing the salt towards him.

'Not here all alone, surely, are you?' he went on easily, catching the eye of another waiter, who hurried up (Victor passed the Waiter Test with honours). 'Where's the rest of the family?'

As usual, he spoke to her as though she were a little girl, enjoying her confusion.

'At the Lakes. At least, Mr and Mrs Wither and Madge are, and Tina and I are down here, only Tina's gone away for the weekend, so I'm alone.'

'What a shame (bring me half a dozen oysters, will you?). Never mind. So am I. We must cheer each other up.'

Pause. He leaned back, and looked leisurely round the room. Most of the people at near-by tables were staring at them, interested by the sudden descent of the smart, authoritative young man on that pretty, dowdy little thing. One or two of the young women looked faintly envious. So did Mrs Brodhurst. It was simply *lovely*. Viola was in heaven.

Victor, not troubling to talk, ate his oysters with an occasional affectionate smile at his companion. He never had much conversation

231

anyhow, unless there were something definite to be said about business or sport. Phyllis had suspected for a long time that old Vic, though a gem, was not overburdened with the grey matter (her words); he talked so little.

Feel as though I'd known her for years – a very bad sign, he thought. But dammit, I can't help it. I had no idea she was here, had I? Last person in the world I expected to see. It's not my fault if the one day I come down here she happens to be here too, is it? I couldn't cut her, could I? Besides, I ought to explain to her . . . That was a very dirty trick; she got as worked up as I did that day. I owe her an apology. He decided that presently he would take her for a moonlit run in the car and give her the apology he owed.

'What will you drink, Violet?'

'Could I have champagne, please?' firmly asked Mrs Wither, who had made up her mind to have everything she wanted on this heavenly occasion; and after all, he had asked her, and though champagne cost a lot, she had always heard, ever since she was a little girl, that he had plenty of money. She stopped herself from saying 'If it isn't too expensive, please,' remembering that Shirley said men hated that sort of remark.

'Feel like that, do you?' opening his hazel eyes wide, and laughing at her. 'You fond of champagne?'

'Oh yes. It's my favourite wine.'

'But don't the bubbles tickle your nose?'

'Oh yes, fearfully, and I always choke when I take the first sip,' derisively.

He had not expected back-chat from the little Wither, and was amused. He ordered the champagne, which came in a silvery bucket misty with ice-dew, and he poured it out.

Fancy me saying that, thought Viola, drinking the champagne with bright eyes looking at him over the top of the glass. Frightful neck. But I can't help it, I'm so happy and I don't feel a bit afraid of him, it's just as though I'd known him for years and years.

Champagne can never be ordered without the temperature shooting up. The dining-room at the White Rock was of course used to champagne, but a tiny quiver of interest went through the near-by tables. *Those people are drinking champagne* – up goes the rocket! Diamonds and orchids . . . thoroughbreds and sables . . . I know for a fact he made a cool fifty grand . . . champagne!

'Come for a run in the car afterwards?' asked Victor suddenly; he wanted to make sure that this evening, so unexpected and so pleasurable, would be prolonged.

'I'd simply *love* to.'

I'd got her all wrong, he thought, filling her glass. She isn't playing any game at all, she's just a kid. But, oh boy, what a temperament! It would be so easy . . . but I think not. No, decidedly not. It would be a damned shame. She's a sweet kid.

Viola made no attempts at sensible conversation, and this kept the atmosphere dreamlike and almost tender. They exchanged a few remarks about the weather, and the number of visitors in Stanton, and Victor casually explained that he had only come down for that afternoon to Bracing Bay on business. Bracing Bay, of course, was a Hole; it was not possible to eat decently in Bracing Bay, and as most of his friends in Stanton were away, he had come in to the White Rock for dinner.

'Great luck I did,' filling her glass. 'You enjoying this stuff?'

'Yes, it's lovely,' tranquilly swallowing.

'Aren't you afraid of getting tight?'

'No. I've got a very good head.'

Victor roared, and one or two people glanced across amusedly.

'You have, have you? What do you usually drink?'

'Oh well, lemon and barley at The Eagles, but of course I've had cocktails and gin and lime and sherry and all those things, and none of them made me tight. I'm very fond of drink, only we don't have much of it at The Eagles,' ended Mrs Wither regretfully.

No, I'll bet you don't, he thought, but he only lifted his glass, laughing across at her, and said nothing. He did not even trouble to say that he was motoring back to town that night. His mother and Hetty were in London for some months, having shopping excursions with the females of the Barlow tribe. The wedding would be in early spring, when the fruit trees were out. Phyl had such artistic ideas; she planned to decorate her bridesmaids with apple blossom.

They finished the champagne in friendly silence, sometimes smiling at each other with bright eyes, a little dazed. Viola had forgotten Tina, absent on her risky weekend, as though her sister-in-law had never existed; she had forgotten all the other Withers, and the marvellous girl Victor was engaged to, and the dead Teddy. There was nothing real in the world except this delightful floating feeling in her head, and Victor's eyes looking fondly at her above the smoke of his cigarette.

'Go and get your coat,' he said at last, glancing at his watch, 'and we'll go for a run – that is, if you'd still like it?'

If she would like it! She floated upstairs; and floated down again, looking like the Snow Queen with her fair curls above the tough white coat.

He led her out to where the car stood, tipped one of the White Rock commissionaires who held the door open, and waved her in. People stood about chatting after dinner in the mild autumn air, waving cigars at the moon. Cars glided up, paused to set women down, glided away again. There was a stimulating atmosphere of money and leisure which Hetty would have recognized as the Smell of Progress.

Victor made for the south cliff road, where the bungalows grew fewer towards a tract of wildish country.

Below the cliff on one side spread the silver-black sea, breathing sadness and a stealthy whispering into the night; on the other side rough fields glided past, their tussocks ghostly in the moonglow. A rabbit dashed out and scooned in front of the car for a hundred yards while Victor hooted indulgently; Viola saw the white glint of its scut as it dashed at last into the hedge. There were not many cars on the road, because Stanton liked sitting indoors playing bridge better than it liked moonlit motoring; and presently they had the road to themselves.

At last Victor stopped, on a lonely stretch of cliff. Far below, the white edges of the waves rippled in a blaze of moonlight on the lonely sands, a haunting whisper came up faintly. He threw away a match and leant back, staring at the moonway on the black water and wishing that he could start kissing her without saying anything.

But he owed her an apology and he wanted to make it. She was a sweet kid. Besides, he had not brought her here to kiss her.

'You know,' he began, still not looking at her, 'I've been wanting to say I'm sorry about what happened in the summer. I'm afraid I hurt your feelings.'

'Well, you did rather,' mildly, 'but it's all right now.'

'Sweet of you.' But still he did not look at her. 'I lost my head, I'm afraid.'

Viola said nothing. Of course, it was nice of him to say he was sorry, but she would have liked it much better if he had started the kissing. What else had he brought her here for?

'You – er – you – I suppose you heard—?'

'About your being engaged? Oh yes.' She went very red, then white. Why bring that up? She began to feel miserable, and wished he would take her home. Everything was getting horrid. An enormous lump rushed into her throat.

'Yes. Oh yes. Yes, we're getting married in the spring.'

In another minute, he thought savagely, I'll be saying I'm sure she'd like Phyl and we must all do a show together some time. Blast. I never ought to have started this. To hell with everything.

Sniff.

'Violet darling, what's the matter? Don't cry. Here, have mine. There – is that better? What's the matter, you funny little object?'

'It's *Viola*, not Violet. You always get it wrong,' crying copiously on his shoulder, 'and you always make me miserable and I think you're a beast. I was quite all right until you started about getting married. And you don't even know my name properly, either. It's' (a kind of wail) 'an *insult*, that's what it is.'

'I'm sorry, darling. There, there,' patting her cautiously the young women in his set did not need patting; or, if they did, they patted themselves. 'Darling, do please stop. I'm awfully sorry.'

'So I should hope.'

Viola blew her nose, speaking as haughtily as possible, but continued to recline on his shoulder. Her hair brushed his cheek and it felt pretty good. The fact is, she gets me where I live, he thought angrily, and I was a fool to bring her. I might have known what would happen. Now of course I can't stop kissing her. But he was not trying very hard.

'That better?' he said at last.

In the pause, they did not hear the desolate whisper of the waves. She nodded.

'Powder for the nose.' He held her case while she powdered, then watched while she combed her curls. Her profile was dark and delicate against the silver path on the sea.

'That's grand,' helpfully.

She said nothing.

Better get her back as quickly as I can. He started the car. I'll never be with her alone like this again . . . I'll see to that. But that's what I said before. He fell back on thinking, hell.

'Well,' he observed at last as they sat in silence with the engine ticking over, 'I'm afraid this evening hasn't been exactly a riot. I'm sorry. (You'll know that noise of mine by heart soon).'

'Oh, I enjoyed the first part, it was *lovely*,' earnestly, 'and I'm sorry I was such an ass. It's all right, really, I mean, I don't mind as much as all that.'

'Don't you?' dejectedly. 'Oh. That's grand. Well, shall we be getting along?'

They got along; and presently there were cars on the road again and bungalows; and the town was near.

'Will you be married at Sible Pelden?' inquired Viola in a martyred voice.

Not if I bloody well know it we won't, with you in the congregation.

'No. In Town.'

'Oh.'

Pause.

'You're not cross, are you?'

'Blast it, Viola,' very crossly indeed, 'shut up. Can't you see what – oh hell. Here, have mine.'

Despite her second outburst, he managed to get back to the White Rock without any more talk. Talk was no use. He supposed that he wanted her so much that it was making him fond of her; it

236

sometimes did, but a weekend soon put that right and he was his own master again. Only in this case there could be no weekend, and he dimly felt that it might be some time before he could risk passing long hours winding wool alone with Mrs Wither.

The car stopped outside the White Rock.

'Here we are. Good night, Viola.' He took her hand in a friendly clasp, with a friendly smile, and moved it up and down in a friendly waggle. 'You go in and get some sleep, and you'll feel quite different in the morning, I expect. So shall I. Moonlight and champagne, you know . . . wonderful what they'll do . . .' He ended in an indescribably dreary tone, 'Well . . . on your way, sailor!'

'I can't go to bed now; it's only nine o'clock,' said Viola sulkily, getting out of the car.

'Well . . . read or something. Goodbye.'

And this time it really is goodbye, he thought, smiling determinedly at the tall forlorn girl lingering on the moonlit steps, looking so sad. This has just about something'd up the whole something works, this has. If I'd gone on kissing her I should have asked her to come away with me and to hell with everything.

And that (thought Victor, driving much too fast along the London road in the moonlight), that's not the frame of mind for a man who's shortly going to be married.

Presently he thought, zooming through Colchester, I'll bet she wouldn't mind having kids.

# CHAPTER XIX

Even Viola's gentle nature felt some indignation after the events of Friday evening. In the midst of the crying fits that occupied much of Saturday and Sunday, she frequently told the pillow that Victor was a beast. That Beast he had now become, instead of He and Him. Of course, it was very kind of him to buy her all that champagne and take her in his car, but why need he start talking about his beastly engagement?

I was just getting over it, and he comes along and stirs it all up again. Now my heart darned well *is* broken and I *do* wish I was dead. I didn't really wish it before because something marvellous might happen and I'd miss it, but now it has happened, and it was beastly and I *do* wish I was dead.

But hotels are not built to cry in. People come popping in and out, carrying clean linen and trying not to look at the desolate figure on the bed; and soon the desolate figure gets up.

Viola's indignation helped her to sit in the Palm Lounge, reading with smarting eyelids, to go for walks by the sea that had suddenly become autumnal and sad, even to accept an invitation to take coffee with Mr Brodhurst on Sunday morning; Mrs Brodhurst had been suddenly recalled to London because her mother was ill. Mr Brodhurst seemed to admire Viola, and that was comforting. He told her that she ought to take up golf, she had the figure for it. Willowy, but rounded, said Mr Brodhurst. She could not help a miserable inward giggle, thinking how Shirley would brand Mr Brodhurst as a D. O. M. and One of The Wandering Hand Brigade.

But even with the help of indignation and Mr Brodhurst, she was very miserable and lonely, and pleased to see Tina back to lunch on Monday.

Tina did not look as a person should look who has been spending a wicked weekend with the invalid husband of an old school friend. She was a little absent in her manner, as Viola had seen her look when she was planning a new outfit or learning a new embroidery stitch, but she was cheerful and calm, noticed at once that something was wrong with her young sister-in-law, and affectionately inquired what. Viola began to cry, and told her all the unhappy little story.

Tina was kind as kind could be. She did not tell Viola to pull herself together and take up some interesting hobby, nor did she say too harsh things about Victor and make Viola want to stick up for him. She took the exciting, comforting point of view that Victor was really in love with Viola and trying not to be.

'Why?' demanded Viola.

'Oh well, I imagine that he thinks you're not suitable – no money, and all that sort of thing.'

'Do you think he minds me having worked in the shop?' reddening.

'I shouldn't be at all surprised. That's the kind of thing people do mind,' bitterly. 'Not so much as they did, of course; nothing like; and intelligent people nowadays don't even think about it. But in the country people mind, and rich people mind, especially people who haven't been rich for very long, like the Springs. Old Spring only made his money in the War, you know.'

'Did he? Oh yes . . . now I seem to remember Dad saying . . .'

'Yes. Jam for the troops or something.'

'Then do you think he'll go on thinking I'm not suitable, and marry her?' tears starting again.

'I'm afraid so, Vi. You see, a man like Victor Spring is *sensible* about marriage, in a way most women simply can't understand. He wants someone who can run a big house, and entertain smart flashy people, and do him credit. Now from what I've seen of that Barlow hag, she could do all that. She's hardly what I'd call a human being at all, but she can do just the things he wants, and he's known her for years (you heard what his cousin said) and – oh, it's all most suitable. *You* couldn't, you know. Run a big place, I mean.'

'Yes I could if I had proper servants. Shirley says that's all it is.'

'You couldn't manage them. You're too soft.'

'I'd let him and a housekeeper manage them.'

'Yes, well, that's an idea. It might work. But I'm afraid he won't give you the chance, my poor dear. It's terribly rough luck, and I think he's behaved quite detestably, but I'm afraid you must just make up your mind to go on caring about him for a long, long time; unless, of course, someone else comes along.'

On this melancholy note the conversation ended, and as Tina had to go off again that very evening to see Elenor, they did not talk about Victor again that day. But though she had depressed Viola's spirits by pointing out how unlikely it was that Victor should marry her, she had raised them by suggesting that he was in love with her. Viola had not dared to think that he might be; she had only hoped that perhaps he might like her, and she was much comforted by the notion that he was struggling with a passion for her. She imagined him looking gaunt and worn and Miss Barlow asking him what was the matter, and him starting and biting his lip until the blood came and muttering 'Nothing,' with a sigh that was almost a groan.

But in spite of these solacing reveries, their last week at Stanton was most depressing, for the weather turned wretched, sending September out in floods of rain, and Adrian Lacey became so ill that not even Tina was allowed to go over and see him; and on the Friday before they went home she told Viola that she had had a telephone message from Elenor to say that poor Adrian had passed away peacefully in his sleep just after lunch. Tina would not go to the funeral; she felt too grieved. Elenor would sell the bungalow and go out to her married sister in Malta.

So that polished off the Laceys; and what with the funeral and the weather and her private grief, Viola was really pleased to see

Saxon drive the car up to the White Rock on Saturday morning, and felt that it was pleasant to be going home. She was looking forward to seeing Polo again, of whom she was fond, and she would be twenty miles nearer Grassmere.

'Good morning, Saxon.'

'Morning, Mrs Theodore.'

Saxon looked so cheerful, brown and well that he might have been to the sea, too.

'Did you have a nice holiday?'

'Extra good, thank you, Mrs Theodore.'

'Where did you go?'

'Vi, be an angel and get my gloves, will you? I must have left them on the office table when I went in to pay the bill,' interrupted Tina, and Viola hurried off to get the gloves, which were afterwards found in the car.

In less than an hour they were home.

Mr and Mrs Wither and Madge had returned the evening before, with health and spirits improved by the Lakeland air, and as Tina and Viola were still in the first flush of interest at being again surrounded by their own possessions, lunch was at first almost a cheerful meal, and even when Viola told everybody about poor Adrian Lacey's death the interesting gloom cast by the recital lasted only for a few moments. Mrs Wither said that she seemed to remember having met Elenor one Prize Day at Tina's old school, wasn't she tall and dark with horn-rimmed glasses, and Tina said yes, and Mrs Wither said poor thing, how sad for her, have they any children, and Tina said no, and just as Mrs Wither was saying that perhaps it was a mercy, Mr Wither interrupted her to ask if she had remembered to order the coal, and the Laceys dropped out of the conversation.

Through the clear glass of the french windows that Annie had polished yesterday against the family's return, Viola stared at the dismal garden. Coal . . , yellow leaves lying on the wet grass . . . withered dahlias. Winter was coming. The faint glow of excitement that she had felt at returning to The Eagles faded as lunch went on, in the dark heavily furnished dining-room with familiar uninteresting faces round the table. Everyone had some story to tell about their holiday, and told it, but heaven knows that such stories are never interesting – unless, of course, one is telling them oneself – and Viola, after saying 'I say, good lord,' once or twice, did not listen.

By tea-time, when she had unpacked and arranged her clothes, and fussed over Polo a bit, and learned from Fawcuss that 'the house was still shut up over at Springs except for the head gardener (Mr Rawlings, that is), he says the family's going to stay in Town over Christmas,' she seemed to have been back at The Eagles for weeks; by dinner-time she might never have been away. The long quiet hours drifted into days, and the days into a week, two weeks. There was no excitement except an occasional meeting with Lady Dovewood in Chesterbourne, or tea with the Parshams, or, rarely, a visit to church with Mr and Mrs Wither on Sunday because Mrs Wither said that she really ought to go; also, she loved the little old church, where she had used to walk with her father sometimes on Sunday afternoons and where she had dreamed of being married to Victor Spring, and though it made her sad to go there, it also, in a queer way, made her happy. She bought a few winter clothes (Mr and Mrs Wither seemed to think that her clothes were brought by the ravens, like Elijah's dinner, for they never asked her where she got the money to buy them), and once she went to Town to see Shirley, very fat and bored and crossly waiting for her baby.

It was a long, dull, sad time. Autumn had come, with mists wandering over the flat, river-threaded countryside that seemed to grow more silent as the winter drew near. There was no news of the Springs, except that they were having a gay time in London; and Viola, with no news, no hope and no one to talk to, now pined indeed.

Her unhappiness was deeper and more genuine than it had been in the summer, and perhaps in her confused way she knew this, for she no longer luxuriated in it, but attempted to occupy her mind and not to give way to grief.

She re-read *Twelfth Night* and *As You Like It*; but although she was comforted by the fact that the other Viola had been crazy about a rich young man who was keen on a marvellous girl, and had been awfully fed up yet had got him in the end, and although *As You Like It* was all about some historical people in a wood that made her think of the little wood across the road, the plays were so difficult to understand when they were not read aloud in her father's fine voice that she did not read them all, as she had planned to do. But she did a good deal of sewing and accepted Tina's offer to teach her simple embroidery stitches and French.

Tina was funny since they had got back from Stanton. She was different. Viola had expected that she would be miserable because Adrian Lacey was dead; but she was cheerful and serene, though sometimes Viola (when she came out of her private unhappiness) caught her with a very worried look. She went for a long walk every day, occasionally with Viola but usually alone. She no longer took driving lessons because they were not necessary; she could now drive so well that she often took the family for long excursions.

Saxon was glum, too. Viola never heard him whistle nowadays and Fawcuss, Annie and Cook hoped that he might be seriously thinking about giving up the old selfish, careless way of living, and going to church regular. There was no doubt, they told one another, that that dreadful quarrel with his mother and that man in the summer, in front of everybody like that, had made a great difference to him. You could see it. It was hard on him, of course, but it was all for the best, no doubt of that.

Tina did not mention Victor except casually when the Springs came up in conversation, and Viola, trying to be sensible, followed her lead. I suppose she thinks I'll never get over it if we're always talking about it, she thought. All the same, I do wish I had someone to talk to. It's awful. I wish she'd be more like she was when I first came. She *is* funny these days. I'm sure there's something up.

She had confided a few details about Victor to Shirley, in the laughing, half-ashamed style used by the Crowd when it had fallen for somebody, but Shirley had only snapped 'Well, if you want him why don't you go all out and get him? It's easy enough,' and then gave some smart, stinging generalizations about Getting Your Man that were not helpful. Poor Shirley, thought Viola, gazing mildly at her friend, she feels like that because she's so enormous.

While the sleep of winter settled over Sible Pelden, the Springs were having a grand time in Town. They were established at the Dorchester, which was close to the Barlows' large luxurious flat, and conveniently near to Buckingham Square, where Phyllis and Victor intended to bespeak one of the most expensive flats in the block that was now shooting up on the site of Buckingham House.

Phyllis was on top of the world. Engaged to a rich and personable young man who let her have her own way in almost everything, surrounded by other young men who would plainly have liked to marry her and showed their regret that they had not won her, her time occupied by fittings, hair-dressing, beauty treatments, dancing, and parties, she had not a moment of the day that was not crammed, and she was seldom in bed before three in the morning. There would be time after Christmas to choose the furniture and scheme of decoration for the flat, but she occasionally looked in at some show of modern furniture or textiles, just to get ideas, and she planned her trousseau and gave some of the orders for part of it, for spring, 1937, would be a busy year for dressmakers. She took all her activities with immense seriousness and was convinced that they were important; and doubtless, as they were all good for trade, they were.

Victor good-naturedly endured the whirl in which his betrothed liked to live. He was working very hard over the Bracing Bay development scheme in the weeks before Christmas; it had had setbacks, but was now progressing, and would be started in the spring. He managed, all the same, to spend enough time with Phyllis to satisfy such conventions as are left, and more than satisfy Miss Barlow, who thought that Vic was certainly coming up to scratch but was rather heavy going.

Phyllis, like her rival down in Essex, was no psychologist, but she did wonder once or twice, impatiently, why she always felt so flat after a party, when she and Victor were driving back in the car, silent and tired. This ought to be the time for a little mush. Sometimes it was; but it was not satisfactory mush. Vic did his best but.

Phyllis, who spoke contemptuously of those loose-living writers, painters and scenic designers who live on the edge of society, did not suspect that she wanted the company, and the mush, of bad men. She was scathing in her condemnation of a man in her set who had taken to the cinema and become an English star and was living a very uninhibited life indeed; she almost cut him when they met. She did not know that, had she not had the sense to snub him, she would have been one of his most willing victims. What she missed in Victor was vice.

However, the lovers got on amiably enough, and Mrs Spring's doubts about the suitability of the match went to sleep; for not only did Vic and Phyl seem to be settling down but Mrs Spring's own health was so much better that she could thoroughly enjoy the Little Season, and this made her take a cheerful view of everything. She was interested in every detail of Phyllis's trousseau and her visits to furnishing and textile shows, and often accompanied her. Sometimes Phyllis's elder sister, Anthea, went with them. She was a restless, smart, hard person of thirty-four, living apart from her husband with one pale, discontented little boy. She was ill-tempered with worry because she was always in debt. Mrs Spring disliked Anthea. When she looked at Anthea (who was outwardly all that Mrs Spring liked a woman to be) she feared that Phyllis might get like that, later on; so she avoided looking at Anthea more than was necessary.

Hetty was excessively bored with the life in London. True, she could sometimes get away by herself to visit bookshops and museums and picture galleries, but not often. Her aunt liked her to be on tap for whatever fun might be going. Hetty would trail round the expensive shops with Mrs Spring, Phyllis and Anthea, bored and silent, a book stuffed in the pocket of her suit, wishing that it was April and she was twenty-one.

Mrs Spring proposed, after the wedding, that Grassmere should be sold and she and her niece take a flat in London, where they

245

would be near to Victor and Phyllis and could lead a more social life than they could in Essex.

But Hetty had other plans. They were vague, but they were precious to her. As soon as she was of age she meant to leave Grassmere, or the flat in London, it did not matter which – for ever; take an attic in Bloomsbury, fill it with books and settle down to the life of a student on her own income. I love learning for its own sake, she thought. I don't want to teach, to write, to criticize, or review or be a poet. I just want to learn.

And while she sprawled in some important shop, watching Phyllis and Anthea sweetly bullyragging the young lady assistants, she was dreaming about a view of red and dark chimneys against the pale blue sky of London in summer, she could smell coffee brewing on the gas-ring and hear the drone, far below, of a busy street; and in fancy her gaze moved over the page of a book, and she was happy.

I suppose they'll let me take my books.

When the first shock's over, I imagine they'll be rather relieved.

Victor was behaving well. He let Phyllis have her way about the decorations for the flat, and agreed that it would be fun to fly to Monte Carlo for the honeymoon. He danced, efficiently, every night after a tiring day. He hardly thought about Viola at all; but when he did, he thought: That kid'll always mean something to me. I nearly fell harder than I've ever fallen in my life. Funny-peculiar.

Presently it occurred to him how well he was behaving. He went on letting Phyllis have her way, in spite of his vow, before they became engaged, that he would not. He gave (it could not be called a loan) Anthea a hundred pounds because Phyllis asked him to, and as he watched it disappear into Anthea's handbag for ever, he thought how *very* well he was behaving. Then he wondered, idly, if Phyl would want to dance every night when they were married. He supposed that he liked dancing as much as the next man, but he also liked billiards, bridge, tennis and squash, and none of these things did he want to do every day. Occasionally, after a heavy spell of Bracing Bay business, he even felt a little tired. Phyl was never tired. He could not remember, in the fifteen years that he had known her, ever having heard Phyllis declare that she was tired.

Would she ever get tired after they were married? He hoped she might, but was pretty sure she would not.

The truth was that the pastimes enjoyed by Phyllis and her set were a little too feminine for Victor's taste. He would have been more content in the social life of fifty years ago, when the pleasures and interests of the sexes were more widely separated. He enjoyed an occasional wild, or stodgy for that matter, evening with men, he enjoyed brooding over a newspaper in the peculiar drugged way that men do, thinking sleepily about the news without discussing it with anyone. He liked watching football or tennis matches by himself, and motoring by himself.

And he kept to himself, from everybody but his mother who had the same views, what he thought about women.

He had stupid, old-fashioned, ultra-masculine views on women. He never lost the feeling (though of course he had to suppress it in front of Phyllis and her friends) that women ought to be kept busy with some entirely feminine occupation like sewing or arranging flowers or nursing children until a man wanted their attention. He had not a shred of admiration (though he had to suppress this, too) for women who flew the larger expanses of sea, won motor-racing trophies, wrote brilliant novels, or managed big businesses.

He admired women only for being pretty, docile, and well dressed. He had to pretend he admired the other achievements because everybody else admired them (or said that they did) but to himself he thought coarsely All a lot of B. And when he got with other men, who agreed with him, they would smile in a certain way, and look at each other, and mutter 'All a lot of B.' Brainy women, sporting women, arty women – all a lot of B. This may have been due to suppressed subconscious jealousy. Or it may have been due to the natural resentment of a healthy creature, existing efficiently in its own sphere, because another creature with different powers and aims was muscling in on a comfortable racket. There are the two points of view.

Vic is really coming along nicely, thought Phyllis complacently. Being no trouble at all.

This was more than she could say of that beastly little Hetty, who was always making snooty remarks about the colour-schemes and furniture that Phyl admired and rooting for those that Phyl thought hideous. Her dislike of Hetty grew every day. They got on each other's nerves so much that they could hardly be civil to one another, and Mrs Spring gave each of them a sharp private lecture that had no effect at all. Phyl wished that Hetty would marry somebody, anybody, and immediately emigrate, and Hetty only wished that Phyl would catch cold and die. Neither thought the other of any use. The fact that Vic was indulgently fond of his old Het-Up made Phyllis dislike her the more; he had no right to support anyone whom his betrothed disliked.

Despite these undercurrents, everyone except Hetty enjoyed the stay in London so much that the Springs decided to stay on until the New Year. Then Phyllis would go to Mürren for three weeks with a party of friends, and when she came back would begin furious preparations for the wedding in April.

One gloomy afternoon early in November Saxon was on his way home through the oak wood. Evening had set in early; mist had lingered all day among the trees, muffling the sound of car wheels on the muddy roads and making the song of a robin who haunted the thickets near The Eagles sound startlingly loud and sweet in the languid gloom. Drip . . . drip . . . drip . . . came the small, heavy noise of fog-drops on wet earth in the Hermit's hollow. The stream was full but clogged with leaves, and crept between its wet, buried banks. Saxon crossed the plank and went up the hill on the other side.

He was thinner, and looked worried and irritable. He stared at the ground as he walked, and once he sighed heavily.

It was almost dark as he went through the last glade of leafless beeches before the cottage, and he had to pick his way carefully by the beam of his torch. Lights shone dimly from the public-house and filling station at the cross-roads, and there was a light in the cottage, too. As he came up, he could see into the parlour, for the curtains were not quite drawn.

The first thing he saw was a bottle and two glasses on the table, then a red arm, flung round a neck covered with thick silver curls.

Saxon kicked open the door. 'You get out,' he said, standing against the misty darkness of the doorway.

Mrs Caker struggled off the Hermit's knees, pulling her blouse together and laughing, but she also looked a little frightened. The Hermit, who appeared to be drunk, returned Saxon's fierce stare with one of extreme, if squintful, dignity, and waved his hand tolerantly as though to dismiss the incident.

'Well, fancy meeting you,' said Mrs Caker, buttoning herself. 'We thought you was over Chesterbourne. Proper sneak you are, comin' in on anybody like that.'

'Get out,' jerking his head at the door and staring at the Hermit.

'Now, now,' said the Hermit mildly, also buttoning, but making no move towards the door. 'None o' that, cock. I'll go when I wantsh, and not before. I bin very good a' you, 'know. Never shaid word. Never ask penny more, never shaid word. You be shenshible. Don't want to give you a shender, like I done before. You le' me alone, I'll le' you alone. Shee? Fairsh fair.'

He poured out some beer, slopping it on the table, and shaking his head reprovingly.

Saxon strode across and gripped him by his thick shoulders. Through the sacking coat with its pads of paper he could feel their power; they were thick as a bull's, massive with bone and firm muscled flesh. His own hands, spread on that bulk, looked thin and helpless.

'Keep your 'ands orf me,' roared the Hermit, staggering up. 'You dare touch me, you little bastard, and I'll cut— By Chrisht, I will.'

He staggered against the table and the beer bottle went over, foaming, fell on the floor and smashed. They struggled clumsily for a minute, breathing hard, slipping in the pool of beer and broken glass. Mrs Caker hovered in the doorway, screaming helpfully.

'Shut up, can't you, you'll have the whole bloody cross-roads here in a minute,' panted Saxon, crimson. The Hermit was forcing him to the door.

'Don't hurt him, now,' begged Mrs Caker, seeing that Saxon was getting the worst of it. 'Let him go, Dick; come on now, let him go.'

'Laid 'andsh on me,' bellowed the Hermit, his tremendous voice echoing over the dark misty valley '– of a boy laid 'andsh on me. All becaush I like a bit, shame as anyone else. Shame ash he doesh, dirty—. Now I *am* going to tell, shee?' slowly pushing the scarlet, sweating and swearing Saxon out through the door. 'Never shaid a word, sho help me, never ashked for a penny up till now, but now I'm a-goin' to, sho help me Chrisht. Goin' right over to Mishter Wither, I am, and I'll shay, your jorter, I'll shay. Thish very ni'. Wot your jorter been up to, eh?' jerking Saxon violently over the threshold, 'with your shuvver, eh? Goin's-on. I know. I shee 'em. Jay after jay, I sheen 'em. Down inna wood' . . . he shook off Saxon as though the tall young man had been a child, and sent him sprawling – 'shee? Like *that*. Now I'm off to Mishter Wither.'

Shouting and singing, he plunged away into the misty darkness, and Saxon, picking himself up and brushing the mud off his uniform with trembling scratched hands, heard him blundering down the hill like a big animal, his bull-voice echoing weirdly through the fog-veiled trees.

'Mishter Wither! Mishter Wither!'

'There. You see,' said Mrs Caker, shrugging her shoulders and sitting down at the table. 'Proper upset, he is. You shouldn't ha' laid hands on him; he's easy upset when he's buzzy wi' the drink.'

She herself was a little mellowed by the drink. Fright and anger had gone from her pretty blue eyes and lurking laughter had come back.

'All messed up, aren't 'ee,' she added, staring at his muddy coat. 'Here,' she got up unsteadily, 'I'll brush 'ee down . . . hold still.'

He twisted angrily away from her, staring into the mist as though he did not know quite what to do. Far away on the other side of the valley a faint voice sounded:

'Mishter Wither!'

'I'd better go over,' muttered Saxon anxiously, as though to himself, and started off along the path leading into the confused, misty blackness of the trees. His mother saw the beam of the torch flash out, making the trees look like ones of stone among the wandering mist-folds; then, as he went deeper into the valley, she lost sight of him.

Mrs Caker, yawning, put the kettle on for some tea. As an afterthought, while waiting for it to boil, she mopped up the broken glass and beer.

# CHAPTER XX

The family at The Eagles was assembled in the drawing-room at that dreary hour when tea is long over and dinner not yet in sight. It was a tranquil scene; it would have annoyed a Communist. Five non-productive members of the bourgeoisie sat in a room as large as a small hall, each breathing more air, warmed by more fire and getting more delight and comfort from the pictures and furniture than was strictly necessary. In the kitchen underneath them three members of the working class swinked ignobly at getting their dinner, bought with money from invested capital. But perhaps this is not a very interesting way of regarding poor Mr Wither and the rest.

Mrs Wither was knitting, Madge was reading a book about dogs' diet, Mr Wither was dozing over the *Morning Post*, Tina was embroidering, and Viola was staring into the fire, her hands idle upon the sewing in her lap. Except for the heavy breathing of Mr Wither, the click of Mrs Wither's needles, the breathless flutter of the flames in the fireplace and the tiny metallic sound as Tina's silk was drawn through her canvas, the room was quiet. The faintest imaginable smell of roasting meat hovered in the air. Suddenly there broke out a loud, continuous knocking at the front door; so loud that it penetrated through the front door itself, across the hall, through the drawing-room door and into the consciousness of the five people sitting round the fire.

Mr Wither opened his eyes with a start and sat up, letting the *Morning Post* slide to the floor.

'What on earth is that?' exclaimed Mr Wither. No one ever knocked at the front door of The Eagles. There was a perfectly good bell.

The four women turned startled gazes on the drawing-room door. Then the bell began to ring. Someone had got their thumb on it. By now Mr Wither was on his feet.

'Whoever can it be?' demanded Mr Wither.

Mrs Wither got up, and rang.

The knocking went on, and now a voice could be heard, shouting.

The scared face of Annie, trying to look correct, came round the drawing-room door after a longish pause.

'You rang, m'm?'

'Annie, what *is* that noise at the front door? Where is Fawcuss? Why doesn't she answer it?'

'Oh, m'm – it's that man. The Hermit, m'm. Fawcuss doesn't like to go to the door, m'm. In case he should be in drink, m'm, I mean.'

Bang! Bang! Bang! 'Mishter Wither! Mishter Wither!' Whirrrrrrrrrr.

'Has Saxon gone home?' demanded Mr Wither, looking rather frightened, as, indeed, they all did. The front door was stout, but the Hermit was strong as an elephant and did not care in the least what he did.

'He's gone home, sir. He went a good half-hour ago.'

'You said he could, Arthur, as it was too foggy to go into Chesterbourne,' murmured Mrs Wither.

Bang! Bang! Bang! The uproar was starting to get on their nerves.

They were all standing up, the women clutching their sewing and exchanging alarmed glances.

'We'd better—' Mr Wither was beginning, when suddenly the knocking stopped.

'Bloody yob,' came a muffled roar, after a pause. '– of a – boy.'

'Tina jumped and went pale, her inside turned over, but before she could say, 'I think Saxon must be out there, too, Father,' Fawcuss came round the drawing-room door at a staid trot, and announced breathlessly:

253

'Saxon's out there with him, m'm, he's just come back, I saw him out of the master's study window, m'm.'

'Saxon's no good, the old brute knocked him out before,' interrupted Madge. 'We'd better phone for the police, hadn't we, Father?'

'No, no, don't want to do that, can't bring the police down here on a night like this just for Falger. No, we'll have to . . .'

'I really think you'd better send for Roberts, Arthur,' said Mrs Wither timidly. (Roberts was the Sible Pelden policeman.)

Mr Wither said nothing. He was listening.

Two voices could be heard loudly arguing, but though everybody strained their hearing, not a word could they make out. By this time they had moved out into the hall, and were standing close to the front door, all bending slightly forward to listen.

'What on earth's up, Tina, you're quivering like an ashpan,' loudly observed Viola, breaking the hush with a giggle. She went on, staring curiously at her sister-in-law. 'I say, do you feel rotten? You look it.'

'I'm all right. Sh'sh.'

They listened again.

'. . . shut yer gab, see,' came the Hermit's voice, obstinate and thick, '. . . don't want yer – money . . .'

Then Saxon's voice, lower, speaking quickly and persuasively.

'Good boy; smart fellow,' nodded Mr Wither. 'He's talking him over, calming him down. Just as well to try a little bribery and corruption, if there's no other way. (I wonder what he wanted. Disgraceful.) Then *I* can deal with him tomorrow . . . it's gone on long enough. That's the best way to deal with these people, you know, drunks, just argue with them, quietly and calmly . . .'

'MISTER WITHER!!!!' a tremendous roar that blew everybody backwards, 'YOUR JORTER'S CARRYING ON WITH YOUR SHUVVER. KISSIN AND YOU-KNOW-WHAT. MISHTER WITHER!!!'

'Shut up, you—!'

There was a scuffle, and a roar of pain from the Hermit.

'Your jorter. Little one. Not the fat one. Carryin' on. Down the wood. Mishter Wither!'

Scuffling.

'*What* did he say?' demanded Madge, who had gone red, looking suspiciously at Tina, who had gone white.

Her father, her mother, the servants – everybody was staring at Tina except Viola, who had suddenly realized what had been going on under her nose for the last two months and, quite white herself with fright and sympathy for poor Tina, was staring fiercely at a giant seascape hanging above her sister-in-law's head.

'Give us a hand, will you?' came Saxon's voice faintly; the battle had moved down the steps.

'Coming up!' shouted another voice heartily. They heard someone running. Then:

'Ah, 'tes you, is ut? dirty owd man. Puttin' the wind up my girl in the wood – Keep off, will yer?'

More roars and scuffling.

'Kissin' and cuddlin',' roared the Hermit, despairingly, as Saxon and the unknown hustled him away. 'Your jorter.'

Then, as the family and the three old servants (for Cook had come ponderously up to join the party) stared in silent horror at the white-faced Tina, who stared steadily back at her mother, there floated back through the foggy night one last, shocking, unmistakable Word.

It was a word known in his youth to Mr Wither, but not spoken by him for nearly forty years, a word which Madge with reddened ears had sometimes overheard the cross-roads louts tossing backwards and forwards in their coarse wise-cracking, a word entirely unknown to Mrs Wither, a word that Shirley had once or twice coolly used to the shocked yet giggling Viola, a word lumped with eight or so similar words by Fawcuss, Annie and Cook as Bad Words, a word sunk miserably from its once plain natural use and made to drudge as a vivid outcast, a poor stout peasant of a word no longer allowed to be a verb and sometimes a noun but used generally as an adjective or an oath, a word slinking below the surface of polite language and boorishly resisting the knight-errantry of certain writers who would willingly restore it to its old homely kinghood.

'—,' bellowed the Hermit, hoarsely, despairingly, from the edge of the wood.

And lest there should be doubt about whom the word referred to—

'Yor jorter and yor shuvver,' came floating faintly through the mist, as he was hauled and pushed away.

At once, with the sound of that word, the group of eight alarmed people in the hall split up; and became five employers and three servants, the employers with a shocking open secret to hide, the servants trying not to look horrified. The Withers made a general movement back towards the drawing-room, turning their embarrassed faces away from the equally embarrassed ones of the maids, and Mrs Wither, looking over her shoulder, said distantly:

'Very well, Fawcuss. I don't think there will be any further trouble. Dinner as usual, Cook.'

Madge shut the drawing-room door and they moved slowly over to their former places. But no one spoke, or sat down. A dreadful question hung in the room. No one could think of anything but: Is it true? And no one looked at Tina, who leant against the carved marble mantelpiece, staring into the fire.

'Beastly cold, isn't it?' said Viola helpfully at last, kneeling and spreading her hands to the flames. But no one answered. The silence grew unbearable; everyone felt that someone *must* speak, yet no one could; it was as if they were all under a spell. And Tina stared into the fire, her lips pressed together and a feverish red in her cheeks.

At last Madge cleared her throat and said in a would-be sensible voice:

'Father, that settles it. You must get something definite done about the old brute. You'd better let Saxon drive—'

She stopped, appalled.

The name fell into the room like the Bad Word itself. Viola actually jumped. Each personality seemed to rush away, crowding with a horrified rustling sound to the door – upstairs – anywhere where the facts could be faced (or ignored) in decent solitude.

But this time the Withers were not going to be allowed to run away. Mr Wither did try. He said a little hoarsely, not looking at anyone:

'Yes, the fellow's a disgrace to the neighbourhood—' Then he stopped, his lips moved uncertainly, and he turned and stared piteously at his wife.

And then Madge, who was not quite such a coward as her parents and whose disgust had been roused by the Hermit's words, said bluntly—

'Look here, Tina, what on earth did he mean? About you and Saxon,' going red, 'about you and Saxon, I mean,' blundering.

Tina looked up quickly. Just for a second her face frightened them, it was so furious, ashamed, despairing, so transformed by passion. Fifteen years of longing for love, of joylessness and cowardice, of trying to be 'nice' as her family wanted everything to be 'nice' and 'decent' (even mating, birth and death), of lies, of gently dying from starvation, of never using a strong word or telling the truth to anyone – she wanted to shriek her sufferings at their three frightened faces.

Then the wild look faded. Trembling, she calmed herself. It was not her family's fault if her youth had been wasted like a cup of water poured into sand. They had done their best for her; her father had given her money to pay for the years at the art school, the journalism school, where she had hoped to meet a husband; her mother had brought her up to be modest, gentle, in careful ignorance, so that if she were to live half her life in starvation, she should at least not realize that she was starved. They had done their best: and if she could not be grateful, she must at least be just.

But she could not help wanting to see how they would take the Hermit's story. A little of her bitterness *would* out. They were so nice, so decent, so ready to believe that she was hopelessly loose. Let them.

'It's true that Saxon and I are lovers,' she said, trying to speak coolly, but trembling as she stared at her sister's red, disgusted face.

'Tina!' cried Mrs Wither, starting forward. 'It isn't true . . . you're joking . . . My little girl . . . my baby . . .' trying to put her arms round her, 'how could you? Oh Tina . . . a common boy . . . out of the village . . .'

Tina shook her off.

'Well, it's beastly, that's all I've got to say,' said Madge loudly, hands in her pockets and her feet apart, her chin stuck out. 'Just beastliness. Of course, we all know you're man-mad, but I didn't think you'd ever go as far as this. You must be off your head . . . carrying on like some tart in the back streets in Chesterbourne. My own sister . . . be jolly for me up at the Club, won't it?'

Mr Wither's face was a mask of frozen, disbelieving horror, his skin was patchy grey and purple. Twice he tried to say something. Then he sat down, trembling, shaking his head dazedly like an old dog that has been hit.

'How long has this been going on?' he almost whispered at last.

'Six months. I fell in love with him the first week he came here. You see, he's so beautiful, and in this house,' Tina's voice was hard and calm, but what exquisite relief there was in letting these warm words come from her lips; the truth, the lovely truth, bare as Venus! 'We're none of us beautiful, and the life we lead isn't beautiful either. He's like the God of Spring. No woman could resist that, you know, Father, especially a woman of my age who's been sexually starved for years—'

'Dammit, Tina, you needn't be disgusting,' cut in Madge.

'—and as I've trained myself to look at the truth in a way that none of you can, I thought it all out and decided it was better to risk having a baby—'

Faint cries and movements from the audience.

'—by Saxon and have the delight of sleeping with him than never sleep with anyone at all, or with someone old and ugly, like we're all getting to be in this house, except Viola.'

Viola, kneeling before the fire and staring at her sister-in-law in fascinated horror, jumped at the sound of her name. Was it Tina, saying these awful, shocking things?

'Oh, Tina,' sobbed Mrs Wither, 'you aren't going to have a – have a—'

'I don't know . . . yet,' said Tina grimly, and lit a cigarette.

'Everybody will know,' muttered Mr Wither, his hands spread on his kneecaps, staring at the floor. 'Everybody. Good God Almighty – you've been brought up decently, given everything you wanted – a good home, pocket money, all this art stuff and writing, free to go anywhere you like – and you go on as though you'd been dragged up – no thought for all we've – your mother and I—'

He was choking, he could not talk for his fury and disgust.

'. . . a boy I took in out of charity, off the streets practically, whose father drank himself to death, his mother taking in washing – I can't believe it, I can't believe that you're my daughter, you're like some girl off the streets – talking like that . . . about sex, like that . . . and that devil shouting it all over the neighbourhood, so that everyone'll know you've gone wrong with the chauffeur . . .' He got up and tramped up and down, shaking his fists over his head '. . . like any bitch—'

'Father,' moaned Mrs Wither.

'—off Piccadilly—'

Tina stood quietly by the mantelpiece, through the storm, staring at him. She felt that she had never seen her father before. The coarse raging words poured from his mouth as though he, too, felt a relief in letting them come. Perhaps I haven't been the only starved one, she thought.

Her own rage was dying. She had vented her anguish for her wasted youth by saying those warm naked words to her family, and now she felt quieter. She was even sorry that she had been so stagey, letting them think that matters were worse than they were.

Madge had started it, blurting at her like that, looking at her with suspicious sly eyes and *wanting* what people called The Worst to be true. Her family were all raw-minded about sex; their natures all had that one secret, sore place and when it was touched, they winced and ran mad. Only they themselves knew what old longings and crushed miseries her warm naked truths had let out of prison.

But millions of people were like that.

Poor wretched human beings, making their best of a bad job. Now she was calm, and a little sad and ashamed of herself. She said quietly, when her father had choked himself into a silence—

'I'm sorry, Father. I ought to have told you at once that we're married.'

'MARRIED?' shrieked everybody, looking more horrified than ever.

'Married? To a chauffeur?' shouted Mr Wither, making a run at his daughter as though he were going to hit her. 'It's a lie, you're lying.'

'No, Father. We were married at Stanton in September.'

'Then *you* must have known about it, you sly little beast.' Madge whirled on Viola. 'You were there.'

'I didn't – I didn't know a thing about it,' stammered Viola. 'She never told me a word.'

'You must have guessed, unless you're a born fool.'

'No, I didn't, and I'm not a born fool, either.'

'Then you're a liar, too, I expect,' said Madge contemptuously. 'Breeding will out. It's like dogs.'

'I'm as good as you are, even if I did work in a shop!' cried Viola hotly.

'Sh – sh—' Mrs Wither held out a distracted hand towards them. 'Tina, is it true?'

'Of course it's true,' impatiently. 'What would be the point of saying so, if it wasn't?'

'Then it's all right about the—'

'Oh, I'm not going to have a baby either, if that's what you mean,' said Tina crossly, stubbing out her cigarette like an early Noël Coward heroine. 'I just said that to shock you. You seemed to want shocking, so I supplied shocks.' She stared moodily into the fire.

'That settles it,' said Mr Wither, breathing heavily. 'You leave this house tonight, and you don't come back – er – you don't come back.'

'What a pity it isn't snowing.'

'What?'

'I said: it's a pity it isn't snowing. Oh well . . .' She straightened herself, turned, and gave one long curious stare round the drawing-room. If she ever saw it again, she would see it through the eyes of a wife, the wife of a young chauffeur keeping them both on three pounds a week. She herself had about seventy pounds.

'All right, Father. I'll go over and collect my husband' (in spite of fear, and wondering how Saxon would take this upheaval, what satisfaction there was in saying *my husband*! She saw disgust, struggling with some other feeling, on her sister's face as she said it). 'Goodbye, Mummy. We'll go to the Coptic, and I'll write you from there as soon as we know what we're going to do. Will you send my clothes on and my books?'

Mrs Wither could only sob. Mr Wither, after staring dazedly round at his womenfolk, lurched out of the room and shut the door. He had gone to his den.

'Oh, Tina,' said Viola eagerly, 'can I help you pack?'

'It would be more help if you'd look up a train for me.'

'I'm awfully sorry, Tina,' apologetically, 'I can't make out those time-table things.'

Tina, half-way up the stairs, looked back impatiently.

'Well, then, ring up the station.'

Fawcuss came slowly out of the door leading to the kitchen stairs, with no expression on her face, waddled across the hall, and began to pong the gong to announce dinner.

Viola went to the telephone and gave the station's number, looking uneasily at Fawcuss out of the corner of her eye. Did Fawcuss know?

Fawcuss, Annie and Cook knew All . . . except that Tina was married. They had heard every word that the Hermit had said, and while setting the table for dinner in the dining-room, Annie had gathered the rest from the loud voices in the drawing-room. Though they were three religious women, whose Vicar (a man with a long experience of village life) was always warning his congregation against the evils of gossip, Annie would have been an angel had she not repeated everything that she heard to Fawcuss and Cook when she got downstairs again and they would not have been human had they not listened.

All three were very shocked and truly grieved. Little Miss Tina! whom Annie had known since her pigtail days, to whom Cook had given dough to make dollies when she was a tiny thing, whom Fawcuss had first seen as a pretty child of ten . . . and Saxon, that nice respectable boy! It didn't seem hardly possible . . . only Miss Tina had said so herself . . . said awful things . . . that made you quite hot to overhear them. And her poor mother crying so, and Miss Madge sounding so hard and angry (she was a hard one, Miss Madge was) and the Master taking on so . . . and now Mrs Theodore was phoning about trains.

Surely the Master wasn't going to turn Miss Tina out on a night like this!

The world seemed coming to an end.

Tina came downstairs in her fur coat, carrying a big suitcase.

'There's an eight o'clock, gets in at nine-twenty,' said Viola. 'I say, can't I come with you?'

'No, thanks awfully. I'm going over to see if I can find Saxon. He's probably on his way back here; he must know there's been a frightful row.'

She paused at the front door, which Viola was holding open, and glanced back across the hall. Fawcuss's solid figure was just disappearing slowly through the door to the basement.

'Fawcuss. Just a minute,' called Tina, a shade nervously.

'Yes, Miss Tina?'

Fawcuss slowly turned and slowly came across the hall, her large pasty face all inquiry, suspicion and grief.

'I just wanted you to know that Saxon and I are married,' said Tina steadily. 'Will you tell the others for me, please? and say good-bye to them? I'm going to London, with Saxon, and I don't quite know when I shall be back.'

'Oh yes, miss . . . Madam, I should say. Well, what a surprise, I'm sure! Good-bye, Madam,' she took Tina's outstretched hand and shook it awkwardly, then added, in a sudden emotional rush, 'I'm so glad for you, Miss Tina, Madam, I should say. I always did say he was a nice respectable boy.'

She slowly retreated again, looking relieved, but also perhaps the least bit disappointed.

'Good-bye, Vi. Thanks awfully. Write to me sometimes, will you? I'm sorry I had to tell you such a lot of lies at Stanton, but it couldn't be helped. I don't know quite what we're going to do, of course; the first thing is for Saxon to get another job, and as soon as he does, I'll let Mother know. I expect Father'll cool down after a bit, but the truth is that I don't care much what he does, or Mother and Madge either. I know it sounds awful, but I never have liked them much.'

To Viola, who had liked her own father better than anyone she had ever known, it sounded worse than awful.

'I just want to get away, and start a normal life with Saxon, and never see this hole again,' Tina went on, staring out into the dark, misty drive. 'The last two months haven't been much fun, you know . . . Well. Good-bye.'

She kissed her hastily, and went quickly down the steps. Viola hurried after her.

'I say, Tina, are you all right for money? I've got seven pounds, if that's any use?'

'Oh no, thanks awfully, I've got about three myself, and Saxon'll have a little and I can get some from the bank in Town tomorrow. Good-bye. Run in, you'll catch cold.'

Viola watched her cross the damp drive by the light from the open door, a small fur-coated figure pulled sideways by the weight of the suitcase. When she saw the beam of Tina's torch flash into the dark wood, she slowly shut the door.

# CHAPTER XXI

Tina went down into the little valley, and the trees closed behind her.

The path was slippery with fog-damp and it was difficult to carry the case, so heavy, in one hand and to poise the torch, so light, steadily in the other. Once or twice she slithered, and only got her balance by leaning against the wet, ridged black bole of an oak. She could see nothing but tree-trunks and slowly writhing mist, but she had known this path all her life, and soon she came to the stream and picked her way across. A fire glowed inside the Hermit's shack. Surely he doesn't sleep down here on nights like this, she thought, vaguely.

She began to climb the hill on the other side, staring steadily at the path under the torch-beam, for no landscape is so wildly confusing as a wood filled with mist, even if the ground be familiar to the traveller, and on this side the path was fainter.

She felt frightened and sad. All her anger had gone. She had cast off her family (well, they had cast her off, actually, but it came to the same thing), the house where she had been born, all the well-known framework of her life, and was going to trust herself to a stranger. That was what Saxon seemed to her as she climbed, drawing the chill, winter-tasting mist into her throat. Their relationship had always been romantic and secret, leading her to compare her husband to young wolves and spring gods, but suddenly these comparisons seemed ridiculous to her, and Saxon just a pleasant, friendly young man whom she took great pleasure in kissing and whom she hoped was going to come up to scratch in the present unpleasant situation.

Her meetings with him since their return from Stanton had also been romantic, taking place in damp autumnal dells and remote teashops on the outskirts of Chesterbourne but both he and she had stopped feeling that they were romantic. It was a confounded nuisance to have to lurk around like someone in an Eberhart thriller when you had the legal right to sit by the fire calling bits to each other out of the books you were reading and sucking toffee.

The feeling between Tina and Saxon, in short, had changed from romantic love to married love.

(It would take too long to argue, and explain, and illustrate the difference. Everybody knows there is one. One love is as worthy of support as the other. It just depends which you prefer.)

The change happened during the holiday at Stanton, and it happened while they were lovers but before they were married. Saxon it was who had first discovered that the natural bond for this new feeling was marriage. He had proposed to Tina and been accepted.

He had wanted to tell Mr Wither at once, for he disliked making love in damp leaves, calling his wife Miss Tina in public, and behaving like a stealthy seducer when he was in fact a respectably married man; but Tina had got, on their return to Sible Pelden, into what used to be known as a State; had dithered weakly, putting off and putting off the day when her family should be told, and even having little quarrels with Saxon about the delay. She had wanted him to get a new job, in London, before telling her father that they were married. She so hated scenes, she hated and dreaded them, and had not wanted the first weeks of her wifehood spoilt by a hideous row with Mr Wither. She had, in fact, been nervous, pettish and thoroughly foolish about the affair. She now saw this plainly, and told herself that she was glad the bomb had burst, the scene was over, and she and Saxon free to take up the burdens and dignity of the married state.

Nevertheless, as she stumbled along the greasy path towards a light shining among the trees, she could not feel relieved and excited. She could only feel extremely depressed. Would Saxon be the same friend and lover now that the last shreds of Romance had blown away, and he had to keep her in corselets and mutton chops?

She put the suitcase down, rubbed her aching arm for a minute, then knocked.

After a little while the door was opened by Mrs Caker, an old jacket huddled over her shoulders, who stared down at Tina in astonishment.

'Good evening, Mrs Caker,' began Tina, remembering how she used to be especially polite when she was a little girl to Mrs Caker when she brought home the maids' washing, because *I hear the Cakers have been having a hard time of it lately.*

'Good evenin'.'

Her gaze wandered sullenly and enviously over the fur coat, its surface dark-pointed with moisture from the mist, but there was a gleam of excitement in her eyes, as well. Mrs Caker enjoyed nothing more than a bit of excitement; she had just had some, and she was now pretty sure that she was going to have some more.

'Is Saxon in?' pursued Tina resolutely, looking up out of big dark eyes in a white, drawn face.

'Nay, he run out a while since. Us had a bit o' trouble to tell yer the truth, Miss Wither. He run down the wood. Count yer might have seen him; 'twasn't long.'

Tina shook her head.

'I didn't. Do you mind if I come in for a little, Mrs Caker, and wait? I must speak to Saxon.'

'O' course yer can.'

She moved aside and opened the door wider, the last trace of sullenness gone. 'Come in an' sit down. Place is all slumocky – ye mustn't mind that. I been washing all day – as per usual. Here . . .' sweeping a pile of dried clothes off the couch, 'sit down and make yerself at home.'

She shut the door, and the stuffy, cottagey smell of old stuffs, boiling clothes, and fresh beer, mingled with dust, closed round Tina, who sat on the edge of the sofa with her small muddy shoes together trying not to stare round at Saxon's home. It was even worse than she had feared. Every moment she felt more alarmed and depressed, more cut off from her old life and shrinking from the new.

But in spite of the squalid room, and the smell, and her mother-in-law's slatternliness, she could feel Mrs Caker's charm. She was so good-natured; an easy warmth was shown in her every movement. She would never disapprove, or condemn, or let anyone die gently of starvation because it was the proper thing to do. Live and let live would be her motto. Good heavens, I like her, thought Tina drearily. I suppose that's just as well.

'Mrs Caker,' she said, looking up at the tall slut leaning against the mantelpiece and staring down at her hat and coat with the liveliest interest, 'you must think it very funny, my coming here like this, and asking for Saxon, but—'

'I know you and maye Saxon's sweet one on t'other – you know – crazy about each other,' interrupted her mother-in-law with an embarrassed, eager smile. 'Count everybody round about here knows that, Miss Wither. Village people's proper owd gossips.' She laughed.

'Do they?' said Tina, discomfited. 'Oh ... well, that doesn't matter now. You see, we're married.'

'Married?' Mrs Caker brought out the word in an immensely long, sweet Essex whine, at the same time flinging up her shapely, reddened hands and taking a couple of steps backwards as though blown by the news, her mouth wide open and her eyes too. '*Married*, are 'ee? Cor, he niver said nothin' about it ter maye, proper cunnin' l'il owd toad he is! Married? In church, were 'ee? Proper married?'

'Well, not in church,' confessed Tina, smiling; there certainly was a taking, a charming, quality in Saxon's mother. 'In a registry office at Stanton, in September. Saxon came there for his holiday, you know, so that we could be there together.'

'Nay, I don't know,' protested Mrs Caker. 'Niver told maye a word, he didn't. So that were it!'

'And now the Herm— now it's come out that we're married and my father's rather upset about it,' went on Tina steadily, blushing as she approached the social delicacies of the situation, 'so I'm going away from home for a bit—'

'Just ter gie him time ter get over it, like,' said Mrs Caker, nodding sympathetically. 'Ah, they do take on so, the old 'uns, don't they? It's nateral, though, ain't it? Yer Dad don't like yer marryin' a shuvver, is that it?' She sat down in her favourite position at the table, her chin in her hands. 'Seems queer ter maye, too. But he's a proper smart boye, Saxon is; he'll make good, as they say. P'raps yer Dad'll git over ut. And we're not so low as some. Mr Caker had his own mill, yer know . . .'

Her indolent, sweetly whining voice went on, telling the silent listener about the mighty mill-wheel with moss and 'toddy blue flowers' growing over it, about her old father's pony trap, and Cis's death, while Tina stared round the ugly untidy little room, brightly lit by one unshaded globe, and felt utterly lonely and desolate, like a traveller lost among strange tribes, far from his home and those who talk his own language.

As she gazed slowly about her, keeping her head down and the brim of her hat lowered so that Mrs Caker should not notice what she was doing, she caught a gleam of dingy red in a half-open cupboard.

The rubbish of years was stuffed in there; old newspapers, and cinema papers, magazines, dirty torn clothes, a scorched ironing blanket and a roll of dirty rope; but the glow of red that caught, and then held her glance in a rapt, disbelieving stare, came from what was left of a sleeveless, stained and ravelled old red jersey.

'Here's Saxon.' Mrs Caker stood up, looking mischievous, as the door opened violently, and Saxon, hatless, pale and untidy, stood staring at his mother and his wife. He was breathing as though he had been running.

'I've been over to get you,' he said to Tina at last. 'Then when I found you'd gone, I tried to see your father. But he wasn't having any. They told me you'd come over here.'

'I've been here about twenty minutes. I'm sorry you've had all that for nothing. I told Mother we'd probably go to London and I'd write her from there. There's a train at eight. That's best, don't you think?'

'I reckon it is. Crikey, this's been a nice old show-up, this has. Never mind; it'll all come out in the wash, as Mother would say,' glancing in a little embarrassment from one to the other. 'You two been making friends? That's right. Mum, put the kettle on; Tina'd like a cup, I expect. I'll go up and get me things.'

He seemed relieved. As he ran up the stairs he called, 'You told her about us, Tina?'

Her own name sounded strange to Tina, sounding through the cluttered dismal little room in a young man's full, self-important voice.

'Aye, she told maye,' shouted Mrs Caker, winking at Tina. 'That's a nice Christmas box, that is. Proper Walton oyster, you are.' She went into the kitchen to put the kettle on again.

Neither she nor Saxon had any anger left about their recent quarrel; Mrs Caker's was too day-by-dayish a nature to brood, and Saxon had other things just now to think about. Tina sat on the sofa listening to the packing and, tea-making, and felt miserable. She would have liked to go upstairs and see Saxon's room, but she did not, because she knew that he would not want her to; he was very sensitive about the poverty and ugliness of his home.

Presently he came down again, carrying a cheap suitcase. He dumped it on the floor, stared at it fiercely, then suddenly looked up and gave her such a delightful smile that her spirits rose to meet it.

'And that's that,' said Saxon. 'Now how about this cup of tea?'

There was just time for the tea before they caught the quarter-past seven bus at the Green Lion, and they gulped it standing up, while Mrs Caker sat at the table sipping hers, and a voice in the corner said that Miss Rita Lambolle would now talk to them about Persian Music while Miss Deirdre Macdonnell would illustrate the talk with songs to the zither.

'Oh no she won't,' said Saxon, turning the switch. 'Mum, here's ten bob. I'll begin sending you regularly again when I've got another job. Can you manage?'

'Seems I'll have to,' winking again at Tina. 'Here, hi, what about the payments on the wireless?'

'I'd like to settle that right up for you, if I may,' said Tina. 'How much is it?'

'Well, that's proper kind of 'ee, I will say. He's got the bills for it put away somewhere, haven't 'ee?'

Saxon tapped his overcoat pocket, looking steadily at Tina over the top of his cup. He was happy, excited and confident. At last they were getting away! out of this one-horse place that he had always wanted to 'show'. Suddenly he hated Sible Pelden, with all its Fatbottoms in it, and did not care if he never 'showed' them, nor saw them again. His boyish ambition to dazzle the disapproving neighbours had died since his marriage. Kid's nonsense, that had been. His business now was to get a job, and make a home for Tina, and show her —— family that he was some good. And he would, too.

So the ambition quietly took another shape; and he did not notice that it had.

Awkward good-byes were said, then Tina and Saxon hurried off into the cold foggy night, while Mrs Caker stood at the door and stared after them with a jeering yet wistful look. She had never had a fur coat, and she never would.

As they waited for the bus under the sickly lights of the Green Lion, where the time-tables hung against the creamy old weather-boarding, Saxon jerked his head at the pub and said:

'I'd take you in to have one, only he's in there, the old swine.'

'Who – the Hermit? (I don't want one, thanks, I'm quite warm, and I should hate being stared at; I always think the barman, or whoever he is in there, looks so cross).'

'That was young Heyrick, up at Springs', gave me a hand with the old devil,' he went on. 'Said he tried something on with his girl, Gladys Davies, down in the wood. So Heyrick was quite ready to beat him up. She's a parlour-maid up at Springs', Gladys Davies.'

*You ought to have married a Gladys Davies*, thought Tina. *I don't think I'm going to be any good to you.* But she swallowed the lump in her throat, and said nothing.

He slipped his arm through her fur-clad one and peered round into her face.

'Cheer up. Everything'll be fine. You see.'

Tina did not feel that everything would be fine. However, she answered sensibly:

'Oh yes, I think we shall be all right. I don't think you'll have much difficulty in getting a job, and I think Father'll come round, too—'

'We're not going to sponge on him,' sharply.

'No, I know, my dear, but it will be much pleasanter if we don't keep up a stupid feud with the family. And I can get a job, too, perhaps.'

'Oh no you don't. Not while I can work.'

He picked up the suitcases. The lights of the bus were coming up steadily through the mist.

'But, Saxon, that's so . . . old-fashioned.'

'You're telling me. It may be prehistoric; it's right. Up you go.'

Tina, sitting dazedly beside him in the bus, understood the feelings of the late Baron Frankenstein.

Her dear monster had certainly taken charge of her affairs. Never having had a job, she had thought that a job might be 'rather fun', as well as being useful. But Saxon had sat on that. Oh well, housekeeping (and she had never housekept, either) might be rather fun, too. In short, her spirits were calmed and cheered by his masterfulness.

And waking in the night in the clock-ticking silence of their neat, impersonal bedroom at the Hotel Coptic in Bloomsbury, with tears on her cheeks from some vague, vast sorrow already receding rapidly into the dream world whence it had come, Tina found with exquisite relief her husband lying quietly beside her, and fell peacefully asleep again.

There had been one: and now there were two: and that (as they say) made all the difference.


Mr Gideon Spurrey, that old acquaintance of Mr Wither's, whom we met early in the story, sat at the window of his house in Buckingham Square, feeling annoyed because his chauffeur, Holt, was dead.

Not only was Holt dead, but before he died he had been ill for a

271

month, and put Mr Spurrey to a lot of trouble and inconvenience. He had put Mr Spurrey to some expense, too, but Mr Spurrey did not mind that, for he was not in the least mean. What he minded was Holt dying like that, and leaving Mr Spurrey at the mercy of strangers.

Holt had been with Mr Spurrey for nearly eighteen years, and knew his ways. Mr Spurrey was used to Holt, and he had mistrusted the fellow they sent to take Holt's place when Holt first got ill; had sent him back again after a day's trial. There was nothing the matter with him except that he was not Holt, but Mr Spurrey was fidgeted by that fact as he sat in his car and decided that he could not go on being fidgeted.

And now Holt was dead and Mr Spurrey would have to spend the morning drafting an advertisement for *The Times* instead of going off to his club, as he usually did every morning.

The room in which he sat was lofty yet dark; heavy curtains of tan velvet looped across the windows, with inner ones of dark creamy net, shut out most of the white glare thrown into the study by the mighty bulk of Buckingham Court, the new flats that were going up opposite Mr Spurrey's residence, on the site of Buckingham House. The walls were covered with stamped tan leather and the ceiling was broken by heavy beams, varnished the same bilious shade, the heavy chairs wore a faded blue and tan tapestry copied from a Jacobean design, the carpet was a Turkey. The place smelled of cigar smoke, and breathed the oppressive atmosphere that only age, wealth and the daily performance of an unchanging domestic ritual can create. The room, the faint scent of tobacco, and Mr Spurrey sitting at the writing table and staring irritably out at the white block of flats, seemed to have been there for ever. *Wanted* (thought Mr Spurrey, staring up at the flats out of his pale grey parroty eyes), *a reliable, respectable, experienced chauffeur, must understand how to drive and* . . .

No. Doesn't sound right, somehow.

*Wanted* . . .

The door opened and the butler came in.

'What is it?' demanded Mr Spurrey, not looking round. Though all his five senses were on the verge of crumbling, they were enjoying an Indian summer, and he was proud of showing Cotton that he could hear him come into the room though his back was to the door. Mr Spurrey was seventy-six, and for the last few weeks had been telling anyone who would listen to him that he had never felt better in his life.

'There's a young man to see you, sir. Name of Caker.'

'Never heard of him,' said Mr Spurrey with satisfaction, still not looking round. 'What's he want? Selling something, eh?'

'He said it was about a Post, sir.'

'A Post? What does he mean? Send him away, Cotton; I'm busy.'

'I took it he might mean the post left vacant by Mr Holt's death, sir.'

'Why didn't you say so at first? I'll see him. Here, wait a bit, Cotton! How did he come to know I want a chauffeur, eh? More in this than meets the eye. You been gossiping, eh?'

'No, sir. I have not mentioned Mr Holt's death outside my own circle, sir. I could not say how he comes to know, sir, I'm sure.'

'Oh. What's he like, eh?'

'He seems respectable enough, sir. Rather a smart young fellow, I should say. A good appearance, sir.'

'All right, send him up.'

A minute later there walked into the room that smart young fellow who had driven Mr Spurrey at the Withers' last summer.

'Hey, so it's you, is it?' cried Mr Spurrey, staring at Saxon, who crossed the room with deliberation and stood, hat in hand, one knee just flexed, staring respectfully yet calmly down at him. 'But your name isn't Caker, no, that wasn't the name your master told me. Saxby, was it? What d'ye want to change your name for, eh? More in this than meets the eye.'

'Saxon's my first name, sir. Mr Wither always called me by my first name.'

'I see. So you've left Mr Wither, have you? What d'ye want to leave him for, eh? No trouble, I hope?' asked Mr Spurrey eagerly, the parroty ones glinting in his yellowish round face as he stared up at Saxon, his little lips primmed together.

'Well, yes, sir. I suppose you might call it that. The fact is, I married Miss Wither, sir. Miss Tina.'

'*Married* her?' exclaimed Mr Spurrey, his face expressing the strongest interest and amazement. 'Old Wither's gel? What, married her, d'ye mean?'

'Yes, sir. She's up here with me now, sir. In Town.'

'Does old Wither know? But of course he does . . . that was why ye left, eh?'

'Yes, sir.'

'Upset, was he, eh?' demanded Mr Spurrey, with a glance of the purest spiteful pleasure. 'Cut up rough, eh?' He bent forward and added, cunningly, 'Took it hard I'm sure. I dare say he did. Don't want to say anything against W., you know, one of my oldest friends, but he's very narrow-minded, eh? Stuffy. Old-fashioned – Victorian. Married her, eh? Well, well. Married old Wither's gel. Bless me.' And Mr Spurrey's face suddenly split up into hundreds of tiny wrinkles, and for quite a minute he shook silently in a fit of malicious laughter, while his round pale eyes stared out glassily from between rolls of yellow fat in a disconcerting way and his little lips compressed themselves more tightly than ever.

Saxon watched him with a respectful, serious expression. Old T – thought Saxon. Old B.

At last Mr Spurrey bent forward and said in a low spluttery voice, his eyes watering with laughter:

'Dare say she was glad enough to get you, eh?'

And off he went again, watching Saxon out of the corner of one eye.

The young man smiled demurely, staring down at the hat he held, but did not answer. At the back of his mind there was a thought, that Tina probably had been glad to get him. So there was no reason why he should mind what Mr Spurrey said; and he did not. As man to man, they had their private joke, and Tina need never know.

'And you haven't much money, I suppose, eh?' pursued Mr Spurrey. Saxon shook his head. Mr Spurrey bent forward once more and lowered his voice:

'She . . . not in the family way, eh? know what I mean?'

'Not yet, sir,' coolly.

Mr Spurrey liked this. He had another fit; then he lit a cigar and became serious.

'How did you come to know I wanted a chauffeur, eh?' he said suspiciously, his eyes fixed steadily on Saxon's face. Mr Spurrey was a malicious old bore, but he was not a fool, and people never imposed upon him; had they been able to, he might have been more popular.

'I didn't know it, sir. But you're the only person in London who's seen me drive, so I came to you because I thought perhaps you might know of someone who wanted somebody, and recommend me.'

'Your wife tell you to come, eh?'

'No, sir. In fact, she was rather against it.'

'I see. Why was that?'

'Well, sir, she thought it might be rather awkward, you see; you might have thought it right to . . . well, to see the situation from Mr Wither's point of view, sir, you see, and not give me your name as a reference.'

'But you didn't think I should, eh?'

'Well, sir, I thought that if I came to you just as a chauffeur, and asked you to recommend me, you would hardly think it necessary to say I was a bad driver just because I occasionally married my employer's daughter.'

'Occasionally "married" your employer's daughter, eh? That's good,' and Mr Spurrey went off again. 'Thinking of doing it again, eh, when you get one with a bit more money?'

Saxon smiled, trying to put into the smile that youthful cynicism and heartless lechery that Mr Spurrey evidently wished to see. Mr Spurrey was enjoying himself by proxy, and Saxon knew it.

'Well, as it happens, I want one myself,' went on the old man. 'My last man, Holt, been with me sixteen years, no, eighteen, nearly eighteen, died last week,' said Mr Spurrey indignantly. 'Went off like *that*,' snapping dry yellow fingers that smelt of cigars. 'No warning. He was getting better, in fact. And that wasn't all . . .'

Saxon had to listen for five minutes while Mr Spurrey related just how inconvenient Holt's illness and death had been.

But at last:

'. . . and I don't see any reason why you shouldn't come to me, hey? What'd old W. give you?'

'Two pounds a week, sir . . . and I did the garden, too, for that.'

'Oh, there's no garden here, no garden or anything of that sort here,' said Mr Spurrey hastily, as though Saxon were pining for rockeries and montbretia. 'Two pounds eh? Not much, is it? Don't want to say anything against W., of course, old friend of mine – but he's pretty near, eh? Close isn't the word. Now I'll give you three-fifteen (that's fifteen shillings more than Holt had, but you're a married man, hee! hee!) and there's your quarters, too. Down the back,' jerking his head. 'Two rooms and a kitchen. Use the servants' bath.'

'Live in, do you mean, sir?'

'Why not? Holt did; made himself very comfortable there. Rent free. Bring old W.'s girl, too, of course. Plenty of room for a double bed,' and Mr Spurrey had another of those fits which Saxon was beginning to find irritating.

'Mind you,' added Mr Spurrey, 'I'd better not know anything about your being married to old W.'s gel, eh? Don't want to get mixed up in any quarrels, no, no, don't want anything of that sort. She'd better keep out of my way, don't you agree? No ill-feeling. Just prudent.'

'Perhaps that would be best, sir.'

Saxon felt that Tina would not be at all sorry to keep out of Mr Spurrey's way.

It was then arranged that he and Tina should move into their new quarters that afternoon and that he would start work tomorrow at nine o'clock. He fluently assured Mr Spurrey that he could drive a Rolls, and knew all about Rollses. This was not true, but Saxon knew that he could soon make it true.

So he said good morning to Mr Spurrey, and hurried away to Tina, who was sitting rather forlornly in an expensive snack-bar in the little market round the corner, and told her coolly that he had a job. Tina wished that the job had been with anyone except Mr Spurrey, but she was too wise to spoil Saxon's satisfaction by saying so: and five minutes later he himself, cautiously prowling round this new development like a handsome tom-cat, observed that it was rather a nuisance its being Mr Spurrey, but a job was a job, and he seemed a spiteful devil who enjoyed doing his old friend W. in the eye and would probably keep on him, Saxon, just out of cussedness.

'Did you see the rooms?' asked Tina casually.

She still felt bewildered, and as though she were living in a dream. Even the table at which they sat, and Saxon's handsome face, were slightly unreal. But she knew that this was an after-effect of nervous strain, so she did not let it worry her, and Saxon's eagerness, affection and reliability shone steadily through the dream and comforted her.

'No. Let's eat; and we can go round after lunch. There'll be plenty to do this afternoon.'

*We'll have to live with the servants*, thought Tina. Well, this is life, my girl. You wanted it; and you've got it.

But the rooms turned out to be a little house in themselves, separated from the back of the big house by a large paved courtyard. They were small, but the sun came into them and they had been redecorated only last year. The furniture was plain and worn, but it could be made pretty with fresh coverings and paint; and after she had opened the windows and stared down into the dirty but picturesque mews below, Tina's spirits suddenly rose; she kissed Saxon, who looked amused, and decided that she liked their first home.

A narrow staircase led down into the garage, where, in a dusk glimmering with the quiet shine of enamel, the wink of chromium, lived the great urbane god to which Saxon was priest. He went down at once to prowl about in the temple.

The garage was cold, clean and silent. All was arranged; there was even a glory-hole for the cleaning rags. The petrol, the oil, the tools, all the complex implements required by an expensive machine, were ranged in cleanly order. He knew his job, thought Saxon, squatting down to look at the underneath of the Rolls, and mentally saluting the dead Holt as a good workman.

277

Mr Spurrey, meanwhile, set forth upon the routine of his day with a feeling of relief, even of pleasure. He had a smart new chauffeur; an up-to-date, go-ahead young fellow, not deaf, not short-sighted and rheumatic, like Holt was getting to be when he died. And that was a good joke on old W., too, giving a job to the chap who had run off with his gel. It was not Mr Spurrey's fault, was it, that he happened to want a new chauffeur, and that the one, the perfectly satisfactory one, who happened to come along, was married to old W.'s gel? Surely old W. would not expect Mr Spurrey to turn down a smart, up-to-date young fellow just because he was married to old W.'s gel? That would not be reasonable. Besides, he enjoyed scoring off old W., stuffy old chap, Victorian, narrow-minded. Why, all kinds of people married their chauffeurs and footmen nowadays, wasn't there that German princess? and nobody minded any more. Must move with the times. Gel was lucky to get a chap like that. Quite natural, too; gel getting a bit long in the tooth, and a nice-looking young fellow like that comes along ... Old W. ought to have seen what was coming. Mr Spurrey would, in his place. And Mr Spurrey, having a fit, sat down in the calm of the club writing-room to write a letter to Mr Wither, casually mentioning that Holt was dead and that he had a new chauffeur, and how were things with Mr Wither? How was Mrs Wither, and the girls? Shaking silently, Mr Spurrey bent over the writing table.

'Saxon.'

'What's the grief?'

Saxon, usually so careful with his English, had a weakness for American. That mocking, curt language, flinging subtle undertones from its pebbly phrases, charmed him as music charms a seal.

'Come up and take these measurements for me, will you? I'm usually good with windows, but my mind won't function this morning.'

'What for?'

'Curtains. These are awful. I'm just going over to Selfridges to get some spotted net ... and the kettle leaks ... and there's no tin-opener.'

Pause.

'*Saxon.*'

'Coming.'

'Do hurry! I've got masses to do.'

'All right; but I must just figure this out; it's interesting.'

Left, mutually figuring.

# CHAPTER XXII

Mr Wither was very, very angry, shocked and disappointed with his daughter, but he had not meant her to go off at once like that.

His 'You leave this house tonight' had met her passionate longing to escape from The Eagles; and she had rushed off sooner than he had meant her to. In fact, he had been so upset that he had scarcely known what he was saying, and when Mrs Wither ventured into his den about eight o'clock with a glass of port and a biscuit on a tray (the Withers met all crises with biscuits, not sandwiches) he was more upset than ever to hear that Tina had gone.

There were a thousand matters to discuss and plan. Everything possible must now be done to make the situation seem as natural as possible: and Tina, by flying off into the night with a suitcase, had made it seem as unnatural as it could be. Fifty years ago, her flight would have been conventional; now, even to Mr Wither, it seemed melodramatic.

'But you told her to go, dear,' said poor Mrs Wither, bewildered.

'You oughtn't to have let her,' was all he would say. 'It'll be all over the neighbourhood that I turned her out.'

He sat staring into the black grate, waving the port away every time Mrs Wither wafted it towards him and looking so ill, with such frozen despair on his purple old face, that Mrs Wither forgot her own grief in her attempts to get him upstairs with a hot-water bottle and two aspirins. She finally did so; and sat beside his bed until he fell asleep.

Then she came down again to the drawing-room, where Madge sat staring sullenly into the fire with pink, swollen eyelids, and they talked until after midnight. Madge would hear no defence of Tina, whom she had always despised. Tina had behaved like a street-girl, disgraced her family, and let down her class. Madge asked what Colonel Phillips would say, and – and Hugh, when his mother wrote to him about it, in India? Everybody would say that if that was the sort of thing the Wither girls did, the whole family must be a bit odd. This was the second thing of this sort that had happened to the family in less than three years; first Teddy, marrying that common little beast, and now Tina. Other families didn't have that sort of thing happening to them, why should the Withers?

Mrs Wither had no answer.

Viola had long since crept up to bed, very unhappy and desolate. Her only friend at The Eagles had gone, and she was suspected of having helped the lovers. Victor did not love her, and he was going to marry someone else. Oh, Dad, darling Dad, I wish you weren't dead. Soon she was crying into the pillow in the dark bedroom, while outside a suddenly awakened wind swept round the house. After a little while she prayed, a thing that she never did unless she wanted something. In the middle of a passionate prayer to God to make everything less rotten, it occurred to her that God must find it rather the limit only being prayed to when you wanted something, so she stopped, started over again, told Him that she was sorry she only prayed to Him when she wanted something, and asked if He would kindly bless everybody, as this seemed the most likely way of settling everybody's troubles and everybody had so many. Comforted, she went to sleep.

Now the winter closed upon Sible Pelden, and a frozen dreary season seemed to have closed, too, upon the people in The Eagles. The days grew shorter and shorter, grey and still without a gleam of sun or swept by gales of freezing rain. For weeks the wind whined round the house like a miserable old dog. From any window, the black trees could be seen fighting against a low, hurrying grey sky, the tall beeches moving slowly and gracefully along their length, the stockier oaks wildly tossing their top branches. The piercing wind tore over the ground, flattening the withered hair of the terrified grass and chilling human flesh to the bone. Outside the house, days and days of such weather passed, and inside the big, dark, quiet rooms sulky little fires burned, and pampas grass and branches of leaves, mummified by Mrs Wither, stood in the vases instead of flowers. Everywhere there were knife-like draughts that gave Viola colds in her head and set up lumbago, neuralgia and kidney troubles in the five older people.

The day after Tina went, Mr and Mrs Wither had a long talk, and decided that their relatives must be told the truth about her marriage, but that friends and acquaintances must be informed that it had been with the consent of her parents, though it had come to them as a surprise, and (naturally) as a slight shock. But girls were so unconventional nowadays (and so self-willed, I shall say, promised Mrs Wither, smiling sourly) that they felt if they did not give their consent, the young people might get married without it!! They were at present staying in London with some friends of Tina's. Their plans were uncertain.

Accordingly, this is what Mrs Wither (Mr Wither standing a little apart in the background, as though under a cloud of helpless paternal shame) told Lady Dovewood when she met her one day in the Free Library in Chesterbourne. (Lady Dovewood had gone there to see if it was true that all the unemployed men in the town used it as a Club. It was true. So Lady Dovewood proposed to do something about it.) Lady Dovewood said the proper things about Tina's naughty, wilful escapade, and when she got home she said to her husband, 'Aubrey, you remember the Wither gairl, the younger one, thin and arty, well, she *has* run off with the chauffeur, just as I always said she would. Just like poor Kitty's gairl. I knew she would. I saw it coming. Now don't say I never told you, because I did.'

Mrs Parsham and Mrs Phillips also said the proper things about Tina, agreeing with Mrs Wither when she stammered that Saxon was such a nice respe— such a nice boy and so devoted to Tina, and helping her to smooth the situation as much as was possible, for they were sorry for the poor woman. They were all the sorrier (so they said) because for years they had been saying what a dreadfully dull life the Withers led, quite unnecessary with all that money, and wondering how the daughters stood it, in these days when all the young people had their 'jobs'. The poor, stupid Withers! they had brought it on themselves by the stifling life they had compelled their children to live; son marries a shopgirl, daughter marries a chauffeur. Now there was only the stout one left. What would the stout one do? Sympathetic but hopeful, Sible Pelden waited.

But Madge did nothing, except go for long tramps in the east wind with Polo, now a fine young dog, rushing after leaves some yards ahead of her. Hugh Phillips's regiment was at last ordered to Waziristan. His next letter to his mother would be written on active service. His young wife and the baby, Ned, would of course stay down country, in safety. 'Polo. Come here,' called Madge, and fondled his ears; the cruel wind made her eyes water and she rubbed them boyishly with her big fists.

The masses in Sible Pelden, however, were not taken in by what Mrs Wither chose to say in the village shop, and to the maids at The Eagles, because they knew the truth. The Hermit had seen to that. He had told everybody in the Green Lion – the cross-roads louts, now grown to manhood, the realist barman, the proprietor Mr Fisher, and Mrs Fisher, and the red-haired postman who was sweet on Davies up at Springs' – that this affair between Saxon and Tina had been going on ever since the summer, and when it was found out by old Shak-per-Swaw and his missus, there hadn't half been a bull-and-cow up The Eagles. He'd been there, and heard it all. Never mind why. On business.

No one was surprised to hear that Saxon and Tina had been carrying on ever since the summer. People had been using their eyes, putting two and two together, comparing notes. Besides, everyone had expected it. The first person who had seen Tina having a driving lesson in the summer had gone home to his wife and said that if something didn't happen there, his name wasn't what it was.

The Withers naturally found the gossip in the village almost the most unpleasant part of their misfortune. Nothing was said directly to them, but they could imagine what was said behind their backs, and once Mr Wither, taking his constitutional on one of the few bright days in December, encountered the Hermit, who to his horror inquired in a shout if he were a grandad yet?

Then there was the problem of Mrs Caker. The Withers felt that something should be done about Mrs Caker, but they did not know what. So they did nothing, except try not to meet Mrs Caker accidentally when they went out. As Mrs Caker did not at all want to meet any of them, they were successful. Mrs Caker was also suffering a little from village gossip; she knew that everyone must be saying it was awful for them up The Eagles to have their daughter married to a boy whose mother took in washing and had got a tramp living in the house. Mrs Caker had never been a naturally respectable woman; but she had once had a love of pretty clothes and gaiety and been the wife of a comfortably-off man, and she could now feel how low she had fallen. So she kept out of the village as much as possible, and when the Hermit came home and told her what people had been saying, she threw water over him, and cried. He would then hit her, and she would hit him but not so efficiently and try to shut him out of the house. Then the Hermit would try to kick the door down and the realist-barman at the Green Lion would remark, 'They're at it again,' in a tone that somehow illuminated the whole problem of the sexes.

Fawcuss, Annie and Cook had to put up with what they described as 'impertinence' from their fellow churchgoers; and all the Wither cousins, including one called Agnes Grice whose hobby was managing other people's affairs, wrote long incoherent letters saying that what had happened was no more than what they had always supposed would happen to Christina ever since she went to that art school, adding that Mr and Mrs Wither must be sure to take care of themselves in this *dreadful weather*, as it would never do to have *illness* added to everything else.

Mr Wither took the disaster very hard. He mentioned Tina no more in public, except when hypocritically backing up Mrs Wither, and when she was mentioned at home, he looked down his nose and was silent. But he allowed Mrs Wither to answer her weekly letters, and gave permission to Viola to send Tina's books, a few pictures of which she was fond that had hung in her bedroom, and the rest of her clothes, to an address in London, care of a Mrs Baumer.

All letters were also to be sent to this Mrs Baumer, and at first the family at The Eagles wondered who she was, but Tina's second letter from Town explained that she was Betti Solomon, who was at school with Tina, and had married David Baumer, the painter. They had three beautiful kids, and were great fun. The Baumers, it appeared, were friends of Mr and Mrs Saxon Caker; Tina had met Betti one day, shopping in Selfridges, and Betti had asked her to come to a party and bring her husband. Now the Cakers went round there a good deal, and the Baumer boys enjoyed messing about with Saxon in the garage. Yes, Saxon had a job, and he and Tina were living over the garage in a mews, but it would be more convenient if letters were sent care of Mrs Baumer; Tina did not say why.

Tina's letters, as the winter went on, were cheerful; nay, they were gay; they were occasionally starred by a Name, for the Baumers knew many minor celebrities, and their parties were comparatively famous even in a party-crazy age. Tina and Saxon went to the Baumer parties and enjoyed them very much. Some colour from this unusual but interesting and satisfying life naturally got into the letters home, and made The Eagles, shut in the gloom of a country winter, seem more dismal than ever.

Writers and painters, Jews and mews; it all sounded very bad indeed to Mr and Mrs Wither and Madge; but Viola believed only half of it, for she had, after long pondering and putting twos together, decided that the business about Adrian Lacey had all been fibs, invented by Tina so that she could be with Saxon, and in future Viola was going to be very careful about old school friends of Tina's.

Mrs Wither thought that Tina was not being punished as she should have been. Impudent, ungrateful Saxon, ungrateful, unnatural Tina! The text about the green bay-tree went through Mrs Wither's mind. All the same, she could not help wishing very much to see Tina's little home, her first married home! even if it was in a mews. It sounded so quaint; Tina had painted the door bright blue! How Mrs Wither would have enjoyed going up to Town 'to see my married daughter', even if that daughter was married to a chauffeur;

and helping to choose curtains and china! But Mr Wither got so upset if she even hinted at going to see Tina that she did not dare to.

It was too bad, the way her children always got married to queer people, in an underhand, sudden sort of way. Just as though their feelings had suddenly got too much for them, thought Mrs Wither. Why couldn't they get married in a nice ordinary way, with engagements, and time to write to cousins living in Jamaica? And Mrs Wither had a little sniffle over Tina's last letter.

The scandal reached the Springs in London some five weeks after it happened, through Bill Courtney (it may be remembered that Bill was in love with Phyllis and had taken her home on the night of the Infirmary Ball) who met his beloved by delightful chance at a cocktail party. Phyllis, amused, passed the news on to the Springs. Mrs Spring could not blame anyone for running away from a house where they gave parties like that one in the summer, even if it was with the chauffeur, though she did wonder what in heaven's name they will live on, the girl's not got a penny of her own, has she? and Victor laughed. He liked a woman to show spirit – if she did not show too much, of course. But it did just occur to him, while he was laughing, that *someone*, at least, had had the guts to cut and run out of a situation that they couldn't stick. Then he wondered how little Viola was getting on. Probably got someone else, by now; *she* won't go begging, thought Victor, as though Sible Pelden was full of someone elses. Then he impatiently thrust away the slight annoyance caused by this thought, and drove off to dance with Phyllis for the third time that week.

Hetty considered that Tina, reared in a nest of neurotics like The Eagles, should have achieved a more subtle escapade than marriage with a handsome oaf, and was disappointed in her accordingly.

Tina and Saxon, meanwhile, were living a peculiar life but a happy one.

Tina, finding herself and her husband on a sandbank, so to speak, between two classes, had gone to the artists. The artists do not mind if one is gentry or a common cad so long as one is neither a snob nor a bore; and the artists, who happened in this case to have that delightful, glowing Jewish warmth that can only be compared to a ripe apricot, received her and her young husband with sympathetic friendliness.

Her own people (who were not so well born, after all, as to excuse their anger) might think that she had disgraced her class; Mr Spurrey's servants might be rude and stand-offish and suspicious; but the Baumers accepted Mr and Mrs Caker as human beings; and Tina, with her husband, her home, and a pleasant social circle, was happier than she had dreamed it possible to be.

Saxon was happy too, though he took to the new life more cautiously than did his wife. He liked his work, and was amused by the Baumers, though he was sometimes embarrassed by their frank speech; and though he wished that Mr Spurrey was not an old friend of Mr Wither's, he was finding his employer easier to get on with as the weeks passed.

Saxon was a sound judge of character, and when he put his mind to the job, he could manage people, as (until his own feelings took a hand) he had managed Tina. Now he began to manage Mr Spurrey.

The old boy loved to jaw. His pet game was trying to put the wind up you, but he liked shooting off his mouth just for the sake of it, and Saxon trained himself to listen and drive at the same time, so that he could make the answers Mr Spurrey wanted. While motoring in London, of course, this was not so easy, but Mr Spurrey did not talk so much on the short drives between his house and the club or from sherry-party to dinner-party. Saxon knew that this was because he did not want any of his swell friends to see him chatting with his chauffeur, and so he was careful never to speak, in Town, unless he was spoken to.

But on those long drives out into the Home Counties, with tea at an expensive road-house on the way back, that Mr Spurrey took for air and exercise every week or so, Mr Spurrey talked nearly all the time, and Saxon drove, listened, and answered.

Cripes! how the old boy jawed. War, politics, money, the old days, modern women, income tax – Saxon had never thought an educated person could talk such rot. Even he, an uneducated chap up from the country, seemed to have read it all before in the papers.

Now those Yid-friends of Tina's, they talked a lot, too, about the same things that the old T. did, but they had something to say. Mad, most of it, but interesting, and it made you think.

Saxon decided that if you were a born fool, education didn't make much difference.

It's funny, thought Saxon, the old boy's got all that money, and I've only got three pounds fifteen a week, yet I feel I'm better than him. Superior. That's because he's stupid, and I'm not. Poor old B.; he hasn't had much of a time, in spite of his money.

He meant that Mr Spurrey had always been lonely. Saxon knew that this was why Mr Spurrey liked to talk; and, with his usual mixture of cool self-seeking and detached kindliness, he encouraged him to talk. It was just as well to keep in with the old chap . . . and somehow you couldn't help feeling sorry for him.

Mr Spurrey was, in fact, lonely as only a crashing bore can be. People were nice to him, as has been explained earlier in the story, but somehow whenever he met someone (unless, of course, he had them pinned in a corner over a meal) that someone had to hurry off somewhere else. This had been happening to Mr Spurrey ever since he could talk; that is, for some seventy-three years. He naturally felt that he had missed something. He did not know what. He only knew that all his life, without realizing it, he had wanted to find someone who would listen while he talked; just listen, without smiling and hurrying away; listen for hours while he frightened them with horrific prophecies, and commented upon the amazing state of the world.

Now he seemed to have found his listener.

Saxon liked his work, found that he could manage his employer, and was happy with his wife; but at the back of his mind there was always the feeling that this odd life they led, between two worlds, was only a temporary one. He felt, too, that his new job was not much better than the old one. He still wanted more money and more responsibility, he was sick of calling old men 'sir' and touching his cap. The undecided, squalid-romantic life at Sible Pelden was as dead to him as a film seen three years ago. It was impossible to believe that *he* had been that raw boy who hoped to squeeze old Wither for a thousand pounds. It made him ashamed to remember.

He was married now, working in London, with educated people for his friends, but that was not enough. Ambition, the strongest note in his nature, sounded night and day in his mind like a far-off bugle, and he was impatient with his present life even while he enjoyed it. He wanted the future to come, and he wanted it to be splendid.

With this vague longing nagging at him, he began to be careful with money. He banked ten shillings a week, sent the usual ten to his mother, gave Tina two pounds ten for housekeeping, and kept only five shillings for himself to buy cigarettes, an occasional beer, and sometimes a second-hand book about the motor industry, in which, as a by-product of his job, he was interested.

He also began to read. He read, cautiously and always with a grain of salt, books about the present state of the world, lent him by the Baumers, who watched his progress with amused sympathy. Presently they noticed that he was more interested by passages about economic conditions than by any others. Facts about trade – transport, geographical advantages and disadvantages, booms and slumps in raw materials caused by wars civil or general – absorbed his attention. He also remembered what he read. David Baumer told Tina that her husband had a good brain.

'. . . A good memory, the power to suspend judgment until he knows more about a subject, able to link up apparently unrelated facts – all good qualities. It's not an original mind; absorbent and retentive rather than creative. One day he'll do something (no, he won't write; at least, I hope not). He'll found an important business, probably. But you beware! he's stopped reading novels!' added the painter, whose own brain darted like a brilliant tri-lingual bee in and out of the ancient flowers of European culture but who was not interested in the present state of the world.

But if Saxon had stopped reading novels, he had not stopped treating his wife as his best friend, and the difficulties they faced together in their half-conventional, half-bohemian life sweetened and deepened their love. It was not a heightened relationship (indeed, Tina sometimes missed the old, dangerous days a little) but it was a true one. Like most working-class men outside the pages of fiction, Saxon did not romanticize his wife; however, he made love to her, and he loved her, and very happy they were. His ambition might trouble him, his brain might bolt and enjoy indigestible facts like a half-starved young goat, but his emotions were at peace.

Viola heard no more about having helped Saxon and Tina while the family was on holiday in the summer, but Mr and Mrs Wither were colder in manner to her after Tina had gone, and she supposed that Madge had been talking to them. They had never approved of her, as we know, but Tina had stood between her and their open dislike. Now that Tina had gone, they showed their feelings in many little ways, and as Christmas drew near, she became steadily more unhappy. There was disturbing news, too, from Miss Cattyman.

Mr Burgess, now head of Burgess and Thompsons, had been going on in the most alarming way lately, talking about getting a New Spirit into the firm, weeding out dead wood, pepping things up and getting a move on. The words zip, hustle, service and sales flew through the lineny-smelling air of Burgess and Thompsons like so many spiteful little bullets. An awful system called Comparison of Selling Ability had been started, in which the respective sales throughout the week of Miss Cattyman, Miss Lint, Miss Russell and the two little 'prentices were compared and commented upon. The two little 'prentices were made to wear dark green silk overalls. Soon the elder assistants were told that they must wear them, as well. With *ecru* bows at the neck. They would cost eighteen shillings each and the money would be stopped out of salaries each week until they were paid for. Time Marches On.

All this alarmed Miss Cattyman very much.

Viola went in to see her one Sunday afternoon, after she had been to see her aunts and give them their Christmas presents (Not To Be Opened Till Christmas Day). Auntie May, the one who was not a district nurse, said at once what a dreadful thing it was your sister-in-law running off with the chauffeur like that and had Viola known what was going on before it happened? Auntie Lizzie, the nurse, had heard it from someone down at the Infirmary whose sister lived in Sible Pelden. Viola had to give all the details, and did so with some pleasure; it was quite nice to have a good old gossip again with Auntie May and Auntie Lizzie. At least when she was with them, she felt like one of the family, which was more than she did at The Eagles. She missed Tina exceedingly.

After drinking two very strong cups of tea with the aunts, she walked round to 19 Carrimore Road, where Miss Cattyman had her bed-sitting-room, and drank two more even stronger, which she made while Miss Cattyman, who had been taking an afternoon nap, lay sideways on the bed, her tiny feet in their carefully darned stockings pulled up under the quilt, her bright old eyes watching Viola moving about.

The blinds were up when Viola came, showing a dreary prospect over the frozen waters of the Central Canal, which ran at the back of Carrimore Road; and the black, monstrous gas works, towering against the quickly fading winter sunset. Viola let the blinds run down and lit the gas.

While they drank the tea (Viola enjoyed that, too; she did not like the China stuff they had at The Eagles) Miss Cattyman told her about Mr Burgess and Comparison of Selling Ability, and ended by saying that 'she could not understand Mr Burgess these days; he was a Changed Man. My work has *always* given satisfaction, Vi,' said Miss Cattyman, with dignity, 'and I must say I don't care for all these new ideas. It's so bad for the children' (the two little 'prentices had been 'the children' to Miss Cattyman since 1907, when the first batch had come) 'to hear Mr Burgess telling me or Miss Lint how to sell silk stockings. What your dear father would have said about it all, Vi, I don't know.'

(I expect he'd have enjoyed it, thought his daughter. Dad loved a bit of change. But she did not say so. People liked to have their own ideas, and never thanked you for butting in.)

'So where it will End,' concluded Miss Cattyman, dipping an Oval Marie into her tea and sucking it, 'I cannot say. I really cannot say, and that's the truth.'

But Viola could have said: and she went home very worried. Dear old Catty, dear kind Catty who had known her since she was a baby and known her mother, Catty, who of course hadn't saved a farthing of her three pounds a week – Catty was going to be sacked.

A few days later Viola found the dismal house and its depressed occupants so unbearable that she suddenly announced she would take sandwiches, and go off all day to the marshes to See The Birds, taking the morning bus from Sible Pelden, and as no one did anything to stop her beyond saying drearily what on earth did she want to go to the marshes for in this awful weather, off she went.

The Birds were about the only interesting thing to be seen near Sible Pelden in the winter. They came from abroad, it was said, thousands of them, as soon as hard weather set in. No one but Giles Bellamy knew their names; and somehow, though the Sible Peldenites often said during the winter, 'The Birds'll be there by now; we really must go and see them this year; remember how interesting they were that time we went, five years ago, was it?' no one ever did go, for it was beastly cold out on the marshes, lonely and desolate, and most people naturally preferred to go to the pictures.

But Viola went, bumping along in the bus with one fat woman for company, through lanes thinly covered with bitter snow, right out to Dovewood Abbey, the last stop. Here the marshes began.

She walked for a good half-hour along the lonely marsh road, passing the ruined Abbey on its hill, looking out across the flat wastes of snowy reeds and grey ice broken by dark, still water. There were not many of The Birds near the road; their huge flocks kept further out, miles away across the saltings where only fishermen, bird-watchers, reed-cutters, and (it was whispered) boats dipping deep into the water with their load of smuggled silk stockings or cameras troubled to go.

But the noise and feeling of birds was all round her; their wild voices sounded near, from clumps of purple shivering reeds and woolly bullrushes; she caught a glimpse of one, big and brownish-grey, wading behind a screen of bent, and once a flock of small ones came sailing across a sheet of water that reflected the grey sky; plump, glowing and summerlike in glossy chestnut and green.

The steady wind blew slowly, like a wall of ice pressed on her cheeks, smelling of reeds, marsh-water and snow. There was no sound except the thin hiss of this wind going against miles of bull-rushes, and water-loving, thick-leaved plants now ginger-brown and withered. Once, far off she saw a mighty cloud of birds go up, dark against the grey sky.

Where the marsh road began to run out in bewildering little tracks, she stopped, unrolled her mackintosh and sat on it to eat her sandwiches. She was chilled and very sad, yet somehow she was enjoying herself. Funny how no one comes here, she thought; it's lovely, really, in spite of being so freezing and not a soul about; and she looked away across the saltings to where the sea was, and as she lifted her face, rosy with the steady smoothing of the cold wind, the sun darted a wild gold beam right across the marshes; the clouds were breaking at sunset.

Suddenly, while she was staring into the glory, she heard a strangely thrilling noise, like the galloping of horses coming nearer and nearer, and yet it was not like the quick thunder of hoofs, it was deeper and more musical, it was unlike any noise that she had ever heard, and so exciting that her heart began to beat quickly, and she stared anxiously round to see what it might be.

Nearer and nearer it came, until suddenly there swept over her head a flock of wild swans, rushing on white-gold wings into the sunset. Laughing with excitement, she ran down the track to follow their flight, but the sunset, and tears, dazzled her, and she could not see.

For some time she stood there, staring yearningly across the distances where they had flown. They were so beautiful! she had never seen anything so beautiful in her whole life. Wouldn't it be wonderful if she could always feel like she had felt when they thundered over her head, not wanting anyone, happy to be quite alone and looking at something as beautiful as those swans?

But the sun had gone behind the clouds again, and the wind was getting up, it was nearly half-past three and the last bus left Dovewood Abbey at four.

She picked up her mackintosh, which was blowing slowly towards a black pool, and put it on, for rain had started to fall.

Hands in pockets, she walked quickly back along the desolate track, her mind already in the everyday world again. Tea would be nice; she might stop for a cup at Lukesedge, and have some hot toast with it, *and* a boiled egg. Hang the expense, be a devil, as Shirley said. There was the bus, just stopping outside the closed pub. Behind her, as she began to run, clouds of birds were streaming across the marshes in their twilight flight.

Well, she had been to the marshes to See The Birds, though she had not actually seen many. P'raps it was the wrong time of the day, or something.

But those swans . . . they were lovely. She would never forget them; she could still hear the noise their wings made, and see their golden necks outstretched, streaming overhead in the sunset like the Swan Princes in the fairy story. They only wanted crowns, to look just like them. Only those swans she had seen were better than the fairy story, because they were real.

They were so beautiful. She would remember them as long as she lived.

Presently the bus stopped at the deserted cross-roads, and she got down. The only other person in sight was the Hermit, and she would not have seen him, for it was dark, had he not been busy at the front door of Mrs Caker's cottage in a glow of light. He was unscrewing a beer bottle, holding it carefully over the doorstep so that the foam should not soil the parlour floor. This done, he retired majestically into the cottage with all the airs of a proprietor, and shut the door.

The days grew ever darker; and presently it was Christmas morning.

# CHAPTER XXIII

Spring was late that year and as usual it was delicious when it came, and enjoyed the more for its lateness.

Viola felt that she had really grown up during this endless, dark, sad winter, brightened only by an occasional letter from Shirley, busy with a baby son. Her father's death, her widowhood, and the first dull weeks at The Eagles had never made her feel so old as had the silent, gloomy days between October and the end of March. She had heard no news of Victor; he might have been dead, and she continued to dream of him in a childish grieving way without trying, as she had at first with Tina's help, to occupy her mind and control her feelings. She had grown thinner, and was quieter nowadays. Life seemed so hopelessly dull and sad, and it would go on like this for ever.

But March was going out, and the evenings were getting longer, with birds singing to one another from the tree-tops, and things began to happen.

Little Merionethshire, who had met Annie at the Staff garden party at Grassmere in the summer, ran into her on their mutual afternoon-off in Chesterbourne, and told her that the Springs were expected back at Grassmere the next day; and then all the maids would have plenty to do, because Mr Victor was getting married on the twenty-fifth, and though it was going to be in Town at St George's where all the posh weddings were, Mrs Spring was going to entertain a lot before it came off, and Miss Barlow was coming down for a few days, and then there was Miss Hetty's twenty-first on the eighteenth, so there'd be plenty to do. Run off our feet, we'll be, said Merionethshire, nodding a black nob of a head on which a white beret just managed to balance. Annie then asked: And when shall we hear of *you* gettin' married, Miss Davies? and little Gladys, who was the sort that causes young men to hang themselves, giggled and said: Never, catch her tying herself up like some girls, but she added hastily that it was not for lack of asking.

Annie repeated most of this conversation to Mrs Theodore. The maids were used to Mrs Theodore by now, she was a known quantity, and her youthful looks and air of wanting something to happen had been so toned down by The Eagles to a proper sobriety that the three felt justified in occasionally indulging in a decorous gossip with her.

The news revived all Viola's misery. The twenty-fifth! less than a month away. Nothing could happen to stop it now. And it was to be in London; she could not even have the unhappy consolation of being there to see him for the last time. Not that I would, really, she hastily thought; I *could* put off going up to see Shirley until the twenty-fifth, of course, and go, but I'm blowed if I do. Tagging round after him. Besides, I should only howl, and everybody would see.

But she made up her mind that she would have the London evening papers for that day, and the morning papers for the following day, in case there were any pictures of the wedding; and after lunch she took the bus into Chesterbourne to order them from a newsagent. She did not want everyone in Sible Pelden knowing that young Mrs Wither up The Eagles had ordered the London papers from Croggs, the sweetshop-tobacconist-newsagent in the village; they would go on wondering why until they guessed.

It was Saturday, a grey day, but quite different from the grey of winter, for the air was soft and the low distant hills beyond the town were distinct and close, as though in a picture, and in all the budding woods and hedges the birds were – not singing, it sounded like an absorbed talking, a discussing and planning in sweet chirrups.

I'll pop in and see Catty, thought Viola, getting off the bus outside the Clock Tower. It's nearly a quarter to three, old Burgess'll be having lunch, and she set off down the High Street, her spirits rising, despite her unhappiness, at the sight of the New Spring Millinery displayed in the shop windows and a sweet mysterious smell that wandered on the soft wind.

There was the usual jam by Woolworths', and as she waited at the crossing, she glanced at a handsome car a little ahead of her in the traffic, and her heart leapt, for in it were Victor and Phyllis. The first thing she noticed was that both were sunburnt; the next was that they were unmistakably having a row.

Victor's face suggested a thundercloud (it slipped into that expression easily these days) and Phyllis's looked lightly, bitterly amused. They snapped remarks at each other, without turning round, while the car waited. Snap, snap snap snap snap snap, snap snap? went Phyllis's mouth, and Victor's retorted with three vicious snap snap *snaps*. Then the car moved on.

Viola could not help being very pleased. She and Shirley had noticed that people who snapped before they were married usually snapped afterwards, and if Victor and Phyllis snapped for two or three years, they might get a divorce. And then perhaps I could have him, thought Mrs Wither, going into Burgess and Thompson's in a more hopeful mood, for her views on marriage, as on everything else, were primitive.

But then she caught sight of Miss Cattyman and forgot Victor, for Miss Cattyman was serving someone (fortunately old Mrs Buckle, who was half blind) with tears running down her face.

Miss Cattyman had been with Burgess and Thompson's for fifty years. She had started with them when she was sixteen, and in a few days now she would be sixty-six. She remembered the firm, of course, long before Viola's father had come into it; she could remember it when it was Patner and Hughes, and the girls had to work as long as Mr Patner wanted them to . . . long before Early Closing and all that came in . . . sweeping about the shop in trailing skirts that picked up the dust and straw blowing in from the unpaved High Street of Chesterbourne, and had to be brushed every evening before, dead tired, the girls crawled into bed.

Though poor Miss Raikes had died of consumption and tight

lacing, and everyone was ashamed to show their feet in those days because they had deformed their toes by wearing shoes a size and a half too small, and as for the state their hair was in, Vi, you wouldn't believe it even if I was to tell you – Miss Cattyman had not a good word to say for the present, and yearned for the past. Weekly shampoos, handfuls of silk and elastic to hold you together, early-closing, Woolworths – Miss Cattyman admitted that all these things were good, but the past was better. She gave no reasons about why it was; it simply was. The past was always better.

Yet Miss Cattyman enjoyed the present, even when, as just now, it was alarming. Miss Cattyman made a drama out of Burgess and Thompson's, and had been doing so for fifty years. Instead of love, courtship, marriage, a home, children, literature and the arts, Miss Cattyman had had Burgess and Thompson's, and had not missed any of the others. Every counter of the shop, every cupboard and box, had some memory for her, sweetened by thoughts of your dear father, Vi, and fifty years of faithful service.

So when Viola saw Miss Cattyman, who had a strong sense of her own dignity and public position, crying openly in front of a customer and Miss Lint, who had only been there twelve years, Viola knew that the worst had happened.

She looked up as Viola strolled in, and her face showed pleasure and relief. She began to roll up red, white and blue ribbons more rapidly, and Viola, smiling patronizingly at Miss Lint, who smiled spitefully back, sat down on one of the long-legged chairs and waited for Catty to finish with Mrs Buckle. The other assistants were at lunch. Once they used to have tea and buns in a den at the back of the shop; now they slipped out to the Bunne Shoppe or Lyons or, when they felt reckless, the Miraflor; and instead of buns and tea they had (tinned) prawn mayonnaise and coffee.

Glancing round the shop, Viola saw many signs of Mr Burgess's drive towards efficiency. Those paper packets whose string had to be undone every time black woollen stockings or woven combs were wanted, had gone. The combs were displayed in a counter-case (that was new, too) and carelessly scattered over them were posies of primroses from Woolworths. As for the black woollen stockings, no one wore *them* any more; they had just vanished. The little wooden case on an overhead wire that used to fly along with bills and change had gone, too. Viola was rather sorry about the little overhead railway; it used to fascinate her when she was a child, and she had always longed to send her tiniest dolls for rides in it. But Catty, left in charge with Viola when everyone else was at lunch, would never allow this. There were smart green bags stamped 'Burgess and Thompson: Everything for Ladies' and Children's Wear' now, instead of the former ordinary brown paper and string that came out of a tin with a hole in the lid; the old worn brown oilcloth had been replaced by a green one and on a far counter (it used to be the Haberdashery, where Viola had cried on the night before her wedding) there was a display of small woollen garments and coloured shoes for the tots and kiddies, and a large Mickey to lull their tremors while being fitted.

I must say it all looks very nice, thought Viola placidly. There was a lot of old junk that ought to have gone years ago. Only I do hope they haven't sacked Catty.

But as the door closed on Mrs Buckle and six yards of red, white and blue ribbons, and Miss Cattyman came over to Viola with her wrinkled face drawn with worry and grief, she knew that they had.

'So glad to see you, Vi, dear,' reaching up to take the kiss that Viola bent to give. She added with dignity, 'Miss Lint, please carry on for me, will you. I'm going into the office to talk to Mrs Wither for a minute.'

Miss Lint nodded. She knew what had happened that very morning to Miss Cattyman, and was sorry. But how that Thompson girl did stick it on; you'd never think she'd been almost born in the shop, and worked there until she'd caught her precious husband.

Viola and Miss Cattyman went into the little office at the back of the shop, where Mr Burgess did the accounts and the girls took their fifteen minutes for tea of an afternoon, and Catty, sighing deeply, sat down, and looked at Viola.

'Well, dear, it's come. This morning,' she said, throwing up her little withered hands and letting them fall (lightly as dead leaves) on her shabby black lap. 'The sack *and* the bag to put it in. I'm to go at the end of this month. He's *very sorry*, of course, hasn't got a word to say against my work, thank him very much—'

'Good lord, I should hope not!' indignantly.

'. . . but the truth is, Vi, I'm just getting too old for the job. That's putting it very bluntly, but there you are; it's the truth, and you can't get away from that, can you? Oh, he was very *nice* about it, I will say that for him . . .'

Her expression changed, she leant forward, her old bluey-brown eyes glinting with amusement, and said in quite another voice, malicious, rich with relish:

'J'ever see a bar of soap in trousers? Well, that's just what he looked like when he told me, dear: a great, big, yellow bar of Sunlight Soap. Oh dear,' wiping her eyes, which suddenly overflowed, 'I do feel so bad about it, Vi; of course I've always known it would have to come one day, but somehow I'd never really thought about it (you know), I've kept me health and me eyesight and always felt so young for me age, and I suppose I didn't notice I was getting into an old woman, but it tells in the work. Other people notice it, if you don't. But I do feel so bad about it, Vi; the years I've been here, and seen the town grow, and Woolworths come and everything and the time that wolf escaped . . . and your dear father, Vi,' wiping again, 'what he'd say I *don't* know. He always promised me I'd die in harness, you know.'

Viola was silent; and there was a pause while Miss Cattyman sniffled and wiped. Viola was remembering the little laughs she and her father used to have about poor old Catty. Old hen, her father used to call Catty; a born old maid, Viola, and then strike an attitude and sing something about *lovely Letty* . . . Viola had forgotten . . . and the last line was *Letty died a maid unloved* . . . oh yes . . . *Her frozen heart her prison proved* . . . what years and years ago that seemed! And now her father was dead; and Catty was the only person who remembered the old life, and she loved Catty because Catty reminded her of her father and how happy they had been together.

Viola wiped her eyes; and wondered how she should get on to the subject of money. Catty was the purest natural snob; *ladies* did not work, *ladies* did not receive salaries, therefore Miss Cattyman's salary must never be mentioned nor must its amount be known. This had been her attitude in 1887, and it was her attitude now. The world had changed beyond belief in fifty years; but still the amount of Catty's salary was a secret to her most intimate friends. Viola, of course, knew that it was three pounds a week, because she and her father had discussed the raising of it to this sum (a handsome one for a head saleswoman, in a small draper's in a small town) and Howard Thompson had had a battle about it with Mr Burgess.

At last Viola said casually:

'Shall you keep on your room?'

'I shall have to see, dear,' retorted Miss Cattyman, a shade sharply. 'Things will be very different, you know. Still,' blithely, 'I dare say I shall manage.'

'Look here, Catty,' blurted Viola, 'I don't want to butt in and you mustn't think it's cheek, I only want to help you so you mustn't mind my asking . . . but . . . have you got anything saved?'

Miss Cattyman looked down at her greenish-black lap and was silent for a little while. Then she said quietly, 'No – no, Vi, not very much, I'm afraid. That is to say, I really have very little. Mother's illness, you know, and the funeral, that took all my savings at the time, and somehow since then I've never managed to get started properly again. And of course,' perking up and speaking indignantly, 'I always expected to die in harness. And so I should have, if some people hadn't got it into their heads to turn everything upside down as though they were the D. of W. himself (though I for one shall always think of him as the P. of W., never could get used to his being called the K., he hadn't the face for it, I always said; ought to have grown a beard at once, and then all this would never have happened) where was I? Oh yes, well, dear, you're not to worry. I dare say I shall manage.'

But as she hastily kissed Catty, patted her, and promised to come in again soon, then hurried away because Mr Burgess would be in any minute and he was not so friendly as he used to be to his dead partner's daughter, Viola was very worried indeed; so worried that for the time her own troubles were driven out of her head.

They returned for a moment while she was ordering the newspapers that might contain pictures of the Spring – Barlow wedding and telling the newsagent that she would call for them; but on the way home she could think of nothing but Catty, and wonder what was to be done about her.

She did have a brief vision of herself pouring out the story to Mr Wither, and Mr Wither blowing his nose violently like people did in books, and saying gruffly that he would allow Miss Cattyman a hundred a year, no doubt he was an old fool to do it but there . . . but somehow when she shut the front door of The Eagles, the vision faded; and suddenly Mrs Wither was hurrying out into the hall, a letter in her hand, mixed indignation and excitement on her face.

'Viola, what *do* you think?' began Mrs Wither at once, speaking in a quite normal and family voice, so plainly was she in need of somebody to speak to. 'That old gentleman, the one Saxon's working for, you know – it's Mr Spurrey.'

'What? *Old* Mr Spurrey? Mr Wither's friend, that was here in the summer, do you mean?'

'There's only one Mr Spurrey, dear,' but she spoke mildly, still staring at the letter. 'Yes, he's been there all this time.'

'But why on earth didn't Tina tell you?'

'That's just what I cannot make out, Viola, and I can't understand why Mr Spurrey didn't mention it, either. It's all so *peculiar*,' said poor Mrs Wither, looking up from the letter with puzzled, faded eyes. 'Why keep it a secret from us like that? Of course, I can't really say that I am surprised at anything that Tina does, after everything that has happened; but I do think that Mr Spurrey might have mentioned it. It's so unfriendly. After all, Mr Wither has known Mr Spurrey for a very long time, they were practically boys together. It's so strange – to keep on writing about how pleased he is with his new chauffeur and asking how Tina was, and saying how sorry he was to hear that she had gone off like that, and all the time – don't you think it very peculiar, Viola, very *unnatural*?'

'I should darned well think so (sorry, it slipped out),' said her daughter-in law heartily, pleased at being brought into the family circle by this crisis. To Viola, almost any affection was better than none. 'Does Mr Wither know about it yet?'

'No. Madge has driven him out to Lukesedge this morning, they went off rather early and the post was late. This,' waving the letter, 'is from Mr Wither's cousin, Agnes Grice, Mrs Grice. She knows Mr Spurrey quite well. She went up to Town, it seems, from Peterborough (she lives at Peterborough) for the day to see her dentist (she's been having trouble with her teeth, poor thing, lately) and she saw Saxon driving Mr Spurrey along Wigmore Street. She waved out of her taxi-window but Mr Spurrey didn't see her, she says . . . or pretended he didn't, more likely. She says he didn't look at all well and she thought he might have been to see a specialist (all the big doctors are round that part, you know, Harley Street and there). I can't get over it. Mr Spurrey! I am afraid Mr Wither will be very upset.'

He was. He came in just as Fawcuss was ponging the gong for lunch, arguing with Madge about the route they had taken. He had wanted to take the usual road home from Lukesedge but Madge had said that another way, known to herself, was quicker. As a result they were almost late for lunch and Mr Wither was already irritable. He had granted Madge's eager request that she might 'take over the car' now that Saxon had gone, partly because he felt that he could never trust a chauffeur again and partly because he found it too much trouble to keep on saying No. Mr Wither was getting old. But drives with Madge were not so soothing as drives with Saxon had been; arguments, innovations, narrow escapes and fluent excuses prevented that.

But it was the same with everything, thought Mr Wither gloomily, coming into the hall, which echoed with the ponging of Fawcuss; there was no peace and no comfort anywhere. Mr Wither put it all down to the War.

Then did Mrs Wither, in silence, hand him Cousin Agnes Grice's letter.

Cousin Agnes was wrong. Mr Spurrey had not been to see a specialist on that bright April morning, haunted by a piercing little wind. He and Saxon, inwardly excited though outwardly composed, were on their way into Buckinghamshire to try out the new Rolls.

Mr Spurrey had been trying for years to buy a new Rolls, but Holt had been against it. Whenever Mr Spurrey, who was not a mean man, hinted at buying a new Rolls, Holt, who was another of the Stay Put Brigade, had made a certain kind of face, sucking in his breath and pushing out his lips. He did not say, 'Shouldn't do that if I was you, sir,' but the face said it, and Mr Spurrey, who did not realize how easily he was dashed, said no more until the next time, when the same thing happened again.

But Saxon's face had lit up at Mr Spurrey's first cautious hint about buying a new Rolls; and he had suggested the very next morning that he should drive down and make some inquiries and get some particulars; and Mr Spurrey decided to go with him. Soon 'a' new Rolls became 'the' new Rolls; then 'it'; and finally, when Mr Spurrey and Saxon glided out on that bright windy morning, riding inside the mighty black beauty as proudly as the men who steered Cleopatra's barge – the Rolls had become She.

This is the life, thought Saxon, at the wheel. Power, bound and obedient and costing a large sum of money, lay under his hands. You sweet, you beauty. Oh, you bird, thought Saxon as they left London and marched rather than ran, so unobtrusive yet splendid was their pace, into the lanes of Buckinghamshire;

Mr Spurrey, too, was content. The sun was shining (Mr Spurrey liked sunshine), there was blue sky, the Rolls was running well, and at home he had Dorothy Sayers's latest story waiting unopened. He would read it that evening, over a decanter. In front sat Saxon, that good boy, and there was a little window that could be opened at any minute if Mr Spurrey wanted someone to talk to.

Presently, while they were honouring Rickmansworth by passing through it, Saxon slid back the little window off his own bat and said cheerfully:

'All right, sir, isn't she?'

'Very good, very good indeed,' agreed Mr Spurrey. 'Splendid, in fact. One can feel the difference, by George, can't one? not only on the hills, though of course one feels it most there, but all the time, eh? Of course, I was getting thoroughly dissatisfied with the other, thoroughly dissatisfied. I remember . . .'

He remembered; while Saxon, his eyes half shut, the empty sunlit lanes steadily advancing, listened, commented and drove.

Mr Spurrey's monologue was of so flavourless a brand, so hesitant, slow and repetitive, so full of microscopic triumphs for his own wit, courage and cunning at the expense of nameless inferior fleas usually described as The Chap or The Feller, so lacking in colour, point and distinction, that no attempt shall be made to report it.

But Saxon was used to the old man's jaw, and it did not get on his nerves now as it used to at first. He could not help feeling a satirical pity for Mr Spurrey, either; all that money (and not a tightwad, either) and no idea how to spend it. Mr Spurrey had always been suspicious of women and rather afraid of them, so he had not had any fun there; and men only tolerated him. Fun and jollity had a way of quietly going off the boil when he came up, even if he did not say a word. He was too sharp to tolerate toadies yet too stupid to please even ordinary kind people, and his habit of trying to frighten his hearers, when he was not excruciatingly boring them, had put the lid on; no one, all his long life, had really wanted to be with Mr Spurrey.

But Saxon, now that he knew him, did not dislike him. For instance, he was generous; nothing of old Wither's save-fivepence-on-the-return-journey about Mr Spurrey. When they stopped the Rolls at last, on a hill looking over the exquisite valley of the Chess, and Mr Spurrey climbed out to stretch his legs, Saxon unpacked a luncheon basket for two that included foie gras sandwiches and a good brand of champagne. Whee! thought Saxon. Last time it was only sparkling muscatel. We're getting on.

'What've they given us, eh?' inquired Mr Spurrey, coming round the majestic black shoulder of the Rolls (one of the minor joys of the rich is that they never know what is in the sandwiches), wrapped in his new spring overcoat against the bitter little wind, and peering into the basket.

Saxon, smiling, held up the bottle.

'Ha! hey! excellent! Ah yes, that was my idea. Thought we'd drink to the new Rolls, eh? Just a little surprise, eh?'

'Very good idea, sir,' said Saxon, and meant it. And he added, guessing that Mr Spurrey would recognize a slang phrase of some years ago, 'And very nice too, as they say.'

'Ha, ha! Very good!' cried Mr Spurrey. '*And very nice too!* Yes, exactly. *And very nice too!*'

Saxon spread a tweed rug on the grass and put Mr Spurrey's waterproofed cushion on it; the rheumatism must always be remembered.

'Comfortable?' he asked, easily.

As he settled another cushion at the old man's back he forgot to 'sir' him, and Mr Spurrey did not notice it. He was only a lonely boring old man to Saxon, at that moment, enjoying the sunshine and chill spring air, looking forward to his first sip of champagne. He was not Saxon's employer any more; he might have been one of the old boys down home who kept the darts parlour warm at the Green Lion; you always asked them how they were keeping . . . for some reason . . . not that you cared a damn. It pleased them and did you no harm.

'Just a little more to the left. That's it. Thank you.'

They sat side by side, leaning against the Rolls, their mouths full, glasses in their chilled hands, staring, as they munched, away across the clear air of the valley. Cloud shadows sailed across the purple ploughed land. The larches were out, pale among the darker trees. The cries of rooks came loudly; then softly, as the wind changed. For a minute Saxon wished that Tina were there; she was so fond of scenery. Then he forgot her, for she would be waiting when he got home that evening and there was no reason for thinking about her.

'Nice bit of country.'

Mr Spurrey, with his mouth full, waved at the prospect before them. It was so delicate, vivid and splendid, glowing through such miraculously clear air, that it was like some marvellous painting.

'Pretty steep, that hill.' Saxon narrowed his eyes. 'About one in four, I sh'd say. How about trying her up that, after lunch?'

Mr Spurrey was agreeable; and after lunch was over and Mr

Spurrey had smoked a little cigar and Saxon a cigarette, they did try her up that, and superbly she did it.

What with trying her up that, and others, and stopping on a hill near Marks Tey to admire the sunset, it was dark before they got back to Buckingham Square; but as he climbed stiffly out of the Rolls and turned to say good night to Saxon, Mr Spurrey felt that it had been one of the pleasantest days he had spent for years. The Rolls had done so well, the champagne had tasted so good drunk under a tree like that, the country had looked so pretty, and that boy, Saxon, was such good company. Nice, sensible boy. Knew his place, yet none of your soft-soaping. No wonder old Wither's gel got smitten.

He turned to give his wrinkled old smile, that years of unconscious self-defence had made malicious, to the young man who sat smiling at the wheel of the splendid car.

'Well, good night, Saxon. Pleasant day, eh?'

'Very pleasant, sir.'

'Must do it again some time, eh?' He paused, nodding, one foot on the step, and added:

'How's your wife these days?'

'Very well, thank you, sir.'

'Ah . . . h'm. Well . . . give her my regards.'

'I will, sir. Thank you. Good night, sir.'

The car glided away into the spring dusk.

Mr Spurrey let himself in, nodding to the butler, and went slowly up the stairs. It had been on the tip of his tongue to suggest to Saxon that he and Tina should come in to dinner one night . . . and damn what the servants thought. Two nice young people . . . why shouldn't he have them in, if he wanted to? But then he thought, no. Women . . . always laughing, making fun of perfectly ordinary remarks, trying to get something out of a man. No. Let her stay where she was. Later on, he might have the boy in, by himself.

Thus did Mr Spurrey hide from himself that he was jealous of Saxon's wife.

There was a good fire in the library after dinner, the decanter of port and the new Dorothy Sayers; but the fresh air had made him so sleepy that his head was nodding before he had read a chapter, and at last he dozed off. When he awoke, with a start, the fire was very low, the room chilly, and nine o'clock striking. He sat up, yawning, the book sliding to the floor. Suddenly the yawn turned to a sneeze; and Mr Spurrey shivered violently. That night in bed he could not get warm.

The next day was mild and calm, the bitter little wind had gone, but Mr Spurrey lay in bed, still trying to get warm; and in the evening Cotton, the butler, took it upon himself to send for the doctor. It was a cold, only a cold, said the doctor (as though anyone cared enough about Mr Spurrey to need reassuring) but Mr Spurrey had best stay in bed. There was a lot of flu about still, and bed was the best place, said the doctor.

The next afternoon it had turned to a feverish cold, and it got steadily worse; slowly, like a rising flood, it crawled through the old body and got hold of one part after another; his limbs ached, he shivered and burned, and then it got to the lungs; suddenly it was pneumonia, with all the stops out, full orchestra, two nurses, and grumblings in the kitchen about extra meals, shaded lights burning all night and straw down outside the house, the doctor calling twice a day and oxygen ready; and at last, on the fifth day, the doctor asking Cotton in a low voice in the hall, 'Isn't there anybody who ought to be told, Cotton?' and Cotton answering almost defiantly, 'No, sir, not that I know of, sir. I believe that Mr Spurrey has some friends living in Essex, sir, but they're not what you might call close friends, sir, and he has no relations. Mr Spurrey is the only son of an only son, sir, or so I always understood him to say.'

But that evening Mr Spurrey rallied a little, and the first person he asked the nurse for, when he had found out where he was and what had happened to him, was Saxon.

Tina and Saxon were at supper when the parlourmaid, looking suspicious and disagreeable, came over to give the message, and he got up at once, eager and embarrassed. He who never had 'feelings' had had a feeling that Mr Spurrey might want to see him. He had also been wondering if he had been long enough with Mr Spurrey for the old man to leave him a legacy if he died. Tina, looking at her husband under her eyelashes, felt a little disturbed. She knew that shrewd, wary look. It meant that the self-seeking strain in his nature was uppermost. She watched him hurry across the courtyard with a dismayed feeling.

The big bedroom was in shadow except for the subdued glow of a lamp by the bed, and in the shadows sat a nurse, watchful and quiet. She looked up as Saxon tip-toed in and said in the softest possible voice:

'Just a few minutes; then you must go.'

Mr Spurrey lay in the bed, looking yellow and very old. All the wrinkles had come into his face to stop now, and his pale protuberant eyes were even bigger than usual; they looked bewildered. He stared up at Saxon for what seemed a very long time, then ran his tongue over his lips and said in a low, strange voice:

'I'm very ill.'

'Yes, sir. We're all very sorry.' Saxon tried to talk quietly yet naturally, bending a little over the bed.

'I'm not going . . . not going . . .' Suddenly tears ran out of his eyes, tiny rivers. Saxon stared, fascinated; then he said quickly:

'No, sir, of course you're not,' in a bright tone, with a merry, stupid smile.

There was a silence.

'Good day that . . . we had . . . eh?'

'Yes, sir, it was. We'll be doing it again soon, don't you worry.'

Mr Spurrey smiled faintly, and shut his eyes. Then he opened them again.

'Want to say . . . so tired . . .' his head lolled to one side, then to the other, 'want to give you something . . . a present . . . good boy . . .'

The nurse glanced up sharply, her face full of professional concern and pure human curiosity, and rose from her chair.

'Now, Mr Spurrey, you mustn't excite . . .'

'Yes, I know . . . I know . . .' waving her away. 'Got a pencil . . .?'

The nurse glanced across at Saxon, nodding meaningly, and he at once moved towards the door, but Mr Spurrey raised his head and peered into the shadows beyond the glow of the lamp.

'Saxon!' he cried weakly. 'Don't go away . . . Saxon!'

'As the young man paused, glancing inquiringly at the nurse, the night nurse rustled in, settling her apron strings, took in what was happening, gave the younger nurse a look and said softly but firmly to Saxon:

'All right. You can stay.'

'Saxon . . .' a whimper from the bed.

Saxon tip-toed forward again, and sat down cautiously. Mr Spurrey, still with those unnaturally large and bewildered eyes turned towards the young man, nodded, and shut them. Presently his hand, the bent fingers stained by nicotine, came out from under the bedclothes and fumbled anxiously about. Half-pitiful, half-ashamed, Saxon took it firmly in his own. Mr Spurrey opened his eyes.

'It's all right, Dad. Don't you worry,' muttered Saxon roughly, and to the comfort of the homely name, with his hand in Saxon's, Mr Spurrey fell into an uneasy sleep.

Presently the night nurse bent over him. After a little pause she smiled at Saxon, and moved her head towards the door. With the greatest care, a fraction of an inch at a time, Saxon got his hand away, stood up, and went softly away. He glanced back once at his employer, lying small and yellow, like a Chinaman, in the big bed while the nurse cautiously pulled the clothes round his chin. He never saw him again.

He went back and told Tina what had happened. He was excited yet ashamed. He kept on telling her that of course it didn't mean anything.

After the funeral, at which Saxon and Tina, the servants, and one old gentleman from Mr Spurrey's club were the only mourners, Mr Spurrey's lawyer assembled the household in the library, where the Dorothy Sayers still lay beside Mr Spurrey's big chair in its bright yellow jacket, and read them Mr Spurrey's Will.

There were generous legacies for Cotton and the maids, a present of a bust of Joseph Chamberlain to Mr Wither, *because he always admired it*, and a small bequest to his Club, but the bulk of his fortune, some hundred and twenty thousand pounds, was left, by a Will dated the day before his death, shakily signed, and witnessed by the two nurses, '*to my chauffeur, Saxon Caker, for companionship and faithful service*'.

# CHAPTER XXIV

It would take Shakespeare and Proust, working in shifts, to cope with the reactions when this piece of news burst upon The Eagles.

Tina telephoned it to her mother just after tea, and Mrs Wither shrieked to Mr Wither as he sat in his den, and he came shuffling out, unable, as the saying is, to believe his ears. Madge and Viola burst out of the drawing-room, having heard only shrieks in which Saxon's name recurred and supposing that he had had an accident with the car and killed Mr Spurrey.

Perhaps nothing but a piece of news about money would have made Mrs Wither so far forget herself as to shriek in front of the maids, who were putting the last touches to the cleared tea-table and setting it for dinner. There was nothing shameful about somebody getting a huge sum of money, and Mrs Wither instinctively felt this. Sex was shameful, and any bit of news about it must be hidden, but money was all right: anyone might hear about that. So Fawcuss and Annie took it all in, and went down and told Cook.

When the excitement had died down a little, the chief feeling at The Eagles was one which may be described as righteous indignation. It was generally felt to be A Bit Too Much. Saxon, having stravagued about the country as a boy, neglected his mother, hypnotized and corrupted Tina, and underhandedly obtained a job with an old friend of Mr Wither's, to say nothing of living in a mews with Jews, was now, as a punishment for all this, a rich man. There was no justice in earth or heaven. Fawcuss, Annie and Cook said it really did seem that those who deserved least got most; of course, Saxon (or Mr Caker, they supposed they ought really to call him now he had all that money) had always been very nice to them; they had no cause for complaint against him, but – a hundred and twenty thousand pounds! It didn't seem right.

Mr Wither was very angry about all sorts of things; with Mr Spurrey, for behaving in so eccentric and unfriendly a manner, with Tina for having again concealed from her family something which they would have liked to know, with Saxon for having (no doubt) lied, sponged and flattered his way into a handsome fortune. But Mr Wither kept a special corner in sorrowful indignation for the bust of Joseph Chamberlain. All he had done, while on a visit once to Mr Spurrey's house, was to remark that the bust was a good likeness. Never given the thing another thought. And here he was, landed with an *objet d'art* weighing goodness-only-knew how much, which would cost heaven-knew-what to bring down from London. And where, when it did reach The Eagles, could it Go? Every cranny was occupied. Besides, it would look so strange, a bust of Joseph Chamberlain about the place. People would always be asking who it was meant to be, and who it was by, and how did Mr Wither come to have it, and Mr Wither, who hated explaining about the furniture, which he liked to take for granted, would have to find out who had done it in order not to be shamed by saying, 'Don't know.'

In short, Mr Wither was so annoyed by the catastrophes brought about by Mr Spurrey's death that he had no real feeling of regret for Mr Spurrey. After all, he and Gideon had drifted apart a good deal since the 'nineties, when a tallow-faced Mr Spurrey and a port-faced Mr Wither had together dared the Empire Promenade, and Mr Spurrey had always backed out at the very last minute with an excuse about last trains while Mr Wither had gone bulldoggishly ahead. Gideon had got such an old woman as he grew older, too, always chin-wagging; and there was that habit of knowing all the disagreeable things that were going to happen weeks before they did. No wonder that Mr Wither, reading a few days later a cutting sent him by some kind friends in London that was headed could not really feel much sorrow for Mr Spurrey.

Even the smallest, meanest legacy would have been less insulting than a bust of Joseph Chamberlain.

But below all Mr Spurrey's angers, there was another feeling. It was a pure and sacred, an almost priestlike longing, to get his fingers on that hundred and twenty thousand pounds and, with the help of Major-General Breis-Cumwitt, manage it. A boy like Saxon, a wild, raw, common boy, would not be capable of managing all that money without expert advice from older and more experienced men. It was an unpleasant, a humiliating, a disagreeable task, but Mr Wither did not really see how he was going to avoid writing to Tina and suggesting that she and Saxon should soon come down to The Eagles for a long weekend. After all, the money did make a difference. Now, Tina was not likely to come asking her father for money; even a wild, raw, common boy would take a month or two to spend a hundred and twenty thousand pounds. Much as Mr Wither shrank from the task, he felt that it was his duty to suggest that weekend.

Tina, hanging up the receiver in the telephone-box at the end of the mews, walked slowly back to her blue front door. The window boxes were blue, as well, and out of them, glowing in the evening sunlight, hung the purple and cherry-red heads of begonias. It was a quaint, inconvenient, charming little place, and she had been sweetly, completely happy there, and now she was never going to be so happy again.

For one of the very few truths of which we may be sure in this world is that Money Makes All The Difference; and Tina, an intelligent woman, knew it. There was a particular feeling of peace that came over her every evening about half-past five, when the sky was beginning to deepen in blue, and the children came out after tea to play in the mews, and she knew that this was the last time she would ever have it. It was only three hours since the Will had been read; but Saxon was already a different person from the cheerful, calm but wary young man who had gone with her that morning to his employer's funeral.

He had gone off with Mr Spurrey's solicitor to his offices, and was not yet back. His manner, as he had nodded to his wife and said that he would try not to be long, adding crisply that perhaps she had better not come, had been such a blend of solemnity, and pompousness, with beneath it an hysterical and almost awed exultation, that Tina had felt stunned.

Saxon had come through the test of Love with honours; apparently it was in the test of Money that he would fail.

He'll be like so many other people, she thought, opening the door; admirable when he's hard up, but just not able to stand oats. She went slowly up the stairs, picturing peace, modest comfort, domestic pleasures and bohemian gaiety flying horror-stricken out of the window, while expensive and dull killtimes, the servant problem, super tax and social climbing came swarming in, like demons, to take their place.

If only he'd left us five hundred a year . . . even three hundred, it would have been perfect, she thought, beginning to slice tomatoes for supper. But this is appalling, it's an avalanche. It's . . . what . . .? . . . six thousand a year. We can't spend a sixth of it, unless we live like film stars.

But that's how he'll want to live. I saw it in his face.

Then, when we've got out into that world where most of the women know how to get men, and don't let anything stop them from trying, someone'll get him away from me.

And I've been looking so plain lately, with this horrible indigestion.

She carefully mixed some bicarbonate of soda and drank it; but it did not do the indigestion any good.

Those women (Tina's fancy was fed on photographs in *Vogue*) will fall for him, too; sure to, because he's so . . . untarnished.

I can see just what's going to happen.

While she let these ripe fancies drift through her head, she was resting by the open window, watching the sunset on the red and creamy chimney-pots of the old houses opposite, and sometimes staring dreamily round the room in which she had been so happy, and as she idly gazed, she saw without realizing it the face of an old friend.

It was *Selene's Daughters*, lying meekly sideways on the top of a row of books on cookery, and books on history and economics, and mere fiction. Viola had sent it on with the rest of Tina's things.

In the midst of her depression and fears about the *Vogue* sirens, Tina smiled. How far off seemed the days when Miss Christina Wither, the earnest student of mental hygiene, had tried to manage her love-life with the help of Doctor Irene Hartmüller! Now Mrs Saxon Caker was up to her neck in Life: and her psychological studies seemed very amusing indeed, and almost endearingly youthful.

And yet, thought Tina, resting by the window, supper waiting on the table, it wasn't altogether silly and a waste of time. Poor little Doctor Irene (I wonder if the Baumers' story is true?) she did teach me to *try* and tell the truth to myself; and if I hadn't done that I should never have tried to get Saxon's friendship, and if I hadn't tried . . .

But here Mrs Saxon Caker (who was even further up to her neck in Life than she suspected) heard her husband coming upstairs.

To her immense relief Saxon came in looking his usual self. He smiled at her, hung up his coat and hat, and said, 'Well, that's that. Sorry I'm late, but I thought they'd never get through. Is there a lot to be done! Well . . . how does it feel to be rich?'

He pulled her out of her chair and kissed her, but as though he were not thinking about her, and she saw that he was still very excited, and, for some reason, angry.

'It doesn't feel too good to me, so far. You're very pleased, aren't you?'

'Oh no . . . I'm broken-hearted.' He sat down heavily, stretched out his legs, and stared at her.

'Now just you remember, before you start picking on me for being "pleased", as you call it (I'm pleased all right . . . feel as though I'd been drinking for a month), that I've wanted this, all my life, more than anything. Ever since I can remember. Got that?'

She nodded, trying not to feel hurt because he had wanted it more than love.

He got up and walked across to the bookcase.

'I can't believe it. It's . . .' He sat down again. 'I can't. I'll wake up.'

He took a biscuit off the table and began to nibble it, then put it down.

'It's all very well for you,' he said roughly. 'You've always had enough to eat. You've never had to pretend you weren't hungry, or smash someone's face for saying your old man boozed.'

'I know, Saxon.'

'All right, then.'

She watched him as he walked restlessly about the little room. He looked too big for it. She suddenly thought, calmly, that their marriage was not going to last.

'And I don't want anyone to be sorry for me, neither,' he said, sitting down again. 'I'm not whining. I've made my own way up till now and I'll go on doing it. I know what you're afraid of. You think I'll go high hat.'

'I do rather, Saxon.'

'Well, I shan't. I've had quite enough this afternoon to cool me down, thank you. Do you know what everybody thinks down at the solicitors'?'

Tina stared at him.

'You won't get it, you mean?'

'Oh, the Will's all right. There isn't a loophole in it. No, they just think I was the old man's boy friend, that's all.'

'Oh, Saxon, they *don't*! People aren't like that . . . just because you've heard a few jokes at the Baumers' . . .'

'They do, I tell you. Those two —— of nurses did, anyway, and so did the clerks down at the office this afternoon.'

'It's because you're so good-looking,' she said thoughtfully, studying him as he sat slouched in the chair. She was always amazed, every time she looked at him, at the romantic beauty of his body and the practical, even commonplace, way his mind worked. He was the truest realist she had ever known. She was beginning to wonder

317

if, when she was forty-five, she might not feel a little thirsty. But perhaps thirst could be avoided by making her own mind work in the same way. If the well was not deep, at least the water was pure.

'Oh . . .' he made an impatient movement. 'Well, that's what they do think, anyway, and that's what everybody'll think. That's enough to keep me from going high-hat. We'll live on five hundred, and I'll put the rest into a business.'

'My dear, I wish you would. There's nothing I'd like better.'

Yet pictures of herself entertaining the quietest but most intelligent people in London in a perfectly furnished house in Westminster left, as they faded, a faint feeling of disappointment.

She went on:

'I'm so glad you're going to be sensible about it. I thought you would, in the long run, only you seemed so excited this afternoon . . .'

'Well, my God, who wouldn't be? It's something to be excited about. You're a queer fish, Tina. What your friend Baumer would call ab-normal, I should say. Most women 'ud want to rush out and buy things.'

'I do,' announced Tina, suddenly getting up. 'I want to go out now, before the shops shut, and get a fur coat for your mother.'

He stared.

'But look here – steady on. I shan't get anything for months, you know, until the Will's gone through Probate, and I've got no job now, remember. We'll have to live on your seventy quid. We can't go—'

'The solicitors will advance you as much as you want, Saxon. Didn't they say so?'

'The old boy did say something, come to think of it, but I was so mad thinking about what he was thinking, I didn't take it in somehow. I suppose they will. God! doesn't it seem . . . here, how much does a fur coat cost?'

'We can get one that will delight your mother for about twenty pounds. I know she wants one; I saw her looking at mine that night.'

'We can't get twenty pounds tonight.'

'I drew out forty this afternoon while you were out – I thought you might want to celebrate.'

'We'll get the coat and then see about that. I do and I don't. Makes me feel – I don't know. Come on.'

They were both excited now, as they hurried through the mews and into Oxford Street. Tina's fears had died down. She allowed herself to imagine a happy future; she even imagined a Child. So far, she had not thought much about a Child, because she and Saxon (she told herself) were enough for one another; also, a Child would cost money and they had had so little. But now she pictured a dark-haired son exactly like Saxon, and the dream was delightful.

Then her thoughts turned naturally to Mr Spurrey, who had been childless.

'Saxon,' she said, as they waited at a pedestrian crossing, 'did you ever think this would happen?'

'Us be rich, do you mean?'

'Mr Spurrey leave you anything, I really meant.'

'Well,' he said, half-smiling, half-defiant, a little ashamed, looking across at the façade of Bumpus's, 'it did just occur to me, you know, after I'd been in to see him that night, that he might. Besides, he said something. I told you. Poor old tw— chap,' he added dutifully.

'But you didn't . . .'

'What?'

'Suck – try to get in with him, Saxon? Hoping he might?'

He was silent for a moment, while the lights changed from amber to green and the pedestrians meekly hurried across the, road. Then he said:

'Not really. I did just think, once or twice, that something might come of it some day if I kept in with him. But that's me, you know,' squeezing her arm and smiling down at her. 'I was like that with you once, and we've turned out all right, haven't we?'

'We have so far,' returned Tina cautiously. She added, 'You're a funny mixture.'

'So's everybody. Now what about this fur coat?'

They chose a full rich squirrel one with a very large collar of fox. There was a sale at the Jew-shop where they found it, and they were assured that it was reduced from seventy-two guineas to twenty-three. Saxon said doubtfully that it looked kind of flashy to him and hadn't they better get something a bit quieter that would Last? But Tina was firm. She said that what his mother would like better than anything was just this fragile, gorgeous, film-starrish coat.

'And grand she'll look in it,' added Tina enthusiastically, her warm fancy glorifying the absent Mrs Caker a little.

'She will if she washes her face first.'

'Don't be cruel.'

'Well, it's all very well, but she never liked me much and I'm not over-struck on her.'

'Saxon . . . we've been so lucky, darling. Think.'

'Oh . . . anything you like. All right. We'll have this one,' to the Jewish salesman, an eloquent, tired-eyed little man who was disguising an intense interest in their conversation under a bored manner.

So the coat set off that night for Essex, wrapped in many sheets of pale-rose tissue paper, and with it went a note from Saxon saying that his employer had just died and left him a bit of money, and this was the first of many good things that his mother might expect.

'Because she's had such a rotten time, Saxon,' his wife informed him, 'and it takes so little to make people happy.'

Saxon did not agree with this. It was taking twenty-three guineas to make Mrs Caker happy in this case; and he knew that the Hermit and a bottle of beer could do the job quite as well. However, he said nothing, and after they had eaten the supper waiting at home, they went out and had a modest five shillings' worth at the Astoria, and that was how Saxon and Tina celebrated coming into a fortune.

The next day after dinner the Hermit and Mrs Caker strolled down to the stream to see how the Hermit's house had weathered the winter. The Hermit himself had weathered it in the cottage, with Mrs Caker, enjoying all the privileges of the late Mr Caker, but the hut had not done so well; it had fallen in.

'There,' observed the Hermit discontentedly, his large broken boots planted among the celandines on the bank. 'Now what'll I do?

Can't leave a place five minutes that something don't 'appen.'

'Stay wi' me?' suggested Mrs Caker, who had grown used to having a man about the place, and hated being alone.

'Can't do that.' The Hermit shook his curls. 'Never do, that wouldn't.'

'What d'ye mean, Dick Falger? Been with maye all winter, haven't 'ee?'

'Ah, but t'ain't winter now. People'll 'ull be comin' round now, hikers and that.'

'What difference 'll that make?'

'They might get torkin'.'

'Let 'em. Gie 'em somethin' ter do.'

'Ah, but my old woman might 'ear about it.'

'What?' screamed Mrs Caker.

'Don't 'oller,' reproved the Hermit. 'My old woman, I says. Beatty. Beatty Falger. Lives near Bedford . . . or did, larst I 'eard of 'er.'

'You said she was dead,' shouted Mrs Caker, in tears, hitting him on the arm.

'Shut up, will yer,' with a blow on the breast that made her stagger. 'Only 'cos you kep' on so, makin' such a bull-and-cow about it. She ain't dead. Leastways, I 'ope not. 'Ope not, I'm sure. Very fond o' Beatty, I used ter be, on'y she fair got on me nerves grizzlin' because she never 'ad no kids (not my fault, I can tell yer). Aw, shut up, carn't yer, Nellie? Snivvlin'. Come on 'ome, and we'll 'ave a cup o' Rosie.'

After they had gone a little way through the trees, Mrs Caker trailing sullenly behind him, he added thoughtfully,

'Shouldn't mind seein' Beatty again. She'll be gettin' on now. Nearin' seventy, Beatty'd be. I ain't seen 'er for 'leven years. Nearer twelve.'

Mrs Caker said nothing.

The blow had made her as angry as a good-natured, feckless woman could be. Fool I was, lettin' that owd toad get on the soft side o' maye. Men! women can have a sight better time without 'em. He's been comfortable enough all winter wi' maye, and now he wants to be off. Feels he'd like a bit of a change. Well, he can go, and dirty water down a bad drain.

It was quite plain that the Hermit did mean to be off.

As soon as they got back to St Edmund's Villas (which was down on the Vicar's visiting list for next week, after long talks with the Vicaress and much irritation and well-George-I-do-feel-that-if-you-don't-no-one-else-willings) the Hermit marched upstairs, and while Mrs Caker was making the tea and feeling more and more angry and unhappy, she heard him clumping about, opening drawers and singing; and presently he came down again, carrying a battered suitcase from Marks and Spencers that looked very small in one leg-o'-mutton hand. His boots were freshly tied up with string and he wore an old coat belonging to Saxon that Mrs Caker had persuaded him to wear instead of the sacking one sewn with newspaper pads, which she had burned.

'Where be goin'?' demanded Mrs Caker, clapping down the teapot.

'I'm off. Been 'ere too lang as it is,' announced the Hermit, pouring half a bottle of milk into a cup and adding four lumps of sugar. 'Now don' take on, Nellie. Me mind's made up.'

'I weren't goin' to take on,' said Mrs Caker fiercely. 'I don't care what 'ee do, Dick Falger. I wonder I got so low as to hev 'ee here, I do. Pity I didn't keep on the way I started wi' 'ee, not lettin' 'ee in the parlour at all.'

'Kitchen does as well fer me, missus,' draining his tea. 'Tain't much of a place, anyways. Drink up, Nellie.'

'It were good enough for 'ee all winter, ungrateful owd toad of a man, an' I'll drink up mie tea when I please. You better be off, if you're goin'. I want to gie the place a bit of a clean up.'

But the Hermit finished his tea without haste, while she sat at the table staring sulkily at her cooling cup. The bruise ached where he had hit her. Outside in the wood, the trees were so bright and the air so clear that they made her feel somehow ashamed of the slumocky place and her dirty dress, and the way that old tramp – he was no more, that he wasn't – stood there swilling tea as though he were lord and master, and once she used to ride beside her father in

322

his own pony-trap, in a sweet white muslin and a hat with poppies and wheat on it. Well, haven't I had enough to make me slumocky, she thought, sighing, and gulped her tea.

The Hermit wiped his mouth.

'Well – so long,' said the Hermit, and, moved at the last, stooped as though to take a kiss. But Mrs Caker dodged, and gave him a push with all her strength that did not even rock him. The one he gave her sent her sprawling.

It would seem that the warm, dark, blood-pulsing intimacy in which the Hermit and Mrs Caker had lived during the winter had fostered neither friendship nor esteem.

Then the Hermit, bawling, 'Serve you right, you—' set out cheerfully for the cross-roads on his way to Beatty. In the suitcase he had his knife for carving, a pair of Saxon's old trousers, a bundle of blackish-yellow visiting cards, bearing the names of Alma-Tadema, J. McNeill Whistler (the butterfly in one corner almost worn away), Edward L'Estrange, and Holman Hunt; also Bear with Cubs and three shillings and twopence, the property of Mrs Caker.

It was three o'clock. The busy quiet of April lay over the oak wood, filled with the chirruping and sudden flight of nesting birds. Mrs Caker staggered to her feet, crying bitterly, sat down at the table again, and rubbed her bruise. Never in all her happy-go-lucky, live-by-moments life had she felt so miserable. A womanly pride, almost buried beneath her natural generosity towards men and her slovenly habits, had been roused by the Hermit's blows and casual departure. I'm gettin' on fer sixty, she thought. Fifty-six, and not a bit o' comfort nor prosperity nowhere. I'll end up in the poorhouse, that's what I'll do. Oh well . . . that won't stop Easter coming.

A noise outside roused her. Someone was coming up the garden path.

She looked up idly. It was Mrs Fisher from the Green Lion, very neat, with her mouth mimmed up. She was carrying, as though it were a snake, a very large cardboard box.

'Arternoon, Mrs Fisher,' said Mrs Caker languidly, but managing to get a smile into her drowned blue eyes. 'Proper loaded up, aren't 'ee. What is ut, in the name o' goodness?'

'It's fer you, Mrs Caker.' Mrs Fisher, still with her mouth mimmed, set the box down heavily on the path. 'Post come up here a while ago, but you was out, so he come down ter us and knocked *us* up. Said he didn't like ter leave it, 'case anyone was ter walk in and take it. Tramps, likely, he meant,' ended Mrs Fisher meaningly.

'If you mean Dick Falger, he's gone and he didn't steal neither,' cried Mrs Caker, unaware of the three and twopence. 'Fer maye? That monster?'

Her languor and depression gone, her eyes sparkling, she ran out and lifted the box, wincing as she pressed it against the bruise. ' 'Tisn't very heavy, anyways.'

'The old man gone?' cried Mrs Fisher.

'Aye. Just went off,' indifferently. 'Felt like a change, I expect. Here, gie us a hand, Mrs Fisher, 'tis all netted up.'

After they had tried for a little while to undo the string, Mrs Fisher's curiosity got the better of her, and she cried:

'Oh, where's a knife? We'll never undo these doddy knots.'

'It's not Saxon's writin',' muttered Mrs Caker, sawing at the string. Together they lifted off the lid, Mrs Fisher's contempt for Mrs Caker forgotten in the excitement.

Sheets of pale rose tissue were revealed.

'Oh, what is ut?' cried Mrs Fisher, hopping.

'Maybe 'tis owd cloes from mie daughter-in-law—' Mrs Caker was beginning, but her voice faded – died into a thunderstruck silence as she slowly, with arms at full length, lifted out a gorgeous dark grey squirrel coat, top-heavy with a collar of smoky fox.

'Mercy preserve us,' whispered Mrs Fisher, and her mouth came unmimmed. Slowly she put out a work-worn hand and touched the fur. Then she said confidently:

' 'Tis a mistake, Mrs Caker. Must be.'

'It's just mie size, Mrs Fisher! Did 'ee ever see – aye, the beauty! I must just try it on.'

'Better not, Mrs Caker,' croaked Mrs Fisher, circling about the coat like a warning raven. 'Ye might soil it.'

But Mrs Caker was slipping her arms, in their dirty torn sleeves, into the silk-lined sleeves of the coat. She drew it round herself, and

the soft, electric warmth of fur caressed her neck as she looked
delightedly down the coat's silvery length.

'Do it suit maye?'

'Looks kind o' funny wi'out a hat.'

'Niver mind; I'll get one next week.'

'You're niver goin' to *keep* it, Nellie Caker?'

'You watch maye, Mrs Fisher!'

'Wait a bit – here's a letter.'

Mrs Fisher had been poking in the wrappings, as though hoping
to find a hat they had overlooked, and held up an envelope.

'Gie it ter maye.' Mrs Caker snatched, and read.

The next instant Mrs Fisher found herself seized by the arm, and
running out of the cottage and down the path. Mrs Caker, the other
hand clutching the coat round herself, was crying—

'It's fer maye, Mrs Fisher, it's fer maye! Saxon bought it fer maye!
He's come into a bit o' money, he says, and it's fer maye! Come on,
quick.'

'Where we goin'?' panted Mrs Fisher.

'Down to yours. You got a long glass, haven't 'ee? Oh, Mrs Fisher,
to think o' maye in a fur coat! Oh, Mrs Fisher, a fur coat! Oh, Mrs
Fisher! A fur coat!'

Viola's first thought on hearing that Saxon had come into all that
money was that perhaps he might help Catty, so she wrote off at
once to Tina, asking her if she would tell him about Catty, and
adding that she, Viola, would be awfully grateful if he would help.

The news by this time was all over the village. Mrs Caker's coat
had been the herald, assisted by Mrs Caker. The village did not at
first know how much Saxon had come in for; of course, Mrs Caker
was swanking all over the place and had said on one occasion (to
the realist-barman at the Green Lion, in fact) that it might be as
much as a thousand pounds. But that was a bit too much, that was,
even when supported by the evidence of the fur coat, and Sible
Pelden, laughing merrily, said 'Oh yeah?' Then Viola met Mrs
Caker in the post-office in Sible Pelden and wishing, because of her
plans for Catty, to stand well with Saxon's family, schoolgirlishly

325

introduced herself. In the course of the awkward conversation that followed, Viola said exactly how much Saxon had got: and Mrs Caker rushed off to the Green Lion to tell.

Sible Pelden laughed louder than ever. Putting its finger against its nose, Sible Pelden refused to believe – until Tina sent her mother-in-law a newspaper cutting mentioning the sum in print, and Sible Pelden was convinced.

And then the village quietly, angrily, withdrew from the Cakers. Like everyone else, Sible Pelden felt that Saxon's luck was Just A Bit Too Much, and refused to discuss it. Mrs Caker found that no one would gossip with her. No one mentioned the event, except obliquely and spitefully. The fur coat was glamorous, and them up The Eagles had written and asked her to tea, but Mrs Caker was not enjoying the first few days of being a rich man's mother.

Tina and Saxon were not completely enjoying their money, either. The Essex village was too innocent to suspect Saxon and his late employer of the modish vice, but it was plain what their neighbours in the mews, the reporters whom Saxon refused to see, and some of the more conventionally loose-minded friends of the Baumers thought. Tina felt angrily amused, but also a little sickened. She thought that everyone who had read the Amazing Will paragraph must have come to the same conclusion. 'Uh-huh,' she could hear the sophisticates gently saying, from Marble Arch to Fitzroy Square. 'Uh-huh.'

Poor Mr Spurrey, innocent old Victorian bawdy! With what outraged amazement he would have gobbled at such an accusation. Perhaps, for more reasons than the obvious one, it was a good thing that he was dead.

So Tina was just in the mood to be a little irritated by Viola's letter. Their fortune had not been theirs a week yet, they had not even actual possession of it, and here was Viola on the make. True, she was on the make for someone else, and in an excellent cause, but that made her request the more irritating because it was the more difficult to refuse.

So Tina wrote back quite crisply, explaining that Saxon was far too busy to be worried just now, and that in any case they had not got the money yet and when they did they would have to think very carefully about what they were going to do with it and could not make any promises. She added that she was very sorry and enclosed a cheque for Catty, value one pound.

Viola was pleased to have the pound but very snubbed by the letter and wondered more than ever what was to be done for poor Catty.

Then the pound gave her an idea. She would write to all the people she knew and try to get together a little Fund for Catty. It could be put into the Post Office and drawn out by Catty when she wanted it. By the time it was all gone she, Viola, might have managed to get some more from somewhere, though she had no idea where from, for that thirty pounds had almost gone, the last fiver having been broken into for her spring outfit, and now she was sure that she would never dare to ask her father-in-law for an allowance.

But she might earn some. Life at The Eagles had become so dismal since Tina had left that Viola was seriously thinking about trying to get a job in London as a salesgirl. Shirley would help her. She was frightened by the idea, but at least a job in London would get her away from this one-horse place, and help her not to go all broody about Him, That Beast. (Only it was getting more and more difficult to think of him as That Beast when all she could remember was how frightfully good-looking he was and oh lord! he was getting married in a fortnight, and back came the pain. No poet has yet compared unhappy love to toothache, yet that is what it undoubtedly most resembles.)

Then she remembered what Tina had said about sublimating your mind (it meant doing something else so that you didn't think about what was making you miserable) and she decided that she would shut herself in the library that very afternoon and write all her letters asking people if they would send a contribution to Catty's Fund.

So at half-past two she came slowly downstairs carrying her fountain-pen in her mouth and a lot of Woolworth notepaper. As she crossed the hall, Mrs Wither met her, looking preoccupied.

'Going to write letters, dear?'

Her tone was absent, but sufficiently kind. The news about Saxon's fortune seemed to have sent Tina further than ever out of her mother's life, and naturally she turned more to Viola. They were all used to Viola now, even Madge. There was a tendency to call her Poor Viola. She was so much quieter and nicer these days, and after all it was a dreadful thing to be widowed so young.

'Yes, Mother.'

'That's right, dear. Well . . . I wish this afternoon were over.' And Mrs Wither sighed.

'I expect you do,' said Viola sympathetically.

'Well, dear, Mr Wither – Father and I felt that it is really the only thing to do. After all, if Saxon is coming down here with Tina to be received as our son-in-law we cannot very well ignore his mother, can we? And it lies with us to make the first move. After all, poor creature, she used to be respectable once. It hasn't been all her fault. And of course, he will be making her an allowance now, as Tina said.'

'Has she stopped doing washing?'

'Oh dear, yes – so I heard from Mrs Parsham. She sent a little boy round to all her people telling them not to send her any more. Well, dear, run along. I shall rely on you to help me.'

And Mrs Wither smiled and went into the drawing-room, to sit and knit and think what a lot of things had happened in the last year, and decide how she was going to cope with Mrs Caker, who was coming to tea at four o'clock.

Viola went into the dingy little library, and shut the door.

An hour passed quietly, while she sat at the table with her pale gold head bent over the paper and the brilliant April sunlight pouring over the faded backs of uninteresting books and the stout, ugly yellow wooden furniture. Everything was quiet except the sparrows who darted to and fro outside the window over the bright green grass. A quarter to four struck sleepily somewhere. Viola put down the pen, yawning. It was tiring, writing letters.

She had written to Shirley, and to Mrs Colonel Phillips, to Mrs Parsham and to the chemist's son with whom she had danced at the Infirmary Ball and whom she had since met once or twice in

Chesterbourne and once had a coffee with. She had written to that friend of Shirley's who kept a dress-shop in London, and to Irene, nicest and most generous of The Crowd (though The Crowd as a whole was anything but mean), and spent a quarter of an hour over the letter to Lady Dovewood, which was very humble and imploring. To each of these persons she had explained that Miss Edith Cattyman who had been at Burgess and Thompson's for fifty years had been dismissed, and was leaving at the end of the month and would have no recourses. She, Viola, would be so grateful if they could see their way to sending a small donation for Miss Cattyman to go into a Fund in the Post Office and she was theirs truly, Viola Wither.

She leant back, looking complacently at the pile of letters. Now was that everybody? Shirley, Parsham, Phillips, Dovewood, Morley, Irene, Mrs Givens . . . *and the Springs. Of course, I ought to write to the Springs.* The thought flew into her mind, and she sat staring at the writing-pad, her heart beating painfully.

Of course I ought. They're so rich, and Tina always said Mrs Spring's got rotten health and that makes her very decent about giving money to hospitals and things. She'd be sure to be sorry for Catty and send a good lot.

And suddenly she was overwhelmed with longing to write to Victor, to put his name with 'dear' in front of it, to sign herself 'yours truly', and stick the stamp very carefully on the envelope the least bit sideways so that it meant a kiss, and go out after tea in the lovely spring evening and post the letter in the box at the cross-roads. She would be able to think, all the next day, 'Perhaps he's opening my letter . . . now he's reading it . . . now he's seen it's from me,' and then, of course, he would have to write back – unless he just sent a cheque with compliments. But even then, there would be the envelope with her name on it in his writing, and she could keep that for ever.

She knew that it would do quite as well if she wrote to Mrs Spring or even to Hetty (who had been so kind that day last summer at the garden party) but the longing to write to Victor was so strong that it defeated her commonsense.

After all, it's quite an ordinary thing to do, she told herself, and it's for Catty. She picked up the pen and bent again over the table.

The letter was short. She was too afraid of boring or annoying him to write much.

My dear Mr Spring,

I am writing to you to ask you if you would kindly send me some money for an old friend of mine, Miss Edith Cattyman. She has just been dismissed from Burgess and Thompson's, a Ladies' Outfitters in Chesterbourne, after being there for fifty years without recourses. Of course the money would be put into a fund in the Post Office.

And then the pen hesitated. She was trying to make it write those wishes for his happiness that she knew she ought to give.

It was no use. The pen would not write. Carefully moving the letter aside, she put her arms down on the table and cried quietly, heart-brokenly, for a moment. Then with tears running down she finished the letter.

I am,
Yours truly,
Viola Wither

and put it into its envelope just as the clock struck four and the front-door bell rang.

The letter's first words, unfortunately, were not true: he was not her dear Mr Spring, but its last ones were true to their last shade of meaning. She was his truly, and always would be. Worse luck, she thought, carefully powdering her nose. Then she went into the drawing-room to help receive Mrs Caker.

Mrs Caker wore the coat, and hat, shoes, stockings, gloves and handbag in grey to match. When Mrs Caker was young, 'all to match' was the height of elegance, and since then she had not been in a position to learn that 'all to match' is now regarded as the depths of dowdiness. But this did not matter, because Mrs Wither was in exactly the same state of ignorance, and she thought that, apart from the fuzzy bits of hair sticking out under her hat and her lack of teeth, Mrs Caker looked very nice. And soon Saxon would give her the money to buy some teeth, and then she would look nicer still.

Mrs Caker was not nervous. She was too interested in her surroundings and in noticing what there was for tea and what Mrs Wither and Viola had on. She kept her feet pressed together at first and would not take her gloves off because her hands were so red, but as no one said anything about her lack of teeth or her washing, she at last took her gloves off, and as no one said anything about her hands being red, she soon forgot them and enjoyed her tea.

Mrs Wither sometimes had gleams of common-sense. They usually came from following her instincts and forgetting what was the proper thing to do. She had one this afternoon. Instead of pretending that Mrs Caker was an ordinary caller and that nothing exciting had happened to bring her into the drawing-room at The Eagles, she plunged at once, as she handed Mrs Caker her first cup of tea, into the realities.

'Well, Mrs Caker,' said Mrs Wither, 'I expect you're feeling as amazed as I am about your boy's wonderful luck,' and Mrs Caker, accepting the tea, replied eagerly, 'That I am, Mrs Wither. Niver had any idea o' such a thing, can't believe ut now,' and then they were well away, comparing notes, discussing the character of Mr Spurrey, wondering where Tina and Saxon would live, and whether Mrs Caker, when she left the cottage, would take a flat or a small house in Chesterbourne, or live in a boarding house, and recalling the personal appearance and habits of Mrs Caker's old father, the same by whose side she used to ride in the poppied hat. They carefully did not discuss (except for a nod and wink or two from Mrs Caker) the late Mr Caker, but otherwise they enjoyed the gossip as though there had been no social barriers between them.

Mrs Caker, indeed, was enjoying it all, sitting there in her new rig-out, eating tea-cake and noticing everything. The squalid little place over the other side of the wood, the bundles of sour-smelling dirty clothes, her recent exuberances with the Hermit, seemed very far away. It's quite like old times, thought Mrs Caker, when I was a bit of a girl with Dad. I wish Dick Falger could see maye now, having arternoon tea. Old bastard; I hope he dies in a ditch. I'm done wi' all that. Goin' ter be respectable now, thought Mrs Caker, her large limpid blue eyes fixed smilingly upon the faded ones of her hostess. Five pound a week, he said. I'll be proper comfortable on that.

This idyll was somewhat clouded by the arrival of Mr Wither, who sidled in, muttered over Mrs Caker's hearty outstretched hand, sipped half a cup of tea and sidled out again, choked by embarrassment and indignation at Fate, who had forced him to receive a washerwoman at The Eagles. Chauffeurs, shopgirls, washerwomen . . . where were the Withers drifting?

And down in the kitchen Fawcuss, Annie and Cook were still discussing whether they should call Mrs Caker Madam. They had been spared this humiliation today because Mrs Wither had in a most irregular manner gone herself to open the door to Mrs Caker (Mrs Wither had guessed what was being said in the kitchen) but sooner or later they were bound to be confronted by Mrs Caker, and then what would they do?

Fawcuss said No. Duty was duty, and of course It Did Say that there was more rejoicing over one sinner that repenteth than over nine and ninety just persons, but after all, how were they to know that Mrs Caker had repented? All she had done was to turn that wicked old man out (and not before it was time, either) and go round in a fur coat that would have kept a poor family for months. No. Fawcuss would say *Mrs Caker*, quite pleasant-like, but Madam she would not.

And Annie and Cook, at the close of this discussion that had gone on ever since they heard, two days ago, that Mrs Caker was coming to tea at The Eagles, decided they would do the same. Annie added a rider to the effect that she did wonder at Her havin' that woman to the house, seein' the whole village knew about her and that wicked old man and so must She, after that awful scene in the yard last summer.

But Mrs Wither, making the best of a bad job, had decided that Mrs Caker was not really so bad. She had apparently turned over a new leaf since Saxon came into the money. Mr Wither reported, from spy-work carried out under his hat-brim while on his constitutional, that the Hermit seemed to have gone; his hut had fallen in and Mr Wither had not seen him outside the Green Lion nor in the cottage. With the Hermit gone, a new wardrobe bought for her by Saxon, her washerwomaning given up and an apparent desire to be thought well of by her betters, Mrs Caker was acceptable, and Mrs Wither parted from her with a pleasant feeling that difficulties had been overcome and the way smoothed for possible future meetings between the two families.

Just before dinner Madge came in, glum and silent. She had been for a long walk with Polo, to avoid seeing Mrs Caker, for she agreed with her father that a washerwoman at The Eagles was a bit too much of a good thing. Mrs Wither had had to apologize for her absence and make some excuse that did not take in Mrs Caker in the least, for she knew Madge's sort through and through.

The long spring evening slowly passed. At half-past eight Viola slipped out to post her letters, loitering, because it was such a beautiful twilight, along the white road that ran beside the little oak wood. The trees were in early leaf, just as they had been on her first evening at The Eagles a year ago; the air was mild and scented by new foliage, one star was out, and down in the dark wood a thrush was singing. It was all enough to break your heart, if your heart had not been broken already.

She posted her letters, keeping Victor's until the end and pushing it slowly through the letter-box, letting it fall at last into the darkness. She heard the little sound as it landed on the other letters below. She stood for a minute, staring at the box, then turned and walked slowly home.

# CHAPTER XXV

The next day was Hetty's twenty-first birthday, and fine and clear, though haunted by one of those bitter little winds that had killed Mr Spurrey. There was to be a garden party in the afternoon with a dinner in the evening for some of the young people living in the neighbourhood. On the breakfast table Hetty found a superb beauty-box, fitted with all the creams in creation, from Victor, and a little necklace of perfectly matched pearls with a platinum and diamond clasp from her aunt. In a discreet little round case was a pair of ear-rings to match.

'They were your mother's,' said Mrs Spring, lifting her face to take Hetty's slightly ashamed kiss, 'and they're real, of course. I had a new clasp put on them and the ear-rings made into clips. You'd better wear them tonight.'

'This is most elaborate, Vic; thank you very much,' said Hetty, examining the beauty-box and wishing irritably that her aunt had not given her a present so semi-sacred and obviously hoarded up for this occasion, for it would make it more difficult to announce, as she meant to do before the day was over, that she was shortly going to leave Grassmere for ever. 'Did you choose it yourself?'

'Yes,' curtly. He was reading the paper with the ill-tempered expression that was natural to him nowadays, 'but it was Phyl's idea. I'm glad you like it.'

'Why? Did Phyl think my beauty needs attention?' Hetty's tone was quiet, but a flush came slowly into her pale cheeks.

'Good God, I don't know what she thought. Can't you two stop picking on each other for five minutes?' and he got up, strewing the paper all round him, and went out of the room. They heard his car start up, and go off.

Hetty went on with her grapefruit, Mrs Spring with hers. Presently, as her aunt sighed, Hetty looked up and said what was expected of her:

'Vic seems very on edge lately. I imagine it's the strain of spending so much time with the betrothed. It would strain me, too.'

'Engagements are always trying,' retorted her aunt sharply, 'and you can see for yourself how on edge Phyl is. She does too much; she'll never keep her looks if she doesn't learn to relax a bit. And that makes her go at Vic, because she's worn out and won't see it. She's not been herself for weeks.'

'An advantage, I cannot but feel,' drawled Hetty, 'were it not that the substitute is, if anything, worse than the original.'

'Don't speak in tha— there, Hetty, I don't want to pick on you on your twenty-first, but you make Phyl worse, you know. She's always nervier when she's been down here an hour or two and bickering with you. Why can't you leave each other alone? I know she's trying, I find her trying myself, I don't quite know why, I think it's because she's so healthy. Anyway, I wish you would try to keep the peace until the twenty-eighth. Then they'll be going off for six weeks and you and I will have time to get ourselves comfortably settled before they come home.'

Here was Hetty's chance, but she did not take it. Better leave it until after the garden party. She observed pensively, finishing her grapefruit:

'I detest her. To me she typifies all the varnished vulgarity and falseness of this horrifying age. Everything that she is, poetry is not. I wish that she would die, preferably violently.'

Before her staggered aunt could reply, in marched the antithesis of Poetry, wearing a becoming shirt-dress. She glittered with superficial health and energy, but she talked faster than she used, and her voice was shriller. The strain of being a minor society beauty, preparing for her wedding, supervising the furnishing of the flat and being engaged to Victor, whom she found daily more maddening, was telling even upon her superb health.

'Many happy returns,' nodding at Hetty. 'Hope you liked your beauty-box. Edna, Vic hasn't *gone*, has he? He is too sickening; he said last night he'd wait until I came down because I wanted to give him that bracelet to take back. The fools have made it too big, it falls off every time I put it on, and I wanted to tell him about the scent, too, I *must* have it for tonight and it won't be in, those fools said, until late this afternoon. Can I have some fresh toast, please? Had any other presents, Hetty? Oh, help . . . books. Who from? What a weird cover.'

'A girl I was at school with. You would not know her.'

'Another of your brainy colleagues, I suppose. Edna, didn't Vic say *anything* about that bracelet? I want to wear it tonight and he knows that perfectly well, and they could easily have made it smaller today and he could have called for it and brought it back this evening if he'd taken it this morning. It really is too sickening. Hetty, I haven't done a thing about your present yet, I've been rushed to death, but I thought you might have my fox, just to go on with. I haven't got it here, Anthea's got it at the minute, but Vic's giving me a new one, and I thought the old one would just do for you.'

'You are very kind,' returned Hetty coolly, going white about the nostrils, 'but I do not much care to wear the skins of dead animals round my neck. When the skin of the dead animal happens to have been worn round your neck for a full two years, I dislike the prospect intensely. And if you give me your fox, I shall burn it.'

There was a shattered silence.

'Or rather,' drawling, 'I shall request Heyrick to burn it. In the incinerator. Then,' concluded Hetty, tapping an egg, 'I need not touch it.'

Phyllis laughed angrily. A red stain had got up into her smooth dark cheeks.

'Well, you needn't be so snooty about it, just because it isn't new. If I hadn't been so frightfully hard up just now I'd have got you a new one. Good thing I didn't, if that's how you feel about it – *you insulting, half-baked, affected little beast*' – her voice going up shrilly.

Hetty rose to her feet

'Be quiet – both of you!' cried Mrs Spring very angrily. 'You ought to be ashamed – squabbling like children! Hetty, apologize to Phyllis at once.'

Hetty shook her head, and walked out of the room.

With this pleasing skirmish the festivities for Hetty's twenty-first birthday were launched, and it was Mrs Spring's task to whip up a gay and carefree atmosphere to greet the guests when they arrived for tea and tennis at three o'clock. As Hetty went about the house still looking white round the nostrils while Phyllis kept up a continual splutter like a catherine-wheel about Victor and the bracelet and the scent and Hetty's extraordinarily amusing behaviour which some people might have taken seriously but thank heaven she, Phyllis, had a sense of humour – Mrs Spring found herself, by four o'clock, with a bad headache and feeling most unlike performing that ritual known as mingling with the guests.

However, she mingled, and by six o'clock tea and cocktails were well away and a party of about thirty people gathered from Stanton, Chesterbourne, Dovewood Abbey and Lukesedge was apparently enjoying itself. So cheerful and talkative and absorbed was everybody, leaping after tennis balls in the chilly sunlight or gossiping, hatless but in coats, on the veranda and in the drawing-room where the wireless was playing, that Hetty saw no reason why she should not slip away for ten minutes to the water-butt in the vegetable garden and cut the pages of *Mithraic Emblems*, which was her schoolfriend's present.

The canopy of pale red and white blossom hung once more over the deserted orchard. The almond-trees were flowering and the cherry, the pear in a waterfall of white stars and the dark pink Siberian crab-apple. Hetty sat down on the three bricks with her back against the water-butt and opened *Mithraic Emblems*; but when she had read a few fiery, jewel-like lines she let the book fall on her lap and, leaning her head against the water-butt, stared up at the pale blue sky.

How difficult life was, how complicated and poisoned! How hard it was to have courage and make steadily for the things one wanted, ignoring everything else until one got them. She had planned to tell Mrs Spring at breakfast that she was going to leave Grassmere; then she had put it off until the party should be over. Now it was half-past six in the evening of her twenty-first birthday, the day that she had been looking forward to for nearly seven years, and she had not told her aunt, and was afraid that she would not. She said to herself: I'll tell her tonight, after the dinner party, but she knew that the words were weak, an escape and a putting off. To give herself courage, she thought of the attic room in Bloomsbury – near, perhaps, to the very house where lived Virginia Woolf herself – with the view across pale and dark chimney pots under the smoky London sky, the noise of traffic coming up faintly, the smell of coffee brewing on the gas-ring and her own eyes moving, in a trance of content, over the pages of a book.

Looking down at *Mithraic Emblems* again with a sigh, she caught the flutter of a white apron moving between the trees. Oh dear, that would be Davies; she had said that she was going down to the orchard for ten minutes' peace and asked the Welsh girl to let her know if people began wondering where she was.

Yes, it was Davies. But there was somebody with her, an elderly, shortish, slender and stooping man, wearing no hat and carrying – surely – a pile of books under one arm. In the other hand he held a round white parcel, stiffly upright.

Now they were coming under the canopy of apple-blossom, and the stranger, who wore glasses, was gazing up at the bloom as though he were more interested in it than in Hetty, who got doubtfully to her feet as they came near.

Little Merionethshire hurried up, while the man followed more slowly.

'Oh, Miss Hetty,' began Davies, 'I hope you won't mind me bringing the gentleman here, indeed, but Madam's talking to Lady Dovewood and as he said it was you he wanted to see I thought I'd best bring him along here—'

'And when I heard that you were down in the vegetable garden reading by the water-butt, I knew that you wouldn't mind my coming,' interrupted the stranger, looking at her with mild yet enthusiastic light eyes behind thick lenses, 'because that's just what your father used to do – steal away with a precious volume whenever he got the chance. I'm his brother, my dear. I'm your uncle, Frank Franklin.'

And, stooping unembarrassedly to put the parcel of books on the ground, he held out his hand, which Hetty bewilderedly took.

'There, Miss Hetty,' smiled Merionethshire, looking from one to the other, 'isn't that a nice birthday present for you? Your uncle.'

'Yes . . . thank you, Davies,' muttered Hetty. She went on staring, all her usual composure gone, at the thin fresh-coloured face of her uncle, in which she could see not the faintest likeness to her own.

'I'd best be getting back, Miss Hetty, if you don't mind?' suggested Davies; 'and if I were you, Miss, I wouldn't stay down here too long, for Madam's sure to ask for you in a minute.'

'All right, Davies. Thanks very much, we'll be along soon,' said Hetty, then looked round confusedly to see if there was anywhere for Uncle Frank Franklin to sit down. But he, without a word, pulled out another three bricks from a pile near by, arranged them neatly, seated himself, and pointed to the other three. Still in silence, Hetty sat down facing him.

'Before I say anything, I want to give you these,' he began eagerly. 'They were my suggestion. You see,' holding out the rounded paper parcel, 'we don't know your tastes yet, Hetty, (though we hope to) but everybody must like violets.'

Opening the parcel with a mutter of thanks she found a bunch of the largest, darkest and finest violets she had ever seen. She breathed in their faint scent, and said warmly:

'I *do* like them. How very kind of you; I could not have had anything that I liked better. You knew it was my birthday, then?'

'They are the famous Windward violets,' he said with a touch of complacence, gazing at the flowers. 'Oh yes – indeed we did. Your Aunt Rose and I have followed your progress (*so far as we could, Hetty*) with deep interest ever since you were a baby. We wanted to adopt you, you know.'

'Oh, are you *that* uncle? I just knew that there was someone . . .'

'Yes. Your Aunt Rose and I, you see, have no children. We . . .

no, we have no family. But your Aunt Spring thought it better for you to go with her, and no doubt it has all been much more comfortable for you . . . you have a beautiful home here, have you not? so spacious.'

'I hate it,' she answered simply.

'Do you? Do you indeed?' he said eagerly, looking pleased. 'Why is that? Perhaps you cannot enjoy it because you are thinking of all the millions who can never hope to have enough to eat, let alone a place like this to live in, is that it?'

'Oh no, it isn't that, I'm afraid, Uncle Frank. It's just that life here is so tedious, and they will not let me do what I want to do.'

'And what is that? dear me, how I am running on, and I haven't yet given you half your Aunt Rose's messages, nor told you how I come to be here today . . . and perhaps you ought to be getting back to your friends?'

'Oh, they can wait, and they aren't my friends anyway, they're Aunt Edna's. I'm so enjoying it here. Do tell me why you came.'

'Well, there happened to be a sale of books this morning at a place called Blackbourne (perhaps you know it, yes) and as I had to come down for that, your Aunt Rose said, Frank, why not take the bull by the horns and call on the Springs and try, at least try, to see Hetty.'

'Uncle Frank,' interrupted Hetty slowly, 'you said you "had" to come down here for a sale of books. Why was that?'

'Well, my dear, I'm a bookseller, you know. Your Aunt Rose and I have a bookshop on the corner of Acre Street in the Charing Cross Road. Did you not know that?'

'No,' said Hetty, staring at the pear-tree.

'Well – but did your Aunt Spring never tell you anything about us?'

'Uncle Frank,' she said steadily, 'I never knew that you existed until five minutes ago. I was always told that my father's people were . . . not very well-off, you know, and bookish . . . and they'd never got on or anything – you know—'

'Made money,' he nodded. 'Yes, I can imagine what you were told. Hetty, before we go any further, I must tell you that your Aunt

Rose is a Communist, an active Communist working for the Revolution in Great Britain, and that I am a Socialist. A Fabian. Yes, well. Now go on.'

'– and I just knew that there were two uncles, and one of them wanted to adopt me—'

'That was me, your Aunt Rose and me. Your other uncle, Henry, is not married. He is a librarian in York.'

'– and I certainly rather got the impression that my father's people didn't care much about me but just—'

'– wanted to adopt you so that they could manage your money,' nodded Uncle Frank. 'Yes. Go on—'

'– I never knew that you kept a *bookshop*,' she ended, 'or else of course I should have written to you years ago. Books are my chief interest in life.'

'Are they, are they indeed. They were your father's too, so that is quite natural. Of course,' went on Uncle Frank, looking at once indignant and pleased, 'your Aunt Rose and I supposed that you never wrote to us *because* of the bookshop. We thought that you were a shocking little bourgeois snob, Hetty, idle and pleasure-loving, a typical product of the capitalist system at its worst. Yet we could not help feeling an interest in you, my dear, because we remembered you as a baby and so we wrote sometimes to your Aunt Spring for news of you.'

'She never told me. I was told nothing. It is *too bad*. Stupid, rude, narrow . . .'

'She did not answer our last three letters, Hetty, and so naturally we did not try to see you, because we thought that you did not wish to see us. Your Aunt Rose it was,' went on Uncle Frank, with relish, 'who first thought that it might have been your Aunt Spring who was keeping you from us. Your Aunt Rose, though an out-and-out materialist in religious matters, of course, has these intuitions occasionally. Divine visionings, I always think of them as. But I do not say so to her, for of course she is rather sensitive about her intuitions.'

'You must have thought me a detestable creature,' said Hetty in a low tone.

'Oh no, Hetty, not that. Just the helpless product of a corrupt and decaying system,' said Uncle Frank tolerantly. 'We are all cogs in it, Hetty, we cannot help ourselves. But we must leave all that for another talk, must we not? The main things now are that I have *seen* you,' checking off the points on one open palm, 'that we have *talked* together, and that the next time you are in London you will come to see us, will you not? and meet your Aunt Rose. Your Aunt Rose, though deeply affectionate, does not give her affection lightly. She needs knowing; I am the first to admit that, but when you do come to know her . . .' He shook his head, as though the visions inside it were too dazzling to be put into words, then got up from the three bricks without difficulty (and anyone who has sat on three bricks will appreciate this achievement), collected his books, and glanced inquiringly first at the way through the orchard and then at Hetty, as though suggesting that it was time they made a move.

But Hetty stood with her back pressed hard against the water-butt and said resolutely:

'Uncle Frank, may I come to live with you and Aunt Rose in London? Paying for myself, I mean? I have a hundred pounds a year of my own and I'm twenty-one today, so it's mine to do as I like with. If I gave you and Aunt Rose a pound a week, could you keep me for that? If you have a spare attic room I should like that better than anything. I wouldn't be any trouble. I only want to read all day, and later on perhaps I might get some kind of a job.'

'Good gracious me, Hetty, you go so fast, I cannot keep up with you!' cried Uncle Frank, looking alarmed and pleased and triumphant all at once. 'You can't arrange things like this in five minutes, you know. And what is your money invested in, my dear? Your Aunt Rose disapproves of invested income, of course, and I am afraid that if it were invested in armaments or anything of that sort she would not for a moment entertain the idea of having you as a paying guest . . . a boarder, shall we say? . . . a *lodger*! How easy it is to be a snob, is it not? Well . . .'

'I never heard my cousin (he looks after my money) say it was in armaments,' said Hetty. 'I think it's mostly in Government stock . . .

I suppose Aunt Rose' (she tried to keep a satirical note from her voice) 'would not approve of that, either?'

'Bad enough, Hetty, but not so bad as armaments.'

'Well, you will try, won't you, Uncle Frank, to persuade Aunt Rose to let me come? You see, I was going to tell Aunt Edna today that I mean to go and live in London and you can see what a difference it would make, can't you, if I could tell her that I was going to live with relations and not with strangers?'

'But your Aunt Rose and I, Hetty, *are* strangers to you,' he pointed out, beginning to lead the way back through the orchard. ('Good gracious, we have been away here nearly an hour!') It is a very big step, you know, to give up all this comfort and luxury and beauty,' glancing round him with a sigh, 'for life in one room over a bookshop.'

'But that's exactly what I've always wanted,' she cried. 'I hate all this. It's dead. I can't be myself in it. It may be other people's kind of beauty; it isn't mine. I want something . . . I don't know yet. Harder.'

He nodded as though he understood.

'And it won't come as a shock to Aunt Edna, either,' she went on. 'She's always known that I wanted to get away from here, and go to college.'

'You won't be able to manage college, my dear, on your income, and keep yourself as well.'

'Then I'll borrow from my capital,' recklessly, 'and pay myself back when I get something to do.'

'Jobs are not so easy to get nowadays, and I don't know what your Aunt Rose would say to a girl with enough invested income to live on trying to get a job. You see, you would be taking the work away from some girl who might need it to keep alive at all.'

Hetty was silent. She had a feeling that she and Aunt Rose might not get on together. Aunt Rose's principles were lofty, her taste in flowers impeccable, but she sounded as though she might be a little difficult to live with.

'But that can be discussed later, of course,' he added. 'Your Aunt Rose will be willing – eager, even, I am sure – to discuss *all* your problems with you at length. Where she gives, she gives unsparingly.

But what we really must decide, before I hurry off to catch my train, is whether you *really do want to come to us*. Now think, Hetty. Take your time. Do you, or do you not, upon reflection, want to come? Speak the truth: I shall not take it the wrong way, or misunderstand, if you change your mind.'

They had instinctively turned aside to walk in the rhododendron shrubbery where Hetty had sat with Viola in the summer, and now halted there, out of sight of the players on the tennis courts above. Hetty looked into her uncle's eager, commonplacishly sensitive face. He was just a little absurd, with his literary way of talking and his veneration for his wife, but Hetty knew that he could be managed, and that at a pinch he would show himself a sensible man. She had no fears about Uncle Frank. Aunt Rose was the snag. Just the kind of earnest, passionately sincere, talkative person that is not easy to deal with, thought Hetty. One is forced to respect their sincerity and that gives them an unfair hold. Suddenly it occurred to her that she could always leave Aunt Rose's house if she did not like it. If she tries to manage my affairs, I shall just walk out, she decided. She said:

'Yes, Uncle Frank, I do.'

'You are sure?'

'Yes. You see, even from the little you have told me I can see that you live the kind of life I have always wanted to live.'

He looked flattered

'Yes, I can understand that. We do know a number of very interesting Left Wingers whom your Aunt Rose has met in her work for the Party – and not only Left Wingers. George Crumley often drops in (you have heard of George Crumley, I am sure, the Miner's Friend, you know, the Quaker) and Alice MacNoughton and E. E. Tyler, and Donat Mulqueen and Roger Brindle—'

'Donat Mulqueen?'

Her tone made him glance at her sharply: then he smiled. She did not return his smile. She thought: No, he is not clever but he is not stupid. He is ingenuous, but it would not be easy to deceive him.

'Do you know his work?' asked Uncle Frank, letting his smile die in deference to her grave, rather bored look.

'I do.'

'And admire it, I gather?'

'Extremely.'

'Yes; well, we know him quite well. He often comes into the shop. Your Aunt Rose feeds him, poor boy.'

'Why? Hasn't he any means?'

'None, I gather, except what he earns by writing, and, of course, the commercialized papers will not touch his stuff because it is difficult, as well as obscene (I personally do not care for it, but your Aunt Rose says that he is the modern Keats) and the other papers, the intellectual ones, pay so badly, they have so little money behind them.'

She said nothing.

'And then,' he went on, 'what he does get, he spends on drink.'

'Does he?'

'All those boys – Roger Brindle, Donat, all of them, they drink all the time, Hetty. They're never completely sober. I've never imagined anything like it. Drink seems to be a kind of religion with them. I cannot describe it to you. Yet they get no pleasure from it, none at all. I find it very distressing, but your Aunt Rose is more tolerant, and she sees it all as a part of the decaying capitalist system – inevitable.'

All this sounded most promising. Nothing could be further from life at Grassmere, where everyone enjoyed their liquor and nothing was allowed to decay.

But who the hell was Aunt Rose, to be tolerant about Donat Mulqueen? And no one but a fool would compare his work to Keats's. It was not like anyone's; it was only like itself.

They were now passing slowly across the lower lawn towards the gates, and Hetty suddenly remembered her manners.

'I am so sorry, Uncle Frank; I was so interested in what you were saying that I quite forgot to ask you if you will have something. Some tea, or a cocktail, perhaps? And of course you must see Aunt Edna.'

'Oh no, thank you, my dear,' he said hastily. 'I had a cup of tea while I was waiting for the bus at Blackbourne and I don't really think I will see your aunt, if you don't mind; there really won't be comfortable time. I am afraid she will think this a most peculiar visit, creeping in like this and creeping out again and upsetting you so thoroughly, but I asked for *you*, you see, in case she should refuse to let me see you.'

'I don't think she would have done that, but I'm very glad that I have been able to see you alone, because of what we've been able to arrange.'

'Yes, well, Hetty, so am I – if your mind is really made up?'

'It really is. You have only put the match to a fire that has been waiting for seven years.' (Uncle Frank looked a little alarmed.) 'Good-bye,' holding out her hand. 'I will write to you as soon as I know what my plans are, and then you can let me know if you can have me.'

'I will do that, Hetty. Frank Franklin, Acre Street, WC2 will always find me. Good-bye.'

She watched him go down the road. When he had gone a little way she called, almost challengingly, 'Oh . . . Uncle Frank . . . give my regards to Aunt Rose,' and he turned, waving and nodding.

She walked slowly back to the party, with the disagreeable feeling in her stomach that some people have when they know that there is going to be a row.

Mrs Spring was sitting on the veranda with one or two older people, a smart figure in black and white with hair admirably dyed to a dark chestnut-red. She had noticed Hetty's lengthy absence, and while she talked, her pain-dulled eyes moved about, trying to find her niece. Her headache was so much worse that she wondered how she was to get through the evening's gaieties, and she felt really bitter with Phyl and Hetty, whose tiresomeness had brought it on.

There was Hetty, lounging down by the geranium beds with a book and looking both untidy and bored. Mrs Spring waved, calling rather tartly, and Hetty sauntered across, still feeling rather bewildered and as though Uncle Frank's visit had been a divine visioning.

As she looked across at her aunt's tired, pain-drawn face that was trying to look serene and gay, Hetty felt both remorseful and angry. Mrs Spring had suppressed letters, snubbed people who only meant to be kind and done everything she could to keep Hetty away from her father's family. Yet it had all been done, Hetty was sure, for Hetty's good. How tiresome people were! how complicated, tortuous and impossible to judge all in one piece. And the simple ones were dull and faintly irritating. Not for the first time, Hetty decided that she preferred books.

Victor, picking up his letters from the bamboo tray in the hall an hour later, was pounced upon by Phyllis, coming quickly downstairs. She was dressed for the evening's party in black and yellow stripes, and suggested a slim, ill-tempered, handsome wasp.

Victor just glanced at her, then back at his letters again. He did it on purpose; he wanted to annoy her. She got on his nerves so badly these days that he really hated the sight of her and had to show it somehow. He supposed that things would be better when they were married; he hoped so, anyway, or it was a cheerful look-out.

Why couldn't she leave him alone? She was everlastingly balling him out about something. Why hadn't he said he liked the new cushions she had chosen for the (ruddy) dining-recess? Couldn't he be there when they demonstrated the televisor; he *ought* to; surely he could get away for an hour in the morning? Blah . . . blah . . . blah . . . and for months he had been overworking steadily on the Bracing Bay scheme.

Women were only there, after all, for one . . .

'Vic,' began Phyllis rapidly, 'I suppose you didn't remember my scent?'

'No, I did not. I haven't been into the West End today, anyway.' He was walking towards the stairs, skimming his letters. He looked tired.

'My dear, don't you think you'd better see a good man or something? This morning you went off before I came down, and you knew perfectly well I'd particularly asked you last night to wait until I'd told you properly about the emerald bracelet. Those fools have made it much too big and it falls off every time I put it on.'

'Oh.'

He was reading the last of his letters. It was written on

347

Woolworth notepaper in a childish and rather vulgar hand, yet it appeared to absorb him.

'Vic.'

'What?'

He put the letter into his pocket and for the first time gave her a smile. It was as near sour as his attractive face could get. 'New dress. Rather nice. Is that what I'm to say?'

The funny, wrongly spelled little letter with its appeal for some old trout he'd never heard of had gone straight into his heart. He was very aware of it, tucked into his pocket. It almost felt warm, lying there. Dear little kid. Funny, sweet little kid. You'd better be careful, his hazel eyes said to Phyllis, giving her the quick summing-up look that women admired. Don't push me too far, you bad-tempered —, said the eyes. *Now* what's biting you?

'You'll be paying for them soon, so it's just as well you approve. Now did you hear a word I said, Vic? About the bracelet?'

'Yes. Too small. Won't go on. Too bad.' He was going upstairs, and said this to annoy her. He had heard what she said.

'Too *big*, I said, not too small. I wish you'd listen when I speak to you. I really think you'd better take it back tomorrow; they always take more notice of a man.'

'I'm rather tied up tomorrow. Can't you go? You're going up, aren't you?'

'I don't know yet. Probably. You know I loathe making plans hours ahead. Anyway—'

'What's the fuss outside?' jerking his head towards the garden.

'Hetty's twenty-first. Don't tell me you'd forgotten?'

'Oh God, so it is. Are any of them staying for dinner?'

'This lot isn't, but some more are coming in about eight-thirty. Can't we go out to Stanton again and dance? I really can't stand a whole evening of your girl cousin; she's too insufferable. What do you think happened this morning? Vic – do listen. Need you walk upstairs while I'm talking to you?'

'Going to change,' he said over his shoulder.

'Well, I do think you ought to do something about Hetty. I wish you'd speak to her – but of course, you never do. You always stick up

for her and of course it's quite enough for *me* to ask you to say anything to her for you to make up your mind you won't.'

He was disappearing down the corridor towards his room.

'I say,' called Phyllis, one foot on the stair, '*did you get the ring?*'

'No. My secretary'll run down tomorrow.'

He went into his room and shut the door.

Phyllis hurried into the morning-room as though she were late
for an appointment, took out her engagement book and studied its
crammed pages, then stared discontentedly out of the window.

Of course, one expected the last days before one's wedding to be
hell; all her young married friends had warned her that they were,
and how right they had been. She had been bridesmaid, too, to
Anthea and Gillian, to say nothing of Rosemary, Jennifer and
Anne, and had observed them getting thinner, crosser and jumpier
as the day drew near. The richer they were, the jumpier they got,
because the wedding was bigger and more of a fuss and the fussier it
was, the more there was to go wrong.

But neither Anthea, Gillian, Jennifer, Rosemary nor Anne had
had a Victor to cope with. *Their* young men had not been so utterly
foul and completely lacking in all decent feeling, so uninterested in
the flat and in plans for the wedding and the honeymoon and everything. It was like being engaged to a stick of firewood, thought
Phyllis furiously, a stupid, stocky, obstinate stick of firewood. And he
hardly ever wanted to kiss her and when he did she didn't feel like
it and he was no good at kissing, anyway. She knew him too well.
She even knew what he was going to say next. Once she had said it
for him, and he was all hurt and surprised and got all mushy. And
when he lost his temper and got bossy, she hated that worst of all,
because she felt that he could knock her down and *make* her do
what he wanted, simply, and only, because he was stronger than she
was. He just made her see red, that was all there was to it. Her mind
went rushing blindly round in a stifling little cage of discontent and
nervous exhaustion like a slim black marmoset as she stood staring
out of the window at the departing guests. All her friends went
through these dark furious fits with their men, of course; many a
time she had listened and given advice and smoked a great many

cigarettes while she did so, but this was the first time that she had really had one about Victor. If only he would be *different*! quite, completely different. But she did not know what she wanted him to be.

And there were a thousand things going wrong about the wedding, too. There were those fools with the bracelet, and now those other fools had dyed the bridesmaid's shoes the wrong colour, and there was the most sickening delay about the hand-quilted coverlets for the twin beds, the miner's wife down in Wales who was to have done them had had to stop work because she had just lost her baby or something, and though of course Phyllis was very sorry about the baby, the wedding was important too, wasn't it, and Phyllis was giving the woman work, wasn't she, and when she, Phyllis, tried to get the firm who employed the woman to give the job to someone else because there was such a rush, the firm was *shocked*, as though Phyllis had suggested something too awful.

Oh, everything was too sickening, and even though Vic didn't help, or take any interest, he'd be the first to bawl if the wedding didn't go off without a hitch; nothing made him more furious than bad staff work.

Sighing, she turned from the window, sat down in a chair with less than her usual athletic grace, and opened *Vogue*.

The guests had all gone, by car or walking out hatless into the lovely evening, and now there was a lull until the new ones arrived about a quarter-past eight.

Mrs Spring came in, followed by Hetty.

'Well, all I can say is,' Mrs Spring was snapping, 'it was a very rude, queer thing to do. Everybody was asking where you were.'

Hetty, who looked pale and excited, did not answer.

'And considering it was your party, I think you might have behaved properly for once,' Mrs Spring went on. 'Where on earth did you get to?'

'She was down in the shrubbery talking to someone who looked like a verger when I saw her,' threw in Phyllis, not looking up from *Vogue*. 'Tim and I were playing tennis, and we saw them lurking down there in the most odd manner.'

'Who was that, Hetty?' asked Mrs Spring, sharply.

'If you must know – and you'll have to know soon – it was Frank Franklin, my uncle, whom you've always been so very careful that I shouldn't meet.'

Phyllis did not look up, but one slender foot in its dark yellow satin slipper stopped swinging.

'Who?' Mrs Spring sat upright. 'Your Uncle Frank was here? This afternoon?' (Hetty nodded.) 'What did he want? Why didn't they tell me he was here? What an extraordinary thing to do. I suppose he came to see you?' looking a little confused. 'He can't have stayed very long. I hope you saw that he had something before he left? Did he want to see you about anything special? I must say I think it's very peculiar – almost sneaky. Why on earth didn't he ask for me?'

'I imagine that he was afraid (and not without reason) that you wouldn't let him see me. He told me that he had written to you three times about me, and you never answered the letters.'

'Oh, I was busy or something, I forget what happened now,' said her aunt, looking more and more embarrassed. 'Now don't make a mountain out of it, Hetty, there was never any reason why you shouldn't see your father's people, except that I'd rather lost touch with them since you were grown up, you know, and as a matter of fact, I didn't particularly want you to see them. They aren't the kind of people who can be useful to a girl. This one keeps a bookshop and the other one has a miserable little job in a public library in the north somewhere. Of course, if you'd wanted to see them, I should never have stopped you, but you never seemed to take the slightest interest in them.' She hurried on almost nervously; as though excusing herself.

'I should have, if I'd had the chance. However, it doesn't matter now; I dare say you did it for the best. And I dare say you'll be furious when you hear what I'm going to do, but I can't help that. I'm going to London, to live with them, with Uncle Frank and Aunt Rose.'

'Rubbish, you're not going to do anything of the kind,' said Mrs Spring, going red under her delicate rouge.

Phyllis at last let *Vogue* fall on her lap and looked up, her eyes sparkling with malice and interest.

'Yes I am, Aunt Edna. You can't stop me. I'm of age, and I've got my own money.'

'Don't you believe it; I put it all into Spanish Liquorice last week and every cent's gone,' Victor assured her, coming in rubbing his hands and apparently in a better humour. He sat on the broad arm of Phyllis's chair and bent over to kiss her, but she dodged.

'Don't paw me, there's a good boy; I don't want to do my face again before dinner.'

'All right.' He got up, and lit a cigarette, then glanced from Hetty, pale and sulky, to his mother, red and cross.

'What's going on here? Not a *row, surely*?'

'Hetty has some absurd plan of going to London to live with her Uncle Frank Franklin,' said his mother.

'Never heard of him.'

'Yes you have, but it was so long ago you've forgotten, and I'm not surprised. He hasn't seen Hetty since she was three, and now he comes sneaking round here this afternoon because he knows she's of age today and has a bit of money of her own and he hopes to get some of it. They're awful people, particularly the wife. Socialists and they keep a shop.'

'I remember now. Do you really want to leave us, Het? Don't you *like* it, here, after all we've done for you?'

'Oh, Vic, do shut up,' snapped Phyllis, sitting up and opening fire. 'It isn't funny. Of course,' to Mrs Spring, '*I've* seen this coming for months, only none of you would ever listen to me. I've *always* thought that Hetty hated living here and wanted to get away.'

'You shut up,' said Hetty fiercely. 'We are quite capable of managing this, thank you, without cerebrations from you.'

'I don't know what you mean, but I suppose you're being clever, as usual. It's my business as much as anyone else's here. If you go and live with these disgusting people you'll always be getting into messes and then Vic will have to get you out, and that will be jolly for me, won't it? I'm not going to sit here and listen to you getting away with anything you like, so don't think it.'

'If I do get into "messes" (by which delicate expression I suppose you mean sexual entanglements; that's the only sort of "mess" your type recognizes) I shall get out of them as I got into them: by myself. And I don't want anyone's help, thank you. From now on, I'm managing my own affairs and the sooner you swallow that, the better.'

'Shut up, you two,' ordered Victor. 'Phyl, you'd better keep out of this, you only put her back up.'

'That's right, that's right, stick up for her!' retorted Phyllis furiously, scrambling out of her chair. 'Let her insult me and say anything she likes – you've always stuck up for her ever since we were kids. That day in the woods when she got lost and you stayed to look for her and made me go home alone – I've never forgotten it, and it's been the same ever since.'

'Oh God. Post-mortems now. Listen, go upstairs or something will you, there's a dear good girl, and let Mother and I manage this? You're only making things worse.'

'No, I will *not*, Victor. This is my affair as much as it is yours, and I won't be ordered upstairs as though I were the housemaid. You're too fond of ordering people about.'

'So are you . . . and since you've raised the point, I'm not your bloody errand-boy. You flew at me like a witch the minute I put my nose round the door this evening about your cursed scent or something.'

'Well, good heavens, I do like that. Just because I ask you a simple—'

'Not only this evening. You're always at it . . . have I got this, did I remember the other. I'm fed up with it.'

'Not half so fed up as I am with the way you go on – not even pretending to be interested in the wedding or anything—'

'God, it isn't my business to worry my guts out about all that, is it? That's your affair. I'm paying for most of it, anyway. That's what I'm for.'

'There! There you go again! Just because Dad couldn't stand us the televisor after all! I could see you were simply furious . . .'

'Well, your sister owes me two hundred and fifty quid. I suppose I can say good-bye to that, and like it.'

353

'You'll get your money back, don't worry,' said Phyllis. 'And here's something else back, too.'

He stared at her outstretched hand. In the palm was his ring.

'Go on . . . take it . . . take it . . . I've been wanting to do this for *months*, ever since before Christmas. Oh, I've been so *bored* with you . . . you're so *dull* . . . night after night, same old places, same old mush that didn't quite come off. I wondered how I'd ever stick it when we were married and I couldn't get away.'

Victor, pale with rage, could only look at his mother as though appealing to her to witness what a beauty he had proposed to marry.

'Go on, take it,' she persisted. 'If you don't, I'll chuck it out of the window.'

'Go on, then.'

It flew glittering through the sunlight and disappeared in a herbaceous border.

'Thank you,' said Victor. 'Now we both feel better. You weren't the only one who was bored; I'd sooner kiss my typist. Now will you get to hell out of here and let me finish what I was saying.'

She went out and slammed the door, but a second later opened it again:

'Edna, I can't stay here after this. I'll phone you in the morning. Send my things on, will you?'

The door slammed again.

'There's a little devil for you,' said Mrs Spring. 'Phyl! Well, I always suspected she had a beast of a temper but – Vic, aren't you going to – don't you want to try and put things right? You'll just catch her, she's gone round to get her car, I expect.'

'You heard what I said. I meant it.'

'Well, I think you've had a very lucky escape,' said his mother. 'You're well out of it, if you ask me. Oh dear . . . now there'll be the invitations to cancel and the presents to send back and the flat and everything – Vic – where are you going – don't go away, dear; we must settle this absurd notion of Hetty's first (all the girls seem to have gone mad lately!). She's not going, of course, that's flat.'

'Yes I am,' said Hetty quietly. 'Now, Aunt Edna, please don't let's quarrel; we've had enough for one evening, surely. I'm sorry if I was rude just now, but this means so much to me. Nothing you can say will make any difference, but I dislike scenes, and I don't want any more. Just think about it quietly for a minute. Vic! isn't this the sensible way to settle it, and do you really see any reason why I shouldn't go?'

'You can go as far as I'm concerned,' he said. He had slouched into a chair and was staring sullenly at his gleaming pumps. 'I think you're a little fool, but anything for peace. I'll go round and vet the place one day next week and see if it isn't too impossible. When do you want to go?'

'Oh, as soon as I can, please?'

'All right.' He got up heavily, and went to the door. 'You write to them, or whatever it is you've arranged to do, and I'll see about getting your money made over entirely to you.'

'Victor, you surely aren't going to let the child go off like this? without discussing it at all?' cried Mrs Spring. 'Hetty – I'm sorry I was irritable – do think it over, my dear. We're going to live in London – oh dear, of course I suppose we shan't go now . . . what a muddle everything is and how sickening . . . well, your life will be dreadfully different, you know. You've always been used to every comfort and it's not so easy to do without the things you're used to.'

'I've done without the things I really wanted for twenty-one years, so I imagine that it won't take me as long as that to get used to doing without my comforts.'

'If she's fed up with us, she's quite right to say so,' said Victor roughly, as he went out of the room. 'Speak right out, never mind whose corns are in the way.'

He slammed the door.

Mrs Spring and Hetty, left together in the exhausted silence that follows a family row, looked at one another, their differences forgotten in a rush of family feeling. Mrs Spring compressed her lips and shook her head, Hetty twisted her mouth and raised her eyebrows.

'Well, *I'm* only glad he's out of it,' began Mrs Spring. 'Of course, you *never* liked her, did you?'

This understatement started the ball rolling, for even Hetty could gossip when she felt at peace because she had got her own way, and for half an hour they chopped Phyllis into messes and were so happily employed that although they heard the noise of her car starting out on the London road, they did not hear Victor at the telephone in the hall.

He stood there in the deepening twilight, frowning, with an ugly look on his attractive face. He was still so sore that he wanted to smash something. Phyllis's taunt about being a bore had got right under his skin and was rankling. He was not only angry with every ounce of masculine vanity in his nature; he was also hurt. Old Phyl, whom he'd known since they were kids and had such grand times with (only probably she'd been 'bored' while he was enjoying them) . . . he could hardly believe it was old Phyl who had said that to him, and called his kisses mush. As he gave the number he had just looked up, he swore softly.

Well, he knew someone who did not find him a bore and his kisses mush. Her letter was still in his pocket; he had changed it over when he changed his clothes. She was not a hard-faced bitch on the make. She was a sweet kid, and he was going to see her this evening and show her, and himself, that there were good times coming. They were going places, he and she. He finished the double whisky he had brought into the hall, and said into the telephone, whence a voice was asking who he wanted:

'May I speak to Mrs Wither, please. Mrs Wither junior.'

# CHAPTER XXVI

It happened that Mr and Mrs Wither and Madge had gone over in the car, with Madge driving, to play bridge with the Doctor Parshams. Viola had not been invited. This was because she did not play bridge, at which the Parshams excelled. So, having dined, she was sitting alone in the drawing-room re-reading *The Lad with Wings*, and sometimes glancing up at the window, where the trees were slowly growing darker against the fading sunset. The drawing-room, with the bearskin glimmering like a patch of snow in front of the empty grate, was in twilight except for the standard lamp by her chair, that sent soft light over her fair hair. She kept looking up at the window, because she hoped she might see a swan flying over; they sometimes did, in the spring, and she had felt an interest in swans ever since her visit to the marshes before Christmas, when the wild ones had rushed over her head. She was thinking a little about the story she was reading and worrying a little about poor Catty, and wondering whether there would be answers to any of her letters by the morning's post and trying not to remember that in exactly a fortnight Victor would be married – when the telephone bell rang.

Telephone calls at The Eagles in the evening were rare enough to make Viola put down her book, glance at the door, and think: who's that? Tina, I expect. Hope nothing awful's happened.

But when Annie, looking rather annoyed at being summoned

from the servants' parlour and the wireless to answer the instrument, came into the drawing-room, she announced—

'You're wanted on the telephone, Mrs Theodore.'

'Oh. Thanks awfully, Annie. Is it Mrs Caker?'

'No, m'm. It's,' Annie managed to keep every whiff of expression out of her face, 'a gentleman, m'm.'

Viola dropped her book on the chair.

'Oh! I wonder who on earth—'

Even as she lifted the receiver, while Annie was slowly retreating to the basement, even when she said 'Hullo?' in her deep soft voice, she did not guess who was at the other end of the line. She had grown up so much since the autumn that she never had day-dreams now. Good lord, who can it be? was her only thought as she spoke.

'Viola? Victor Spring here. I say, I got your note. I want to talk to you about it. Can you meet me in the wood, the one down the hill, in about ten minutes?'

She hung on to the receiver, that came slowly down towards her (it was the old-fashioned kind), as though it, too, were nearly fainting. But she managed to say:

'All right. But where? Where shall I meet you, I mean?'

'By the stream. Near that little hut. In ten minutes, then. 'Bye.'

He rang off.

Good lord, thought Viola, standing by the telephone with shaking knees and staring up at the long pale blur that was the landing window. I *say* – good lord. And just for a second she thought that she would not go. It was getting dark, and the maids would be sure to see her, and—

She hesitated, but suddenly thought: If he gets there and I'm not there, he'll think I'm not coming, and she turned and tore upstairs to get her coat.

A moment later she slipped out, shutting the door noiselessly.

It was that most mysterious of lights called owl-light, in which it is possible to imagine anything. All white things looked startlingly white; the road, a bush of may on the edge of the wood, Viola's shoes, and some flowers growing out of the ditch, were white as starch. But the trees were very dark, with a bloom that was not green nor black. The night seemed to be hiding in them, not coming out of the darkness.

She crossed the road and went down into the wood, and as she went, it got quieter and the trees shut the path in with layers of motionless leaves standing stiffly in the dusk air. An owl went leisurely over her head, flying low. Then she heard the noise of the stream, April-full, rippling over roots and the fall of stones and saw a white shirt front glimmering between the trees, and he waved to her.

He was hatless and wore a light overcoat over evening dress. She could not help being pleased at the evening dress, it was so romantic, but she saw with dismay that he looked angry.

He helped her across the stream, and as she reached the other side, kept her hand in his and pulled her towards him. She went without protest, and clung to him silently for a little while, returning his kisses with her eyes closed.

At last he moved away a little, but still held her, and looked down into her lifted face. Then he started kissing her again. Neither spoke; but thoughts whirled in Viola's head. It was so quiet and ghostly all round them, and he was so strange, his kisses were almost angry. She wanted to break the silence, but was afraid to, and as his love-making grew rougher, almost brutal, she was suddenly afraid of him. Exhausted, she pulled away from him, whispering:

'I say, don't. Please don't.'

'Why not?' he muttered.

'I'm frightened.'

'Come away with me, Viola, will you?'

She stared at him. She could not believe that he had said it. He gave her a little shake.

'Did you hear what I said? I want you so much. You *must* come. Make some excuse, and we'll get away somehow. We'll fly. Go to Paris – just you and me.'

'But you – what about her, I mean? That girl?'

'Oh, that's all off, thank God,' he said roughly.

'You aren't going to marry her, do you mean?'

'No, I'm not.'

'Really? It's true? It isn't – a joke, is it?'

'No, it is not. Can't you understand English? I want you to come away with me, next weekend. I've had enough of this,' and he made to take her again.

But she moved away from him a little, and fearfully, gently, put out her fingers and held his arm. It was so dark that he could only see her eyes as shadows in the pale blur that was her face. In a voice shaking with doubt, hope, longing she said:

'You – you don't want to marry me, do you?'

'Thanks,' he retorted, startlingly loud, 'but I'm not getting tied up again just yet.'

She burst into tears, stumbling wildly away from him.

'Oh, oh, how can you be so horrible, so beastly to me! I've never done anything to you, I came when you asked me to . . . you just pick me up and drop me whenever you think you will . . . you're so *cruel* . . . I've been so fed up I wished I was dead . . . asking me to go to Paris . . . *Paris* . . . a place like Paris . . . everybody knows what that means . . . as though I was one of those girls . . . you know . . . you don't care a damn about me, you think because I'm a widow and I worked in a shop you can say anything to me and I won't mind . . . you think I'm a bad girl, that's what you think, but I'm not . . . I'm not . . . Oh, oh, I can't *bear* it . . . you ought to have known, you ought . . . *I'm not that kind of girl!*'

She turned, stumbling, sobbing, hands in her pockets and head bent, and ran up the path that led home. He made two steps after her; then stopped, shrugged, and took out his cigarette case. He could just see her white figure, silent now, hurrying out of sight among the trees.

Sobered, doubtful, more than a little ashamed, he inhaled and sat down dejectedly on a tree-stump, so tired and depressed that he did not even think the moss would ruin his clothes. A long exhausting day, and on top of it a violent fit of rage and one of desire, had left him worn out. He yawned, sunk his chin in his hands, and shut his eyes. He could have gone off to sleep where he sat. Tomorrow there would be the flat to dispose of, the invitations to cancel, presents to return, Phyl's father on the telephone and if he knew anything about Phyl's mother, her mother too, and Hetty's new stunt to see to . . .

He yawned again. It was quite dark. A delicious fresh smell floated from the spring foliage but he only smelled cigarette smoke. Women. No wonder everybody said they were the devil. What *did* they want? Most girls would have jumped at the chance. How was he to know she was straight? Hardly any of them were nowadays. It had given him a shock, the shock in her voice. Made him feel a swine. Poor little kid, she did cry. Such a strong wave of desire, shame and longing suddenly swept him that he got up quickly, stamped out his cigarette, and began to walk back, as quickly as he could in the confusing shadows. When he was nearly at the house he saw, from the wood's edge, four young people getting out of a car, and remembered, with fury, the party.

He sneaked into the house and up to his room, where he lay on the bed until he heard them go into dinner, then he rang and had some food brought up. He ate it in front of the electric fire, for he was cold, and every now and then he yawned savagely. For almost the first time in his successful, sunny, well-organized life he was miserable.

One thought him a bore and the other thought him a blackguard.

We live and learn, he mused, with his mouth full of smoked salmon. I shouldn't have said I was either.

Poor little thing. She did cry. She was shaking all over. Pretty decent of her, in a way, turning me down like that, because I'm sure it wasn't because she didn't want to come. No. She's just straight, that's all. There aren't so many about nowadays. Little —, most of them. No, she just didn't think it was right, and so she said no. Er . . . pure, that's what she is. Funny I had her all wrong. But she likes kissing me all right, she isn't like Phyl.

She's a good girl, that's what she is. Well, my lad, you've often wondered what they were like, and now you know.

I don't suppose she'll ever speak to me again.

I suppose I oughtn't to have asked her, but hell, how was I to know?

361

She did cry. She wasn't sticking it on.

Oh blast. Better have a bath.

He had it.

Viola crept up the steps very quietly so that the maids should not hear her, and unlocked the front door. She was shivering with cold and her eyes were so gummed up with crying that she could only just see where she was going. The dimly lit hall with its tiled floor struck chillier than the spring twilight outside; she felt as though she could never get warm again. She only longed to creep into bed and go to sleep. He thought she was bad . . . he thought she was a bad girl . . .

Aching as though she had been beaten, without one clear thought in her head, she climbed slowly to her room, and shut herself in.

At half-past ten the revellers returned, having passed an enjoyable evening. If the writer knew anything about bridge, here is a grand chance for some twinkling asides, but as the writer was never able to make bridge out the reader must do with the bare bones that Mr Wither was five shillings up, Mrs Wither three shillings and twopence up, and Madge six shilling and tenpence down.

'I suppose Viola has gone to bed,' observed Mrs Wither, straightening the cushion in Viola's chair and putting *The Lad with Wings* back on the shelf. 'Left the light on too, careless girl. Well, dear, that was very enjoyable on the whole, was it not? Lemonade? or a little glass of port? It's quite chilly.'

Mr Wither had the port, which he sipped for ten minutes while Mrs Wither sipped icy lemonade and Madge ate a mass of biscuits, surely the most unsustaining form of nourishment known to mankind.

The Withers felt more or less at peace. They were about to be reconciled to Tina, who was the wife of a man with a hundred and twenty thousand pounds, Madge had driven them to and from the Parsham home without mishap, the summer was coming, and they had won eight and twopence by gambling.

Accordingly they filed up to bed at ten minutes to eleven in a mood of mild content. Mr Wither even forgot, as he undressed and tweaked the blind sharply so that the crescent moon should not peep in at him and Mrs Wither, to wonder how his money was getting on, and Madge hummed a tune as she brushed her closely cropped hair and put on pyjamas with very wide stripes.

When Fawcuss, Annie and Cook had also gone up to bed and the house was in utter darkness because the crescent moon had gone down behind the trees of the little wood, a bedroom door slowly opened, and someone went quickly downstairs. Right down to the back door they went, which they fumbled at, cursed, and finally opened.'

'Sh-sh,' they said, warningly, to something else, that was plainly very pleased to see them. 'Sh-sh,' and they picked the something up, and told it to be quiet. It obeyed, and the person went cautiously upstairs again.

Something settled comfortably at the foot of a bed and two contented creatures fell asleep.

Three hours passed. The moon had gone, but the sleeping countryside was lit by thin ethereal starlight, rarest of all radiances, like darkness itself shining. And as last year, and the year before, and so back into the natural yet unutterably romantic shades of history – the wood rang with wild beautiful singing that no one heard.

Suddenly Polo began to bark.

Madge sat up in bed.

'Shut up,' she whispered furiously. 'Shut *up*, Polo. Down. Good dog . . . quiet.'

He went on barking. He was crouching at the door, his nose to the floor, whining, wildly excited. His body shook as Madge bent over him. There was something wrong. She had had him up in her room, every night for months, and he had never done this before.

'What is it, boy?'

Upstairs, Annie suddenly sat bolt upright in bed. That dog . . . waking everybody up . . . what was the matter . . .

She sniffed, staring at the darkened window, where one thin line of starlit sky showed.

Smoke . . . the frightening acrid smell creeping under her door, and a queer crackling noise like sticks rattling together.

363

Annie sniffed again. The dog was barking wildly now, and she could hear confused sounds on the next floor. Suddenly, staring now at the door, she saw a light out in the passage. It died and flared again in a horrifying red glare.

Scrambling out of bed, Annie shrieked wildly—

'Fire! Fire! Fire!'

As she was stumbling to the door, having stubbed her toe in the dark and feeling (as she afterwards narrated) quite sick with the pain, the door was flung violently open and Cook stood there, screaming.

'Annie? Are you there? For the dear Lord's sake come on! The place is on fire! It's in the old box-room – the whole place is blazing. There's no time for that—' Annie was tugging at the chest of drawers where she kept her few treasures. 'Come *on!*'

Snatching up a coat from behind the door, Annie ran.

The corridor was full of smoke. The red glare came from one end.

'Where's Renie?' (Fawcuss had been christened Irene).

'She ain't up yet. Slep' right through it. You go and get her, I'm going down to the master. My Lord, Annie, the old box-room's over Miss Madge! Pray heaven the ceiling don't fall in!'

But Fawcuss, roused by the barking and the shrieks, was already coming out of her room at the end of the passage. On seeing the smoke and the glare she gave one brief, very loud shriek, then went composedly back to her room and collected her Bible, a photograph of her mother, sevenpence halfpenny and her new summer combinations. These she swept into a face towel and pattered downstairs.

The hall was full of people. White, alarmed faces still heavy with sleep gaped up at Fawcuss as she hurried down, bundle in hand. Thank the dear Lord, everybody was there, M'm, Miss Madge, Mrs Theodore. The master, with one slipper on, was at the telephone. Miss Madge had something funny under her arm; it heaved, and out of the blanket came an intelligent head, ears cocked, eyes very bright. It was That Dog. Well I never.

'Give me the Fire Brigade. Yes . . . fire. Here . . . here. At The Eagles, near Sible Pelden, near the cross-roads. Wither is the name . . . I don't know. It seems to be spreading . . .'

Crash! Something fell in upstairs.

'That'll be the box-room ceiling. A blessing you was out of it, Miss Madge!' cried Annie.

'*Sh-sh!*' from the telephone. 'Yes, will you? At once.'

He hung up the receiver.

'Oh, Arthur,' quavered Mrs Wither, 'isn't there time for anything . . . my garnet brooch? Hadn't we better try and put it out . . . it mayn't be so bad as—'

Crash! Something else fell in. As they stood staring up at the staircase, shivering with sick excitement, a great puff of black smoke came round the corner and rolled slowly, insolently, right down the stairs. Down it came, terrifyingly unreal, into the neat chilly hall and slowly spread in a dark haze along the walls. Coughing and choking, they retreated to the front door, which Annie opened. The sweet night air blew in.

Polo, struggling, began to bark, and Madge put him down and slipped her dressing-gown cord through his collar.

'Oh, can't we do *anything?*'

Mrs Wither was weeping. Tears ran down her small face, on each side of which hung a little grey pigtail. 'Oh, Arthur – the house! All the furniture!'

The telephone bell rang, and everybody jumped.

'Yes?' Mr Wither's hand shook as he held the receiver. 'In half an *hour?* Can't they? Oh, all right. Yes, it seems to be. Must have got a hold.'

'Oh, Miss Madge!' called Fawcuss, who had gone down into the drive. 'It's coming out of your window!'

Everybody ran down the steps and across the drive and stood staring at the fantastic spectacle of the flames leaping like devils behind the neatly curtained windows of one of the front bedrooms. The curtains were drawn, but the hellish glow could be seen between them.

'Wonder how it started?' said Madge, who had picked up Polo again. 'It was in the old box-room, did you say, Annie?'

'Yes, Miss Madge. In the old—'

'Then it must have been the Men,' said Mr Wither excitedly.

'They must have got smoking up there and dropped ash and it must have smouldered all this afternoon and then broken out—'

The Men had been in that morning to finish mending a leak in the roof, widened by the recent heavy rains.

'Yes, that must be it,' said everybody, staring and shivering and thinking dismally of their own little possessions shrivelling in the flames.

'Mum, you *must* have something . . . you'll catch your death,' said Madge suddenly. Though the house was blazing, and no one could think of anything else for the moment, she did not want her father suddenly to realize that Polo had been spending the night at the foot of her bed. True, it was he who had roused the house and probably saved their lives, but one never knew how Mr Wither was going to take anything. He might say that Polo had started the fire.

She shoved the end of his improvised lead into Viola's hand and ran up the steps.

'Margaret! Come back!' roared Mr Wither.

She waved and shouted something and vanished into the smoky hall.

Two minutes later she appeared at the window furthest from the flames, which had been Tina's room, but was now a dump for things that were going to the Church Army and the P.S.L.

'It's all right here! Safe as houses – well, safe, anyway!' roared Madge, who appeared to be rather enjoying the fire.

'Houses aren't very safe just now, ha! ha! Vi, come up and give me a hand, will you? There's just time—'

She vanished.

Viola passed Polo to Fawcuss and, ignoring the roars of Mr Wither and the whimpers of his wife, ran up the steps. She felt as if this was a nightmare, for she was still dazed from the heavy sleep Madge had roused her from, and she wore only a thin sleeveless nightgown. Her feet were bare and her teeth chattered with cold. Of course, the house *must* catch on fire tonight, when she felt so awful and only wanted to stay asleep as long as possible! Tears overflowed again as she ran, holding up her nightgown, up the smoke-filled staircase.

Madge met her half-way along the undamaged corridor, carrying a load of old blankets.

'Here . . .' dumping them on Viola, 'I'm going back to get a lot of Father's shoes, we can all get into those. Is Polo all right?' coughing.

'Fine. Hurry up, it's getting louder.'

For the fire, up till now almost silent, was starting to make a horrifying noise, like the caverns of hell sucking. The glare crept steadily along, masked behind thick, fat, evil-smelling smoke. The old furniture, polished for thirty years with inflammable waxes, burned fiercely. As Viola waited at the stairhead, her eyes pricking with smoke, a sudden fierce wall of heat rushed at her.

'Madge!' she shrieked, terrified. 'Oh, be quick!'

'I'm coming – hold your horses!'

Her sister-in-law's heavy body, wrapped in a blanket, charged head down through the smoke, sending a cascade of shoes down the stairs, and they stumbled after them, stopping long enough at the bottom to collect them, then hurried down the steps into the garden.

The women were huddled on the other side of the road, where the wood began, staring up at the now blazing second floor, the flickering red light on their pale faces, but Mr Wither had gone round to the garage to get the car. Shivering, gripping his blanket round himself, his old heart banging, Mr Wither fumbled with the garage door and thought about insurance money.

'Don't cry, Mum.' Madge put her stout arms round Mrs Wither. 'It might have been a damn sight worse,' patting her. 'After all, we're all alive' (thankful murmurs, in which references to the Dear Lord could be distinguished, from Fawcuss, Annie and Cook). 'We might have been burned in our beds if' (defiantly, bursting with pride) 'it hadn't been for Polo!'

But Mrs Wither was not listening.

'Oh, Madgie – my lovely home! Your father and I were so proud of it . . . all gone.'

'No it isn't, Mum. They'll manage to save some of it, I expect. Don't cry, there's a dear.'

Everyone suddenly felt cold and exhausted. Viola rubbed her

smarting eyes, and covered her face with black smears. And suddenly, far off on the Chesterbourne road, sounded the thrilling, clanging bell of the fire-engine.

The party at Grassmere was still going strong at two o'clock. Mrs Spring had not intended that it should be so late, for the excitements of the evening had so worsened her headache that she meant to pack the guests off as early as she decently could, and go to bed: but the guests were not having any. Hetty, exhilarated by the knowledge that her fight was won, had asked if they might have champagne, and that put everybody into a party mood, and there happened to be an especially good programme of dance music that night and they danced to that until late and after London Regional had closed down they fiddled about and hit on a band in Budapest and danced to that, and Mrs Spring, though still unhappy and disturbed about Hetty's rebellion, and dreading the fusses there were sure to be tomorrow about the broken engagement, surprisingly found herself enjoying the evening about twelve o'clock, and her headache gone. She was really very pleased that dear old Vic was not going to marry that little harridan, and perhaps the next one would not mind giving her a grandchild!

At ten o'clock Victor came rather sulkily into the drawing-room, explaining that he had been working upstairs and was sorry he could not get down before, and drank a good deal of champagne. In his low state it had little effect on his sobriety, but it helped to pass the time and kept him from thinking, and that was something. He danced with the prettiest of the girls, and she made him laugh once or twice, and he stayed on, instead of going upstairs to bed as he had meant to. At one o'clock a lot more delicious and exciting food was discovered laid out in the morning-room, and everybody sat about, with young faces flushed with laughter and exercise, and ate while they insulted one another. Mrs Spring smiled on the scene in a dress sparkling with black sequins, and Victor sat with his arm round the prettiest girl, sharing her champagne. Everyone enjoyed themselves.

But at two o'clock someone said they really must go home and that broke up the party. The boys collected their coats, the girls tied handkerchiefs, fisher-wise, over their carefully cherished curls, and everyone went out to the front of the house where the cars were parked.

In one of those pauses in the ragging and laughing, someone looked up and saw a glare in the sky above the oak wood, and at the same instant, far off, they heard the clang of fire-bells.

'Must be a fire somewhere.'

'That? That's the sleigh bells. Always try out the sleighs round here in the small hours. Didn't you know there was a sleigh factory—'

'Sparkling, aren't you? Look! There – can't you see? Over there – there it is again! It must be quite near.'

'It must be at The Eagles,' exclaimed Mrs Spring, standing on the doorstep in a fur cape and peering up at the sky. 'Yes – look, Vic, it's quite bright . . . there! It must be The Eagles – that's the only house over there.'

'I say, how about beetling over?' suggested one amateur in thrills. But Victor was already running to the garage.

Afterwards he said it was the champagne: then, he only knew that he felt sick. It was not an over-statement; he thought that any instant he would be sick. Of course she's all right, he thought, climbing into the car, starting up, swerving out of the garage and tearing away up the road past the astonished faces at the gate ('Hi! wait for baby!') Of course she's all right. Making a damn fool of myself . . . I'll just see if I can do anything and get back. Perhaps it isn't there, at all . . .

The car, zooming round a curve, screeched as it just missed the solid back parts of a fire engine. Everything was lit with a beautiful demoniac rosy glow from the gold and black furnace that had been the house. The flames burned in enormous long golden plumes, with a solemn roaring noise. The road was flooded. Four solid hissing curves of silver water, steady as bridges, sighed their way into the heart of the fire. A little crowd, sooty-faced and staring, stood at the edge of the wood on the other side of the road; there were two or three cars parked there, and Doctor Parsham was bounding about accompanied by Chappy, who was not being much use as all he did was to sniff loudly at people's bare ankles and frighten them even worse than they were already. But Doctor Parsham was doing his stuff, prescribing for shock, patting people, and offering to put up some of the homeless Withers for the night, a proposal which was most gratefully accepted.

But she was not there.

Victor pushed his way through the little crowd to Mr Wither, who was staring dismally out of the car's window at the destruction of The Eagles.

'Where's Viola?' demanded Victor.

Mr Wither was so agitated that it did not strike him as at all strange that young Spring should appear from nowhere, demanding where was Viola.

'Good heavens, isn't she here?' cried Mr Wither, falling with fatal ease into a state. 'She was here a minute ago, I saw her, I'm sure I did, I thought everybody was safe, Emmy, Emmy, here's Mr Spring can't find Viola anywhere, have you seen her?'

'She was over by the path just now, sir,' volunteered Fawcuss, speaking respectfully from the depths of a very old Church Army blanket with ironing-stains on it. 'By the wood, sir, I mean,' and Fawcuss retreated once more into her tent.

Victor hurried off.

But she was not by the path. Was that her, down in the smoky depths of the wood where the rosy flickering light faded into confusing shadows? It might be. He blundered down into the dusk, shouting, 'Viola – are you there?' Presently he felt the ground sloping under his feet, caught the red glare in the sky reflected in water among the dark trees, and found that he was where he had parted from her, seven hours – a hundred years – ago.

It was not quite dark. The hollow was full of an indescribable dim light, half from the fire, half from the stars. The smell of smoke, the delicious perfume of young leaves, came in gusts. It was very cold down there, and suddenly – the strangest possible sound at that hour and in that place – a bird sang four or five very loud and beautiful clear notes from somewhere overhead in the dim, faintly reddened boughs. Startled, Victor glanced up, then down again; and there

Viola was, sitting on the tree-stump where he had sat earlier in the evening, wrapped in a blanket, her face hidden in her hands.

'Darling – thank God you're all right,' he said, kneeling down beside her and putting his arms round her in the ragged old blanket. 'Darling,' he muttered, trying to pull her hands away from her face, 'I've been feeling such a swine. Will you forgive me? I didn't mean to hurt you – I didn't, truly. Please, Viola. I'm sorry.'

She resisted, holding her hands against her face in silence.

'Darling. Viola. Will you marry me? I mean it. Please, Viola, do. I . . . I love you, as a matter of fact. (Must have all the time, I suppose.) Please, Viola, will you? I don't want anyone but you. I do love you so much. Will you, Viola?'

Then her hands came away, slowly and cautiously, from her sooty little face. She looked at him, then nodded, twice.

# CHAPTER THE LAST

On a Saturday afternoon late that summer, the old church at Sible Pelden is decorated for a wedding. The ceremony is over, and the wedding guests are waiting for the bride and bridegroom to come out of the vestry.

It is a beautiful day, with a blue sky, and brilliant sunlight tempered by a soft wind. The lanes round the church are full of glowing wild roses and the elms looking over its walls are laden with splendid masses of summer leaves. It is difficult to realize that Hugh Phillips has been killed in Waziristan.

The church is full, and (which is very convenient) nearly all the people in the story are there.

There are Mr and Mrs Wither, looking older and more shrunken than they did some months ago; the burning of The Eagles has been a great shock, and they still feel bewildered and forlorn in the furnished house which they have taken in Chesterbourne until their new home, a smaller and more convenient version of The Eagles, shall rise like a phoenix upon the site by the oak wood. Were it not for the fact that Fawcuss, Annie and Cook have followed them to 13, Croftmere Gardens, and are slowly building up a Wither atmosphere there, Mr and Mrs Wither would feel that their old life had been completely destroyed on the night of the fire. But already the furniture (though it is of course not so good as that at The Eagles) is acquiring a well-polished gleam, and Annie has found a dungeon for the Vim under the sink. Mrs Wither has mummified some leaves, ready for the autumn, and the three maids are hard at work on things for the Give What You Like stall. Of course, they find it a nuisance being a bus ride from church, but M'm always has cold supper on Sunday evenings so that they can ride out together to this very church where they now sit, and they are quite getting into the way of it. All three have been given leave to come to the wedding today; 13, Croftmere Gardens is locked up for the afternoon, and there will be high tea instead of an elaborate dinner.

Fawcuss, Annie and Cook are soberly pleased about Mrs Theodore's good fortune. She is a nice young lady, and they wish her every happiness. Since her engagement to Mr Spring, so rich and respected, the three naturally think of her as a young lady. A year ago they found it difficult to think of her as Mrs Theodore: money certainly does make a difference.

Mrs Wither, looking round the packed church, has a vague feeling that her daughter-in-law has played some kind of a dirty trick. For months she went about so quiet and subdued and apparently contented with her lot: then suddenly burst out into an engagement with Victor Spring, a gorgeous trousseau, and all the pleasure and excitement of a smart wedding with half the county to see! White roses and violas all over the church, a smart, tired woman journalist from London taking the names of guests in the porch, press photographers, a honeymoon in Paris and a flat in town . . . Mrs Spring feels that all this is a kind of insult to poor Teddy's memory. Why, Viola looks so young and so happy that she might never have been married before! Mrs Wither thinks that Viola must have been very underhand, very cunning, to have carried on this affair with young Spring under her mother-in-law's nose without Mrs Wither guessing.

Madge sits between her parents, sturdy and upright in a light coat and skirt that make her look twice her size. She is thinking about Polo, who is waiting for her out in the churchyard, tied to the railings of somebody's tomb under the eye of Mrs Fisher up the Green Lion. Polo does not need the eye of Mrs Fisher, for he is now so well trained that even Colonel Phillips can find no fault in him, and, as we know, Madge holds Colonel Phillips's opinion very high indeed.

But Mrs Fisher has offered to 'see no one don't run off with him', and Madge, flattered by Mrs Fisher's obvious admiration for Polo, accepts. Lately, Madge and Colonel Phillips have been talking seriously about going into partnership. The Colonel thinks that Madge's enthusiasm, common sense and capacity for hard work would be very useful in his kennels, and Madge can think of no career that would give her more satisfaction. A nice, sensible woman, Madge Wither, thinks Colonel Phillips. No nonsense about her. And Madge thinks, I shall see quite a lot of the kid, I expect. Hugh's kid. Funny that sounds. I suppose they'll make a soldier of him, too. Best life for a boy. When he's a lot older and can manage a dog, I might give him Polo, only Polo'll be pretty ancient by then, of course.

The young widow and the baby, Ned, will be home next week. The spare room is all ready; and the nursery has been repapered and Hugh's toys hunted out (though they will not be needed for years, the Phillipses tell each other), and some new ones bought. And Mrs Colonel Phillips is trying to remember her few sentences of Urdu, for the ayah will feel so strange just at first, poor thing. And Mrs Colonel Phillips, glancing at a new white tablet in the ancient wall above their pew, sighs and goes off into a reverie.

Mr Wither, on Madge's other side, is enjoying the wedding, the fine weather, and the knowledge that yet another person whom he knows well has managed to get near a lot of money. Even Mr Wither cannot hope that he will ever be able to manage Victor Spring's money, because Victor manages it so well himself, but there is satisfaction for Mr Wither in the thought that Victor does do it so well. It is a beautiful sight, Victor's money. It grows: it runs healthily round the country like a sound bloodstream: it never suffers from the palpitations and nerve storms that affect Mr Wither's money. Mr Wither is planning to get many sound tips from Viola, when she comes to see Mrs Wither, about where to invest, and when. Victor is sure to tell her that sort of thing, thinks Mr Wither complacently. The fellow is head over heels, anyone can see that. And Saxon, too; Saxon listened with real appreciation when Mr Wither gave him that little talk about investing. He must remember to ask Tina, after this business is all over, whether Saxon had yet taken his advice.

Tina, sitting near the door in case she feels faint and wearing a discreet but becoming dress, is not really very interested in the wedding. She is pleased, of course, that old Vi has got young Spring after all, but she rather wishes she were spending this lovely day in the garden of their new house in Maida Vale, exquisitely embroidering a robe for the baby (like all people who have never had a baby, Tina does not really believe that babies are ever sick). She finds this return to the scene of her own romance curiously unreal and, frankly, just a little dull. The present, to Tina, is much more interesting just now than the past. Sible Pelden might seem more interesting if Saxon were here, and they could smile at each other as they passed lanes that had amusing youthful memories, but Saxon is much too busy nowadays to go to weddings.

One's own house, one's husband and peacefully developing baby are, after all, the most interesting objects in the world, thinks Tina. The supervision of two well-trained (and paid) maids, the catering, the shall-you-be-in-to-dinnering – how absorbing and interesting is the routine, when it comes late in life! I must be the most contented woman in England, thinks Tina. She uses the word deliberately. She feels that 'content' perhaps expresses her state of mind better than 'happiness', She has grown calm so *suddenly*. Is this pleasant preoccupation with the business of everyday living, this pleasure in Saxon's company, this tender but composed interest in the baby . . . happiness? Is it natural to be so tranquil, at thirty-six?

Whether it be natural or no, it is the state she finds herself in, and she is too lazy nowadays to fight against it. She says to herself sometimes, 'After all, I'm nearly forty.' Her youth, her romance, was crammed into a few feverish months, and violent delights have violent ends. She and Saxon are very fortunate to have salvaged their affectionate friendship from their odd, secretive love affair. But I do wish, thinks Tina, that he hadn't got to wear glasses.

Yes, the cool grey eyes are not very strong, and he has made them weaker by over-reading, and over-working in the factory at Slough. The greater part of his capital has been sunk into this factory that he and another small capitalist have bought. It will make cheap beauty products for the chain of beauty parlours that Saxon and his partner propose to establish all over Great Britain, under the name 'Glamour, Limited.' His hard working-class common-sense and his ambition are driving him steadily along the conventional path taken by successful men. Once Tina hoped that he might do something unusual with his talents; but as the years go on, she becomes used to seeing him do nothing but make more and more money, which he spends prudently, without much delight. He is a handsome, sober, rather humourless man, whose good looks have fortunately been passed on to their only daughter, Zoë.

Zoë is to be the chief pleasure and joy in Tina's life, as the years pass. She is an only child, for Tina had such a Bad Time with her that a lot of expensive doctors forbade her to have any more. And she does not really want any more. Zoë, who inherits her father's looks and her mother's honesty and courage, shall be all that a girl with a rich yet sensible mother can be; and oddly enough, Zoë is.

Saxon and Tina are happy. She is still, to the end of their lives, his best friend. But as they grow older, and Saxon is more and more successful as a money-spinner, they think and talk less and less about their shady courtship. Was that really us? they think, exchanging a guilty glance when something reminds them of the lanes round Sible Pelden, the nights at Rackwater.

Saxon will always work unnecessarily hard, and Tina will never quite realize why. He himself does not know that he overworks because he dimly feels that his success was earned, not by his own hands and brain and determination, but by the fascination his beauty exerted upon a love-starved woman and a lonely old man. The finer part of his vanity, that was willing to work to justify itself, has never had a chance to do so, and so he feels vaguely that he has been cheated. The Fatbottoms have been shown, indeed, but they only talk about some people having all the luck and do not admire him at all; and for years, until the past grows dim, he will wonder every time he and Tina go out to dinner whether people think that he was Mr Spurrey's boy friend.

He and Tina and Zoë will lead a rather quiet, domestically satisfying and socially dull life. Sometimes Tina will smile faintly to remember that she once feared Saxon would go high hat. Saxon . . . that nice respectable boy whom she now knows to be about as much like a young wolf and a spring god as the Bank of England! We live; and we learn.

Mrs Caker is also sitting by the door, because she arrived late and the front pews were full. She and Tina have exchanged shy but friendly smiles. It is Mrs Caker's conviction that, because she now lives in a small block of flats in Chesterbourne with a series of flighty and impudent girls to 'do' for her, she is respectable. But no one else thinks so. She has made friends with one or two publicans' widows and dubious grass widows of her own age and class; and how they do enjoy themselves! They are known to most of the commercial travellers in Essex and also to most of the saloon bars. They rush round the country in taxis or in cars belonging to the travellers, they have all-night parties about which the neighbours complain, and they never stop slapping at one another and screaming with laughter. They will be one of the talks of Chesterbourne for many years yet, which of course pleases them very much.

As time goes on, Mrs Caker realizes that she has been quietly 'dropped' by her son and daughter-in-law, but as the money continues to come regularly, with a handsome cheque at Christmas and photographs of Zoë, she does not really mind. It is understood that she never goes to the house in Maida Vale, and they never motor down to Avion Mansions (known to the travellers, with bellows, as 'Ave One Mansions).

'Ye see, mie boy, he's very well off,' Mrs Caker explains to the travellers and publicans' wives, her pretty, fading blue eyes laughing over the top of a glass. 'Fact is, he's a bit too posh fer maye, and so's she. Oh, they're all *right*, I suppose,' shaking her head with an indescribable face that conveys just how all wrong they are, 'but they're not my sort. Stuck-up. Well, not exactly stuck-up, but stiff. You know. A la-ish. Oh, we get on very well as we are.'

The acquaintanceship between Mrs Caker and the Withers has also been allowed quietly to fade. When they leave the church this morning, they will say 'good morning' to her pleasantly enough, and

Tina will exchange a few friendly words with her, but it is felt, on all sides, that this is quite enough.

Very respectable and comfortable feels Mrs Caker, sitting by the door in a gaudy dress and, despite the heat, the coat. She idly wonders for an instant what Dick Falger would say if he could see her now and hear about her good luck; but it is only for a second. Dick Falger! Hope he died in a ditch long ago! and Mrs Caker's thoughts drift away to other matters.

But the Hermit has not died in a ditch. He has tramped to the village in Bedfordshire where Beatty was last living, and finds her living there still, in a tiny, dirty, overcrowded cottage where nesting swallows are slowly but surely pulling the thatch to pieces. Beatty is living on the charity of some good ladies in the village and her old age pension, and is not very pleased to see the Hermit. Neither are the good ladies, nor the Vicar, nor the retired naval man who acts as squire.

None of this upsets the Hermit. He settles into the cottage with the protesting Beatty; and there, a nuisance to the community and perfectly happy, he enters upon the sunset of his years, even mellowing sufficiently to be described by the Vicar as an Old Character. Bear with Cubs, which he never persuades anyone to buy, stays on the crowded mantelpiece until the day of his death.

Really, everything looks very well and went off most satisfactorily, thinks Lady Dovewood, sitting near the front of the church next to a small snuffy old woman in a black silk coat. She seems a noticeably nice gairl, not out of the top drawer, of course, but one is used to that nowadays, and after all, the Springs aren't, either. So nice of her, I thought, writing about that old creature . . . (the old creature is sitting beside Lady Dovewood), I really must try to get Aubrey pinned down about the Over Sixty Club, we *do* need it, England must have millions of women like that poor old creature, nice respectable bodies with not a halfpenny in the world and too old to work . . . I never did like that Barlow gairl. I know a bad-tempered woman when I see one. I don't wonder young Spring shied at the fence.

Phyllis is not in church. She has been invited, but is playing in a tournament at Bournemouth and cannot get away, she writes. She and Victor made up their quarrel weeks ago, Phyllis being the first to make advances. She has apologized and so has he; Heyrick has found the ring among the delphiniums and zinnias and Victor has passed it on to her as a peace-offering, suggesting that she shall sell it and buy herself a snappy pair of ear-rings with the plunder. And she does, but although they seem to be once more on their old casual friendly footing, Victor never again feels quite comfortable with Phyllis. Whenever he is with her he wonders if he is boring her, and gradually their friendship cools until it reaches the Oh-yes-I-knew-her-quite-well-at-one-time stage. Phyllis never visits Grassmere again after the row; she and Mrs Spring talk pleasantly over the telephone, but somehow Phyllis always is too busy to come down. She does this to avoid Viola. She feels really bitter about Viola. Something *must* have been going on all the time Phyllis and Victor were engaged; the whole business was too quick. Sly little beast, thinks Phyllis. Unsporting. Common.

She feels bitter with Victor, too, because he has had the chance of marrying her and let it slip without one word. If she hurt his vanity, he hurt her pride almost as deeply, and it is not until nearly two years later, when she gets engaged to an ambitious and intelligent M.P., that her self-confidence is quite restored. Her married life is busy, expensive, highly social, over-occupied and completely commonplace. The M.P. shares her views on child-bearing and so she can keep her admired figure unimpaired. Of course, life would be more fun if they had more money, and poor Anthea is a very large mote in the ointment, having taken at forty to lovers, drugs and necromancy, and even Phyllis's vitality begins to flag a little, as the full years press past, under the pace at which she lives. If she were not steadily sustained by her belief in the importance of her activities, she would sometimes get depressed. Sometimes when she and the M.P. are going home from a party at five in the morning she observes to the M.P. that life is very different from what you thought it was going to be when you were a kid. But the M.P. is too tired to ask her what she thought it was going to be, and even if he did, it is possible that she could not remember.

Miss Cattyman can remember. Right from the time she was a tot Miss Cattyman always expected that something exciting was going to happen, and something always has. There was that time Mr Buttrick fell dead right across the Corsets and Liberty Bodices, and the time Mrs Woods had to be taken away from the shop in Mr Casement's carriage, straight to the hospital to be operated on for appendicitis just like King Edward (that was 1907, Vi, you wouldn't remember that, of course) and your dear father standing at the shop door on that Saturday afternoon when the first Walls ice-cream man in Chesterbourne came down the High Street and your dear father Stopping him and Buying One for all us girls, well, girls I say, women really, and poor Miss Miller and that dreadful madman, and having the electric light put in and how it always went out in the early days . . .

It is exciting, too, to be getting on for seventy years old when the happiest day of your life comes; for this day, with the church decorated with all those exquisite blooms (flowers are always blooms to Miss Cattyman), the crowd of familiar, excited faces, the music, the dressy smell of fine clothes and scent, the rustling and the whispers, is undoubtedly Miss Cattyman's high spot. Howard Thompson's daughter is being married to a rich, handsome and dashing young man, and this is all the more exciting because Miss Cattyman, fond though she is of Viola, never did think Viola would marry, let alone marry twice, and the second time so well! Vi was so quiet, a dear sweet girl, of course, but not *lively*, no *go*, and men do like go. Shirley (Cissie, really, never could think of her as Shirley) was the one the fellows all liked. It just shows you never can tell, that's all.

And after the wedding there will be Viola's letters to look forward to; and later on, the babies. The babies will be more exciting than anything. Viola may colour up and say, 'Good lord, Catty, I don't know, you are awful,' when the babies are mentioned, but Catty is sure that she is longing for them and certainly Catty is. Viola may laugh, but Catty has started knitting a matinée jacket.

Victor is allowing Catty a hundred and fifty pounds a year. He is without a trace of meanness, he can afford it, and Viola has only to remind him that it was her letter about Catty that really brought them together, and he says yes. One of the natural considerations at the back of his mind is that the poor old trout won't last long, anyway.

However, the old trout does. The fire in Catty that loved watching Howard Thompson act, and could find drama in the daily routine at Burgess and Thompson's, burns cheerfully for another twenty-five years, and when Catty dies peacefully of old age at just over ninety, she has had from Victor some three thousand seven hundred and fifty pounds. Her will is on a form bought at a stationer's and witnessed by the landlady and her husband, and it leaves the two hundred pounds she has saved to Viola's youngest daughter ('my baby, because it is right the money should go back where it came'). Up to the week before Catty's death Viola writes to her, and sends her picture papers that Catty is too blind to see.

Nearly everybody in Sible Pelden is outside the church, except the realist-barman at the Green Lion. When asked if he did not want to go to the wedding, the barman spat and observed not him, he'd had enough o' weddin's to last him a lifetime, he had. But Mrs Fisher is there, as we have already seen, and Mr Fisher, and some of the servants from Grassmere, who have slipped away for twenty minutes from the preparations for the wedding breakfast. Little Merionethshire is standing on a tombstone and leaning on the shoulder of the tormented but adoring Heyrick, her print skirt and her black Welsh curls blowing in the wind. None of her Essex admirers gets little Davies in the end; she is called home to nurse her mother, and marries a local farmer.

Doctor Parsham is in church, and the chemist's ill-tempered son from Chesterbourne, who sent Viola two guineas for Catty with a long and rather wild letter about the foolishness and criminal folly of encouraging useless people to live and ending with a dark reference to personal unhappiness which Viola perfectly understands and giggles over. He has come because he must, though he feels as if he were biting on an aching tooth. However, he gets a kick out of sneering at the decorations and the barbarous, indecent bourgeois ostentation of it all. He stares round him with a bitter smile, and several women are talking about him in indignant whispers. Why does he come at all, if he isn't enjoying it?

Most of the people in the church are women. This wedding is not just the marriage of one Chesterbourne girl to Victor Spring. Viola is the type of all those girls in shops and offices, banks and cafés, Woolworths and Boots and Marks and Spencers, who have all dreamed, just a little, about a wedding with Victor Spring, and naturally, when she married him, they all feel that they must be there. Their wistful, envious, interested eyes take in the tiniest detail, the finest shade of expression, the last shred of meaning, in everything that happens. It is very tiring to be a woman.

That is what Hetty is thinking, sitting in the front pew in a dress of white chiffon printed with sprays of lilac and a floppy hat that does not become her. She feels ridiculous in this get-up, but Viola has sentimentally insisted upon having her as bridesmaid, and as Mrs Spring also wants it, Hetty has given way. She still feels grateful, in her reserved ungracious way, to her aunt and Victor for having let her go to live in London with so little opposition, and she wants to show her gratitude.

She is grateful because the life she now leads, though exhausting, frightening and unhappy, is absorbing and satisfying as she had never dreamed life could be. Of all the people in the story who have escaped from lives they hated, Hetty is the only one who has found ecstasy. This is because she is the only one capable of finding it.

If ecstasy means to live to the full, she has this, and she knows it. She feels dimly, too, that the experiences now happening to her are so important that they will colour and influence her life to come for many years. Some day she will think that they were worth having, but at present she only knows that they are agonizing and cannot be escaped, and that they may end in darkness and despair. She must use her reserved, half-poetic, half-sceptical nature to its fullest powers and for the first time in her life she is doing so.

Between Hetty and Donat Mulqueen a bitter, painful and difficult love is growing. It is the most miserable of affairs. Hetty, who has some common sense and detachment left, sometimes thinks what a depressing pair they must look, idling over Hampstead Heath or down Charlotte Street to the pub; an untidy plump pale girl and a gaunt, black-haired young giant almost in rags, dirty (she has given up trying to get him to wash, indeed, his example has persuaded her, never too sudsy, to cut down her own washing), the soles of his shoes flapping, and his body shaken by a terrifying cough that is half exaggerated and half frighteningly real. He has huge full grey eyes and the beautiful mouth that poets often have. Everywhere he goes he is stared at, which he pretends he hates, but in truth he loves to attract attention and hates himself for this love.

He also hates himself for needing Hetty. Their lovemaking is like the snarling of two dogs; tenderness is unthinkable; there must be nothing but lust and merciless sincerity. Hetty, whose gentleness has always been rather due to good manners than to instinct, is rapidly losing what little she had, and tenderness she buries deep in her spirit, because he shrinks with such horror from any signs of it. His whole life is one agonized effort to harden himself. He has cast off his family. He is a Communist, and twenty-four years old.

What is the matter with him? He does not know, and neither does she. She cannot get him to talk about himself. The glimpses she has had into his nature appal her; there seems nothing within but hatred and horror. She cannot forget an evening when they rode on the top of the bus to Richmond. They had both been silent, but at last she said something about the beauty of some leaves above a street lamp. Then he whispered, half turning to look at her, 'Shut up,' in a voice that turned her sick with despair and a strange shame.

In spite of himself he has (so odd is human nature) a large number of friends. Hetty, who finds herself capable of a degradingly strong jealousy, learns from these that she is what they call with the fashionable candour 'Donat's first woman'. It appears that he has had some horror of sex, among all his other horrors, and Hetty has been able to put an end to this. All his friends (kind as it is possible for human beings to be, most of them desperately unhappy, very hard drinkers and talkers and *not* domesticated) congratulate her upon this achievement, but she can feel no emotion except this ceaseless desire to serve him, to keep him writing poetry, and to lend (or rather give) him what money she can, so that he will go on writing poetry.

The room in Bloomsbury with the chimney pots, the coffee brewing and a contented Hetty curled up with a book has not come off. After a month at Aunt Rose's, Hetty took herself off to a ratty, beetley attic next to Donat's in an old house somewhere in the back streets off Leicester Square, and here she lives in a sluttishness that does not trouble her at all. To tidy up takes time, and she wants all her time for wolfing books, dreaming violently, and putting Donat to bed when he is drunk, which is often.

Guinness and Dewar, how these people drink! Hetty had thought that the Grassmere set drank plenty, but they are teetotallers compared to the set that goes, night after night, to the one or two public houses they use as clubs. All their parties flow with drink; they do not seem able to pass half an hour without a frenzied search for drink, they make long pilgrimages to one another's dens for drink in hopes that A may have some when B has run out. No one could call them drunkards: they just drink. A good deal of Hetty's money goes on drink for Donat and his friends. 'My bloody little capitalist friend will pay,' he says, and she does.

Uncle Frank is very distressed about all this, but Aunt Rose says calmly, looking at Hetty with her fanatic blue eyes, that it is all unavoidable. Hetty is not the bourgeois, domestic, maternal type. She is the neurotic type that sacrifices itself to a man of genius, without holding anything back; a decadent and inevitable product of a social system based on Individualism, says Aunt Rose, looking up from a pamphlet she is writing against the Fascists. She must find herself – if she can – in her own way. Aunt Rose helps Hetty to hide from Aunt Spring the fact that she is no longer living with her relations, and sometimes drops a hard word of advice about Donat, that Hetty finds sound, and gives the young people carrier-bags full of food, or an occasional bottle that is appreciated much more. Hetty dislikes Aunt Rose, but thoroughly respects her. She is a little mad, but never a fool.

Mrs Spring is beginning to suspect that things are very wrong with Hetty, because the girl is so silent and looks so pale and shabby, and years older, but she will not ask her what is the matter. Hetty has taken her own road, and must walk on it by herself. For over twenty years Mrs Spring has tried to alter Hetty; now she tries no more. Hetty's failure to be like her dead mother has been the great disappointment of Mrs Spring's life, and she feels more than a little bitter towards her niece. And with Viola so charming and everything that a girl should be – it is small wonder that Mrs Spring leaves Hetty to manage her own affairs. After all, she has always wanted to.

Viola is the daughter for whom Mrs Spring has always longed, whom Hetty and Phyllis failed to be. Mrs Spring, surprised and dismayed at first by Victor's lightning decision to marry a shopgirl with no money, finds herself, from Viola's first afternoon alone with her, agreeably soothed and stimulated by the girl's company. True, she is rather artless and young for her age and her clothes are dreadful, but she is so friendly, so fully sensible of her immense good fortune, and so much in love with Victor; above all, so biddable and without the wish to dominate and excel, that Mrs Spring's good will is won. Her taste in dress, after all, can be influenced, her complexion, figure and style of hairdressing only need a little attention from experts and she will be transformed into the prettiest and most charming of young-marrieds.

She seems to have none of the traditional fear and antagonism towards her mother-in-law, and asks her advice about her trousseau and the furnishing of her flat in the most flattering way. So beguiled is Mrs Spring, in fact, that it is not for some years that it dawns upon her how many of those small alterations that Viola made at her suggestion have been quietly altered back again to the way Viola first preferred them. Then, having become devoted to Viola and the children, Mrs Spring is more amused than annoyed and thinks of Viola as a clever little thing.

Those Davises, for example. Mrs Spring had from the first quietly but firmly discouraged Viola from being friends with that loud-voiced, vulgar, showy Shirley Davis, who had nothing to recommend her but a fine head of red hair, and Viola had cheerfully allowed herself to be discouraged. It was not until Viola and Vic have been married three years and the second baby, Gloria, is on the way, that Mrs Spring, out one day in her car, sees Viola and that

Shirley creature together in a taxi, laughing uproariously and plainly enjoying each other's company very much.

There was a funny little bit of deceit for you!

But Mrs Spring is a wise woman, if only worldly-wise, and knows when to stop a molehill from growing, so she says nothing about these little rear-guard actions of Viola's, and the Springs are a most harmonious and happy family.

Lady Spring keeps her curls, her slenderness and her habit of saying, 'I say, good Lord!' when surprised. She never has any difficulty in remembering that she was once a dampish nobody, and she never ceases to enjoy, for they are the sweeter by contrast, the privileges and pleasures that her marriage has brought.

It may here be said, to relieve probable anxiety, that Viola makes a serene success of being Lady Spring. As she had once said to Tina, long ago, that she would do, she leaves the housekeeping to an expensive and competent housekeeper, does not stint on wages, makes her maids comfortable and happy, and does not worry if the bills for electricity and alcohol are heavy. She takes Shirley's advice about oiling the old war-horse and lets Mrs Spring imagine that she is having her own way, gives in to Victor on every occasion except when she feels that he would enjoy a little wifely opposition, and sets herself, with what intelligence she has, to be what he wants her to be.

The task is made easy for her. She was already, before he married her, what he wanted a woman to be; and he is a good husband, romantic yet monogamous, taking great pride and pleasure in his four handsome, healthy children. He asks nothing of his wife but that she shall love him, dress well, and entertain his friends. She goes down very well with his friends; the coarse well-living men like her freshness and respect her virtue (they are all great prudes) and the women like her because she does not try to steal their husbands.

She has no wish to. There is no one in the world like Vic; so handsome, so clever, so kind. He says the sweetest things to her, and she tells him how sweet she finds them (Phyllis would have knocked all the suppressed romance out of Victor in six months, and then have been aggrieved and astonished because he gave her grounds for divorce within a year) and they tease one another about still being sweethearts, and so do the children, whom Victor will not allow to become hard-boiled. The simple truth is that these two remain in love with one another all the days of their lives.

But all this is years and years away: and now there bursts out the Wedding March, gayest and most triumphant tune in the world, and down the church on her husband's arm comes Viola Thompson-Wither-Spring, diffusing a strong odour of *Love in Paris* from her pale lilac wedding dress and looking very pleased with herself, as well she may. Her husband's bright brown head is bent a little towards her so that he can watch her happiness and all the women notice this and coo over it.

It must be odd to be as happy as that, thinks Hetty, following them down the church between the ranks of smiling, moved, wistful faces. I'd sooner have my life than hers. I wonder if he's drunk yet?

The verger has swung back the doors of the church, and out into the sunshine and the laughing cheering crowd, the showers of confetti and silver horseshoes, goes Viola on Victor's arm. All the birds of summer seem calling to welcome her, as though the landscape itself were singing (they love a land like Essex, flat and wooded and watery) yet it is not so much a singing as a busy chirruping, a subdued recalling of springtime among the trees whence the white stars of the pear, the dark pink crab-apple flowers and the cherry-blossom have long since fallen. All the birds of summer seem to be calling; but the courting season is over, and one voice is silent.